ROBERT LOUIS STEVENSON

THE MASTER OF BALLANTRAE

A WINTER'S TALE

Edited with an Introduction and Notes by

ADRIAN POOLE

PENGUIN BOOKS

PENGUIN BOOKS

Published by the Penguin Group
Penguin Books Ltd, 80 Strand, London WC2R 0RL, England
Penguin Putnam Inc., 375 Hudson Street, New York, New York 10014, USA
Penguin Books Australia Ltd, 250 Camberwell Road, Camberwell, Victoria 3124, Australia
Penguin Books Canada Ltd, 10 Alcorn Avenue, Toronto, Ontario, Canada M4V 3B2
Penguin Books India (P) Ltd, 11 Community Centre, Panchsheel Park, New Delhi – 110 017, India
Penguin Books (NZ) Ltd, Cnr Rosedale and Airborne Roads, Albany, Auckland, New Zealand
Penguin Books (South Africa) (Pty) Ltd, 24 Sturdee Avenue, Rosebank 2196, South Africa

Penguin Books Ltd, Registered Offices: 80 Strand, London WC2R 0RL, England

www.penguin.com

First published 1889

This edition published in Penguin Classics 1996
19

Set in 10/12.5pt Monotype Baskerville
Typeset by Rowland Phototypesetting Ltd, Bury St Edmunds, Suffolk
Printed in England by Clays Ltd, St Ives plc

ISBN-13: 978–0–14–043446–0

www.greenpenguin.co.uk

CONTENTS

PENGUIN CLASSICS

THE MASTER OF BALLANTRAE

ROBERT LOUIS STEVENSON was born in Edinburgh in 1850. The son of a prosperous civil engineer, he was expected to follow in the family profession but finally was allowed to study law at Edinburgh University. Stevenson reacted violently against the Presbyterian respectability of the city's professional classes and this led to painful clashes with his parents. In his early twenties he became afflicted with a severe respiratory illness from which he was to suffer for the rest of his life; it was at this time that he determined to become a professional writer. The harsh nature of the Scottish climate forced him to spend long periods abroad and he eventually became settled in Samoa, where he died on 3 December 1894.

Stevenson's Calvinistic upbringing gave him a preoccupation with predestination and a fascination with the presence of evil. In *Dr Jekyll and Mr Hyde* he explores the darker side of the human psyche, and the character of the Master in *The Master of Ballantrae* (1889) was intended to be 'all I know of the Devil'. Stevenson is well known for his novels of historical adventure, including *Treasure Island* (1883), *Kidnapped* (1886), *The Black Arrow* (1888) and *Catriona* (1893). As Walter Allen in *The English Novel* comments, 'His rediscovery of the art of narrative, of conscious and cunning calculations in telling a story so that the maximum effect of clarity and suspense is achieved, meant the birth of the novel of action as we know it.' But these works also reveal his knowledge and feeling for the Scottish cultural past. During the last years of his life Stevenson's creative range developed considerably and *The Beach of Falesá* brought to fiction the kind of scene now associated with Conrad and Maugham. At the time of his death Robert Louis Stevenson was working on his unfinished masterpiece, *Weir of Hermiston*, which is at once a romantic historical novel and an emotional reworking of one of Stevenson's own most distressing experiences, the conflict between father and son.

ADRIAN POOLE is Reader in English and Comparative Literature and a Fellow of Trinity College, Cambridge. He has written widely on nineteenth-century novelists such as George Eliot, Hardy, Gissing, James and Kipling. He has also published a book on Greek and Shakespearean tragedy and is co-editor of *The Oxford Book of Classical Verse in Translation*. He was born in Edinburgh and is distantly related to the Stevenson family through his maternal grandmother.

INTRODUCTION

In 1913 the French novelist André Gide recorded his puzzled admiration for *The Master of Ballantrae*. A curious book, he thought: it was all excellent, but such a heterogeneous mixture, like a sample-card, a display of the writer's best wares.[1] Twelve years later, Gide took it with him to the Congo and read a few pages at a time with delight.

The Master of Ballantrae stands at the centre of Stevenson's career, midway between the writing of *Treasure Island* in 1881 and the unfinished *Weir of Hermiston* in 1894. It looks back to the summer in the Scottish highlands when he wrote two of his finest tales, 'Thrawn Janet' and 'The Merry Men', and dreamt up Long John Silver for what he later called 'My First Book'. There are pirates and buried treasure in *The Master*; there is also superstition and nightmare and magic. It looks forward to the last years of Stevenson's life in Samoa, when he cast back to his Scottish origins in the fragments of *Weir* and *St Ives* and *Heathercat*, but also dwelt on the squalor at the margins of empire, in 'The Beach of Falesá' and *The Ebb-Tide*. There is history and romance and tragedy in *The Master*; there is also an artful and reflective shrewdness. Gide was right about its diversity, and right to be delighted.

In May 1887 Stevenson's father died. Financially independent for the first time in his life, and avid as always for a climate kind to his unreliable lungs, Stevenson left Bournemouth with his family a few months later and travelled to North America. They found a cabin for the winter at Saranac Lake in the wilds of the Adirondacks, close to the Canadian border. And here, as the temperature sank lower and lower, so that the mercury in their thermometer curled up into the bulb 'like a hibernating bear',[2] Stevenson was gripped by an icy conception. He thought of it as 'The Familiar Incubus' or 'The Brothers' before fastening on 'The Master of Ballantrae'; he toyed with sub-titles such as 'A Romantic Tale', 'A Fantastic Tale', 'A Fantasy'.[3] By the middle of December he was outlining the contents to Edward L. Burlingame, his editor at *Scribner's Magazine*; by Christmas Eve he had written ninety-two pages at high speed and was telling Sidney Colvin that it was 'to me a most seizing tale; there are some fantastic elements; the most is a dead genuine human problem – human tragedy, I should say rather'. The Master himself, he said, was 'all I know of the devil'.[4] His plot was provided by the division of the Durie family in the Jacobite rising of 1745, and he had his cast of principal characters, the two brothers James and Henry and their father old Lord Durrisdeer, the kinswoman with beauty and money who loves one brother but marries the other, the faithful steward Mackellar, and the Irish Jacobite, Chevalier Burke. Only Secundra Dass had not yet occurred to him. Mackellar would be his main narrator, seconded by the Chevalier. Above all, he had a bold contrast in mind between the restless vagrancy of the outlawed heir and the sedentary sadness of his propertied brother. Though he saw the conclusion from the outset, the first surge of inspiration took him up to the exact mid-point of the tale, a candle-lit duel between the two brothers in the long shrubbery and the second 'death' of the Master. And there, in the spring of 1888, he left things in the air.

Stevenson liked to pause. *Treasure Island* might never have been finished had he not been committed to serial publication, and the same is true of *The Master*. He was a great beginner of things, as the litter of fragments and scenarios testifies. But when he set sail from San Francisco that summer, *The Master* could not be shrugged off and it dogged him across the Pacific. There were two further bursts of writing, first in Tahiti, between the end of September and Christmas, then finally in Hawaii, inch by inch to the bitter end, from February to May 1889. He complained that the ending hung over him like the arm of the gallows, and when at last he had buried *The Master*, he rejoiced to a friend that 'his body's under hatches – his soul, if there is any hell to go to, gone to Hell; and I forgive him; it is harder to forgive Burlingame for having induced me to begin the publication, or myself for suffering the induction.'[5]

These disruptions in the space and time of the novel's composition may well have influenced its distinctive shape and accentuated its 'heterogeneity'. But for all we know, it might have turned out just the same if Stevenson had stayed at Saranac and carried on writing without a break. It is more to the point that Stevenson positively courted the abrupt and the discontinuous, and made it, in this tale as nowhere else, part of his subject. If only writing could be as risky as living, like a hazard or gamble or toss of the coin. He complained about the demands of serialization, but they extorted from him a precious concentration, for these conditions pose with peculiar urgency, for writer and reader alike, the question of mastery. Whether by instinct or design or a happy combination of the two, Stevenson created for himself the sensation of flight and pursuit on which his own writing thrived.

He claimed to have taken inspiration from a supernatural thriller of Captain Marryat's. *The Phantom Ship* (1839) tells a version of the Flying Dutchman legend that sprawls promiscuously through time and space, across oceans and continents. It was exactly this sense of the fugitive and volatile that Stevenson wanted at the heart of his own novel, a wild and erratic energy, virtually devoid of intelligible motive, swaying on the edge of the crazy. This took the form of James Durie, the Master, who is only at home in peril on the sea, swinging up and down on the brink of the elements.

Up and down, here and there, to and fro: these are the movements by which Stevenson's tale is shaped, endless and repetitive, but – to what end? In one of the drafts for his 'Note' on the novel (see Appendix), he says that his aim was to 'carry the reader to and fro', in space and time. This deceptively simple phrase recurs to telling effect in the novel itself. It is Henry Durie's most characteristic attitude, as it were, the pale replica of his brother's more vigorous but no more productive surges across the face of the globe. While James travels the world in perpetual motion, Henry tosses to and fro in the family home of Durrisdeer, until his mind begins to wander in mimicry of his brother's body. As the moment approaches when Durrisdeer must be abandoned, we see him 'racing to and fro in one end of the room like a half-lunatic' (p. 137). His good servant Mackellar shares his restlessness. When Mackellar has bidden farewell to his master and mistress, he spends the rest of the night pacing 'to and fro on the smooth highway' (p. 146). Meanwhile the eery figure of Secundra Dass is 'continually travelling to and fro in the house' (p. 150). All this nervous, unfocused movement is partly that of the novel itself. Stevenson foments it as much as he seeks to allay it, or rather he makes the question of its control a feature of the novel's own subject. It is to Mackellar that this impossible task is consigned. And it is Mackellar who has to record, after so much aimlessness, the sudden, belated directness with which the novel marches to its brutal conclusion, 'along a path whose every stage was mile-stoned with a mutilated corpse' (p. 206). So much for any paths marked out by the arts and graces of the Duries, or the culture, education, and trade of the colonizing powers with which their fortunes are entangled.

Stevenson saw his beginning in the old Scottish house on the edge of the sea and his ending in the American wilderness, and he bound them together with the elements of winter, with wind and storm and the stricture of frost. The context for which he initially designed his tale has a certain influence on it. *Scribner's Magazine* during these years was full of articles on and images of the North American wilderness, rivers and valleys and lakes, from Colorado to Quebec. In the issue for December 1888 there is a piece called 'Winter in the Adirondacks' with lots of engravings of snow and trees. There are endless pieces on the railway and associated feats of engineering, and also on ocean liners, on electricity, telegraphy and photography. Nature is being conquered and annexed in various ways. There are the tunnels and bridges that penetrate and cross the landscape. There is the 'natural space' being opened up for sport and leisure: a piece on 'Nepigon River Fishing', for instance, where one learns that 'Canada is now the goal for American sportsmen, as for cashiers . . .' (September 1889). At the same time, there is a distinct appetite for old world houses and castles: there are illustrated features on Birr Castle in Ireland, on Castle Life in the Middle Ages, on 'The Picturesque

Quality of Holland: Interiors and Bric-à-brac'. There is a specific interest in the houses of famous writers: Tennyson, Goethe and Scott. The issue that carried the fourth instalment of *The Master* (February 1889) opened with a big spread on 'Walter Scott at Work'. These juxtapositions of wild nature and old culture are reproduced in the series of illustrations that accompany Stevenson's novel in *Scribner's*. These were important to Stevenson (see 'Summary of Events During the Master's Wanderings', note 11), and he was so enthusiastic about the effects achieved by William Hole's illustrations (all except one) that he persuaded Scribner to retain them for the first American issue in book form; English readers of the Cassell first edition had to manage without.[6]

Stevenson had been surprised by the welcome he received in America. He was a celebrity, it seemed. He was moderately abashed by the amount of money magazine proprietors were ready to pay him, though he got over this. We get a clue to the way in which he shaped his tale for a new kind of market from a *Scribner's* piece by Charles Eliot Norton, entitled 'The Lack of Old Homes in America' (May 1889). Norton's observation is scarcely original, but the scale of the phenomenon to which he is pointing is new and his response will be an influential one. 'Since the days of the great wanderings of the nations,' he writes, 'there has been nothing like the movement of migration from Europe to America, and the shifting of residence of the American people during the last fifty years.' Norton's tone is one of anxiety and elegy, marked by his use of a language unintelligible to the majority of these migrants: 'Nos patriae fines et dulcia linquimus arva;/Nos patriam fugimus'.[7] Virgil is the classic poet of migration, and we shall see that he was an important point of reference for Stevenson. But Stevenson's whole novel was conceived around a double image deeply appealing to the readership at which *Scribner's* was aimed: the idea of the old home and the new wilderness. And the dark fable of eviction, uprooting and exile that he developed, while it certainly drew on some of his own deepest feelings, was also designed for readers attuned to Norton's patrician melancholy: 'Attachment to the native soil, affection for the home of one's youth, the claims of kindred, the bonds of social duty, have not proved strong enough to resist the allurements of hope, the promise of bettering fortune, and the love of adventure.'

This was not the first time that the idea and experience of emigration had entered Stevenson's writing. The brave and reckless journey he took to California in 1879 had furnished him with the matter of *The Amateur Emigrant*. The structure of his work, as Jonathan Raban observes, is that of a rite of passage.[8] It moves through the purgation of two hellish crossings, first of the ocean and then of the continent, to the symbolic rebirth of daybreak in San Francisco. In *Kidnapped* (1886), the figure of the emigrant features to quite different effect. David Balfour emerges from the symbolic death of shipwreck and exposure on the west coast of Scotland, and as he begins his long journey home to claim his inheritance, he encounters an emigrant ship on the point of departure for the American colonies. It is a great scene of collective mourning. The chief singer in the boat that is carrying David strikes into 'a melancholy air' which is taken up by the emigrants themselves and those they are leaving behind, 'so that it sounded from all sides like a lament for the dying'. David himself does not join in, though he confesses to finding the scene 'highly affecting' (Ch. 16). The emigrant ship marks exactly the fate that will not be his own. Towards the end of the novel there is a bit of banter about the genre to which David belongs, whether ballad or epic, but whatever it is, his is the story of the exile returned and reborn, the beggar who comes into his kingdom, who can say at the end: 'I was a man of means and had a name in the country' (Ch. 29).

Whether rebirth is to be found in the old world or the new, it is just such a narrative of regeneration that *The Master* invokes only to reject. The rejection is a cold-blooded one, and some readers have always flinched from it. Andrew Lang, for instance, to whom the novel seemed more like Zola than Scott. And if this was tragedy, Lang asked, the tragedy of 'a little Scottish Theban line', then where was Antigone, and 'where the hope that goes with the passing of Oedipus?' It was, he concluded, 'a very modern gloom that broods over the roof-tree of Durisdeer'.[9] The model to which Stevenson's sub-title makes formal allusion is not in fact Greek but Shakespearean, yet this certainly deceives the reader into some distinct hope for the future.

The Winter's Tale offers exactly the pattern of generational change and renewal on which so much nineteenth-century fiction depends. This novel will surely follow that pattern. But it does not, with a vengeance. There are two children, but they are never lost and never found; they simply wither away, glimpsed in the Preface as they wait for death, the last lord and his old-maid sister, long after the events of the novel itself. Their mother also, who begins with such fire and passion, hurling a coin through the family shield in the window, is never to be a reviving Hermione, but simply and quietly sinks away. It is winter in the old Scottish house and it is winter in the American wilderness, with the same icy wind blowing through both. Stevenson told his friend Sidney Colvin: 'I have always feared the sound of wind beyond everything: in my hell it would always blow a gale'.[10] Many years earlier, in the depth of his troubles with his parents, he had written to Fanny Sitwell that it was 'just the old story, only sudden revelations of a whole Hell between people', and again that 'There's no place like H—, you know – which you may understand as you will'[11] (*Letters* 1, 411). *The Master* is the tale of a home that is hell, and of a family who take their hell with them wherever they go, turning the world all around them to winter.

There is then a bitter disappointment written into the structure of the novel. Right from the start this was part of Stevenson's conception, that there would be no return and no rebirth. It had to end in the wilderness (though he did not foresee that both brothers would die). How exactly he would get there was another matter, and it would prove a real difficulty. He got some assistance from Virgil's *Aeneid.* In Bournemouth in 1886 he had started reading Books 5 and 6, the latter for the first time, and he enthused: 'That is one of the most astonishing pieces of literature, or rather it contains the best, I ever met with. We are all damned small fry, and Virgil is one of the tops of human achievement . . .'[12] In October 1887 he asked Charles Scribner to send him an *Aeneid* at Saranac, and over the next few years Virgil went with him around and about the South Seas. In *The Ebb-Tide* (1894) Herrick knows his Virgil, amongst other things.

The Master makes four explicit allusions to Virgil's epic (see 'Summary of Events During the Master's Second Absence', note 3; 'The

Enemy in the House', note 4; 'Passages at New York', note 4; 'The Journey in the Wilderness', note 7). The first stands at the centre of the novel and recalls a moment from the centre of the *Aeneid.* The last words of old Lord Durrisdeer repeat Aeneas's plea to the Sibyl near the start of Book 6 for permission to descend to the underworld and see his father again. This is the very fulcrum of Aeneas's journey, from darkness to light, from the destruction of Troy to the foundation of Rome. He does not shrink from the visions of pain and torment, and he is granted a glimpse of the future he will help to create. This is the great narrative of recovery to which the House of Durrisdeer will never live up. There is indeed a desperate nocturnal flight from the old home, but there will be no new beginning. When the Master compares his own escape from India to such a flight from Troy, it is not his father on his back, but Secundra Dass (p. 180). When he regales his nephew with tales of his escapades, he makes Mackellar think of him as 'a diabolical Aeneas' and the boy as a little Dido (p. 143). And when Mackellar finds a Virgilian phrase to express his grief at the transformation of his beloved master, the words serve rather to mark the distance between a Hector and a Henry Durie. There is more to be said about Mackellar's efforts to strike the right note and genre for the telling of his story, especially its ending.

But first one should recognize a larger kind of irony in these Virgilian allusions. From the 1690s onwards, so Murray Pittock has demonstrated, Jacobite writers tried hard and to a large extent succeeded in appropriating the *Aeneid* as their own, 'deepening the Stuart text of Vergilian celebration into a whole code of exile and return'.[13] There is a certain historical propriety, then, in Stevenson's re-activation of such a code for a tale set in the years following the catastrophe of the '45. And yet, of course, his novel does not seek for a moment to give renewed credibility to such myths. The House of Durrisdeer has never been truly engaged in the Stuart cause or indeed any other, nor are its fortunes in any real sense connected with the Jacobite tropes of treacherous invaders and abandoned homes and courageous exiles. The vicious turn that Stevenson gives to his Virgilian allusions makes the House of Durrisdeer destroy itself from within. The intruder who evicts the family from its ancient residence is not a foreigner, but the true heir himself, at once hateful and deeply beloved.

And above all, charming. When all is said and done, the Master is a brilliant fake. For if the old Jacobite tropes are still alive in the air that Stevenson's novel breathes, these are now the wan spectres of Victorian nostalgia, a specific branch of the developing heritage industry set in motion by James Hogg's *Jacobite Relics* (1819–21).[14] This is the age in which Queen Victoria was able to adopt Balmoral 'as a centre for the display of Hanoverian identity reforged in the Stuart image'.[15] Stevenson's novel analyses this kind of forgery through the charismatic figure of the Master, the 'bonnie laddie' who goes out to fight for one side, comes back to spy for the other, and is never deflected for an instant from a single-minded devotion to himself. If there is any sense of Virgilian duty, piety, and self-sacrifice, it is only to be found in Mackellar. But the family whose life he tries to preserve is determined to destroy itself.

So this is a tale of exile that signally fails to conclude in triumphant restoration. But then the whole novel is a collection of failing narratives, some of them dashing but all of them dashed, like the members of the dying family of Duries, merely held together by the iron will of Mackellar. In the big world beyond Durrisdeer, there are all sorts of adventures. There are pirates and buried treasure, there are Jacobite exiles and smugglers and Indians from more than one continent. The Master's tongue and the Chevalier's pen try to turn these into stories, yet they all more or less peter out. Buried treasure is never dug up. Nothing comes to fruition. Nothing, that is, except the tragedy of the Duries.

If the Master is a character in search of a story, the Duries are a family in search of history. Their house is like an island, occasionally grazed by a world elsewhere with which no trading of value or meaning ever takes place. No wonder that Henry Durie gazes longingly at the life of adventure embodied by the smugglers he sees in the distance, looking out from a high window. The money comes in and Mackellar counts it and more money goes out. The novel repeats the Duries' fleeting collisions with history, with the grand narrative of the '45, with the spectacular stories of colonial conflict in India and North

America. The Master ensures that their actual participation is only with the seamiest elements of these stories, with the Jessie Brouns and 'the dregs of colonial rascality'. The dutiful Henry and his steward Mackellar have no effective means of resistance. They are eventually drawn to the place where the Master is amongst his own kind, the colonial frontier town of Albany, where the inhabitants are 'like all the smugglers in the world, spies and agents ready-made for either party' (p. 53). The Duries contribute no more to the building of empires, whether British or French, than they do to the establishment of monarchies, Stuart or Hanoverian. But the natives on whose lands they intrude do insist on their place in the novel, and there is a savage narrative logic that brings together at the novel's climax the North American Indians and Secundra Dass. They represent the two extremes of native reaction to the incursion of colonialism: on the one hand, savage resistance, and on the other, slavish devotion. What visible logic governs the difference between them? No more than the toss of a coin, one may think.

Stevenson chose the title of this novel with care.[16] 'Ballantrae' has a glamorous ring to it, and on several occasions it is brought close enough to the word 'gallantry' for the reader to hear a rhyme, each time as it happens by the Chevalier Burke (pp. 33, 43, 130). (Stevenson noted that 'Ballantrae' was to be stressed on the first syllable.) Less flamboyantly, there is 'balance' in the name, and more ominously, the word 'betrayal'. Perhaps the Master's most significant triumph occurs on board the ship to New York when he succeeds in 'charming' the phlegmatic Mackellar. He tells a sinister tale of murderous intrigue in the Roman campagna – there is more than a shade of Hawthorne – but this is not in itself what makes Mackellar feel 'giddy and vacant'. It is the way he tells it, swinging up and down, one moment high above his mesmerized listener, the next beneath his feet. He is the epitome of perilous grace, of everything that Mackellar is not and has not, as he sits there 'fitting the swing of the ship with an exquisite balance' (p. 164). This is a moment of poetry: Stevenson creates a perfectly crafted line of verse, a dactylic pentameter, for this most crafty of creatures ('fitting the/swíng of the/shíp with an/ éxquisite/bálance'). It is a brilliant balancing act, both the Master's and his creator's. No wonder the Master makes everyone around him betray feelings they did not even realize they had. Like the earlier moment when Mackellar exclaims: 'I had never seen the man so beautiful' (p. 94). Or the moment now, when he thinks to himself '*I were liker a man if I struck this creature down*' (p. 164). In the presence of the Master, other men find themselves wondering what it is to be a 'man'.

Yet the title itself is a kind of fake. Henley was the first to point this out: 'In naming his book Mr Stevenson has committed a blunder, strange, indeed, in a Scotsman.'[17] This is not an entirely disinterested observation. Stevenson's friendship with Henley had exploded in resentment and recrimination in the spring of 1888, and it never recovered. Henley's point is that 'Master' is the courtesy title accorded the heir apparent to a Scottish peerage, and this means that James Durie should properly have been called 'the Master of Durrisdeer'. He might have been called '*Marquis* of Ballantrae', like the historical Marquis of Tullibardine, heir to the first Duke of Atholl, whose sons' divided allegiances provided an important impetus to the tale (see 'Summary of Events During the Master's Wanderings', note 9). But a mere Marquis was no good to Stevenson. Scott had given him a clue with the darkly passionate Master of Ravenswood, whose disinheritance drives the action of *The Bride of Lammermoor* (and one may see Mackellar as a rewriting of the loyal old steward of Ravenswood, Caleb Balderstone). The attraction for Stevenson was exactly the way in which the special Scots meaning of 'Master' runs athwart the dominant meanings of the word in English. These of course connote the presence of power and authority rather than its promise. It was exactly these questions – about the real location and workings of 'mastery' – that Stevenson found so happily coiled in the word.

How can one tell the difference between a lord and master and Master? One may read the distinction between those upper and lower cases but one cannot hear it. A flickering comedy plays round these endless tiny confusions, as when Henry tries to put the Master in his place by saying: 'my lord here is the master', or the Master tells Mackellar, 'Your master has chosen this way, and not I', or Mackellar says to the old lord, 'I am here to plead the cause of my master'. As the devoted family servant and the tale's main teller, Mackellar tries to control this potential confusion, indeed to master it. In the father of the family he has a lord and in Henry Durie he has a master, and when Henry succeeds to the title he has a lord and master. But the one thing that Henry Durie will never be is the Master, hard as Mackellar tries to stiffen him up to it. This is Henry's tragedy, but it is also Mackellar's and that of the family he serves, and perhaps beyond that of the larger world across which the Master imperiously roams, extorting admiration, fear and envy. This at least is Mackellar's conclusion in the verdict he inscribes on the brothers' joint tombstone. The 'mastership of arts' he brings with him from Edinburgh College is not without substance, as we shall see. But in the epitaph he creates for James Durie he acknowledges the extra qualification before which his own arts must bow: 'A MASTER OF THE ARTS AND GRACES'.

Stevenson's decision to tell his tale mainly through the mouth and pen of Mackellar was an inspired one. It created difficulties for him, most notably in the novel's final phase in the wilderness, and at one point he lost his nerve and considered abandoning the whole strategy. In February 1888 he told *Scribner's* that he was going to recast the whole thing in the third person: 'this version is one large error'.[18] Fortunately he changed his mind again, and, although he was never completely convinced of his success, he made the difficulties he faced with Mackellar part of the novel's own questioning of 'mastery'.

There is an obvious level on which the novel depends on the rivalry between the two brothers and all that they may be thought to represent. Critics have read into them all kinds of symbolic value. They have been taken to represent a Scotland divided between Jacobite and Hanoverian, Highlands and Lowlands, Heart and Head, Nature and Culture, Passion and Prudence, and so on. They have been referred to a recurrent dualism in Stevenson's writings, which manifests itself most famously in the intimate affinities between Dr Jekyll and Mr Hyde, and between David Balfour and Alan Breck. The Master himself evidently makes one of a gallery of charming rogues or lovable scoundrels that begins lightly enough with Long John Silver and darkens at the end into Adam Weir, Lord Hermiston. There is, it has often been said, a mythic quality about such figures, and this is true enough. But in *The Master* the very ways in which such mythic force is created and sustained become the novel's own subject (as they are the subject of the Shakespearean tragedy to which the Master himself at one point alludes, *Coriolanus*). The exploration of this subject is conducted not by the rivalry between the brothers but between the Master and Mackellar.

The Master himself does not write. He acts of course, in both senses of the word, but he also talks and, on a couple of critical occasions, he sings. He is above all the performer, and it is the art and grace of his presence that Mackellar so envies, readily hates, reluctantly admires and perhaps secretly loves. Mackellar thinks of himself as born old, and he does not dispute Mrs Henry's description of him as an old maid. Critics feel comfortable when they identify him as an 'unreliable narrator', but this should go without saying. He betrays his partialities at every twist and turn, his identification with his master Henry, his mistrust of all women except his mother and his Aunt Dickson, his furtive admiration for the Master. Douglas Gifford has argued for his debt to a specifically Scots tradition of the self-condemning dramatic monologue, which runs down to Stevenson from Burns's 'Holy Willie' through John Galt and James Hogg.[19] We are certainly supposed to perceive his little self-deceptions and self-betrayals, his sense of having things to hide and to justify, as for instance when he protests 'the moderation of my part in these affairs, a thing which some have called recklessly in question' (p. 113). But though they are masked and oblique, he also has large ambitions, for himself and for the story he leaves behind him. These are not quite in tune with each other because his feelings about the Master are so violently mixed. He is attracted by the Master's charisma and repelled by his own attraction. He is tempted by the role of tragic chorus, the narrator of the Fall of the House of Durie, but he tries to hold on to his more down-to-earth sense of the sordid realities. The story he tells is at least partly the confession and self-justification of a man who succumbs to temptation.

The novel loses a good deal if the reader is not prepared to share Mackellar's ambivalence towards the Master. Francis Hart robustly contends that readers should no more be taken in by the Master than by any of Stevenson's other Glittering Scoundrels: 'Those who glamorise James's diabolism, including some romantic critics, are victims of his ingenious deceits.'[20] But fakes have real effects, and the Master is exactly what we now call a 'reality effect'. Of course we should see through him, just as Mackellar knows that he should hang on to his sense, on board the *Nonesuch*, that there is nothing behind the man's mask. Yet it is hard to prevent credulity creeping back in again. For the Master is more than a fictional figure; he is a figure for physical presence itself, above all for presence as voice.

Through the rivalry between Mackellar's pen and the Master's tongue, Stevenson is dramatizing his own fascination with the disjunctions between writing and voice. He makes Mackellar acutely attentive to the range of sound, both human and inhuman, from the wildness of wind to the magic of song. The Master is a brilliant talker and teller of tales. He can cast a 'glamour' over anyone whose ear he can catch, like Mrs Henry, who looks on the ground 'like a person lost in listening' (p. 90). His magic finds a faint repetition for the reader in the charm of these sounds, as if to listen means that one is bound to be lost. But it is when he rises into song that his listeners are most spell-bound, when he sings the old ballad called 'Shule Aroon' to his family, and then as he leaves Durrisdeer with Mackellar, the song called 'Wandering Willie' (see 'Persecutions Endured by Mr Henry', note 18, and 'Mr Mackellar's Journey with the Master', note 2). These moments are the equivalents of that crucial scene in *Kidnapped*, when David Balfour hears the emigrants and those they are leaving behind sing together 'Lochaber no more'. The sentiments of mourning and exile and loss are real enough here in their effects on the listeners, Mackellar and the family, but the singer himself is entirely indifferent, a pure, heartless performer. To express his sense of the Master's unique delivery, Mackellar finds himself coining a new verb or giving a twist to an old one. He says that the words 'were sung (or rather "soothed") to me by a master-singer' (p. 154). Normally, the verb 'to soothe' is used to describe the effect of the verb's subject on its object. Here, however, it is the means by which an effect is produced. Yet to imagine the Master as 'soothing' the words of the song is wonderfully appropriate in its mixed connotations of sooth and falsehood, of the true power of persuasion and blandishment. There is an added irony at work here. Mackellar does not recall hearing elsewhere the words that the Master sings to 'the saddest of our country tunes'. But this is unsurprising. Stevenson has composed them himself (see 'Mr Mackellar's Journey with the Master', note 2).

Stevenson himself wrote of the verse contained in *Underwoods*, the volume published in 1887 shortly before he left for America, that it was the work of 'a man who talks, not one who sings'.[21] He did not think of himself as a poet at all, at least not a poet like Virgil; Horace and Martial were more his style – conversational, chatty, occasional. He wrote a Preface for this novel that he decided not to publish on its first appearances in serial and volume form, and then he revived it, or planned to, for the collected Edinburgh Edition (see Note on the Text). It provides something notably absent from the tale itself: the tone of cosy conversation between equals. Stevenson is drawing, with a certain nostalgia, on the idiom of ingenious banter that he enjoyed with his old friend Charles Baxter. But it serves to measure the loneliness of Mackellar's writing, the paucity and perversion of linguistic exchange in the novel itself. We get only occasional glimpses of such intimate dialogue. Old Lord Durrisdeer and Mrs Henry chat away in the ingle-nook after dinner, sentimentalizing over the Master. But we are kept at a distance from that warm fireplace, with the pitiful Henry and the anxious Mackellar. They too share some shy and broken confidences with each other. But most speech in the novel is a matter of open or furtive or oblique combat, of vicious duels and the casting of spells. And if Mackellar's writing has the last word over living speech, it is a desolate triumph: the epitaphs on an improvised tombstone in the cold middle of nowhere.

Mackellar, the master of arts, is determined at the end to impose an order on the heterogeneous materials in his hands. He insists that they conform to a genre and the genre will be tragedy. But there is another story for us to read between the lines of the one he proposes. It is what Stevenson's good friend Henry James liked to call 'the story of the story'.

Mackellar is proud of his command of Latin. Early in the telling he quotes Horace to his master Mr Henry, and he gets on well with the old Lord Durrisdeer whose favourite occupation is to sit in the great carved chimney reading his Livy; indeed the dying man presents him with one of his Latin books. Mackellar's diction is influenced by the education that permits him to relish such Latinate words as 'pretermit' and 'prededicate' and 'immixture'. He would have made a good lawyer, like Mr Rankeillor in *Kidnapped.* His speech sets him sharply apart from the lower classes, or tries to, from the servants John Paul and Macconochie, and the foul-mouthed harridan, Jessie Broun. An important rivalry is lost when these marginal Scots-speaking figures are banished from the novel. They belong only to the earlier stages, when the Duries can still be (barely) located in a collective landscape, a local and national history. But they are evicted, paid off and forgotten, and this leaves Mackellar unchallenged from beneath, free to indulge his aspiring cultural instincts and tastes. The death of the old Lord Durrisdeer also increases his freedom; he is now the only one left to quote Virgil.

In the Master's first spell at Durrisdeer, Mackellar can see through his degeneracy: he is 'the discredited hero of romance' (p. 89). But there is a marked change on the occasion of the Master's second return with Secundra Dass. Mackellar sees that his own master Henry has shrunk and regressed, while the Master has remained – an important word for Mackellar – 'erect': 'He had all the gravity and something of the splendour of Satan in the *Paradise Lost*' (p. 139). Within the next few pages Mackellar thinks of him as 'a diabolical Aeneas' and he glancingly compares himself to Caius Martius Coriolanus (see 'The Enemy in the House', note 7). Milton, Virgil, Shakespeare: not a bad trio to support your literary standing.

On the sea-voyage to New York the question of 'reading' is explicitly pursued. In a kind of literary duel Mackellar reads the Bible and the Master *Clarissa.* Mackellar shrewdly observes that the Master treats all texts in the same way. He is a connoisseur for whom words are empty referents, and the differences between Richardson's novel and the Book of Job are merely a matter of style, 'a source of entertainment only' (p. 156). In a passage that seems to owe something to Melville, Mackellar is struck with horror at the man's inner vacancy, as if he were 'a man of pasteboard'.[22] It is as if the idea of the world that he represents has no more solidity than the swamp and the touchwood with which he was earlier associated. This image of pure treachery is more than Mackellar can bear; he tries to destroy it and fails. He continues to dispute the Master's fine words: '. . . these warlike similitudes are something too high-sounding for the matter in hand. You want some dirty money' (p. 166). But the Master's boast, as they near New York, will turn out to be true, that 'I never yet failed to charm a person when I wanted' (p. 169).

In the latter stages it is the note of tragic pathos towards which Mackellar is irresistibly drawn. Not that the reader need remain unmoved by the plangency of an allusion to Virgil, nor the pity that overbears the writer, 'a pity almost approaching the passionate, not for my master alone, but for the sons of man' (p. 190). But one should note the collision of diction and cultural code in the reference just before this to a different form of tragic expression, the stark ballad of the 'Twa Corbies', the closing lines of which Henry Durie endlessly repeats (see 'The Journey in the Wilderness', note 6):

> And over his banes when they are bare
> The wind sall blaw for evermair!

Something similar occurs near the end of *Kidnapped* in this juxtaposition of popular ballad and classical Latin. Alan Breck teaches David Balfour the little fragment of a Highland air that will serve as a signal between them, before David goes to Mr Rankeillor. Then David takes a decisive step into the lawyer's confidence by recognizing the first of the Latin quotations with which his speech will be peppered. There are two distinct codes here and David has to negotiate between them, to master the different kinds of signal and act as a broker between the fugitive outlaw and the pillar of the community. It is a precarious balancing act. Stevenson leaves David in some confusion, with 'a cold gnawing in my inside like a remorse for something wrong', but also at the doors of the bank, 'his hand upon his fortune' (Ch. 30). The remorse from which Mackellar also suffers at the end of his tale is more complicated. But it has something to do with the popular ballad that has taken possession of his master. As if in penance for his

Virgilian allusion, the next moment Mackellar does the rare thing, for him, of using a good Scots word for the sight of his master's face, 'all swollen and begrutten like a child's'.

The double epitaph with which Mackellar concludes his narrative is full of falsehoods. The least of these is his inclusion of Mrs Henry in an act for which he must take full responsibility (would she have agreed to these words?). The most shocking aspect of his last piece of writing is simply the difference between the two inscriptions, the magniloquence of the one and the pinched understatement of the other. Is this really, after all we have seen and heard, the summation of what Mackellar thinks and feels about the two brothers? Or is it more like the brothers' own self-estimates, as Mackellar intuits them? Whatever else may be said of the admiration the Master has commanded, it is a rank falsehood to assert that he 'acquired' or 'accomplished' anything. But then it is Mackellar who is responsible for the story's ending. This is the point of the dispute he has with Sir William Johnson, the authority in charge of the expedition, who washes his hands of responsibility. Of the ending of the tale, the events and also their telling, Mackellar is the forlorn master.

It is the drama of this masterful servant's divided loyalties that holds the tale together. This is the answer to Gide's proper query about its 'heterogeneity'. In the Gospel according to St Matthew we read that no man can serve two masters. But Mackellar upholds this novel by the service he renders no less than three masters: both James and Henry Durie, and the writer who imagined them. It is, in all sorts of ways, Stevenson's master-piece.

NOTES TO THE INTRODUCTION

1. Gide wrote in his journal for 17 November 1913: 'Curieux livre, où tout est excellent, mais hétérogène, au point qu'il semble la carte d'échantillons de tout ce où peut exceller Stevenson' (*Journal 1889–1939* (Paris, 1940)).
2. *Letters* 6, 77. All references to Stevenson's letters are to *The Letters of Robert Louis Stevenson*, 8 vols., ed. Bradford A. Booth and Ernest Mehew (New Haven and London, 1994–5).

3. Roger Swearingen, *The Prose Writings of Robert Louis Stevenson: A Guide* (London and Basingstoke, 1980), p. 120.

4. *Letters* 6, 81–2, 86–7.

5. *Letters* 6, 302.

6. On 3 February 1889 Stevenson enthused to Cassell's: '. . . Mr Hole has been doing those that have already appeared in a style so magnificent that I could not bear the whole volume should not be similarly adorned' (*Letters* 6, 244). But although later English editions carried these adornments, the first did not; nor did the Edinburgh Edition.

7. Virgil, *Eclogues* 1, 3–4 ('We are leaving our country's borders and its pleasant fields; we are taking flight from our homeland').

8. Jonathan Raban, Introduction to *The Amateur Emigrant* (London, 1984). For the complicated textual history of this work, first published in its complete form in the Edinburgh Edition (1895), see Swearingen, *Prose Writings*, pp. 42–5.

9. [Andrew Lang], unsigned review, *Daily News*, 5 October 1889; reprinted in *Robert Louis Stevenson: The Critical Heritage*, ed. Paul Maixner (London, Boston and Henley, 1981), pp. 344–6.

10. *Letters* 7, 59.

11. *Letters* 1, 307, 411.

12. *Letters* 5, 235–6.

13. Murray G. H. Pittock, *Poetry and Jacobite Politics in Eighteenth-Century Britain and Ireland* (Cambridge, 1994), p. 38.

14. See for example *The Jacobite Songs and Ballads of Scotland from 1688 to 1746*, ed. Charles Mackay (London and Glasgow, 1861), and *Jacobite Songs and Ballads*, ed. Gilbert S. Macquoid, published in the same year that Stevenson was working on this novel (London, 1888). Of collections such as these William Donaldson asks: 'Is there anything, then, to prevent the conclusion that they are fakes, brilliant fakes, perhaps, but fakes notwithstanding?' (*The Jacobite Song: Political Myth and National Identity* (Aberdeen, 1988), p. 4).

15. Pittock, *Poetry and Jacobite Politics*, p. 240. See also Pittock's *The Invention of Scotland: The Stuart myth and the Scottish identity, 1638 to the present* (London and New York, 1991), especially Chapters 3 and 4.

16. Fanny Stevenson says that he thought its 'flowing, mellifluous sound . . . gave an impression of elegance and smooth duplicity' (Prefatory Note to Tusitala Edition, vol. 10 (1924)).

17. [W. E. Henley], unsigned review, *Scots Observer*, 12 October 1889; reprinted in *The Critical Heritage*, ed. Maixner, p. 352.

18. *Letters* 6, 121.

19. Douglas Gifford, 'Myth, Parody and Dissociation: Scottish Fiction 1814–1914', in *The History of Scottish Literature, Volume 3: Nineteenth Century*, ed. Douglas Gifford (Aberdeen, 1988), p. 245.

20. Francis R. Hart, 'Robert Louis Stevenson in Prose', in *The History of Scottish Literature, Volume 3: Nineteenth Century*, ed. Gifford, p. 302.

21. *Letters* 6, 65.

22. For the comparison with Melville, see Frank McLynn, *Robert Louis Stevenson: A Biography* (London, 1993), p. 308.

NOTE ON THE TEXT

The Master of Ballantrae was first issued in twelve monthly instalments in *Scribner's Magazine*, beginning in November 1888 and concluding in October 1889. Ten of these carried illustrations by William Hole. In September 1889 it was published in volume form, with some revisions, by Scribner's Sons in New York and by Cassell and Company in London. After Stevenson's death in 1894, the novel was issued in the Edinburgh Edition of his works as vol. 6 of *Romances* (vol. 15 of issue) in January 1896, with a note by the editor, Sidney Colvin, to the effect that: 'The present text follows a copy of the first edition corrected by the author before his death.' Some of the differences between serial version, first edition and Edinburgh Edition are the subject of a separate note on 'Textual Variants'. Stevenson had written a Preface for the first edition which he suppressed at the time, but he planned to reinstate it for the Edinburgh Edition. Colvin says that the manuscript temporarily went astray, but the text was recovered in time to be published in 1898 in the Appendix to the Edinburgh Edition (vol. 28). The subsequent collected editions in the main follow the text of the Edinburgh Edition: Pentland (1906–7), Swanston (1911–12), Vailima (1922–3) and Tusitala (1923–4). Stevenson also drafted a Note on the novel, which has been issued in fragments (see Appendix to this edition).

The present edition follows the text of the Edinburgh Edition. With one specific exception, there is no good reason to doubt Colvin's assurance that the text he printed in 1896 had Stevenson's approval. Over the spelling of Scots words, however, to which Stevenson brought a native solicitude, Colvin's English ear is not to be trusted.

In the present text therefore the spelling of certain Scots words reverts to that of the first edition of 1889.

There is, however, one particularly good reason to keep faith with the Edinburgh Edition. It follows, as all later editions do not, Stevenson's directive that the sections of the narrative should not be numbered. In a letter of May 1889 to his editor at *Scribner's*, accompanying the last serial instalment, Stevenson asked Burlingame to 'see that the book runs through *without any numeral division* according to the MS and without regard to the magazine dislocations' (his own italics; *Letters* 6, 299). Though the first American edition followed his wishes, the first English edition did not. But the Edinburgh Edition does preserve the effect Stevenson had in mind, of renouncing the consequentiality of chapter numbers. It also reunites the opening and closing sections, both of which had been divided in serial form, so that instead of twelve numbered chapters, it presents ten unnumbered sections distinguished only by title. Stevenson had followed a similar format in *The Strange Case of Dr Jekyll and Mr Hyde*, of which it has been well observed that 'the chapter titles on the contents page might be mistaken for a collection of short stories rather than a sequence of events' (Colin Manlove, '"Closer than an Eye": The Interconnection of Stevenson's *Dr Jekyll and Mr Hyde*', *Studies in Scottish Literature*, 23 (1988), 87–103). This is clearly an effect that Stevenson wanted to repeat in *The Master of Ballantrae.* To number this collection of narratives from 1 to 12 is to impose an air of editorial control on them, of mastery, such as he wanted expressly to avoid.

Footnotes indicated by an asterisk are Stevenson's own.

SELECT BIBLIOGRAPHY

(Place of publication is London unless otherwise stated.)

BIBLIOGRAPHY

Roger G. Swearingen, *The Prose Writings of Robert Louis Stevenson: A Guide*, 1980.

OTHER NOVELS, TALES AND ESSAYS

For comparison with *The Master of Ballantrae*, the following are particularly relevant:

Kidnapped, 1886.

'Thrawn Janet' and 'The Merry Men', in *The Merry Men and Other Tales and Fables*, 1887.

Catriona, 1893.

The Amateur Emigrant, 1895.

Weir of Hermiston, 1896.

Robert Louis Stevenson: The Scottish Stories and Essays, ed. Kenneth Gelder, Edinburgh, 1989.

LETTERS

Henry James and Robert Louis Stevenson: A Record of Friendship and Criticism, ed. Janet Adam Smith, 1948.

RLS: Stevenson's Letters to Charles Baxter, ed. De Lancey Ferguson and Marshall Waingrow, New Haven, Connecticut, 1956.

The Letters of Robert Louis Stevenson, 8 vols., ed. Bradford A. Booth and Ernest Mehew, New Haven and London, 1994–5.

BIOGRAPHY

Ian Bell, *Dreams of Exile: Robert Louis Stevenson*, Edinburgh, 1992.

Jenni Calder, *RLS: A Life Study*, 1980.

Elsie Noble Caldwell, *Last Witness for Robert Louis Stevenson*, Norman, Oklahoma, 1960.

David Daiches, *Robert Louis Stevenson and His World*, 1973.

J. C. Furnas, *Voyage to Windward: The Life of Robert Louis Stevenson*, 1951.

Frank McLynn, *Robert Louis Stevenson: A Biography*, 1993.

James Pope Hennessy, *Robert Louis Stevenson*, 1974.

CRITICISM

Robert E. Bonds, 'The Mystery of *The Master of Ballantrae*', *English Literature in Transition, 1880–1920*, 7.1 (1964), 8–11.

Jenni Calder (ed.), *Stevenson and Victorian Scotland*, Edinburgh, 1981.

Joseph E. Egan, 'From History to Myth: A Symbolic Reading of *The Master of Ballantrae*', *Studies in English Literature 1500–1900*, 8.4 (1968), 699–710.

Edwin M. Eigner, *Robert Louis Stevenson and Romantic Tradition*, Princeton, New Jersey, 1966.

Nathaniel Elliott, 'Robert Louis Stevenson and Scottish Literature', *English Literature in Transition, 1880–1920*, 12.2 (1969), 79–85.

Leslie Fiedler, 'R. L. S. Revisited', in *No! in Thunder: Essays on Myth and Literature*, 1963.

Douglas Gifford, 'Stevenson and Scottish Fiction: The Importance of *The Master of Ballantrae*', in Calder (ed.), *Stevenson and Victorian Scotland*.

'Myth, Parody and Dissociation: Scottish Fiction 1814–1914', in *The*

History of Scottish Literature. Volume 3: Nineteenth Century, ed. Douglas Gifford, Aberdeen, 1988.

Francis R. Hart, *The Scottish Novel: A Critical Survey*, 1978.

'Robert Louis Stevenson in Prose', in *The History of Scottish Literature. Volume 3: Nineteenth Century*, ed. Douglas Gifford, Aberdeen, 1988.

Robert Kiely, *Robert Louis Stevenson and the Fiction of Adventure*, Cambridge, Massachusetts, 1964.

James F. Kilroy, 'Narrative techniques in *The Master of Ballantrae*', *Studies in Scottish Literature*, 5.2 (1967), 98–106.

Paul Maixner (ed.), *Robert Louis Stevenson: The Critical Heritage*, London, Boston and Henley, 1981.

Karl Miller, *Doubles*, 1985.

Carol Mills, '*The Master of Ballantrae*: An Experiment with Genre', in Noble (ed.), *Robert Louis Stevenson*.

Andrew Noble (ed.), *Robert Louis Stevenson*, 1983.

Facsimile of the title page of the first edition (1889), reproduced from a copy in the Cambridge University Library by permission of the Syndics of Cambridge University Library.

THE

MASTER OF BALLANTRAE.

A Winter's Tale.

BY

ROBERT LOUIS STEVENSON,

Author of "Kidnapped," "Treasure Island,"
&c. &c. &c.

CASSELL & COMPANY, LIMITED

LONDON, PARIS, NEW YORK & MELBOURNE.

1889.

TO

SIR PERCY FLORENCE AND LADY SHELLEY[1]

Here is a tale which extends over many years and travels into many countries. By a peculiar fitness of circumstance the writer began, continued it, and concluded it among distant and diverse scenes. Above all, he was much upon the sea. The character and fortune of the fraternal enemies, the hall and shrubbery of Durrisdeer, the problem of Mackellar's homespun and how to shape it for superior flights; these were his company on deck in many star-reflecting harbours, ran often in his mind at sea to the tune of slatting canvas, and were dismissed (something of the suddenest) on the approach of squalls. It is my hope that these surroundings of its manufacture may to some degree find favour for my story with seafarers and sea-lovers like yourselves.

And at least here is a dedication from a great way off: written by the loud shores of a subtropical island near upon ten thousand miles from Boscombe Chine and Manor: scenes which rise before me as I write, along with the faces and voices of my friends.

Well, I am for the sea once more; no doubt Sir Percy also. Let us make the signal B. R. D.!

R. L. S.
Waikiki, May 17th, 1889.

PREFACE[1]

Although an old, consistent exile, the editor of the following pages revisits now and again the city of which he exults to be a native; and there are few things more strange, more painful, or more salutary, than such revisitations. Outside, in foreign spots, he comes by surprise and awakens more attention than he had expected; in his own city, the relation is reversed, and he stands amazed to be so little recollected. Elsewhere he is refreshed to see attractive faces, to remark possible friends; there he scouts the long streets, with a pang at heart, for the faces and friends that are no more. Elsewhere he is delighted with the presence of what is new, there tormented by the absence of what is old. Elsewhere he is content to be his present self; there he is smitten with an equal regret for what he once was and for what he once hoped to be.

He was feeling all this dimly, as he drove from the station, on his last visit; he was feeling it still as he alighted at the door of his friend Mr Johnstone Thomson, W.S.,[2] with whom he was to stay. A hearty welcome, a face not altogether changed, a few words that sounded of old days, a laugh provoked and shared, a glimpse in passing of the snowy cloth and bright decanters and the Piranesis[3] on the dining-room wall, brought him to his bed-room with a somewhat lightened cheer, and when he and Mr Thomson sat down a few minutes later, cheek by jowl, and pledged the past in a preliminary bumper, he was already almost consoled, he had already almost forgiven himself his two unpardonable errors, that he should ever have left his native city, or ever returned to it.

'I have something quite in your way,' said Mr Thomson. 'I wished to do honour to your arrival; because, my dear fellow, it is my own youth that comes back along with you; in a very tattered and withered state, to be sure, but – well! – all that's left of it.'

'A great deal better than nothing,' said the editor. 'But what is this which is quite in my way?'

'I was coming to that,' said Mr Thomson: 'Fate has put it in my power to honour your arrival with something really original by way of dessert. A mystery.'

'A mystery?' I repeated.

'Yes,' said his friend, 'a mystery. It may prove to be nothing, and it may prove to be a great deal. But in the meanwhile it is truly mysterious, no eye having looked on it for near a hundred years; it is highly genteel, for it treats of a titled family; and it ought to be melodramatic, for (according to the superscription) it is concerned with death.'

'I think I rarely heard a more obscure or a more promising annunciation,' the other remarked. 'But what is It?'

'You remember my predecessor's, old Peter M'Brair's business?'

'I remember him acutely; he could not look at me without a pang of reprobation, and he could not feel the pang without betraying it. He was to me a man of a great historical interest, but the interest was not returned.'

'Ah well, we go beyond him,' said Mr Thomson. 'I daresay old Peter knew as little about this as I do. You see, I succeeded to a prodigious accumulation of old law-papers and old tin boxes, some of them of Peter's hoarding, some of his father's, John, first of the dynasty, a great man in his day. Among other collections, were all the papers of the Durrisdeers.'

'The Durrisdeers!' cried I. 'My dear fellow, these may be of the greatest interest. One of them was out in the '45; one had some strange passages with the devil – you will find a note of it in Law's *Memorials*,[4] I think; and there was an unexplained tragedy, I know not what, much later, about a hundred years ago—'

'More than a hundred years ago,' said Mr Thomson. 'In 1783.'[5]

'How do you know that? I mean some death.'

'Yes, the lamentable deaths of my lord Durrisdeer and his brother, the Master of Ballantrae (attainted in the troubles),' said Mr Thomson with something the tone of a man quoting. 'Is that it?'

'To say truth,' said I, 'I have only seen some dim reference to the things in memoirs; and heard some traditions dimmer still, through my uncle (whom I think you knew). My uncle lived when he was a boy in the neighbourhood of St Bride's; he has often told me of the avenue closed up and grown over with grass, the great gates never opened, the last lord and his old maid sister who lived in the back parts of the house, a quiet, plain, poor, hum-drum couple it would seem – but pathetic too, as the last of that stirring and brave house – and, to the country folk, faintly terrible from some deformed traditions.'

'Yes,' said Mr Thomson. 'Henry Graeme Durie, the last lord, died in 1820; his sister, the Honourable Miss Katharine Durie, in '27; so much I know; and by what I have been going over the last few days, they were what you say, decent, quiet people, and not rich. To say truth, it was a letter of my lord's that put me on the search for the packet we are going to open this evening. Some papers could not be found; and he wrote to Jack M'Brair suggesting they might be among those sealed up by a Mr Mackellar. M'Brair answered, that the papers in question were all in Mackellar's own hand, all (as the writer understood) of a purely narrative character; and besides, said he, "I am not bound to open them before the year 1889." You may fancy if these words struck me: I instituted a hunt through all the M'Brair repositories; and at last hit upon that packet which (if you have had enough wine) I propose to show you at once.'

In the smoking-room, to which my host now led me, was a packet, fastened with many seals and enclosed in a single sheet of strong paper thus endorsed:

Papers relating to the lives and lamentable deaths of the late Lord Durrisdeer, and his elder brother James, commonly called Master of Ballantrae, attainted in the troubles: entrusted into the hands of John M'Brair in the Lawnmarket of Edinburgh, W.S.; this 20th day of September Anno Domini 1789; by him to be kept secret until the revolution of one hundred years complete, or until the 20th day of September 1889: the same compiled and written by me,

EPHRAIM MACKELLAR,[6]
For near forty years Land Steward on the estates of His Lordship.

As Mr Thomson is a married man, I will not say what hour had struck when we laid down the last of the following pages; but I will give a few words of what ensued.

'Here,' said Mr Thomson, 'is a novel ready to your hand: all you have to do is to work up the scenery, develop the characters, and improve the style.'

'My dear fellow,' said I, 'they are just the three things that I would rather die than set my hand to. It shall be published as it stands.'

'But it's so bald,' objected Mr Thomson.

'I believe there is nothing so noble as baldness,'[7] replied I, 'and I am sure there is nothing so interesting. I would have all literature bald, and all authors (if you like) but one.'

'Well, well,' said Mr Thomson, 'we shall see.'

SUMMARY OF EVENTS DURING THE MASTER'S WANDERINGS

The full truth of this odd matter is what the world has long been looking for, and public curiosity is sure to welcome. It so befell that I was intimately mingled with the last years and history of the house; and there does not live one man so able as myself to make these matters plain, or so desirous to narrate them faithfully. I knew the Master; on many secret steps of his career I have an authentic memoir in my hand; I sailed with him on his last voyage almost alone; I made one upon that winter's journey of which so many tales have gone abroad; and I was there at the man's death. As for my late Lord Durrisdeer, I served him and loved him near twenty years; and thought more of him the more I knew of him. Altogether, I think it not fit that so much evidence should perish; the truth is a debt I owe my lord's memory; and I think my old years will flow more smoothly, and my white hair lie quieter on the pillow, when the debt is paid.

The Duries of Durrisdeer and Ballantrae[1] were a strong family in the south-west from the days of David First.[2] A rhyme still current in the countryside –

> Kittle[3] folk are the Durrisdeers,
> They ride wi' ower mony spears –

bears the mark of its antiquity; and the name appears in another, which common report attributes to Thomas of Ercildoune[4] himself – I cannot say how truly, and which some have applied – I dare not say with how much justice – to the events of this narration:

Twa Duries in Durrisdeer,
  Ane to tie[5] and ane to ride.
An ill day for the groom
  And a waur[6] day for the bride.

Authentic history besides is filled with their exploits, which (to our modern eyes) seem not very commendable: and the family suffered its full share of those ups and downs to which the great houses of Scotland have been ever liable. But all these I pass over, to come to that memorable year 1745, when the foundations of this tragedy were laid.

At that time there dwelt a family of four persons in the house of Durrisdeer, near St Bride's, on the Solway shore; a chief hold of their race since the Reformation. My old lord, eighth of the name, was not old in years, but he suffered prematurely from the disabilities of age; his place was at the chimney side; there he sat reading, in a lined gown, with few words for any man, and wry words for none: the model of an old retired housekeeper; and yet his mind very well nourished with study, and reputed in the country to be more cunning than he seemed. The Master of Ballantrae, James in baptism, took from his father the love of serious reading; some of his tact, perhaps, as well, but that which was only policy in the father became black dissimulation in the son. The face of his behaviour was merely popular and wild: he sat late at wine, later at the cards; had the name in the country of 'an unco[7] man for the lasses'; and was ever in the front of broils. But for all he was the first to go in, yet it was observed he was invariably the best to come off; and his partners in mischief were usually alone to pay the piper. This luck or dexterity got him several ill-wishers, but with the rest of the country enhanced his reputation; so that great things were looked for in his future, when he should have gained more gravity. One very black mark he had to his name; but the matter was hushed up at the time, and so defaced by legends before I came into these parts that I scruple to set it down. If it was true, it was a horrid fact in one so young; and if false, it was a horrid calumny. I think it notable that he had always vaunted himself quite implacable, and was taken at his word; so that he had the addition among his neighbours of 'an ill man to cross.' Here was altogether a young nobleman (not yet twenty-four in the year '45) who had made a figure in the country beyond his time of life. The less marvel if there were little heard of the second son, Mr Henry (my late Lord Durrisdeer), who was neither very bad nor yet very able, but an honest, solid sort of lad, like many of his neighbours. Little heard, I say; but indeed it was a case of little spoken. He was known among the salmon fishers in the firth, for that was a sport that he assiduously followed; he was an excellent good horse-doctor besides; and took a chief hand, almost from a boy, in the management of the estates. How hard a part that was, in the situation of that family, none knows better than myself; nor yet with how little colour of justice a man may there acquire the reputation of a tyrant and a miser. The fourth person in the house was Miss Alison Graeme, a near kinswoman, an orphan, and the heir to a considerable fortune which her father had acquired in trade. This money was loudly called for by my lord's necessities; indeed, the land was deeply mortgaged; and Miss Alison was designed accordingly to be the Master's wife, gladly enough on her side; with how much good-will on his is another matter. She was a comely girl, and in those days very spirited and self-willed; for the old lord having no daughter of his own, and my lady being long dead, she had grown up as best she might.

To these four came the news of Prince Charlie's landing,[8] and set them presently by the ears. My lord, like the chimney-keeper that he was, was all for temporising. Miss Alison held the other side, because it appeared romantical; and the Master (though I have heard they did not agree often) was for this once of her opinion. The adventure tempted him, as I conceive; he was tempted by the opportunity to raise the fortunes of the house, and not less by the hope of paying off his private liabilities, which were heavy beyond all opinion. As for Mr Henry, it appears he said little enough at first; his part came later on. It took the three a whole day's disputation before they agreed to steer a middle course, one son going forth to strike a blow for King James, my lord and the other staying at home to keep in favour with King George.[9] Doubtless this was my lord's decision; and, as is well known, it was the part played by many considerable families. But the one dispute settled, another opened. For my lord, Miss Alison, and Mr Henry all held the one view: that it was the cadet's[10] part to go out; and the Master, what with restlessness and vanity, would at no rate consent to stay at home. My lord pleaded, Miss Alison wept, Mr Henry was very plain spoken: all was of no avail.

'It is the direct heir of Durrisdeer that should ride by his King's bridle,' says the Master.

'If we were playing a manly part,' says Mr Henry, 'there might be sense in such talk. But what are we doing? Cheating at cards!'

'We are saving the house of Durrisdeer, Henry,' his father said.

'And see, James,' said Mr Henry, 'if I go, and the Prince has the upper hand, it will be easy to make your peace with King James. But if you go, and the expedition fails, we divide the right and the title. And what shall I be then?'

'You will be Lord Durrisdeer,' said the Master. 'I put all I have upon the table.'

'I play at no such game,' cries Mr Henry. 'I shall be left in such a situation as no man of sense and honour could endure. I shall be neither fish nor flesh!' he cried. And a little after he had another expression, plainer perhaps than he intended. 'It is your duty to be here with my father,' said he. 'You know well enough you are the favourite.'

'Ay?' said the Master. 'And there spoke Envy! Would you trip up my heels – Jacob?' said he, and dwelled upon the name maliciously.

Mr Henry went and walked at the low end of the hall[11] without reply; for he had an excellent gift of silence. Presently he came back.

'I am the cadet, and I *should* go,' said he. 'And my lord here is the master, and he says I *shall* go. What say ye to that, my brother?'

'I say this, Harry,' returned the Master, 'that when very obstinate folk are met, there are only two ways out: Blows – and I think none of us could care to go so far; or the arbitrament of chance – and here is a guinea piece. Will you stand by the toss of the coin?'

'I will stand and fall by it,' said Mr Henry. 'Heads, I go; shield, I stay.'

The coin was spun, and it fell shield. 'So there is a lesson for Jacob,' says the Master.

'We shall live to repent of this,' says Mr Henry, and flung out of the hall.

As for Miss Alison, she caught up that piece of gold which had just sent her lover to the wars, and flung it clean through the family shield in the great painted window.

'If you loved me as well as I love you, you would have stayed,' cried she.

' "I could not love you, dear, so well, loved I not honour more," '[12] sang the Master.

'O!' she cried, 'you have no heart – I hope you may be killed!' and she ran from the room, and in tears, to her own chamber.

It seems the Master turned to my lord with his most comical manner, and says he, 'This looks like a devil of a wife.'

'I think you are a devil of a son to me,' cried his father, 'you that have always been the favourite, to my shame be it spoken. Never a good hour have I gotten of you since you were born; no, never one good hour,' and repeated it again the third time. Whether it was the Master's levity, or his insubordination, or Mr Henry's word about the favourite son, that had so much disturbed my lord, I do not know: but I incline to think it was the last, for I have it by all accounts that Mr Henry was more made up to from that hour.

Altogether it was in pretty ill blood with his family that the Master rode to the North; which was the more sorrowful for others to remember when it seemed too late. By fear and favour he had scraped together near upon a dozen men, principally tenants' sons; they were all pretty full when they set forth, and rode up the hill by the old abbey, roaring and singing, the white cockade in every hat. It was a desperate venture for so small a company to cross the most of Scotland unsupported; and (what made folk think so the more) even as that poor dozen was clattering up the hill, a great ship of the King's navy, that could have brought them under with a single boat, lay with her broad ensign streaming in the bay. The next afternoon, having given the Master a fair start, it was Mr Henry's turn; and he rode off, all by himself, to offer his sword and carry letters from his father to King George's Government. Miss Alison was shut in her room, and did little but weep, till both were gone; only she stitched the cockade upon the Master's hat, and (as John Paul told me) it was wetted with tears when he carried it down to him.

In all that followed, Mr Henry and my old lord were true to their bargain. That ever they accomplished anything is more than I could learn; and that they were anyway strong on the King's side, more than I believe. But they kept the letter of loyalty, corresponded with my Lord President,[13] sat still at home, and had little or no commerce with the Master while that business lasted. Nor was he, on his side, more communicative. Miss Alison, indeed, was always sending him expresses, but I do not know if she had many answers. Macconochie rode for her once, and found the Highlanders before Carlisle,[14] and the Master riding by the Prince's side in high favour; he took the letter (so Macconochie tells), opened it, glanced it through with a mouth like a man whistling, and stuck it in his belt, whence, on his horse passageing,[15] it fell unregarded to the ground. It was Macconochie who picked it up; and he still kept it, and indeed I have seen it in his hands. News came to Durrisdeer of course, by the common report, as it goes travelling through a country, a thing always wonderful to me. By that means the family learned more of the Master's favour with the Prince, and the ground it was said to stand on: for by a strange condescension in a man so proud – only that he was a man still more ambitious – he was said to have crept into notability by truckling to the Irish. Sir Thomas Sullivan,[16] Colonel Burke, and the rest, were his daily comrades, by which course he withdrew himself from his own country-folk. All the small intrigues he had a hand in fomenting; thwarted my Lord George[17] upon a thousand points; was always for the advice that seemed palatable to the Prince, no matter if it was good or bad; and seems upon the whole (like the gambler he was all through life) to have had less regard to the chances of the campaign than to the greatness of favour he might aspire to, if, by any luck, it should succeed. For the rest, he did very well in the field; no one questioned that: for he was no coward.

The next was the news of Culloden,[18] which was brought to Durrisdeer by one of the tenants' sons – the only survivor, he declared, of all those that had gone singing up the hill. By an unfortunate chance John Paul and Macconochie had that very morning found the guinea piece – which was the root of all the evil – sticking in a holly bush; they had been 'up the gait,'[19] as the servants say at Durrisdeer, to the change-house; and if they had little left of the guinea, they had less of their wits. What must John Paul do but burst into the hall where the family sat at dinner, and cry the news to them that 'Tam Macmorland was but new lichtit[20] at the door, and – wirra, wirra[21] – there were nane to come behind him'?

They took the word in silence like folk condemned; only Mr Henry carrying his palm to his face, and Miss Alison laying her head outright upon her hands. As for my lord, he was like ashes.

'I have still one son,' says he. 'And, Henry, I will do you this justice – it is the kinder that is left.'

It was a strange thing to say in such a moment; but my lord had never forgotten Mr Henry's speech, and he had years of injustice on his conscience. Still it was a strange thing, and more than Miss Alison could let pass. She broke out and blamed my lord for his unnatural words, and Mr Henry because he was sitting there in safety when his brother lay dead, and herself because she had given her sweetheart ill words at his departure, calling him the flower of the flock, wringing her hands, protesting her love, and crying on him by his name – so that the servants stood astonished.

Mr Henry got to his feet, and stood holding his chair. It was he that was like ashes now.

'O!' he burst out suddenly, 'I know you loved him.'

'The world knows that, glory be to God!' cries she; and then to Mr Henry: 'There is none but me to know one thing – that you were a traitor to him in your heart.'

'God knows,' groans he, 'it was lost love on both sides.'

Time went by in the house after that without much change; only they were now three instead of four, which was a perpetual reminder of their loss. Miss Alison's money, you are to bear in mind, was highly needful for the estates; and the one brother being dead, my old lord soon set his heart upon her marrying the other. Day in, day out, he would work upon her, sitting by the chimney-side with his finger in his Latin book, and his eyes set upon her face with a kind of pleasant intentness that became the old gentleman very well. If she wept, he would condole with her like an ancient man that has seen worse times and begins to think lightly even of sorrow; if she raged, he would fall to reading again in his Latin book, but always with some civil excuse; if she offered, as she often did, to let them have her money in a gift, he would show her how little it consisted with his honour, and remind her, even if he should consent, that Mr Henry would certainly refuse. *Non vi sed sæpe cadendo*[22] was a favourite word of his; and no doubt this quiet persecution wore away much of her resolve; no doubt, besides, he had a great influence on the girl, having stood in the place of both her parents; and, for that matter, she was herself filled with the spirit of the Duries, and would have gone a great way for the glory of Durrisdeer; but not so far, I think, as to marry my poor patron, had it not been – strangely enough – for the circumstance of his extreme unpopularity.

This was the work of Tam Macmorland. There was not much harm in Tam; but he had that grievous weakness, a long tongue; and as the only man in that country who had been out – or, rather, who had come in again – he was sure of listeners. Those that have the underhand in any fighting, I have observed, are ever anxious to persuade themselves they were betrayed. By Tam's account of it, the rebels had been betrayed at every turn and by every officer they had; they had been betrayed at Derby, and betrayed at Falkirk; the night march was a step of treachery of my Lord George's; and Culloden was lost by the treachery of the Macdonalds. This habit of imputing treason grew upon the fool, till at last he must have in Mr Henry also. Mr Henry (by his account) had betrayed the lads of Durrisdeer; he had promised to follow with more men, and instead of that he had ridden to King George. 'Ay, and the next day!' Tam would cry. 'The puir bonnie Master, and the puir kind lads that rade wi' him, were hardly ower the scaur[23] or he was aff – the Judis! Ay, weel – he has his way o't: he's to be my lord, nae less, and there's mony a cold corp amang the Hieland heather!' And at this, if Tam had been drinking, he would begin to weep.

Let any one speak long enough, he will get believers. This view of Mr Henry's behaviour crept about the country by little and little; it was talked upon by folk that knew the contrary, but were short of topics; and it was heard and believed and given out for gospel by the ignorant and the ill-willing. Mr Henry began to be shunned; yet a while, and the commons began to murmur as he went by, and the women (who are always the most bold because they are the most safe) to cry out their reproaches to his face. The Master was cried up for a saint. It was remembered how he had never any hand in pressing the tenants; as, indeed, no more he had, except to spend the money. He was a little wild perhaps, the folk said; but how much better was a natural, wild lad that would soon have settled down, than a skinflint and a sneckdraw,[24] sitting with his nose in an account-book to persecute poor tenants! One trollop, who had had a child to the Master, and by all accounts been very badly used, yet made herself a kind of champion of his memory. She flung a stone one day at Mr Henry.

'Whaur's the bonnie lad that trustit ye?' she cried.

Mr Henry reined in his horse and looked upon her, the blood flowing from his lip. 'Ay, Jess?' says he. 'You too? And yet ye should ken me better.' For it was he who had helped her with money.

The woman had another stone ready, which she made as if she would cast; and he, to ward himself, threw up the hand that held his riding-rod.

'What, would ye beat a lassie, ye ugly—?' cries she, and ran away screaming as though he had struck her.

Next day word went about the country like wildfire that Mr Henry had beaten Jessie Broun within an inch of her life. I give it as one instance of how this snowball grew, and one calumny brought another; until my poor patron was so perished in reputation that he began to keep the house like my lord. All this while, you may be very sure, he uttered no complaints at home; the very ground of the scandal was too sore a matter to be handled; and Mr Henry was very proud, and strangely obstinate in silence. My old lord must have heard of it, by John Paul, if by no one else; and he must at least have remarked the altered habits of his son. Yet even he, it is probable, knew not how high the feeling ran; and as for Miss Alison, she was ever the last person to hear news, and the least interested when she heard them.

In the height of the ill-feeling (for it died away as it came, no man could say why) there was an election forward in the town of St Bride's, which is the next to Durrisdeer, standing on the Water of Swift; some grievance was fermenting, I forget what, if ever I heard: and it was currently said there would be broken heads ere night, and that the sheriff had sent as far as Dumfries for soldiers. My lord moved that Mr Henry should be present, assuring him it was necessary to appear, for the credit of the house. 'It will soon be reported,' said he, 'that we do not take the lead in our own country.'

'It is a strange lead that I can take,' said Mr Henry; and when they had pushed him further, 'I tell you the plain truth,' he said: 'I dare not show my face.'

'You are the first of the house that ever said so,' cries Miss Alison.

'We will go all three,' said my lord; and sure enough he got into his boots (the first time in four years – a sore business John Paul had to get them on), and Miss Alison into her riding-coat, and all three rode together to St Bride's.

The streets were full of the riff-raff of all the countryside, who had no sooner clapped eyes on Mr Henry than the hissing began, and the hooting, and the cries of 'Judas!' and 'Where was the Master?' and 'Where were the poor lads that rode with him?' Even a stone was cast; but the more part cried shame at that, for my old lord's sake, and Miss Alison's. It took not ten minutes to persuade my lord that Mr Henry had been right. He said never a word, but turned his horse about, and home again, with his chin upon his bosom. Never a word said Miss Alison; no doubt she thought the more; no doubt her pride was stung, for she was a bone-bred Durie; and no doubt her heart was touched to see her cousin so unjustly used. That night she was never in bed; I have often blamed my lady – when I call to mind that night I readily forgive her all; and the first thing in the morning she came to the old lord in his usual seat.

'If Henry still wants me,' said she, 'he can have me now.' To himself she had a different speech: 'I bring you no love, Henry; but God knows, all the pity in the world.'

June the 1st, 1748, was the day of their marriage. It was December of the same year that first saw me alighting at the doors of the great house; and from there I take up the history of events as they befell under my own observation, like a witness in a court.

I made the last of my journey in the cold end of December, in a mighty dry day of frost, and who should be my guide but Patey Macmorland, brother of Tam! For a tow-headed, bare-legged brat of ten, he had more ill tales upon his tongue than ever I heard the match of; having drunken betimes in his brother's cup. I was still not so old myself; pride had not yet the upper hand of curiosity; and indeed it would have taken any man, that cold morning, to hear all the old clashes of the country, and be shown all the places by the way where strange things had fallen out. I had tales of Claverhouse[25] as we came through the bogs, and tales of the devil as we came over the top of the scaur. As we came in by the abbey I heard somewhat of the old monks, and more of the free-traders, who use its ruins for a magazine, landing for that cause within a cannon-shot of Durrisdeer; and along all the road the Duries and poor Mr Henry were in the first rank of slander. My mind was thus highly prejudiced against the family I was about to serve, so that I was half surprised when I beheld Durrisdeer itself, lying in a pretty, sheltered bay, under the Abbey Hill; the house most commodiously built in the French fashion, or perhaps Italianate, for I have no skill in these arts; and the place the most beautified with gardens, lawns, shrubberies, and trees I had ever seen. The money sunk here unproductively would have quite restored the family; but as it was, it cost a revenue to keep it up.

Mr Henry came himself to the door to welcome me: a tall dark young gentleman (the Duries are all black men) of a plain and not cheerful face, very strong in body, but not so strong in health; taking me by the hand without any pride, and putting me at home with plain kind speeches. He led me into the hall, booted as I was, to present me to my lord. It was still daylight; and the first thing I observed was a lozenge of clear glass in the midst of the shield in the painted window, which I remember thinking a blemish on a room otherwise so handsome, with its family portraits, and the pargeted[26] ceiling with pendants, and the carved chimney, in one corner of which my old lord sat reading in his Livy. He was like Mr Henry, with much the same plain countenance, only more subtle and pleasant, and his talk a thousand times more entertaining. He had many questions to ask me, I remember, of Edinburgh College,[27] where I had just received my mastership of arts, and of the various professors, with whom and their proficiency he seemed well acquainted; and thus, talking of things that I knew, I soon got liberty of speech in my new home.

In the midst of this came Mrs Henry into the room; she was very far gone, Miss Katharine being due in about six weeks, which made me think less of her beauty at the first sight; and she used me with more of condescension than the rest; so that, upon all accounts, I kept her in the third place of my esteem.

It did not take long before all Patey Macmorland's tales were blotted out of my belief, and I was become, what I have ever since remained, a loving servant of the house of Durrisdeer. Mr Henry had the chief part of my affection. It was with him I worked; and I found him an exacting master, keeping all his kindness for those hours in which we were unemployed, and in the steward's office not only loading me with work, but viewing me with a shrewd supervision. At length one day he looked up from his paper with a kind of timidness, and says he, 'Mr Mackellar, I think I ought to tell you that you do very well.' That was my first word of commendation; and from that day his jealousy of my performance was relaxed; soon it was 'Mr Mackellar' here, and 'Mr Mackellar' there, with the whole family; and for much of my service at Durrisdeer I have transacted everything at my own time, and to my own fancy, and never a farthing challenged. Even while he was driving me, I had begun to find my heart go out to Mr Henry; no doubt, partly in pity, he was a man so palpably unhappy. He would fall into a deep muse over our accounts, staring at the page or out of the window; and at those times the look of his face, and the sigh that would break from him, awoke in me strong feelings of curiosity and commiseration. One day, I remember, we were late upon some business in the steward's room. This room is in the top of the house, and has a view upon the bay, and over a little wooded cape, on the long sands; and there, right over against the sun, which was then dipping, we saw the free-traders, with a great force of men and horses, scouring on the beach. Mr Henry had been staring straight west, so that I marvelled he was not blinded by the sun; suddenly he frowns, rubs his hand upon his brow, and turns to me with a smile.

'You would not guess what I was thinking,' says he. 'I was thinking I would be a happier man if I could ride and run the danger of my life with these lawless companions.'

I told him I had observed he did not enjoy good spirits; and that it was a common fancy to envy others and think we should be the better of some change; quoting Horace to the point, like a young man fresh from college.

'Why, just so,' said he. 'And with that we may get back to our accounts.'

It was not long before I began to get wind of the causes that so much depressed him. Indeed, a blind man must have soon discovered there was a shadow on that house, the shadow of the Master of Ballantrae. Dead or alive (and he was then supposed to be dead) that man was his brother's rival: his rival abroad, where there was never a good word for Mr Henry, and nothing but regret and praise for the Master; and his rival at home, not only with his father and his wife, but with the very servants.

They were two old serving-men that were the leaders. John Paul, a little, bald, solemn, stomachy man, a great professor of piety and (take him for all in all) a pretty faithful servant, was the chief of the Master's faction. None durst go so far as John. He took a pleasure in disregarding Mr Henry publicly, often with a slighting comparison. My lord and Mrs Henry took him up, to be sure, but never so resolutely as they should; and he had only to pull his weeping face and begin his lamentations for the Master – 'his laddie,' as he called him – to have the whole condoned. As for Henry, he let these things pass in silence, sometimes with a sad and sometimes with a black look. There was no rivalling the dead, he knew that; and how to censure an old serving-man for a fault of loyalty was more than he could see. His was not the tongue to do it.

Macconochie was chief upon the other side; an old, ill-spoken, swearing, ranting, drunken dog; and I have often thought it an odd circumstance in human nature that these two serving-men should each have been the champion of his contrary, and blackened their own faults, and made light of their own virtues, when they beheld them in a master. Macconochie had soon smelled out my secret inclination, took me much into his confidence, and would rant against the Master by the hour, so that even my work suffered. 'They're a' daft here,' he would cry, 'and be damned to them! The Master – the deil's in their thrapples[28] that should call him sae! it's Mr Henry should be master now! They were nane sae fond o' the Master when they had him, I'll can tell ye that. Sorrow on his name! Never a guid word did I hear on his lips, nor naebody else, but just fleering and flyting[29] and profane cursing – deil hae him! There's nane kennt his wickedness: him a gentleman! Did ever ye hear tell, Mr Mackellar, o' Wully White the wabster?[30] No? Aweel, Wully was an unco praying kind o' man; a dreigh[31] body, nane o' my kind, I never could abide the sight o' him; onyway he was a great hand by his way of it, and he up and rebukit the Master for some of his ongoings. It was a grand thing for the Master o' Ball'ntrae to tak up a feud wi' a wabster, wasnae't?' Macconochie would sneer; indeed, he never took the full name upon his lips but with a sort of a whine of hatred. 'But he did! A fine employ it was: chapping[32] at the man's door, and crying "boo" in his lum,[33] and puttin' poother[34] in his fire, and pee-oys* in his window; till the man thocht it was Auld Hornie was come seekin' him. Weel, to mak a lang story short, Wully gaed gyte.[35] At the hinder end they couldnae get him frae his knees, but he just roared and prayed and grat straucht[36] on, till he got his release. It was fair murder, a'body said that. Ask John Paul – he was brawly ashamed o' that game, him that's sic a Christian man! Grand doin's for the Master o' Ball'ntrae!' I asked him what the Master had thought of it himself. 'How would I ken?' says he. 'He never said naething.' And on again in his usual manner of banning and swearing, with every now and again a 'Master of Ballantrae' sneered through his nose. It was in one of these confidences that he showed me the Carlisle letter, the print of the horse-shoe still stamped in the paper. Indeed, that was our last confidence; for he then expressed himself so ill-naturedly of Mrs Henry that I

* A kind of firework made with damp powder.

had to reprimand him sharply, and must thenceforth hold him at a distance.

My old lord was uniformly kind to Mr Henry; he had even pretty ways of gratitude, and would sometimes clap him on the shoulder and say, as if to the world at large: 'This is a very good son to me.' And grateful he was, no doubt, being a man of sense and justice. But I think that was all, and I am sure Mr Henry thought so. The love was all for the dead son. Not that this was often given breath to; indeed, with me but once. My lord had asked me one day how I got on with Mr Henry, and I had told him the truth.

'Ay,' said he, looking sideways on the burning fire, 'Henry is a good lad, a very good lad,' said he. 'You have heard, Mr Mackellar, that I had another son? I am afraid he was not so virtuous a lad as Mr Henry; but dear me, he's dead, Mr Mackellar! and while he lived we were all very proud of him, all very proud. If he was not all he should have been in some ways, well, perhaps we loved him better!' This last he said looking musingly in the fire; and then to me, with a great deal of briskness, 'But I am rejoiced you do so well with Mr Henry. You will find him a good master.' And with that he opened his book, which was the customary signal of dismission. But it would be little that he read, and less that he understood; Culloden field and the Master, these would be the burthen of his thought; and the burthen of mine was an unnatural jealousy of the dead man for Mr Henry's sake, that had even then begun to grow on me.

I am keeping Mrs Henry for the last, so that this expression of my sentiment may seem unwarrantably strong: the reader shall judge for himself when I have done. But I must first tell of another matter, which was the means of bringing me more intimate. I had not yet been six months at Durrisdeer when it chanced that John Paul fell sick and must keep his bed; drink was the root of his malady, in my poor thought; but he was tended, and indeed carried himself, like an afflicted saint; and the very minister, who came to visit him, professed himself edified when he went away. The third morning of his sickness Mr Henry comes to me with something of a hang-dog look.

'Mackellar,' says he, 'I wish I could trouble you upon a little service. There is a pension we pay; it is John's part to carry it, and now that he is sick I know not to whom I should look, unless it was yourself. The matter is very delicate; I could not carry it with my own hand for a sufficient reason; I dare not send Macconochie, who is a talker, and I am – I have – I am desirous this should not come to Mrs Henry's ears,' says he, and flushed to his neck as he said it.

To say truth, when I found I was to carry money to one Jessie Broun, who was no better than she should be, I supposed it was some trip of his own that Mr Henry was dissembling. I was the more impressed when the truth came out.

It was up a wynd[37] off a side street in St Bride's that Jessie had her lodging. The place was very ill inhabited, mostly by the free-trading sort. There was a man with a broken head at the entry; half-way up, in a tavern, fellows were roaring and singing, though it was not yet nine in the day. Altogether, I had never seen a worse neighbourhood, even in the great city of Edinburgh, and I was in two minds to go back. Jessie's room was of a piece with her surroundings, and herself no better. She would not give me the receipt (which Mr Henry had told me to demand, for he was very methodical) until she had sent out for spirits, and I had pledged her in a glass; and all the time she carried on in a light-headed, reckless way – now aping the manners of a lady, now breaking into unseemly mirth, now making coquettish advances that oppressed me to the ground. Of the money she spoke more tragically.

'It's blood-money!' said she; 'I take it for that: blood-money for the betrayed! See what I'm brought down to! Ah, if the bonnie lad were back again, it would be changed days. But he's deid – he's lyin' deid amang the Hieland hills – the bonnie lad, the bonnie lad!'

She had a rapt manner of crying on the bonnie lad, clasping her hands and casting up her eyes, that I think she must have learned of strolling players; and I thought her sorrow very much of an affectation, and that she dwelled upon the business because her shame was now all she had to be proud of. I will not say I did not pity her, but it was a loathing pity at the best; and her last change of manner wiped it out. This was when she had had enough of me for an audience, and had set her name at last to the receipt. 'There!' says she, and, taking the most unwomanly oaths upon her tongue, bade me begone and carry it to the Judas who had sent me. It was the first time I had heard the name applied to Mr Henry; I was staggered besides at her sudden vehemence of word and manner, and got forth from the room, under this shower of curses, like a beaten dog. But even then I was not quit, for the vixen threw up her window, and, leaning forth, continued to revile me as I went up the wynd; the free-traders, coming to the tavern door, joined in the mockery, and one had even the inhumanity to set upon me a very savage small dog, which bit me in the ankle. This was a strong lesson, had I required one, to avoid ill company; and I rode home in much pain from the bite, and considerable indignation of mind.

Mr Henry was in the steward's room, affecting employment, but I could see he was only impatient to hear of my errand.

'Well?' says he, as soon as I came in; and when I had told him something of what passed, and that Jessie seemed an undeserving woman, and far from grateful: 'She is no friend to me,' said he; 'but indeed, Mackellar, I have few friends to boast of, and Jessie has some cause to be unjust. I need not dissemble what all the country knows: she was not very well used by one of our family.' This was the first time I had heard him refer to the Master, even distantly; and I think he found his tongue rebellious even for that much, but presently he resumed – 'This is why I would have nothing said. It would give pain to Mrs Henry . . . and to my father,' he added, with another flush.

'Mr Henry,' said I, 'if you will take a freedom at my hands, I would tell you to let that woman be. What service is your money to the like of her? She has no sobriety and no economy – as for gratitude, you will as soon get milk from a whinstone; and if you will pretermit your bounty, it will make no change at all but just to save the ankles of your messengers.'

Mr Henry smiled. 'But I am grieved about your ankle,' said he the next moment, with a proper gravity.

'And observe,' I continued, 'I give you this advice upon consideration; and yet my heart was touched for the woman in the beginning.'

'Why, there it is, you see!' said Mr Henry. 'And you are to remember that I knew her once a very decent lass. Besides which, althoug' I speak little of my family, I think much of its repute.'

And with that he broke up the talk, which was the first we had together in such confidence. But the same afternoon I had the proof that his father was perfectly acquainted with the business, and that it was only from his wife that Mr Henry kept it secret.

'I fear you had a painful errand to-day,' says my lord to me, 'for which, as it enters in no way among your duties, I wish to thank you, and to remind you at the same time (in case Mr Henry should have neglected) how very desirable it is that no word of it should reach my daughter. Reflections on the dead, Mr Mackellar, are doubly painful.'

Anger glowed in my heart; and I could have told my lord to his face how little he had to do, bolstering up the image of the dead in Mrs Henry's heart, and how much better he were employed to shatter that false idol; for by this time I saw very well how the land lay between my patron and his wife.

My pen is clear enough to tell a plain tale; but to render the effect of an infinity of small things, not one great enough in itself to be narrated; and to translate the story of looks, and the message of voices when they are saying no great matter; and to put in half a page the essence of near eighteen months – this is what I despair to accomplish. The fault, to be very blunt, lay all in Mrs Henry. She felt it a merit to have consented to the marriage, and she took it like a martyrdom; in which my old lord, whether he knew it or not, fomented her. She made a merit, besides, of her constancy to the dead, though its name, to a nicer conscience, should have seemed rather disloyalty to the living; and here also my lord gave her his countenance. I suppose he was glad to talk of his loss, and ashamed to dwell on it with Mr Henry. Certainly, at least, he made a little coterie apart in that family of three, and it was the husband who was shut out. It seems it was an old custom when the family were alone in Durrisdeer, that my lord should take his wine to the chimney-side, and Miss Alison, instead of withdrawing, should bring a stool to his knee, and chatter to him privately; and after she had become my patron's wife the same manner of doing was continued. It should have been pleasant to behold this ancient gentleman so loving with his daughter, but I was too much a partisan of Mr Henry's to be anything but wroth at his exclusion. Many's the time I have seen him make an obvious resolve, quit the table, and go and join himself to his wife and my Lord Durrisdeer; and on their part, they were never backward to make him welcome, turned to him smilingly as to an intruding child, and took him into their talk with an effort so ill-concealed that he was soon back again beside me at the table, whence (so great is the hall of Durrisdeer) we could but hear the murmur of voices at the chimney. There he would sit and watch, and I along with him; and sometimes by my lord's head sorrowfully shaken, or his hand laid on Mrs Henry's head, or hers upon his knee as if in consolation, or sometimes by an exchange of tearful looks, we would draw our conclusion that the talk had gone to the old subject and the shadow of the dead was in the hall.

I have hours when I blame Mr Henry for taking all too patiently; yet we are to remember he was married in pity, and accepted his wife upon that term. And, indeed, he had small encouragement to make a stand. Once, I remember, he announced he had found a man to replace the pane of the stained window, which, as it was he that managed all the business, was a thing clearly within his attributions. But to the Master's fanciers that pane was like a relic; and on the first word of any change the blood flew to Mrs Henry's face.

'I wonder at you!' she cried.

'I wonder at myself,' says Mr Henry, with more of bitterness than I had ever heard him to express.

Thereupon my old lord stepped in with his smooth talk, so that before the meal was at an end all seemed forgotten; only that, after dinner, when the pair had withdrawn as usual to the chimney-side, we could see her weeping with her head upon his knee. Mr Henry kept up the talk with me upon some topic of the estates – he could speak of little else but business, and was never the best of company; but he kept it up that day with more continuity, his eye straying ever and again to the chimney, and his voice changing to another key, but without check of delivery. The pane, however, was not replaced; and I believe he counted it a great defeat.

Whether he was stout enough or no, God knows he was kind enough. Mrs Henry had a manner of condescension with him, such as (in a wife) would have pricked my vanity into an ulcer; he took it like a favour. She held him at the staff's end; forgot and then remembered and unbent to him, as we do to children; burthened him with cold kindness; reproved him with a change of colour and a bitten lip, like one shamed by his disgrace: ordered him with a look of the eye, when she was off her guard; when she was on the watch, pleaded with him for the most natural attentions, as though they were unheard-of favours. And to all this he replied with the most unwearied service; loving, as folk say, the very ground she trod on, and carrying that love in his eyes as bright as a lamp. When Miss Katharine was to be born, nothing would serve but he must stay in the room behind the head of the bed. There he sat, as white (they tell me) as a sheet, and the sweat dropping from his brow; and the handkerchief he had in his hand was crushed into a little ball no bigger than a musket-bullet. Nor could he bear the sight of Miss Katharine for many a day; indeed, I doubt if he was ever what he should have been to my young lady; for the which want of natural feeling he was loudly blamed.

Such was the state of this family down to the 7th April 1749, when there befell the first of that series of events which were to break so many hearts and lose so many lives.

On that day I was sitting in my room a little before supper, when John Paul burst open the door with no civility of knocking, and told me there was one below that wished to speak with the steward; sneering at the name of my office.

I asked what manner of man, and what his name was; and this disclosed the cause of John's ill-humour; for it appeared the visitor refused to name himself except to me, a sore affront to the major-domo's consequence.

'Well,' said I, smiling a little, 'I will see what he wants.'

I found in the entrance-hall a big man, very plainly habited, and wrapped in a sea-cloak, like one new landed, as indeed he was. Not far off Macconochie was standing, with his tongue out of his mouth and his hand upon his chin, like a dull fellow thinking hard, and the stranger, who had brought his cloak about his face, appeared uneasy. He had no sooner seen me coming than he went to meet me with an effusive manner.

'My dear man,' said he, 'a thousand apologies for disturbing you, but I'm in the most awkward position. And there's a son of a ramrod there that I should know the looks of, and more, betoken, I believe that he knows mine. Being in this family, sir, and in a place of some responsibility (which was the cause I took the liberty to send for you), you are doubtless of the honest party?'

'You may be sure at least,' says I, 'that all of that party are quite safe in Durrisdeer.'

'My dear man, it is my very thought,' says he. 'You see, I have just been set on shore here by a very honest man, whose name I cannot remember, and who is to stand off and on for me till morning, at some danger to himself; and, to be clear with you, I am a little concerned lest it should be at some to me. I have saved my life so often, Mr—, I forget your name, which is a very good one – that, faith, I would be very loth to lose it after all. And the son of a ramrod, whom I believe I saw before Carlisle . . .'

'O, sir,' said I, 'you can trust Macconochie until to-morrow.'

'Well, and it's a delight to hear you say so,' says the stranger. 'The truth is, that my name is not a very suitable one in this country of Scotland. With a gentleman like you, my dear man, I would have no concealments of course; and by your leave I'll just breathe it in your ear. They call me Francis Burke – Colonel Francis Burke; and I am here, at a most damnable risk to myself, to see your masters – if you'll excuse me, my good man, for giving them the name, for I'm sure it's a circumstance I would never have guessed from your appearance. And if you would just be so very obliging as to take my name to them, you might say that I come bearing letters which I am sure they will be very rejoiced to have the reading of.'

Colonel Francis Burke was one of the Prince's Irishmen,[38] that did his cause such an infinity of hurt, and were so much distasted of the Scots at the time of the rebellion; and it came at once into my mind how the Master of Ballantrae had astonished all men by going with that party. In the same moment a strong foreboding of the truth possessed my soul.

'If you will step in here,' said I, opening a chamber door, 'I will let my lord know.'

'And I am sure it's very good of you, Mr What's-your-name,' says the Colonel.

Up to the hall I went, slow-footed. There they were, all three – my old lord in his place, Mrs Henry at work by the window, Mr Henry (as was much his custom) pacing the low end. In the midst was the table laid for supper. I told them briefly what I had to say. My old lord lay back in his seat. Mrs Henry sprang up standing with a mechanical motion, and she and her husband stared at each other's eyes across the room; it was the strangest, challenging look these two exchanged, and as they looked, the colour faded in their faces. Then Mr Henry turned to me; not to speak, only to sign with his finger; but that was enough, and I went down again for the Colonel.

When we returned, these three were in much the same position I had left them in; I believe no word had passed.

'My Lord Durrisdeer, no doubt?' says the Colonel, bowing, and my lord bowed in answer. 'And this,' continues the Colonel, 'should be the Master of Ballantrae?'

'I have never taken that name,' said Mr Henry; 'but I am Henry Durie, at your service.'

Then the Colonel turns to Mrs Henry, bowing with his hat upon his heart and the most killing airs of gallantry. 'There can be no mistake about so fine a figure of a lady,' says he. 'I address the seductive Miss Alison, of whom I have so often heard?'

Once more husband and wife exchanged a look.

'I am Mrs Henry Durie,' said she; 'but before my marriage my name was Alison Graeme.'

Then my lord spoke up. 'I am an old man, Colonel Burke,' said he, 'and a frail one. It will be mercy on your part to be expeditious. Do you bring me news of—' he hesitated, and then the word broke from him with a singular change of voice – 'my son?'

'My dear lord, I will be round with you like a soldier,' said the Colonel. 'I do.'

My lord held out a wavering hand; he seemed to wave a signal, but whether it was to give him time or to speak on, was more than we could guess. At length he got out the one word, 'Good?'

'Why, the very best in the creation!' cries the Colonel. 'For my good friend and admired comrade is at this hour in the fine city of Paris, and as like as not, if I know anything of his habits, he will be drawing in his chair to a piece of dinner. – Bedad, I believe the lady's fainting.'

Mrs Henry was indeed the colour of death, and drooped against the window-frame. But when Mr Henry made a movement as if to run to her, she straightened with a sort of shiver. 'I am well,' she said, with her white lips.

Mr Henry stopped, and his face had a strong twitch of anger. The next moment he had turned to the Colonel. 'You must not blame yourself,' says he, 'for this effect on Mrs Durie. It is only natural; we were all brought up like brother and sister.'

Mrs Henry looked at her husband with something like relief, or even gratitude. In my way of thinking, that speech was the first step he made in her good graces.

'You must try to forgive me, Mrs Durie, for indeed and I am just an Irish savage,' said the Colonel; 'and I deserve to be shot for not breaking the matter more artistically to a lady. – But here are the Master's own letters; one for each of the three of you; and to be sure (if I know anything of my friend's genius) he will tell his own story with a better grace.'

He brought the three letters forth as he spoke, arranged them by their superscriptions, presented the first to my lord, who took it greedily, and advanced towards Mrs Henry holding out the second.

But the lady waved it back. 'To my husband,' says she, with a choked voice.

The Colonel was a quick man, but at this he was somewhat nonplussed. 'To be sure!' says he; 'how very dull of me! To be sure!' But he still held the letter.

At last Mr Henry reached forth his hand, and there was nothing to be done but give it up. Mr Henry took the letters (both hers and his own), and looked upon their outside, with his brows knit hard, as if he were thinking. He had surprised me all through by his excellent behaviour; but he was to excel himself now.

'Let me give you a hand to your room,' said he to his wife. 'This has come something of the suddenest; and, at any rate, you will wish to read your letter by yourself.'

Again she looked upon him with the same thought of wonder; but he gave her no time, coming straight to where she stood. 'It will be better so, believe me,' said he; 'and Colonel Burke is too considerate not to excuse you.' And with that he took her hand by the fingers, and led her from the hall.

Mrs Henry returned no more that night; and when Mr Henry went to visit her next morning, as I heard long afterwards, she gave him the letter again, still unopened.

'O, read it and be done!' he had cried.

'Spare me that,' said she.

And by these two speeches, to my way of thinking, each undid a great part of what they had previously done well. But the letter, sure enough, came into my hands, and by me was burned, unopened.

To be very exact as to the adventures of the Master after Culloden, I wrote not long ago to Colonel Burke, now a Chevalier of the Order of St Louis, begging him for some notes in writing, since I could scarce depend upon my memory at so great an interval. To confess the truth, I have been somewhat embarrassed by his response; for he sent me the complete memoirs of his life, touching only in places on the Master; running to a much greater length than my whole story, and not everywhere (as it seems to me) designed for edification. He begged in his letter, dated from Ettenheim,[39] that I would find a publisher for the whole, after I had made what use of it I required; and I think I shall best answer my own purpose and fulfil his wishes by giving certain parts of it in full. In this way my readers will have a detailed, and, I believe, a very genuine account of some essential matters; and if any publisher should take a fancy to the Chevalier's manner of narration, he knows where to apply for the rest, of which there is plenty at his service. I put in my first extract here, so that it may stand in the place of what the Chevalier told us over our wine in the hall of Durrisdeer; but you are to suppose it was not the brutal fact, but a very varnished version that he offered to my lord.

THE MASTER'S WANDERINGS

From the Memoirs of the Chevalier de Burke[1]

. . . I left Ruthven[2] (it's hardly necessary to remark) with much greater satisfaction than I had come to it: but whether I missed my way in the deserts, or whether my companions failed me, I soon found myself alone. This was a predicament very disagreeable; for I never understood this horrid country or savage people, and the last stroke of the Prince's withdrawal had made us of the Irish more unpopular than ever. I was reflecting on my poor chances, when I saw another horseman on the hill, whom I supposed at first to have been a phantom, the news of his death in the very front at Culloden being current in the army generally. This was the Master of Ballantrae, my Lord Durrisdeer's son, a young nobleman of the rarest gallantry and parts, and equally designed by nature to adorn a Court and to reap laurels in the field. Our meeting was the more welcome to both, as he was one of the few Scots who had used the Irish with consideration, and as he might now be of very high utility in aiding my escape. Yet what founded our particular friendship was a circumstance, by itself as romantic as any fable of King Arthur.

This was on the second day of our flight, after we had slept one night in the rain upon the inclination of a mountain. There was an Appin man, Alan Black Stewart[3] (or some such name,* but I have seen him since in France), who chanced to be passing the same way, and had a

* *Note by Mr Mackellar*. – Should not this be Alan *Breck* Stewart, afterwards notorious as the Appin murderer? The Chevalier is sometimes very weak on names.

jealousy of my companion. Very uncivil expressions were exchanged; and Stewart calls upon the Master to alight and have it out.

'Why, Mr Stewart,' says the Master, 'I think at the present time I would prefer to run a race with you.' And with the word claps spurs to his horse.

Stewart ran after us, a childish thing to do, for more than a mile; and I could not help laughing, as I looked back at last and saw him on a hill, holding his hand to his side, and nearly burst with running.

'But all the same,' I could not help saying to my companion, 'I would let no man run after me for any such proper purpose, and not give him his desire. It was a good jest, but it smells a trifle cowardly.'

He bent his brows at me. 'I do pretty well,' says he, 'when I saddle myself with the most unpopular man in Scotland, and let that suffice for courage.'

'O, bedad,' says I, 'I could show you a more unpopular with the naked eye. And if you like not my company, you can "saddle" yourself on some one else.'

'Colonel Burke,' says he, 'do not let us quarrel; and, to that effect, let me assure you I am the least patient man in the world.'

'I am as little patient as yourself,' said I. 'I care not who knows that.'

'At this rate,' says he, reining in, 'we shall not go very far. And I propose we do one of two things upon the instant: either quarrel and be done; or make a sure bargain to bear everything at each other's hands.'

'Like a pair of brothers?' said I.

'I said no such foolishness,' he replied. 'I have a brother of my own, and I think no more of him than of a colewort.[4] But if we are to have our noses rubbed together in this course of flight, let us each dare to be ourselves like savages, and each swear that he will neither resent nor deprecate the other. I am a pretty bad fellow at bottom, and I find the pretence of virtues very irksome.'

'O, I am as bad as yourself,' said I. 'There is no skim-milk in Francis Burke. But which is it to be? Fight or make friends?'

'Why,' says he, 'I think it will be the best manner to spin a coin for it.'

This proposition was too highly chivalrous not to take my fancy; and, strange as it may seem of two well-born gentlemen of to-day, we span a half-crown (like a pair of ancient paladins) whether we were to cut each other's throats or be sworn friends. A more romantic circumstance can rarely have occurred; and it is one of those points in my memoirs, by which we may see the old tales of Homer and the poets are equally true to-day – at least, of the noble and genteel. The coin fell for peace, and we shook hands upon our bargain. And then it was that my companion explained to me his thought in running away from Mr Stewart, which was certainly worthy of his political intellect. The report of his death, he said, was a great guard to him; Mr Stewart having recognised him, had become a danger; and he had taken the briefest road to that gentleman's silence. 'For,' says he, 'Alan Black is too vain a man to narrate any such story of himself.'

Towards afternoon we came down to the shores of that loch for which we were heading; and there was the ship, but newly come to anchor. She was the *Sainte-Marie-des-Anges*, out of the port of Havre-de-Grace. The Master, after we had signalled for a boat, asked me if I knew the captain. I told him he was a countryman of mine, of the most unblemished integrity, but, I was afraid, a rather timorous man.

'No matter,' says he. 'For all that, he should certainly hear the truth.'

I asked him if he meant about the battle? for if the captain once knew the standard was down, he would certainly put to sea again at once.

'And even then!' said he; 'the arms are now of no sort of utility.'

'My dear man,' said I, 'who thinks of the arms? But, to be sure, we must remember our friends. They will be close upon our heels, perhaps the Prince himself, and if the ship be gone, a great number of valuable lives may be imperilled.'

'The captain and the crew have lives also, if you come to that,' says Ballantrae.

This I declared was but a quibble, and that I would not hear of the captain being told; and then it was that Ballantrae made me a witty answer, for the sake of which (and also because I have been blamed myself in this business of the *Sainte-Marie-des-Anges*) I have related the whole conversation as it passed.

'Frank,' says he, 'remember our bargain. I must not object to your holding your tongue, which I hereby even encourage you to do; but, by the same terms, you are not to resent my telling.'

I could not help laughing at this; though I still forewarned him what would come of it.

'The devil may come of it for what I care,' says the reckless fellow. 'I have always done exactly as I felt inclined.'

As is well known, my prediction came true. The captain had no sooner heard the news than he cut his cable and to sea again; and before morning broke, we were in the Great Minch.[5]

The ship was very old; and the skipper, although the most honest of men (and Irish too), was one of the least capable. The wind blew very boisterous, and the sea raged extremely. All that day we had little heart whether to eat or drink; went early to rest in some concern of mind; and (as if to give us a lesson) in the night the wind chopped suddenly into the north-east, and blew a hurricane. We were awaked by the dreadful thunder of the tempest and the stamping of the mariners on deck; so that I supposed our last hour was certainly come; and the terror of my mind was increased out of all measure by Ballantrae, who mocked at my devotions. It is in hours like these that a man of any piety appears in his true light, and we find (what we are taught as babes) the small trust that can be set in worldly friends: I would be unworthy of my religion if I let this pass without particular remark. For three days we lay in the dark in the cabin, and had but a biscuit to nibble. On the fourth the wind fell, leaving the ship dismasted and heaving on vast billows. The captain had not a guess of whither we were blown; he was stark ignorant of his trade, and could do naught but bless the Holy Virgin; a very good thing too, but scarce the whole of seamanship. It seemed, our one hope was to be picked up by another vessel; and if that should prove to be an English ship, it might be no great blessing to the Master and myself.

The fifth and sixth days we tossed there helpless. The seventh some sail was got on her, but she was an unwieldy vessel at the best, and we made little but leeway. All the time, indeed, we had been drifting to the south and west, and during the tempest must have driven in that direction with unheard-of violence. The ninth dawn was cold and black, with a great sea running, and every mark of foul weather. In this situation we were overjoyed to sight a small ship on the horizon, and to perceive her go about and head for the *Sainte-Marie.* But our gratification did not very long endure; for when she had laid-to and lowered a boat, it was immediately filled with disorderly fellows, who sang and shouted as they pulled across to us, and swarmed in on our deck with bare cutlasses, cursing loudly. Their leader was a horrible villain, with his face blacked and his whiskers curled in ringlets; Teach his name;[6] a most notorious pirate. He stamped about the deck, raving and crying out that his name was Satan, and his ship was called Hell. There was something about him like a wicked child or a half-witted person, that daunted me beyond expression. I whispered in the ear of Ballantrae that I would not be the last to volunteer, and only prayed God they might be short of hands; he approved my purpose with a nod.

'Bedad,' said I to Master Teach, 'if you are Satan, here is a devil for ye.'

The word pleased him; and (not to dwell upon these shocking incidents) Ballantrae and I and two others were taken for recruits, while the skipper and all the rest were cast into the sea by the method of walking the plank. It was the first time I had seen this done; my heart died within me at the spectacle; and Master Teach or one of his acolytes (for my head was too much lost to be precise) remarked upon my pale face in a very alarming manner. I had the strength to cut a step or two of a jig, and cry out some ribaldry, which saved me for that time; but my legs were like water when I must get down into the skiff among these miscreants; and what with my horror of my company and fear of the monstrous billows, it was all I could do to keep an Irish tongue and break a jest or two as we were pulled aboard. By the blessing of God, there was a fiddle in the pirate ship, which I had no sooner seen than I fell upon; and in my quality of crowder[7] I had the heavenly good luck to get favour in their eyes. *Crowding Pat* was the name they dubbed me with: and it was little I cared for a name so long as my skin was whole.

What kind of a pandemonium that vessel was I cannot describe, but she was commanded by a lunatic, and might be called a floating

Bedlam. Drinking, roaring, singing, quarrelling, dancing, they were never all sober at one time; and there were days together when, if a squall had supervened, it must have sent us to the bottom; or if a King's ship had come along, it would have found us quite helpless for defence. Once or twice we sighted a sail, and, if we were sober enough, overhauled it, God forgive us! and if we were all too drunk, she got away, and I would bless the saints under my breath. Teach ruled, if you can call that rule which brought no order, by the terror he created; and I observed the man was very vain of his position. I have known marshals of France – ay, and even Highland chieftains – that were less openly puffed up; which throws a singular light on the pursuit of honour and glory. Indeed, the longer we live, the more we perceive the sagacity of Aristotle and the other old philosophers; and though I have all my life been eager for legitimate distinctions, I can lay my hand upon my heart, at the end of my career, and declare there is not one – no, nor yet life itself – which is worth acquiring or preserving at the slightest cost of dignity.

It was long before I got private speech of Ballantrae; but at length one night we crept out upon the boltsprit,[8] when the rest were better employed, and commiserated our position.

'None can deliver us but the saints,' said I.

'My mind is very different,' said Ballantrae; 'for I am going to deliver myself. This Teach is the poorest creature possible; we make no profit of him, and lie continually open to capture; and,' says he, 'I am not going to be a tarry pirate for nothing, nor yet to hang in chains if I can help it.' And he told me what was in his mind to better the state of the ship in the way of discipline, which would give us safety for the present, and a sooner hope of deliverance when they should have gained enough and should break up their company.

I confessed to him ingenuously that my nerve was quite shook amid these horrible surroundings, and I durst scarce tell him to count upon me.

'I am not very easy frightened,' said he, 'nor very easy beat.'

A few days after there befell an accident which had nearly hanged us all; and offers the most extraordinary picture of the folly that ruled in our concerns. We were all pretty drunk: and some bedlamite spying a sail, Teach put the ship about in chase without a glance, and we began to bustle up the arms and boast of the horrors that should follow. I observed Ballantrae stood quiet in the bows, looking under the shade of his hand; but for my part, true to my policy among these savages, I was at work with the busiest, and passing Irish jests for their diversion.

'Run up the colours!' cried Teach. 'Show the —s the Jolly Roger!'

It was the merest drunken braggadocio at such a stage, and might have lost us a valuable prize; but I thought it no part of mine to reason, and I ran up the black flag with my own hand.

Ballantrae steps presently aft with a smile upon his face.

'You may perhaps like to know, you drunken dog,' says he, 'that you are chasing a King's ship.'

Teach roared him the lie; but he ran at the same time to the bulwarks, and so did they all. I have never seen so many drunken men struck suddenly sober. The cruiser had gone about, upon our impudent display of colours; she was just then filling on the new tack; her ensign blew out quite plain to see; and even as we stared, there came a puff of smoke, and then a report, and a shot plunged in the waves a good way short of us. Some ran to the ropes, and got the *Sarah* round with an incredible swiftness. One fellow fell on the rum-barrel, which stood broached upon the deck, and rolled it promptly overboard. On my part, I made for the Jolly Roger, struck it, tossed it in the sea; and could have flung myself after, so vexed was I with our mismanagement. As for Teach, he grew as pale as death, and incontinently went down to his cabin. Only twice he came on deck that afternoon; went to the taffrail;[9] took a long look at the King's ship, which was still on the horizon heading after us; and then, without speech, back to his cabin. You may say he deserted us; and if it had not been for one very capable sailor we had on board, and for the lightness of the airs that blew all day, we must certainly have gone to the yard-arm.

It is to be supposed Teach was humiliated, and perhaps alarmed for his position with the crew; and the way in which he set about regaining what he had lost was highly characteristic of the man. Early next day we smelled him burning sulphur in his cabin and crying out of 'Hell, hell!'[10] which was well understood among the crew, and filled their minds with apprehension. Presently he comes on deck, a perfect figure of fun, his face blacked, his hair and whiskers curled, his belt stuck full of pistols; chewing bits of glass so that the blood ran down his chin, and brandishing a dirk.[11] I do not know if he had taken these manners from the Indians of America, where he was a native; but such was his way, and he would always thus announce that he was wound up to horrid deeds. The first that came near him was the fellow who had sent the rum overboard the day before; him he stabbed to the heart, damning him for a mutineer; and then capered about the body, raving and swearing and daring us to come on. It was the silliest exhibition; and yet dangerous too, for the cowardly fellow was plainly working himself up to another murder.

All of a sudden Ballantrae stepped forth. 'Have done with this play-acting,' says he. 'Do you think to frighten us with making faces? We saw nothing of you yesterday, when you were wanted; and we did well without you, let me tell you that.'

There was a murmur and a movement in the crew, of pleasure and alarm, I thought, in nearly equal parts. As for Teach, he gave a barbarous howl, and swung his dirk to fling it, an art in which (like many seamen) he was very expert.

'Knock that out of his hand!' says Ballantrae, so sudden and sharp that my arm obeyed him before my mind had understood.

Teach stood like one stupid, never thinking on his pistols.

'Go down to your cabin,' cries Ballantrae, 'and come on deck again when you are sober. Do you think we are going to hang for you, you black-faced, half-witted, drunken brute and butcher? Go down!' And he stamped his foot at him with such a sudden smartness that Teach fairly ran for it to the companion.[12]

'And now, mates,' says Ballantrae, 'a word with you. I don't know if you are gentlemen of fortune for the fun of the thing, but I am not. I want to make money, and get ashore again, and spend it like a man. And on one thing my mind is made up: I will not hang if I can help it. Come, give me a hint; I'm only a beginner! Is there no way to get a little discipline and common sense about this business?'

One of the men spoke up: he said by rights they should have a quartermaster; and no sooner was the word out of his mouth than they were all of that opinion. The thing went by acclamation; Ballantrae was made quartermaster, the rum was put in his charge, laws were passed in imitation of those of a pirate by the name of Roberts,[13] and the last proposal was to make an end of Teach. But Ballantrae was afraid of a more efficient captain, who might be a counter-weight to himself, and he opposed this stoutly. Teach, he said, was good enough to board ships and frighten fools with his blacked face and swearing; we could scarce get a better man than Teach for that; and besides, as the man was now disconsidered, and as good as deposed, we might reduce his proportion of the plunder. This carried it; Teach's share was cut down to a mere derision, being actually less than mine; and there remained only two points: whether he would consent, and who was to announce to him this resolution.

'Do not let that stick you,' says Ballantrae, 'I will do that.'

And he stepped to the companion and down alone into the cabin to face that drunken savage.

'This is the man for us,' cried one of the hands. 'Three cheers for the quartermaster!' which were given with a will, my own voice among the loudest, and I daresay these plaudits had their effect on Master Teach in the cabin, as we have seen of late days how shouting in the streets may trouble even the minds of legislators.

What passed precisely was never known, though some of the heads of it came to the surface later on; and we were all amazed, as well as gratified, when Ballantrae came on deck with Teach upon his arm, and announced that all had been consented.

I pass swiftly over those twelve or fifteen months in which we continued to keep the sea in the North Atlantic, getting our food and water from the ships we overhauled, and doing on the whole a pretty fortunate business. Sure, no one could wish to read anything so ungenteel as the memoirs of a pirate, even an unwilling one like me! Things went extremely better with our designs, and Ballantrae kept his lead, to my admiration, from that day forth. I would be tempted to suppose that a gentleman must everywhere be first, even aboard a rover; but my birth is every whit as good as any Scottish lord's, and I am not ashamed to confess that I stayed Crowding Pat until the end, and was not much better than the crew's buffoon. Indeed, it was no scene to bring out my merits. My health suffered from a variety of reasons; I was more at home to the last on a horse's back than a ship's deck; and, to be ingenuous, the fear of the sea was constantly in my mind, battling with the fear of my companions. I need not cry myself up for courage; I have done well on many fields under the eyes of famous generals, and earned my late advancement by an act of the most distinguished valour before many witnesses. But when we must proceed on one of our abordages, the heart of Francis Burke was in his boots; the little egg-shell skiff in which we must set forth, the horrible heaving of the vast billows, the height of the ship that we must scale, the thought of how many might be there in garrison upon their legitimate defence, the scowling heavens which (in that climate) so often looked darkly down upon our exploits, and the mere crying of the wind in my ears, were all considerations most unpalatable to my valour. Besides which, as I was always a creature of the nicest sensibility, the scenes that must follow on our success tempted me as little as the chances of defeat. Twice we found women on board; and though I have seen towns sacked, and of late days in France some very horrid public tumults, there was something in the smallness of the numbers engaged, and the bleak dangerous sea-surroundings, that made these acts of piracy far the most revolting. I confess ingenuously I could never proceed unless I was three parts drunk; it was the same even with the crew; Teach himself was fit for no enterprise till he was full of rum; and it was one of the most difficult parts of Ballantrae's performance to serve us with liquor in the proper quantities. Even this he did to admiration; being upon the whole the most capable man I ever met with, and the one of the most natural genius. He did not even scrape favour with the crew, as I did, by continual buffoonery made upon a very anxious heart; but preserved on most occasions a great deal of gravity and distance; so that he was like a parent among a family of young children, or a schoolmaster with his boys. What made his part the harder to perform, the men were most inveterate grumblers: Ballantrae's discipline, little as it was, was yet irksome to their love of licence; and, what was worse, being kept sober they had time to think. Some of them accordingly would fall to repenting their abominable crimes; one in particular, who was a good Catholic, and with whom I would sometimes steal apart for prayer; above all in bad weather, fogs, lashing rain, and the like, when we would be the less observed; and I am sure no two criminals in the cart have ever performed their devotions with more anxious sincerity. But the rest, having no such grounds of hope, fell to another pastime, that of computation. All day long they would be telling up their shares or glooming over the result. I have said we were pretty fortunate. But an observation falls to be made: that in this world, in no business that I have tried, do the profits rise to a man's expectations. We found many ships, and took many; yet few of them contained much money, their goods were usually nothing to our purpose – what did we want with a cargo of ploughs, or even of tobacco? – and it is quite a painful reflection how many whole crews we have made to walk the plank for no more than a stock of biscuit or an anker or two of spirits.

In the meanwhile our ship was growing very foul,[14] and it was high time we should make for our *port de carénage*,[15] which was in the estuary of a river among swamps. It was openly understood that we should then break up and go and squander our proportions of the spoil; and this made every man greedy of a little more, so that our decision was delayed from day to day. What finally decided matters was a trifling accident, such as an ignorant person might suppose incidental to our way of life. But here I must explain: on only one of all the ships we boarded, the first on which we found women, did we meet with any genuine resistance. On that occasion we had two men killed and several injured, and if it had not been for the gallantry of Ballantrae we had surely been beat back at last. Everywhere else the defence (where there was any at all) was what the worst troops in Europe would have laughed at; so that the most dangerous part of our employment was to clamber up the side of the ship: and I have even known the poor souls on board to cast us a line, so eager were they to volunteer instead of walking the plank. This constant immunity had made our fellows very soft, so that I understood how Teach had made so deep a mark upon their minds; for indeed the company of that lunatic was the chief danger in our way of life. The accident to which

I have referred was this: – We had sighted a little full-rigged ship very close under our board in a haze; she sailed near as well as we did – I should be nearer truth if I said, near as ill; and we cleared the bowchaser to see if we could bring a spar or two about their ears. The swell was exceedingly great; the motion of the ship beyond description; it was little wonder if our gunners should fire thrice and be still quite broad of what they aimed at. But in the meanwhile the chase had cleared a stern gun, the thickness of the air concealing them; and being better marksmen, their first shot struck us in the bows, knocked our two gunners into mince-meat, so that we were all sprinkled with the blood, and plunged through the deck into the forecastle, where we slept. Ballantrae would have held on; indeed, there was nothing in this *contretemps* to affect the mind of any soldier; but he had a quick perception of the men's wishes, and it was plain this lucky shot had given them a sickener of their trade. In a moment they were all of one mind: the chase was drawing away from us, it was needless to hold on, the *Sarah* was too foul to overhaul a bottle, it was mere foolery to keep the sea with her; and on these pretended grounds her head was incontinently put about and the course laid for the river. It was strange to see what merriment fell on that ship's company, and how they stamped about the deck jesting, and each computing what increase had come to his share by the death of the two gunners.

We were nine days making our port, so light were the airs we had to sail on, so foul the ship's bottom; but early on the tenth, before dawn, and in a light lifting haze, we passed the head. A little after, the haze lifted, and fell again, showing us a cruiser very close. This was a sore blow, happening so near our refuge. There was a great debate of whether she had seen us, and if so whether it was likely they had recognised the *Sarah*. We were very careful, by destroying every member of those crews we overhauled, to leave no evidence as to our own persons; but the appearance of the *Sarah* herself we could not keep so private; and above all of late, since she had been foul, and we had pursued many ships without success, it was plain that her description had been often published. I supposed this alert would have made us separate upon the instant. But here again that original genius of Ballantrae's had a surprise in store for me. He and Teach (and it was the most remarkable step of his success) had gone hand in hand since the first day of his appointment. I often questioned him upon the fact, and never got an answer but once, when he told me he and Teach had an understanding 'which would very much surprise the crew if they should hear of it, and would surprise himself a good deal if it was carried out.' Well, here again he and Teach were of a mind; and by their joint procurement the anchor was no sooner down than the whole crew went off upon a scene of drunkenness indescribable. By afternoon we were a mere shipful of lunatical persons, throwing of things overboard, howling of different songs at the same time, quarrelling and falling together, and then forgetting our quarrels to embrace. Ballantrae had bidden me drink nothing, and feign drunkenness, as I valued my life; and I have never passed a day so wearisomely, lying the best part of the time upon the forecastle and watching the swamps and thickets by which our little basin was entirely surrounded for the eye. A little after dusk Ballantrae stumbled up to my side, feigned to fall, with a drunken laugh, and before he got to his feet again, whispered me to 'reel down into the cabin and seem to fall asleep upon a locker, for there would be need of me soon.' I did as I was told, and coming into the cabin, where it was quite dark, let myself fall on the first locker. There was a man there already: by the way he stirred and threw me off, I could not think he was much in liquor; and yet when I had found another place, he seemed to continue to sleep on. My heart now beat very hard, for I saw some desperate matter was in act. Presently down came Ballantrae, lit the lamp, looked about the cabin, nodded as if pleased, and on deck again without a word. I peered out from between my fingers, and saw there were three of us slumbering, or feigning to slumber, on the lockers: myself, one Dutton, and one Grady, both resolute men. On deck the rest were got to a pitch of revelry quite beyond the bounds of what is human; so that no reasonable name can describe the sounds they were now making. I have heard many a drunken bout in my time, many on board that very *Sarah*, but never anything the least like this, which made me early suppose the liquor had been tampered with. It was a long while before these yells and howls died out into a sort of miserable moaning, and then to silence; and it seemed a long while after that before Ballantrae came down again, this time with Teach upon his heels. The latter cursed at the sight of us three upon the lockers.

'Tut,' says Ballantrae, 'you might fire a pistol at their ears. You know what stuff they have been swallowing.'

There was a hatch in the cabin floor, and under that the richest part of the booty was stored against the day of division. It fastened with a ring and three padlocks, the keys (for greater security) being divided; one to Teach, one to Ballantrae, and one to the mate, a man called Hammond. Yet I was amazed to see they were now all in the one hand; and yet more amazed (still looking through my fingers) to observe Ballantrae and Teach bring up several packets, four of them in all, very carefully made up, and with a loop for carriage.

'And now,' says Teach, 'let us be going.'

'One word,' says Ballantrae. 'I have discovered there is another man besides yourself who knows a private path across the swamp; and it seems it is shorter than yours.'

Teach cried out, in that case, they were undone.

'I do not know for that,' says Ballantrae. 'For there are several other circumstances with which I must acquaint you. First of all, there is no bullet in your pistols, which (if you remember) I was kind enough to load for both of us this morning. Secondly, as there is some one else who knows a passage, you must think it highly improbable I should saddle myself with a lunatic like you. Thirdly, these gentlemen (who need no longer pretend to be asleep) are those of my party, and will now proceed to gag and bind you to the mast; and when your men awaken (if they ever do awake after the drugs we have mingled in their liquor), I am sure they will be so obliging as to deliver you, and you will have no difficulty, I daresay, to explain the business of the keys.'

Not a word said Teach, but looked at us like a frightened baby as we gagged and bound him.

'Now you see, you moon-calf,'[16] says Ballantrae, 'why we made four packets. Heretofore you have been called Captain Teach, but I think you are now rather Captain Learn.'

That was our last word on board the *Sarah*. We four, with our four packets, lowered ourselves softly into a skiff, and left that ship behind us as silent as the grave, only for the moaning of some of the drunkards. There was a fog about breast-high on the waters; so that Dutton, who knew the passage, must stand on his feet to direct our rowing; and this, as it forced us to row gently, was the means of our deliverance. We were yet but a little way from the ship, when it began to come grey, and the birds to fly abroad upon the water. All of a sudden Dutton clapped down upon his hams, and whispered us to be silent for our lives, and hearken. Sure enough, we heard a little faint creak of oars upon one hand, and then again, and farther off, a creak of oars upon the other. It was clear we had been sighted yesterday in the morning; here were the cruiser's boats to cut us out; here were we defenceless in their very midst. Sure, never were poor souls more perilously placed; and as we lay there on our oars, praying God the mist might hold, the sweat poured from my brow. Presently we heard one of the boats where we might have thrown a biscuit in her. 'Softly, men,' we heard an officer whisper; and I marvelled they could not hear the drumming of my heart.

'Never mind the path,' said Ballantrae; 'we must get shelter anyhow; let us pull straight ahead for the sides of the basin.'

This we did with the most anxious precaution, rowing, as best we could, upon our hands, and steering at a venture in the fog, which was (for all that) our only safety. But Heaven guided us; we touched ground at a thicket; scrambled ashore with our treasure; and having no other way of concealment, and the mist beginning already to lighten, hove down the skiff and let her sink. We were still but new under cover when the sun rose; and at the same time, from the midst of the basin, a great shouting of seamen sprang up, and we knew the *Sarah* was being boarded. I heard afterwards the officer that took her got great honour; and it's true the approach was creditably managed, but I think he had an easy capture when he came to board.*

I was still blessing the saints for my escape, when I became aware

* *Note by Mr Mackellar.* – This Teach of the *Sarah* must not be confused with the celebrated *Blackbeard.* The dates and facts by no means tally. It is possible the second Teach may have at once borrowed the name and imitated the more excessive part of his manners from the first. Even the Master of Ballantrae could make admirers.

we were in trouble of another kind. We were here landed at random in a vast and dangerous swamp; and how to come at the path was a concern of doubt, fatigue, and peril. Dutton, indeed, was of opinion we should wait until the ship was gone, and fish up the skiff; for any delay would be more wise than to go blindly ahead in that morass. One went back accordingly to the basin-side and (peering through the thicket) saw the fog already quite drunk up, and English colours flying on the *Sarah*, but no movement made to get her under way. Our situation was now very doubtful. The swamp was an unhealthful place to linger in; we had been so greedy to bring treasures that we had brought but little food; it was highly desirable, besides, that we should get clear of the neighbourhood and into the settlements before the news of the capture went abroad; and against all these considerations there was only the peril of the passage on the other side. I think it not wonderful we decided on the active part.

It was already blistering hot when we set forth to pass the marsh, or rather to strike the path, by compass. Dutton took the compass, and one or other of us three carried his proportion of the treasure. I promise you he kept a sharp eye to his rear, for it was like the man's soul that he must trust us with. The thicket was as close as a bush; the ground very treacherous, so that we often sank in the most terrifying manner, and must go round about; the heat, besides, was stifling, the air singularly heavy, and the stinging insects abounded in such myriads that each of us walked under his own cloud. It has often been commented on, how much better gentlemen of birth endure fatigue than persons of the rabble; so that walking officers, who must tramp in the dirt beside their men, shame them by their constancy. This was well to be observed in the present instance; for here were Ballantrae and I, two gentlemen of the highest breeding, on the one hand; and on the other, Grady, a common mariner, and a man nearly a giant in physical strength. The case of Dutton is not in point, for I confess he did as well as any of us.* But as for Grady, he began early to lament his case, tailed in the rear, refused to carry Dutton's packet when it

* *Note by Mr Mackellar.* – And is not this the whole explanation? since this Dutton, exactly like the officers, enjoyed the stimulus of some responsibility.

came his turn, clamoured continually for rum (of which we had too little), and at last even threatened us from behind with a cocked pistol, unless we should allow him rest. Ballantrae would have fought it out, I believe; but I prevailed with him the other way; and we made a stop and ate a meal. It seemed to benefit Grady little; he was in the rear again at once, growling and bemoaning his lot; and at last, by some carelessness, not having followed properly in our tracks, stumbled into a deep part of the slough where it was mostly water, gave some very dreadful screams, and before we could come to his aid had sunk along with his booty. His fate, and above all these screams of his, appalled us to the soul; yet it was on the whole a fortunate circumstance, and the means of our deliverance, for it moved Dutton to mount into a tree, whence he was able to perceive and to show me, who had climbed after him, a high piece of the wood, which was a landmark for the path. He went forward the more carelessly, I must suppose; for presently we saw him sink a little down, draw up his feet and sink again, and so twice. Then he turned his face to us, pretty white.

'Lend a hand,' said he, 'I am in a bad place.'

'I don't know about that,' says Ballantrae, standing still.

Dutton broke out into the most violent oaths, sinking a little lower as he did, so that the mud was nearly to his waist, and plucking a pistol from his belt, 'Help me,' he cries, 'or die and be damned to you!'

'Nay,' says Ballantrae, 'I did but jest. I am coming.' And he set down his own packet and Dutton's, which he was then carrying. 'Do not venture near till we see if you are needed,' said he to me, and went forward alone to where the man was bogged. He was quiet now, though he still held the pistol; and the marks of terror in his countenance were very moving to behold.

'For the Lord's sake,' says he, 'look sharp.'

Ballantrae was now got close up. 'Keep still,' says he, and seemed to consider; and then, 'Reach out both your hands!'

Dutton laid down his pistol, and so watery was the top surface that it went clear out of sight; with an oath he stooped to snatch it; and as he did so, Ballantrae leaned forth and stabbed him between the shoulders. Up went his hands over his head – I know not whether with the pain or to ward himself; and the next moment he doubled forward in the mud.

Ballantrae was already over the ankles; but he plucked himself out, and came back to me, where I stood with my knees smiting one another. 'The devil take you, Francis!' says he. 'I believe you are a half-hearted fellow, after all. I have only done justice on a pirate. And here we are quite clear of the *Sarah*! Who shall now say that we have dipped our hands in any irregularities?'

I assured him he did me injustice; but my sense of humanity was so much affected by the horridness of the fact that I could scarce find breath to answer with.

'Come,' said he, 'you must be more resolved. The need for this fellow ceased when he had shown you where the path ran; and you cannot deny I would have been daft to let slip so fair an opportunity.'

I could not deny but he was right in principle; nor yet could I refrain from shedding tears, of which I think no man of valour need have been ashamed; and it was not until I had a share of the rum that I was able to proceed. I repeat, I am far from ashamed of my generous emotion; mercy is honourable in the warrior; and yet I cannot altogether censure Ballantrae, whose step was really fortunate, as we struck the path without further misadventure, and the same night, about sundown, came to the edge of the morass.

We were too weary to seek far; on some dry sands, still warm with the day's sun, and close under a wood of pines, we lay down and were instantly plunged in sleep.

We awaked the next morning very early, and began with a sullen spirit a conversation that came near to end in blows. We were now cast on shore in the southern provinces, thousands of miles from any French settlement;[17] a dreadful journey and a thousand perils lay in front of us; and sure, if there was ever need for amity, it was in such an hour. I must suppose that Ballantrae had suffered in his sense of what is truly polite; indeed, and there is nothing strange in the idea, after the sea-wolves we had consorted with so long; and as for myself, he fubbed me off unhandsomely, and any gentleman would have resented his behaviour.

I told him in what light I saw his conduct; he walked a little off, I following to upbraid him; and at last he stopped me with his hand.

'Frank,' says he, 'you know what we swore; and yet there is no oath invented would induce me to swallow such expressions, if I did not regard you with sincere affection. It is impossible you should doubt me there: I have given proofs. Dutton I had to take, because he knew the pass, and Grady because Dutton would not move without him; but what call was there to carry you along? You are a perpetual danger to me with your cursed Irish tongue. By rights you should now be in irons in the cruiser. And you quarrel with me like a baby for some trinkets!'

I considered this one of the most unhandsome speeches ever made; and indeed to this day I can scarce reconcile it to my notion of a gentleman that was my friend. I retorted upon him with his Scots accent, of which he had not so much as some, but enough to be very barbarous and disgusting, as I told him plainly; and the affair would have gone to a great length, but for an alarming intervention.

We had got some way off upon the sand. The place where we had slept, with the packets lying undone and the money scattered openly, was now between us and the pines; and it was out of these the stranger must have come. There he was at least, a great hulking fellow of the country, with a broad axe on his shoulder, looking open-mouthed, now at the treasure, which was just at his feet, and now at our disputation, in which we had gone far enough to have weapons in our hands. We had no sooner observed him than he found his legs and made off again among the pines.

This was no scene to put our minds at rest: a couple of armed men in sea-clothes found quarrelling over a treasure, not many miles from where a pirate had been captured – here was enough to bring the whole country about our ears. The quarrel was not even made up; it was blotted from our minds; and we got our packets together in the twinkling of an eye, and made off, running with the best will in the world. But the trouble was, we did not know in what direction, and must continually return upon our steps. Ballantrae had indeed collected what he could from Dutton; but it's hard to travel upon hearsay;

and the estuary, which spreads into a vast irregular harbour, turned us off upon every side with a new stretch of water.

We were near beside ourselves, and already quite spent with running, when, coming to the top of a dune, we saw we were again cut off by another ramification of the bay. This was a creek, however, very different from those that had arrested us before; being set in rocks, and so precipitously deep that a small vessel was able to lie alongside, made fast with a hawser; and her crew had laid a plank to the shore. Here they had lighted a fire, and were sitting at their meal. As for the vessel herself, she was one of those they build in the Bermudas.

The love of gold and the great hatred that everybody has to pirates were motives of the most influential, and would certainly raise the country in our pursuit. Besides, it was now plain we were on some sort of straggling peninsula, like the fingers of a hand; and the wrist, or passage to the mainland, which we should have taken at the first, was by this time not improbably secured. These considerations put us on a bolder counsel. For as long as we dared, looking every moment to hear sounds of the chase, we lay among some bushes on the top of the dune; and having by this means secured a little breath and recomposed our appearance, we strolled down at last, with a great affectation of carelessness, to the party by the fire.

It was a trader and his negroes, belonging to Albany, in the province of New York, and now on the way home from the Indies with a cargo; his name I cannot recall. We were amazed to learn he had put in here from terror of the *Sarah*; for we had no thought our exploits had been so notorious. As soon as the Albanian heard she had been taken the day before, he jumped to his feet, gave us a cup of spirits for our good news, and sent his negroes to get sail on the Bermudan. On our side, we profited by the dram to become more confidential, and at last offered ourselves as passengers. He looked askance at our tarry clothes and pistols, and replied civilly enough that he had scarce accommodation for himself; nor could either our prayers or our offers of money, in which we advanced pretty far, avail to shake him.

'I see, you think ill of us,' says Ballantrae, 'but I will show you how well we think of you by telling you the truth. We are Jacobite fugitives, and there is a price upon our heads.'

At this the Albanian was plainly moved a little. He asked us many questions as to the Scots war, which Ballantrae very patiently answered. And then, with a wink, in a vulgar manner, 'I guess you and your Prince Charlie got more than you cared about,' said he.

'Bedad, and that we did,' said I. 'And, my dear man, I wish you would set a new example and give us just that much.'

This I said in the Irish way, about which there is allowed to be something very engaging. It's a remarkable thing, and a testimony to the love with which our nation is regarded, that this address scarce ever fails in a handsome fellow. I cannot tell how often I have seen a private soldier escape the horse,[18] or a beggar wheedle out a good alms, by a touch of the brogue. And, indeed, as soon as the Albanian had laughed at me I was pretty much at rest. Even then, however, he made many conditions, and – for one thing – took away our arms, before he suffered us aboard; which was the signal to cast off; so that in a moment after we were gliding down the bay with a good breeze, and blessing the name of God for our deliverance. Almost in the mouth of the estuary, we passed the cruiser, and a little after the poor *Sarah* with her prize crew; and these were both sights to make us tremble. The Bermudan seemed a very safe place to be in, and our bold stroke to have been fortunately played, when we were thus reminded of the case of our companions. For all that, we had only exchanged traps, jumped out of the frying-pan into the fire, run from the yard-arm to the block, and escaped the open hostility of the man-of-war to lie at the mercy of the doubtful faith of our Albanian merchant.

From many circumstances, it chanced we were safer than we could have dared to hope. The town of Albany was at that time[19] much concerned in contraband trade across the desert with the Indians and the French. This, as it was highly illegal, relaxed their loyalty, and as it brought them in relation with the politest people on the earth, divided even their sympathies. In short, they were like all the smugglers in the world, spies and agents ready-made for either party. Our Albanian, besides, was a very honest man indeed, and very greedy; and, to crown our luck, he conceived a great delight in our society. Before we had reached the town of New York we had come to a full agreement, that he should carry us as far as Albany upon his ship, and thence put us on a way to pass the boundaries and join the French. For all this we were to pay at a high rate; but beggars cannot be choosers, nor outlaws bargainers.

We sailed then, up the Hudson River, which, I protest, is a very fine stream, and put up at the 'King's Arms' in Albany. The town was full of the militia of the province, breathing slaughter against the French. Governor Clinton[20] was there himself, a very busy man, and, by what I could learn, very near distracted by the factiousness of his Assembly. The Indians on both sides were on the war-path; we saw parties of them bringing in prisoners and (what was much worse) scalps, both male and female, for which they were paid at a fixed rate; and I assure you the sight was not encouraging. Altogether, we could scarce have come at a period more unsuitable for our designs; our position in the chief inn was dreadfully conspicuous; our Albanian fubbed us off with a thousand delays, and seemed upon the point of a retreat from his engagements; nothing but peril appeared to environ the poor fugitives, and for some time we drowned our concern in a very irregular course of living.

This, too, proved to be fortunate; and it's one of the remarks that fall to be made upon our escape, how providentially our steps were conducted to the very end. What a humiliation to the dignity of man! My philosophy, the extraordinary genius of Ballantrae, our valour, in which I grant that we were equal – all these might have proved insufficient without the Divine blessing on our efforts. And how true it is, as the Church tells us, that the Truths of Religion are, after all, quite applicable even to daily affairs! At least, it was in the course of our revelry that we made the acquaintance of a spirited youth by the name of Chew. He was one of the most daring of the Indian traders, very well acquainted with the secret paths of the wilderness, needy, dissolute, and, by a last good fortune, in some disgrace with his family. Him we persuaded to come to our relief; he privately provided what was needful for our flight, and one day we slipped out of Albany, without a word to our former friend, and embarked, a little above, in a canoe.

To the toils and perils of this journey it would require a pen more elegant than mine to do full justice. The reader must conceive for himself the dreadful wilderness which we had now to thread; its thickets, swamps, precipitous rocks, impetuous rivers, and amazing waterfalls. Among these barbarous scenes we must toil all day, now paddling, now carrying our canoe upon our shoulders; and at night we slept about a fire, surrounded by the howling of wolves and other savage animals. It was our design to mount the headwaters of the Hudson, to the neighbourhood of Crown Point, where the French had a strong place in the woods, upon Lake Champlain.[21] But to have done this directly were too perilous; and it was accordingly gone upon by such a labyrinth of rivers, lakes, and portages[22] as makes my head giddy to remember. These paths were in ordinary times entirely desert; but the country was now up, the tribes on the war-path, the woods full of Indian scouts. Again and again we came upon these parties when we least expected them; and one day, in particular, I shall never forget how, as dawn was coming in, we were suddenly surrounded by five or six of these painted devils, uttering a very dreary sort of cry, and brandishing their hatchets. It passed off harmlessly, indeed, as did the rest of our encounters; for Chew was well known and highly valued among the different tribes. Indeed, he was a very gallant, respectable young man; but even with the advantage of his companionship, you must not think these meetings were without sensible peril. To prove friendship on our part, it was needful to draw upon our stock of rum – indeed, under whatever disguise, that is the true business of the Indian trader, to keep a travelling public-house in the forest; and when once the braves had got their bottle of *scaura* (as they call this beastly liquor), it behoved us to set forth and paddle for our scalps. Once they were a little drunk, good-bye to any sense or decency; they had but the one thought, to get more *scaura*. They might easily take it in their heads to give us chase, and had we been overtaken, I had never written these memoirs.

We were come to the most critical portion of our course, where we might equally expect to fall into the hands of French or English, when a terrible calamity befell us. Chew was taken suddenly sick with symptoms like those of poison, and in the course of a few hours expired in the bottom of the canoe. We thus lost at once our guide, our interpreter, our boatman, and our passport, for he was all these in one; and found ourselves reduced, at a blow, to the most desperate and irremediable distress. Chew, who took a great pride in his knowledge, had indeed often lectured us on the geography; and Ballantrae, I believe, would listen. But for my part I have always found such information highly tedious; and beyond the fact that we were now in the country of the Adirondack Indians, and not so distant from our destination, could we but have found the way, I was entirely ignorant. The wisdom of my course was soon the more apparent; for, with all his pains, Ballantrae was no further advanced than myself. He knew we must continue to go up one stream; then, by way of a portage, down another; and then up a third. But you are to consider, in a mountain country, how many streams come rolling in from every hand. And how is a gentleman, who is a perfect stranger in that part of the world, to tell any one of them from any other? Nor was this our only trouble. We were great novices, besides, in handling a canoe; the portages were almost beyond our strength, so that I have seen us sit down in despair for half an hour at a time without one word; and the appearance of a single Indian, since we had now no means of speaking to them, would have been in all probability the means of our destruction. There is altogether some excuse if Ballantrae showed something of a glooming disposition; his habit of imputing blame to others, quite as capable as himself, was less tolerable, and his language it was not always easy to accept. Indeed, he had contracted on board the pirate ship a manner of address which was in a high degree unusual between gentlemen; and now, when you might say he was in a fever, it increased upon him hugely.

The third day of these wanderings, as we were carrying the canoe upon a rocky portage, she fell, and was entirely bilged.[23] The portage was between two lakes, both pretty extensive; the track, such as it was, opened at both ends upon the water, and on both hands was enclosed by the unbroken woods; and the sides of the lakes were quite impassable with bog: so that we beheld ourselves not only condemned to go without our boat and the greater part of our provisions, but to plunge at once into impenetrable thickets and to desert what little guidance we still had – the course of the river. Each stuck his pistols in his belt, shouldered an axe, made a pack of his treasure and as much food as he could stagger under; and deserting the rest of our possessions, even to our swords, which would have much embarrassed us among the woods, we set forth on this deplorable adventure. The labours of Hercules, so finely described by Homer,[24] were a trifle to what we now underwent. Some parts of the forest were perfectly dense down to the ground, so that we must cut our way like mites in a cheese. In some the bottom was full of deep swamp, and the whole wood entirely rotten. I have leaped on a great fallen log and sunk to the knees in touchwood;[25] I have sought to stay myself, in falling, against what looked to be a solid trunk, and the whole thing has whiffed at my touch like a sheet of paper. Stumbling, falling, bogging to the knees, hewing our way, our eyes almost put out with twigs and branches, our clothes plucked from our bodies, we laboured all day, and it is doubtful if we made two miles. What was worse, as we could rarely get a view of the country, and were perpetually justled from our path by obstacles, it was impossible even to have a guess in what direction we were moving.

A little before sundown, in an open place with a stream, and set about with barbarous mountains, Ballantrae threw down his pack. 'I will go no further,' said he, and bade me light the fire, damning my blood in terms not proper for a chairman.[26]

I told him to try to forget he had ever been a pirate, and to remember he had been a gentleman.

'Are you mad?' he cried. 'Don't cross me here!' And then, shaking his fist at the hills, 'To think,' cries he, 'that I must leave my bones in this miserable wilderness! Would God I had died upon the scaffold like a gentleman!' This he said ranting like an actor; and then sat biting his fingers and staring on the ground, a most unchristian object.

I took a certain horror of the man, for I thought a soldier and a gentleman should confront his end with more philosophy. I made him no reply, therefore, in words; and presently the evening fell so chill that I was glad, for my own sake, to kindle a fire. And yet God knows, in such an open spot, and the country alive with savages, the act was little short of lunacy. Ballantrae seemed never to observe me; but at last, as I was about parching a little corn, he looked up.

'Have you ever a brother?' said he.

'By the blessing of Heaven,' said I, 'not less than five.'

'I have the one,' said he, with a strange voice; and then presently, 'He shall pay me for all this,' he added. And when I asked him what was his brother's part in our distress, 'What!' he cried, 'he sits in my place, he bears my name, he courts my wife; and I am here alone with a damned Irishman in this tooth-chattering desert! O, I have been a common gull!' he cried.

The explosion was in all ways so foreign to my friend's nature that I was daunted out of all my just susceptibility. Sure, an offensive expression, however vivacious, appears a wonderfully small affair in circumstances so extreme! But here there is a strange thing to be noted. He had only once before referred to the lady with whom he was contracted. That was when we came in view of the town of New York, when he had told me, if all had their rights, he was now in sight of his own property, for Miss Graeme enjoyed a large estate in the province. And this was certainly a natural occasion; but now here she was named a second time; and what is surely fit to be observed, in this very month, which was November, '47, and *I believe upon that very day as we sat among these barbarous mountains*, his brother and Miss Graeme were married. I am the least superstitious of men; but the hand of Providence is here displayed too openly not to be remarked.*

The next day, and the next, were passed in similar labours; Ballantrae often deciding on our course by the spinning of a coin; and once, when I expostulated on this childishness, he had an odd remark that I have never forgotten. 'I know no better way,' said he, 'to express my scorn of human reason.' I think it was the third day that we found the body of a Christian, scalped and most abominably mangled, and lying in a pudder of his blood; the birds of the desert screaming over him, as thick as flies. I cannot describe how dreadfully this sight affected us; but it robbed me of all strength and all hope for this world. The same day, and only a little after, we were scrambling over a part of the forest that had been burned, when Ballantrae, who was

* *Note by Mr Mackellar.* – A complete blunder: there was at this date no word of the marriage: see above in my own narration.

a little ahead, ducked suddenly behind a fallen trunk. I joined him in this shelter, whence we could look abroad without being seen ourselves; and in the bottom of the next vale beheld a large war-party of the savages going by across our line. There might be the value of a weak battalion present; all naked to the waist, blacked with grease and soot, and painted with white lead and vermilion, according to their beastly habits. They went one behind another like a string of geese, and at a quickish trot; so that they took but a little while to rattle by, and disappear again among the woods. Yet I suppose we endured a greater agony of hesitation and suspense in these few minutes than goes usually to a man's whole life. Whether they were French or English Indians, whether they desired scalps or prisoners, whether we should declare ourselves upon the chance, or lie quiet and continue the heart-breaking business of our journey: sure, I think these were questions to have puzzled the brains of Aristotle himself. Ballantrae turned to me with a face all wrinkled up, and his teeth showing in his mouth, like what I have read of people starving; he said no word, but his whole appearance was a kind of dreadful question.

'They may be of the English side,' I whispered; 'and think! the best we could then hope, is to begin this over again.'

'I know – I know,' he said. 'Yet it must come to a plunge at last.' And he suddenly plucked out his coin, shook it in his closed hands, looked at it, and then lay down with his face in the dust.

Addition by Mr Mackellar. – I drop the Chevalier's narration at this point because the couple quarrelled and separated the same day; and the Chevalier's account of the quarrel seems to me (I must confess) quite incompatible with the nature of either of the men. Henceforth they wandered alone, undergoing extraordinary sufferings; until first one and then the other was picked up by a party from Fort St Frederick. Only two things are to be noted. And first (as most important for my purpose) that the Master, in the course of his miseries, buried his treasure, at a point never since discovered, but of which he took a drawing in his own blood on the lining of his hat. And second, that on his coming thus penniless to the Fort, he was welcomed like a brother by the Chevalier, who thence paid his way to France. The simplicity of Mr Burke's character leads him at this point to praise the Master exceedingly; to an eye more worldly-wise, it would seem it was the Chevalier alone that was to be commended. I have the more pleasure in pointing to this really very noble trait of my esteemed correspondent, as I fear I may have wounded him immediately before. I have refrained from comments on any of his extraordinary and (in my eyes) immoral opinions, for I know him to be jealous of respect. But his version of the quarrel is really more than I can reproduce; for I knew the Master myself, and a man more insusceptible of fear is not conceivable. I regret this oversight of the Chevalier's, and all the more because the tenor of his narrative (set aside a few flourishes) strikes me as highly ingenuous.

PERSECUTIONS ENDURED BY MR HENRY

You can guess on what part of his adventures the Colonel principally dwelled. Indeed, if we had heard it all, it is to be thought the current of this business had been wholly altered; but the pirate ship was very gently touched upon. Nor did I hear the Colonel to an end even of that which he was willing to disclose; for Mr Henry, having for some while been plunged in a brown study,[1] rose at last from his seat and (reminding the Colonel there were matters that he must attend to) bade me follow him immediately to the office.

Once there, he sought no longer to dissemble his concern, walking to and fro in the room with a contorted face, and passing his hand repeatedly upon his brow.

'We have some business,' he began at last; and there broke off, declared we must have wine, and sent for a magnum of the best. This was extremely foreign to his habitudes; and, what was still more so, when the wine had come, he gulped down one glass upon another like a man careless of appearances. But the drink steadied him.

'You will scarce be surprised, Mackellar,' says he, 'when I tell you that my brother – whose safety we are all rejoiced to learn – stands in some need of money.'

I told him I had misdoubted as much; but the time was not very fortunate, as the stock was low.

'Not mine,' said he. 'There is the money for the mortgage.'

I reminded him it was Mrs Henry's.

'I will be answerable to my wife,' he cried violently.

'And then,' said I, 'there is the mortgage.'

'I know,' said he; 'it is on that I would consult you.'

I showed him how unfortunate a time it was to divert this money from its destination; and how, by so doing, we must lose the profit of our past economies, and plunge back the estate into the mire. I even took the liberty to plead with him; and when he still opposed me with a shake of the head and a bitter dogged smile, my zeal quite carried me beyond my place. 'This is midsummer madness,' cried I; 'and I for one will be no party to it.'

'You speak as though I did it for my pleasure,' says he. 'But I have a child now; and, besides, I love order; and to say the honest truth, Mackellar, I had begun to take a pride in the estates.' He gloomed for a moment. 'But what would you have?' he went on. 'Nothing is mine, nothing. This day's news has knocked the bottom out of my life. I have only the name and the shadow of things – only the shadow; there is no substance in my rights.'

'They will prove substantial enough before a court,' said I.

He looked at me with a burning eye, and seemed to repress the word upon his lips; and I repented what I had said, for I saw that while he spoke of the estate he had still a side-thought to his marriage. And then, of a sudden, he twitched the letter from his pocket, where it lay all crumpled, smoothed it violently on the table, and read these words to me with a trembling tongue: – ' "My dear Jacob" – This is how he begins!' cries he – ' "My dear Jacob, I once called you so, you may remember; and you have now done the business, and flung my heels as high as Criffel."[2] What do you think of that, Mackellar,' says he, 'from an only brother? I declare to God I liked him very well; I was always staunch to him; and this is how he writes! But I will not sit down under the imputation' – walking to and fro – 'I am as good as he; I am a better man than he, I call on God to prove it! I cannot give him all the monstrous sum he asks; he knows the estate to be incompetent; but I will give him what I have, and it is more than he expects. I have borne all this too long. See what he writes further on; read it for yourself: "I know you are a niggardly dog." A niggardly dog! I niggardly? Is that true, Mackellar? You think it is?' I really thought he would have struck me at that. 'O, you all think so! Well, you shall see, and he shall see, and God shall see. If I ruin the estate and go barefoot, I shall stuff this bloodsucker. Let him ask all – all, and he shall have it! It is all his by rights. Ah!' he cried, 'and I foresaw all this, and worse, when he would not let me go.' He poured out another glass of wine, and was about to carry it to his lips, when I made so bold as to lay a finger on his arm. He stopped a moment. 'You are right,' said he, and flung glass and all in the fireplace. 'Come, let us count the money.'

I durst no longer oppose him; indeed, I was very much affected by the sight of so much disorder in a man usually so controlled; and we sat down together, counted the money, and made it up in packets for the greater ease of Colonel Burke, who was to be the bearer. This done, Mr Henry returned to the hall, where he and my old lord sat all night through with their guest.

A little before dawn I was called and set out with the Colonel. He would scarce have liked a less responsible convoy, for he was a man who valued himself; nor could we afford him one more dignified, for Mr Henry must not appear with the free-traders. It was a very bitter morning of wind, and as we went down through the long shrubbery the Colonel held himself muffled in his cloak.

'Sir,' said I, 'this is a great sum of money that your friend requires. I must suppose his necessities to be very great.'

'We must suppose so,' says he, I thought drily; but perhaps it was the cloak about his mouth.

'I am only a servant of the family,' said I. 'You may deal openly with me. I think we are likely to get little good by him?'

'My dear man,' said the Colonel, 'Ballantrae is a gentleman of the most eminent natural abilities, and a man that I admire, and that I revere, to the very ground he treads on.' And then he seemed to me to pause like one in a difficulty.

'But for all that,' said I, 'we are likely to get little good by him?'

'Sure, and you can have it your own way, my dear man,' says the Colonel.

By this time we had come to the side of the creek, where the boat awaited him. 'Well,' said he, 'I am sure I am very much your debtor for all your civility, Mr Whatever-your-name-is; and just as a last word, and since you show so much intelligent interest, I will mention a small circumstance that may be of use to the family. For I believe my friend omitted to mention that he has the largest pension on the Scots Fund[3] of any refugee in Paris; and it's the more disgraceful, sir,' cries the Colonel, warming, 'because there's not one dirty penny for myself.'

He cocked his hat at me, as if I had been to blame for this partiality; then changed again into his usual swaggering civility, shook me by the hand, and set off down to the boat, with the money under his arms, and whistling as he went the pathetic air of *Shule Aroon*.[4] It was the first time I had heard that tune; I was to hear it again, words and all, as you shall learn, but I remember how that little stave of it ran in my head after the free-traders had bade him 'Wheesht, in the deil's name,' and the grating of the oars had taken its place, and I stood and watched the dawn creeping on the sea, and the boat drawing away, and the lugger lying with her foresail backed awaiting it.

The gap made in our money was a sore embarrassment, and, among other consequences, it had this: that I must ride to Edinburgh, and there raise a new loan on very questionable terms to keep the old afloat; and was thus, for close upon three weeks, absent from the house of Durrisdeer.

What passed in the interval I had none to tell me, but I found Mrs Henry, upon my return, much changed in her demeanour. The old talks with my lord for the most part pretermitted; a certain deprecation visible towards her husband, to whom I thought she addressed herself more often; and, for one thing, she was now greatly wrapped up in Miss Katharine. You would think the change was agreeable to Mr Henry; no such matter! To the contrary, every circumstance of alteration was a stab to him; he read in each the avowal of her truant fancies. That constancy to the Master of which she was proud while she supposed him dead, she had to blush for now she knew he was alive, and these blushes were the hated spring of her new conduct. I am to conceal no truth; and I will here say plainly, I think this was the period in which Mr Henry showed the worst. He contained himself, indeed, in public; but there was a deep-seated irritation visible underneath. With me, from whom he had less concealment, he was often grossly unjust, and even for his wife he would sometimes have a sharp retort: perhaps when she had ruffled him with some unwonted kindness; perhaps upon no tangible occasion, the mere habitual tenor of the man's annoyance bursting spontaneously forth. When he would thus forget himself (a thing so strangely out of keeping with the terms of their relation), there went a shock through the whole company, and the pair would look upon each other in a kind of pained amazement.

All the time, too, while he was injuring himself by this defect of temper, he was hurting his position by a silence, of which I scarce know whether to say it was the child of generosity or pride. The free-traders came again and again, bringing messengers from the Master, and none departed empty-handed. I never durst reason with Mr Henry; he gave what was asked of him in a kind of noble rage. Perhaps because he knew he was by nature inclining to the parsimonious, he took a backforemost pleasure in the recklessness with which he supplied his brother's exigence. Perhaps the falsity of the position would have spurred a humbler man into the same excess. But the estate (if I may say so) groaned under it; our daily expenses were shorn lower and lower; the stables were emptied, all but four roadsters; servants were discharged, which raised a dreadful murmuring in the country, and heated up the old disfavour upon Mr Henry; and at last the yearly visit to Edinburgh must be discontinued.

This was in 1756. You are to suppose that for seven years this bloodsucker had been drawing the life's blood from Durrisdeer, and that all this time my patron had held his peace. It was an effect of devilish malice in the Master that he addressed Mr Henry alone upon the matter of his demands, and there was never a word to my lord. The family had looked on, wondering at our economies. They had lamented, I have no doubt, that my patron had become so great a miser – a fault always despicable, but in the young abhorrent, and Mr Henry was not yet thirty years of age. Still, he had managed the business of Durrisdeer almost from a boy; and they bore with these changes in a silence as proud and bitter as his own, until the coping-stone of the Edinburgh visit.

At this time I believe my patron and his wife were rarely together, save at meals. Immediately on the back of Colonel Burke's announcement Mrs Henry made palpable advances; you might say she had laid a sort of timid court to her husband, different, indeed, from her former manner of unconcern and distance. I never had the heart to blame Mr Henry because he recoiled from these advances; nor yet to censure the wife, when she was cut to the quick by their rejection. But the result was an entire estrangement, so that (as I say) they rarely spoke, except at meals. Even the matter of the Edinburgh visit was first broached at table, and it chanced that Mrs Henry was that day ailing and querulous. She had no sooner understood her husband's meaning than the red flew in her face.

'At last,' she cried, 'this is too much! Heaven knows what pleasure I have in my life, that I should be denied my only consolation. These shameful proclivities must be trod down; we are already a mark and an eyesore in the neighbourhood. I will not endure this fresh insanity.'

'I cannot afford it,' says Mr Henry.

'Afford?' she cried. 'For shame! But I have money of my own.'

'That is all mine, madam, by marriage,' he snarled, and instantly left the room.

My old lord threw up his hands to Heaven, and he and his daughter, withdrawing to the chimney, gave me a broad hint to be gone. I found Mr Henry in his usual retreat, the steward's room, perched on the end of the table, and plunging his penknife in it with a very ugly countenance.

'Mr Henry,' said I, 'you do yourself too much injustice, and it is time this should cease.'

'O!' cries he, 'nobody minds here. They think it only natural. I have shameful proclivities. I am a niggardly dog,' and he drove his knife up to the hilt. 'But I will show that fellow,' he cried with an oath, 'I will show him which is the more generous.'

'This is no generosity,' said I; 'this is only pride.'

'Do you think I want morality?' he asked.

I thought he wanted help, and I should give it him, willy-nilly; and no sooner was Mrs Henry gone to her room than I presented myself at her door and sought admittance.

She openly showed her wonder. 'What do you want with me, Mr Mackellar?' said she.

'The Lord knows, madam,' says I, 'I have never troubled you before with any freedoms; but this thing lies too hard upon my conscience, and it will out. Is it possible that two people can be so blind as you and my lord? and have lived all these years with a noble gentleman like Mr Henry, and understand so little of his nature?'

'What does this mean?' she cried.

'Do you not know where his money goes to? his – and yours – and the money for the very wine he does not drink at table?' I went on. 'To Paris – to that man! Eight thousand pounds has he had of us in seven years, and my patron fool enough to keep it secret!'

'Eight thousand pounds!' she repeated. 'It is impossible; the estate is not sufficient.'

'God knows how we have sweated farthings to produce it,' said I. 'But eight thousand and sixty is the sum, beside odd shillings. And if you can think my patron miserly after that, this shall be my last interference.'

'You need say no more, Mr Mackellar,' said she. 'You have done most properly in what you too modestly call your interference. I am much to blame; you must think me indeed a very unobservant wife' (looking upon me with a strange smile), 'but I shall put this right at once. The Master was always of a very thoughtless nature; but his heart is excellent; he is the soul of generosity. I shall write to him myself. You cannot think how you have pained me by this communication.'

'Indeed, madam, I had hoped to have pleased you,' said I, for I raged to see her still thinking of the Master.

'And pleased,' said she, 'and pleased me of course.'

That same day (I will not say but what I watched) I had the satisfaction to see Mr Henry come from his wife's room in a state most unlike himself; for his face was all bloated with weeping, and yet he seemed to me to walk upon the air. By this, I was sure his wife had made him full amends for once. 'Ah,' thought I to myself, 'I have done a brave stroke this day.'

On the morrow, as I was seated at my books, Mr Henry came in softly behind me, took me by the shoulders and shook me in a manner of playfulness. 'I find you are a faithless fellow after all,' says he, which was his only reference to my part; but the tone he spoke in was more to me than any eloquence of protestation. Nor was this all I had effected; for when the next messenger came (as he did, not long afterwards) from the Master, he got nothing away with him but a letter. For some while back it had been I myself who had conducted these affairs; Mr Henry not setting pen to paper, and I only in the driest and most formal terms. But this letter I did not even see; it would scarce be pleasant reading, for Mr Henry felt he had his wife behind him for once, and I observed, on the day it was despatched, he had a very gratified expression.

Things went better now in the family, though it could scarce be pretended they went well. There was now at least no misconception; there was kindness upon all sides; and I believe my patron and his wife might again have drawn together if he could but have pocketed his pride, and she forgot (what was the ground of all) her brooding on another man. It is wonderful how a private thought leaks out; it is wonderful to me now how we should all have followed the current of her sentiments; and though she bore herself quietly, and had a very even disposition, yet we should have known whenever her fancy ran to Paris. And would not any one have thought that my disclosure must have rooted up that idol? I think there is the devil in women: all these years passed, never a sight of the man, little enough kindness to remember (by all accounts) even while she had him, the notion of his death intervening, his heartless rapacity laid bare to her; that all should not do, and she must still keep the best place in her heart for this accursed fellow, is a thing to make a plain man rage. I had never much natural sympathy for the passion of love; but this unreason in my patron's wife disgusted me outright with the whole matter. I remember checking a maid because she sang some bairnly kickshaw[5] while my mind was thus engaged; and my asperity brought about my ears the enmity of all the petticoats about the house; of which I recked very little, but it amused Mr Henry, who rallied me much upon our joint unpopularity. It is strange enough (for my own mother was certainly one of the salt of the earth, and my Aunt Dickson, who paid my fees at the University, a very notable woman), but I have never had much toleration for the female sex, possibly not much understanding; and being far from a bold man, I have ever shunned their company. Not only do I see no cause to regret this diffidence in myself, but have invariably remarked the most unhappy consequences follow those who were less wise. So much I thought proper to set down, lest I show myself unjust to Mrs Henry. And, besides, the remark arose naturally, on a re-perusal of the letter which was the next step in these affairs, and reached me, to my sincere astonishment, by a private hand, some week or so after the departure of the last messenger.

Letter from Colonel BURKE *(afterwards Chevalier)*
to MR MACKELLAR.

TROYES IN CHAMPAGNE,
July 12, 1756.

MY DEAR SIR, – You will doubtless be surprised to receive a communication from one so little known to you; but on the occasion I had the good fortune to rencounter you at Durrisdeer, I remarked you for a young man of a solid gravity of character: a qualification which I profess I admire and revere next to natural genius or the bold chivalrous spirit of the soldier. I was, besides, interested in the noble family which you have the honour to serve, or (to speak more by the book) to be the humble and respected friend of; and a conversation I had the pleasure to have with you very early in the morning has remained much upon my mind.

Being the other day in Paris, on a visit from this famous city, where I am in garrison, I took occasion to inquire your name (which I profess I had forgot) at my friend, the Master of B.; and, a fair opportunity occurring, I write to inform you of what's new.

The Master of B. (when we had last some talk of him together) was in receipt, as I think I then told you, of a highly advantageous pension on the Scots Fund. He next received a company, and was soon after advanced to a regiment of his own. My dear sir, I do not offer to explain this circumstance; any more than why I myself, who have rid at the right hand of Princes, should be fubbed off with a pair of colours and sent to rot in a hole at the bottom of the province. Accustomed as I am to Courts, I cannot but feel it is no atmosphere for a plain soldier; and I could never hope to advance by similar means, even could I stoop to the endeavour. But our friend has a particular aptitude to succeed by the means of ladies; and if all be true that I have heard, he enjoyed a remarkable protection. It is like this turned against him; for when I had the honour to shake him by the hand, he was but newly released from the Bastille, where he had been cast on a sealed letter; and, though now released, has both lost his regiment and his pension. My dear sir, the loyalty of a plain Irishman will ultimately succeed in the place of craft; as I am sure a gentleman of your probity will agree.

Now, sir, the Master is a man whose genius I admire beyond expression, and, besides, he is my friend; but I thought a little word of this revolution in his fortunes would not come amiss, for, in my opinion, the man's desperate. He spoke, when I saw him, of an adventure upon India (whither I am myself in some hope of accompanying my illustrious countryman, Mr Lally);[6] but for this he would require (as I understood) more money than was readily at his command. You may have heard a military proverb: that it is a good thing to make a bridge of gold to a flying enemy? I trust you will take my meaning, and I subscribe myself, with proper respects to my Lord Durrisdeer, to his son, and to the beauteous Mrs Durie,

My dear Sir,

Your obedient humble Servant,

FRANCIS BURKE.

This missive I carried at once to Mr Henry; and I think there was but the one thought between the two of us: that it had come a week too late. I made haste to send an answer to Colonel Burke, in which I begged him, if he should see the Master, to assure him his next messenger would be attended to. But with all my haste I was not in time to avert what was impending: the arrow had been drawn; it must now fly. I could almost doubt the power of Providence (and certainly His will) to stay the issue of events; and it is a strange thought, how many of us had been storing up the elements of this catastrophe, for how long a time, and with how blind an ignorance of what we did.

From the coming of the Colonel's letter, I had a spy-glass in my room, began to drop questions to the tenant folk, and as there was no great secrecy observed, and the free-trade (in our part) went by force as much as stealth, I had soon got together a knowledge of the signals in use, and knew pretty well to an hour when any messenger might be expected. I say, I questioned the tenants; for with the traders themselves, desperate blades that went habitually armed, I could never bring myself to meddle willingly. Indeed, by what proved in the sequel an unhappy chance, I was an object of scorn to some of these braggadocios; who had not only gratified me with a nickname, but catching me one night upon a by-path, and being all (as they would have said) somewhat merry, had caused me to dance for their diversion. The method employed was that of cruelly chipping at my toes with naked cutlasses, shouting at the same time 'Square-toes'; and though they did me no bodily mischief, I was none the less deplorably affected, and was indeed for several days confined to my bed: a scandal on the state of Scotland on which no comment is required.

It happened on the afternoon of November 7th, in this same unfortunate year, that I espied, during my walk, the smoke of a beacon fire upon the Muckleross.[7] It was drawing near time for my return; but the uneasiness upon my spirits was that day so great that I must burst through the thickets to the edge of what they call the Craig Head. The sun was already down, but there was still a broad light in the west, which showed me some of the smugglers treading out their signal fire upon the Ross, and in the bay the lugger[8] lying with her sails brailed up.[9] She was plainly but new come to anchor, and yet the skiff was already lowered and pulling for the landing-place at the end of the long shrubbery. And this I knew could signify but one thing – the coming of a messenger for Durrisdeer.

I laid aside the remainder of my terrors, clambered down the brae – a place I had never ventured through before – and was hid among the shore-side thickets in time to see the boat touch. Captain Crail himself was steering, a thing not usual; by his side there sat a passenger; and the men gave way with difficulty, being hampered with near upon half a dozen portmanteaus, great and small. But the business of landing was briskly carried through; and presently the baggage was all tumbled on shore, the boat on its return voyage to the lugger, and the passenger standing alone upon the point of rock, a tall slender figure of a gentleman, habited in black, with a sword by his side and a walking-cane upon his wrist. As he so stood, he waved the cane to

Captain Crail by way of salutation, with something both of grace and mockery that wrote the gesture deeply on my mind.

No sooner was the boat away with my sworn enemies than I took a sort of half courage, came forth to the margin of the thicket, and there halted again, my mind being greatly pulled about between natural diffidence and a dark foreboding of the truth. Indeed, I might have stood there swithering[10] all night, had not the stranger turned, spied me through the mists, which were beginning to fall, and waved and cried on me to draw near. I did so with a heart like lead.

'Here, my good man,' said he, in the English accent, 'here are some things for Durrisdeer.'

I was now near enough to see him, a very handsome figure and countenance, swarthy, lean, long, with a quick, alert, black look, as of one who was a fighter, and accustomed to command; upon one cheek he had a mole, not unbecoming; a large diamond sparkled on his hand; his clothes, although of the one hue, were of a French and foppish design; his ruffles, which he wore longer than common, of exquisite lace; and I wondered the more to see him in such a guise when he was but newly landed from a dirty smuggling lugger. At the same time he had a better look at me, toised[11] me a second time sharply, and then smiled.

'I wager, my friend,' says he, 'that I know both your name and your nickname. I divined these very clothes upon your hand of writing, Mr Mackellar.'

At these words I fell to shaking.

'O,' says he, 'you need not be afraid of me. I bear no malice for your tedious letters; and it is my purpose to employ you a good deal. You may call me Mr Bally: it is the name I have assumed; or rather (since I am addressing so great a precisian)[12] it is so I have curtailed my own. Come now, pick up that, and that' – indicating two of the portmanteaus. 'That will be as much as you are fit to bear, and the rest can very well wait. Come, lose no more time, if you please.'

His tone was so cutting that I managed to do as he bid by a sort of instinct, my mind being all the time quite lost. No sooner had I picked up the portmanteaus than he turned his back and marched off through the long shrubbery, where it began already to be dusk, for the wood is thick and evergreen. I followed behind, loaded almost to the dust, though I profess I was not conscious of the burthen; being swallowed up in the monstrosity of this return, and my mind flying like a weaver's shuttle.

On a sudden I set the portmanteaus to the ground and halted. He turned and looked back at me.

'Well?' said he.

'You are the Master of Ballantrae?'

'You will do me the justice to observe,' says he, 'that I have made no secret with the astute Mackellar.'

'And in the name of God,' cries I, 'what brings you here? Go back, while it is yet time.'

'I thank you,' said he. 'Your master has chosen this way, and not I; but since he has made the choice, he (and you also) must abide by the result. – And now pick up these things of mine, which you have set down in a very boggy place, and attend to that which I have made your business.'

But I had no thought now of obedience; I came straight up to him. 'If nothing will move you to go back,' said I; 'though, sure, under all the circumstances, any Christian, or even any gentleman, would scruple to go forward . . .'

'These are gratifying expressions,' he threw in.

'If nothing will move you to go back,' I continued, 'there are still some decencies to be observed. Wait here with your baggage, and I will go forward and prepare your family. Your father is an old man; and . . .' I stumbled . . . 'there are decencies to be observed.'

'Truly,' said he, 'this Mackellar improves upon acquaintance. But look you here, my man, and understand it once for all – you waste your breath upon me, and I go my own way with inevitable motion.'

'Ah!' says I. 'Is that so? We shall see then!'

And I turned and took to my heels for Durrisdeer. He clutched at me, and cried out angrily, and then I believe I heard him laugh, and then I am certain he pursued me for a step or two, and (I suppose) desisted. One thing at least is sure, that I came but a few minutes later to the door of the great house, nearly strangled for the lack of breath, but quite alone. Straight up the stair I ran, and burst into the hall, and stopped before the family without the power of speech; but I must have carried my story in my looks, for they rose out of their places and stared on me like changelings.

'He has come,' I panted out at last.

'He?' said Mr Henry.

'Himself,' said I.

'My son?' cried my lord. 'Imprudent, imprudent boy! O, could he not stay where he was safe!'

Never a word says Mrs Henry; nor did I look at her, I scarce knew why.

'Well,' said Mr Henry, with a very deep breath, 'and where is he?'

'I left him in the long shrubbery,' said I.

'Take me to him,' said he.

So we went out together, he and I, without another word from any one; and in the midst of the gravelled plot encountered the Master strolling up, whistling as he came, and beating the air with his cane. There was still light enough overhead to recognise, though not to read, a countenance.

'Ah! Jacob,' says the Master. 'So here is Esau back.'

'James,' says Mr Henry, 'for God's sake, call me by my name. I will not pretend that I am glad to see you; but I would fain make you as welcome as I can in the house of our fathers.'

'Or in *my* house? or *yours*?' says the Master. 'Which were you about to say? But this is an old sore, and we need not rub it. If you would not share with me in Paris, I hope you will yet scarce deny your elder brother a corner of the fire at Durrisdeer?'

'That is very idle speech,' replied Mr Henry. 'And you understand the power of your position excellently well.'

'Why, I believe I do,' said the other, with a little laugh. And this, though they had never touched hands, was (as we may say) the end of the brothers' meeting; for at this the Master turned to me and bade me fetch his baggage.

I, on my side, turned to Mr Henry for a confirmation; perhaps with some defiance.

'As long as the Master is here, Mr Mackellar, you will very much oblige me by regarding his wishes as you would my own,' says Mr Henry. 'We are constantly troubling you: will you be so good as send one of the servants?' – with an accent on the word.

If this speech were anything at all, it was surely a well-deserved reproof upon the stranger; and yet, so devilish was his impudence, he twisted it the other way.

'And shall we be common enough to say "Sneck up"?'[13] inquires he softly, looking upon me sideways.

Had a kingdom depended on the act, I could not have trusted myself in words; even to call a servant was beyond me; I had rather serve the man myself than speak; and I turned away in silence and went into the long shrubbery, with a heart full of anger and despair. It was dark under the trees, and I walked before me and forgot what business I was come upon, till I nearly broke my shin on the portmanteaus. Then it was that I remarked a strange particular; for whereas I had before carried both and scarce observed it, it was now as much as I could do to manage one. And this, as it forced me to make two journeys, kept me the longer from the hall.

When I got there, the business of welcome was over long ago; the company was already at supper; and, by an oversight that cut me to the quick, my place had been forgotten. I had seen one side of the Master's return; now I was to see the other. It was he who first remarked my coming in and standing back (as I did) in some annoyance. He jumped from his seat.

'And if I have not got the good Mackellar's place!' cries he. 'John, lay another for Mr Bally; I protest he will disturb no one, and your table is big enough for all.'

I could scarce credit my ears, nor yet my senses, when he took me by the shoulders and thrust me, laughing, into my own place – such an affectionate playfulness was in his voice. And while John laid the fresh place for him (a thing on which he still insisted), he went and leaned on his father's chair and looked down upon him, and the old man turned about and looked upwards on his son, with such a pleasant mutual tenderness that I could have carried my hand to my head in mere amazement.

Yet all was of a piece. Never a harsh word fell from him, never a sneer showed upon his lip. He had laid aside even his cutting English accent, and spoke with the kindly Scots tongue, that set a value on affectionate words; and though his manners had a graceful elegance mighty foreign to our ways in Durrisdeer, it was still a homely courtliness, that did not shame but flattered us. All that he did throughout the meal, indeed, drinking wine with me with a notable respect, turning about for a pleasant word with John, fondling his father's hand, breaking into little merry tales of his adventures, calling up the past with happy reference – all he did was so becoming, and himself so handsome, that I could scarce wonder if my lord and Mrs Henry sat about the board with radiant faces, or if John waited behind with dropping tears.

As soon as supper was over, Mrs Henry rose to withdraw.

'This was never your way, Alison,' said he.

'It is my way now,' she replied: which was notoriously false, 'and I will give you a good-night, James, and a welcome – from the dead,' said she, and her voice dropped and trembled.

Poor Mr Henry, who had made rather a heavy figure through the meal, was more concerned than ever; pleased to see his wife withdraw, and yet half displeased, as he thought upon the cause of it; and the next moment altogether dashed by the fervour of her speech.

On my part, I thought I was now one too many; and was stealing after Mrs Henry, when the Master saw me.

'Now, Mr Mackellar,' says he, 'I take this near on an unfriendliness. I cannot have you go: this is to make a stranger of the prodigal son; and let me remind you where – in his own father's house! Come, sit ye down, and drink another glass with Mr Bally.'

'Ay, ay, Mr Mackellar,' says my lord, 'we must not make a stranger either of him or you. I have been telling my son,' he added, his voice brightening as usual on the word, 'how much we valued all your friendly service.'

So I sat there, silent, till my usual hour; and might have been almost deceived in the man's nature but for one passage, in which his perfidy appeared too plain. Here was the passage; of which, after what he knows of the brothers' meeting, the reader shall consider for himself. Mr Henry sitting somewhat dully, in spite of his best endeavours to carry things before my lord, up jumps the Master, passes about the board, and claps his brother on the shoulder.

'Come, come, *Hairry lad*,' says he, with a broad accent, such as they must have used together when they were boys, 'you must not be downcast because your brother has come home. All's yours, that's sure enough, and little I grudge it you. Neither must you grudge me my place beside my father's fire.'

'And that is too true, Henry,' says my old lord, with a little frown, a thing rare with him. 'You have been the elder brother of the parable[14] in the good sense; you must be careful of the other.'

'I am easily put in the wrong,' said Mr Henry.

'Who puts you in the wrong?' cried my lord, I thought very tartly for so mild a man. 'You have earned my gratitude and your brother's many thousand times: you may count on its endurance; and let that suffice.'

'Ay, Harry, that you may,' said the Master; and I thought Mr Henry looked at him with a kind of wildness in his eye.

On all the miserable business that now followed, I have four questions that I asked myself often at the time, and ask myself still: – Was the man moved by a particular sentiment against Mr Henry? or by what he thought to be his interest? or by a mere delight in cruelty such as cats display and theologians tell us of the devil? or by what he would have called love? My common opinion halts among the three first; but perhaps there lay at the spring of his behaviour an element of all. As thus: – Animosity to Mr Henry would explain his hateful usage of him when they were alone; the interests he came to serve would explain his very different attitude before my lord; that and some spice of a design of gallantry, his care to stand well with Mrs Henry; and the pleasure of malice for itself, the pains he was continually at to mingle and oppose these lines of conduct.

Partly because I was a very open friend to my patron, partly because in my letters to Paris I had often given myself some freedom of remonstrance, I was included in his diabolical amusement. When I was alone with him, he pursued me with sneers; before the family he used me with the extreme of friendly condescension. This was not only painful in itself; not only did it put me continually in the wrong; but there was in it an element of insult indescribable. That he should thus leave me out in his dissimulation, as though even my testimony were too despicable to be considered, galled me to the blood. But what it was to me is not worth notice. I make but memorandum of it here; and chiefly for this reason, that it had one good result, and gave me the quicker sense of Mr Henry's martyrdom.

It was on him the burthen fell. How was he to respond to the public advances of one who never lost a chance of gibing him in private? How was he to smile back on the deceiver and the insulter? He was condemned to seem ungracious. He was condemned to silence. Had he been less proud, had he spoken, who would have credited the truth? The acted calumny had done its work; my lord and Mrs Henry were the daily witnesses of what went on; they could have sworn in court that the Master was a model of long-suffering good-nature, and Mr Henry a pattern of jealousy and thanklessness. And ugly enough as these must have appeared in any one, they seemed tenfold uglier in Mr Henry; for who could forget that the Master lay in peril of his life, and that he had already lost his mistress, his title, and his fortune?

'Henry, will you ride with me?' asks the Master one day.

And Mr Henry, who had been goaded by the man all morning, raps out: 'I will not.'

'I sometimes wish you would be kinder, Henry,' says the other wistfully.

I give this for a specimen; but such scenes befell continually. Small wonder if Mr Henry was blamed; small wonder if I fretted myself into something near upon a bilious fever; nay, and at the mere recollection feel a bitterness in my blood.

Sure, never in this world was a more diabolical contrivance: so perfidious, so simple, so impossible to combat. And yet I think again, and I think always, Mrs Henry might have read between the lines; she might have had more knowledge of her husband's nature; after all these years of marriage she might have commanded or captured his confidence. And my old lord, too – that very watchful gentleman – where was all his observation? But, for one thing, the deceit was practised by a master hand, and might have gulled an angel. For another (in the case of Mrs Henry), I have observed there are no persons so far away as those who are both married and estranged, so that they seem out of earshot, or to have no common tongue. For a third (in the case of both of these spectators), they were blinded by old ingrained predilection. And for a fourth, the risk the Master was supposed to stand in (supposed, I say – you will soon hear why) made it seem the more ungenerous to criticise; and, keeping them in a perpetual tender solicitude about his life, blinded them the more effectually to his faults.

It was during this time that I perceived most clearly the effect of manner, and was led to lament most deeply the plainness of my own. Mr Henry had the essence of a gentleman; when he was moved, when there was any call of circumstance, he could play his part with dignity and spirit; but in the day's commerce (it is idle to deny it) he fell short of the ornamental. The Master (on the other hand) had never a movement but it commended him. So it befell that when the one appeared gracious and the other ungracious, every trick of their bodies seemed to call out confirmation. Not that alone: but the more deeply Mr Henry floundered in his brother's toils, the more clownish he grew; and the more the Master enjoyed his spiteful entertainment, the more engagingly, the more smilingly, he went! So that the plot, by its own scope and progress, furthered and confirmed itself.

It was one of the man's arts to use the peril in which (as I say) he was supposed to stand. He spoke of it to those who loved him with a gentle pleasantry, which made it the more touching. To Mr Henry he used it as a cruel weapon of offence. I remember his laying his finger on the clean lozenge of the painted window one day when we three were alone together in the hall. 'Here went your lucky guinea, Jacob,' said he. And when Mr Henry only looked upon him darkly, 'O!' he added, 'you need not look such impotent malice, my good fly. You can be rid of your spider when you please. How long, O Lord? When are you to be wrought to the point of a denunciation, scrupulous brother? It is one of my interests in this dreary hole. I ever loved experiment.' Still Mr Henry only stared upon him with a glooming brow, and a changed colour; and at last the Master broke out in a laugh and clapped him on the shoulder, calling him a sulky dog. At this my patron leaped back with a gesture I thought very dangerous; and I must suppose the Master thought so too, for he looked the least in the world discountenanced, and I do not remember him again to have laid hands on Mr Henry.

But though he had his peril always on his lips in the one way or the other, I thought his conduct strangely incautious, and began to fancy the Government – who had set a price upon his head – was gone sound asleep. I will not deny I was tempted with the wish to denounce him; but two thoughts withheld me: one, that if he were thus to end his life upon an honourable scaffold, the man would be canonised for good in the minds of his father and my patron's wife; the other, that if I was anyway mingled in the matter, Mr Henry himself would scarce escape some glancings of suspicion. And in the meanwhile our enemy went in and out more than I could have thought possible, the fact that he was home again was buzzed about all the country-side, and yet he was never stirred. Of all those so-many and so-different persons who were acquainted with his presence, none had the least greed – as I used to say in my annoyance – or the least loyalty; and the man rode here and there – fully more welcome, considering the lees of old unpopularity, than Mr Henry – and, considering the free-traders, far safer than myself.

Not but what he had a trouble of his own; and this, as it brought about the gravest consequences, I must now relate. The reader will scarce have forgotten Jessie Broun; her way of life was much among the smuggling party; Captain Crail himself was of her intimates; and she had early word of Mr Bally's presence at the house. In my opinion, she had long ceased to care two straws for the Master's person; but it was become her habit to connect herself continually with the Master's name; that was the ground of all her play-acting; and so now, when he was back, she thought she owed it to herself to grow a haunter of the neighbourhood of Durrisdeer. The Master could scarce go abroad but she was there in wait for him; a scandalous figure of a woman, not often sober; hailing him wildly as 'her bonnie laddie,' quoting pedlar's poetry, and, as I receive the story, even seeking to weep upon his neck. I own I rubbed my hands over this persecution; but the

Master, who laid so much upon others, was himself the least patient of men. There were strange scenes enacted in the policies.[15] Some say he took his cane to her, and Jessie fell back upon her former weapons – stones. It is certain at least that he made a motion to Captain Crail to have the woman trepanned,[16] and that the Captain refused the proposition with uncommon vehemence. And the end of the matter was victory for Jessie. Money was got together; an interview took place, in which my proud gentleman must consent to be kissed and wept upon; and the woman was set up in a public of her own, somewhere on Solway side (but I forget where), and, by the only news I ever had of it, extremely ill-frequented.

This is to look forward. After Jessie had been but a little while upon his heels, the Master comes to me one day in the steward's office, and with more civility than usual, 'Mackellar,' says he, 'there is a damned crazy wench comes about here. I cannot well move in the matter myself, which brings me to you. Be so good as to see to it: the men must have a strict injunction to drive the wench away.'

'Sir,' said I, trembling a little, 'you can do your own dirty errands for yourself.'

He said not a word to that, and left the room.

Presently came Mr Henry. 'Here is news!' cried he. 'It seems all is not enough, and you must add to my wretchedness. It seems you have insulted Mr Bally.'

'Under your kind favour, Mr Henry,' said I, 'it was he that insulted me, and, as I think, grossly. But I may have been careless of your position when I spoke; and if you think so when you know all, my dear patron, you have but to say the word. For you I would obey in any point whatever, even to sin, God pardon me!' And thereupon I told him what had passed.

Mr Henry smiled to himself; a grimmer smile I never witnessed. 'You did exactly well,' said he. 'He shall drink his Jessie Broun to the dregs.' And then, spying the Master outside, he opened the window, and, crying to him by the name of Mr Bally, asked him to step up and have a word.

'James,' said he, when our persecutor had come in and closed the door behind him, looking at me with a smile, as if he thought I was to be humbled, 'you brought me a complaint against Mr Mackellar, into which I have inquired. I need not tell you I would always take his word against yours; for we are alone, and I am going to use something of your own freedom. Mr Mackellar is a gentleman I value; and you must contrive, so long as you are under this roof, to bring yourself into no more collisions with one whom I will support at any possible cost to me or mine. As for the errand upon which you came to him, you must deliver yourself from the consequences of your own cruelty, and none of my servants shall be at all employed in such a case.'

'My father's servants, I believe,' said the Master.

'Go to him with this tale,' said Mr Henry.

The Master grew very white. He pointed at me with his finger. 'I want that man discharged,' he said.

'He shall not be,' said Mr Henry.

'You shall pay pretty dear for this,' says the Master.

'I have paid so dear already for a wicked brother,' said Mr Henry, 'that I am bankrupt even of fears. You have no place left where you can strike me.'

'I will show you about that,' says the Master, and went softly away.

'What will he do next, Mackellar?' cries Mr Henry.

'Let me go away,' said I. 'My dear patron, let me go away; I am but the beginning of fresh sorrows.'

'Would you leave me quite alone?' said he.

We were not long in suspense as to the nature of the new assault. Up to that hour the Master had played a very close game with Mrs Henry; avoiding pointedly to be alone with her, which I took at the time for an effect of decency, but now think to have been a most insidious art; meeting her, you may say, at meal-time only; and behaving, when he did so, like an affectionate brother. Up to that hour, you may say he had scarce directly interfered between Mr Henry and his wife; except in so far as he had manœuvred the one quite forth from the good graces of the other. Now all that was to be changed; but whether really in revenge, or because he was wearying of Durrisdeer, and looked about for some diversion, who but the devil shall decide?

From that hour, at least, began the siege of Mrs Henry; a thing so deftly carried on that I scarce know if she was aware of it herself, and that her husband must look on in silence. The first parallel[17] was opened (as was made to appear) by accident. The talk fell, as it did often, on the exiles in France; so it glided to the matter of their songs.

'There is one,' says the Master, 'if you are curious in these matters, that has always seemed to me very moving. The poetry is harsh; and yet, perhaps because of my situation, it has always found the way to my heart. It is supposed to be sung, I should tell you, by an exile's sweetheart; and represents perhaps not so much the truth of what she is thinking, as the truth of what he hopes of her, poor soul! in these far lands.' And here the Master sighed. 'I protest it is a pathetic sight when a score of rough Irish, all common sentinels, get to this song; and you may see, by their falling tears, how it strikes home to them. It goes thus, father,' says he, very adroitly taking my lord for his listener, 'and if I cannot get to the end of it, you must think it is a common case with us exiles.' And thereupon he struck up the same air as I had heard the Colonel whistle;[18] but now to words, rustic indeed, yet most pathetically setting forth a poor girl's aspirations for an exiled lover; of which one verse indeed (or something like it) still sticks by me:–

> O, I will dye my petticoat red,
> With my dear boy I'll beg my bread,
> Though all my friends should wish me dead,
> For Willie among the rushes, O!

He sang it well, even as a song; but he did better yet as a performer. I have heard famous actors, when there was not a dry eye in the Edinburgh theatre; a great wonder to behold; but no more wonderful than how the Master played upon that little ballad, and on those who heard him, like an instrument, and seemed now upon the point of failing, and now to conquer his distress, so that words and music seemed to pour out of his own heart and his own past, and to be aimed directly at Mrs Henry. And his art went further yet; for all was so delicately touched, it seemed impossible to suspect him of the least design; and so far from making a parade of emotion, you would have sworn he was striving to be calm. When it came to an end, we all sat silent for a time; he had chosen the dusk of the afternoon, so that none could see his neighbour's face; but it seemed as if we held our breathing; only my old lord cleared his throat. The first to move was the singer, who got to his feet suddenly and softly, and went and walked softly to and fro in the low end of the hall, Mr Henry's customary place. We were to suppose that he there struggled down the last of his emotion; for he presently returned and launched into a disquisition on the nature of the Irish (always so much miscalled, and whom he defended) in his natural voice; so that, before the lights were brought, we were in the usual course of talk. But even then, methought Mrs Henry's face was a shade pale; and for another thing, she withdrew almost at once.

The next sign was a friendship this insidious devil struck up with innocent Miss Katharine; so that they were always together, hand in hand, or she climbing on his knee, like a pair of children. Like all his diabolical acts, this cut in several ways. It was the last stroke to Mr Henry, to see his own babe debauched against him; it made him harsh with the poor innocent, which brought him still a peg lower in his wife's esteem; and (to conclude) it was a bond of union between the lady and the Master. Under this influence, their old reserve melted by daily stages. Presently there came walks in the long shrubbery, talks in the Belvedere,[19] and I know not what tender familiarity. I am sure Mrs Henry was like many a good woman; she had a whole conscience, but perhaps by the means of a little winking. For even to so dull an observer as myself, it was plain her kindness was of a more moving nature than the sisterly. The tones of her voice appeared more numerous; she had a light and softness in her eye; she was more gentle with all of us, even with Mr Henry, even with myself; methought she breathed of some quiet melancholy happiness.

To look on at this, what a torment it was for Mr Henry! And yet it brought our ultimate deliverance, as I am soon to tell.

The purport of the Master's stay was no more noble (gild it as they might) than to wring money out. He had some design of a fortune in the French Indies,[20] as the Chevalier wrote me; and it was the sum required for this that he came seeking. For the rest of the family it spelled ruin; but my lord, in his incredible partiality, pushed ever for the granting. The family was now so narrowed down (indeed, there were no more of them than just the father and the two sons) that it was possible to break the entail and alienate a piece of land.[21] And to this, at first by hints, and then by open pressure, Mr Henry was brought to consent. He never would have done so, I am very well assured, but for the weight of the distress under which he laboured. But for his passionate eagerness to see his brother gone, he would not thus have broken with his own sentiment and the traditions of his house. And even so, he sold them his consent at a dear rate, speaking for once openly, and holding the business up in its own shameful colours.

'You will observe,' he said, 'this is an injustice to my son, if ever I have one.'

'But that you are not likely to have,' said my lord.

'God knows!' says Mr Henry. 'And considering the cruel falseness of the position in which I stand to my brother, and that you, my lord, are my father, and have the right to command me, I set my hand to this paper. But one thing I will say first: I have been ungenerously pushed, and when next, my lord, you are tempted to compare your sons, I call on you to remember what I have done and what he has done. Acts are the fair test.'

My lord was the most uneasy man I ever saw; even in his old face the blood came up. 'I think this is not a very wisely chosen moment, Henry, for complaints,' said he. 'This takes away from the merit of your generosity.'

'Do not deceive yourself, my lord,' said Mr Henry. 'This injustice is not done from generosity to him, but in obedience to yourself.'

'Before strangers . . .' begins my lord, still more unhappily affected.

'There is no one but Mackellar here,' said Mr Henry; 'he is my friend. And, my lord, as you make him no stranger to your frequent blame, it were hard if I must keep him one to a thing so rare as my defence.'

Almost I believe my lord would have rescinded his decision, but the Master was on the watch.

'Ah! Henry, Henry,' says he, 'you are the best of us still. Rugged and true! Ah! man, I wish I was as good.'

And at that instance of his favourite's generosity my lord desisted from his hesitation, and the deed was signed.

As soon as it could be brought about, the land of Ochterhall was sold for much below its value, and the money paid over to our leech and sent by some private carriage into France. And now here was all the man's business brought to a successful head, and his pockets once more bulging with our gold; and yet the point for which we had consented to this sacrifice was still denied us, and the visitor still lingered on at Durrisdeer. Whether in malice, or because the time was not yet come for his adventure to the Indies, or because he had hopes of his design on Mrs Henry, or from the orders of the Government, who shall say? but linger he did, and that for weeks.

You will observe I say: 'from the orders of the Government'; for about this time the man's disreputable secret trickled out.

The first hint I had was from a tenant, who commented on the Master's stay, and yet more on his security; for this tenant was a Jacobitish sympathiser, and had lost a son at Culloden, which gave him the more critical eye. 'There is one thing,' said he, 'that I cannot but think strange; and that is how he got to Cockermouth.'[22]

'To Cockermouth?' said I, with a sudden memory of my first wonder on beholding the man disembark so *point-de-vice*[23] after so long a voyage.

'Why, yes,' says the tenant, 'it was there he was picked up by Captain Crail. You thought he had come from France by sea? And so we all did.'

I turned this news a little in my head, and then carried it to Mr Henry. 'Here is an odd circumstance,' said I, and told him.

'What matters how he came, Mackellar, so long as he is here?' groans Mr Henry.

'No, sir,' said I, 'but think again! Does not this smack a little of some Government connivance? You know how much we have wondered already at the man's security.'

'Stop,' said Mr Henry. 'Let me think of this.' And as he thought, there came that grim smile upon his face that was a little like the Master's. 'Give me paper,' said he. And he sat without another word and wrote to a gentleman of his acquaintance – I will name no unnecessary names, but he was one in a high place. This letter I despatched by the only hand I could depend upon in such a case – Macconochie's; and the old man rode hard, for he was back with the reply before even my eagerness had ventured to expect him. Again, as he read it, Mr Henry had the same grim smile.

'This is the best you have done for me yet, Mackellar,' says he. 'With this in my hand I will give him a shog.[24] Watch for us at dinner.'

At dinner accordingly Mr Henry proposed some very public appearance for the Master; and my lord, as he had hoped, objected to the danger of the course.

'O!' says Mr Henry, very easily, 'you need no longer keep this up with me. I am as much in the secret as yourself.'

'In the secret?' says my lord. 'What do you mean, Henry? I give you my word, I am in no secret from which you are excluded.'

The Master had changed countenance, and I saw he was struck in a joint of his harness.

'How?' says Mr Henry, turning to him with a huge appearance of surprise. 'I see you serve your masters very faithfully; but I had thought you would have been humane enough to set your father's mind at rest.'

'What are you talking of? I refuse to have my business publicly discussed. I order this to cease,' cries the Master very foolishly and passionately, and indeed more like a child than a man.

'So much discretion was not looked for at your hands, I can assure you,' continued Mr Henry. 'For see what my correspondent writes' – unfolding the paper – ' "It is, of course, in the interests both of the Government and the gentleman whom we may perhaps best continue to call Mr Bally, to keep this understanding secret; but it was never meant his own family should continue to endure the suspense you paint so feelingly; and I am pleased mine should be the hand to set these fears at rest. Mr Bally is as safe in Great Britain as yourself." '

'Is this possible?' cries my lord, looking at his son, with a great deal of wonder, and still more of suspicion in his face.

'My dear father,' says the Master, already much recovered. 'I am overjoyed that this may be disclosed. My own instructions, direct from London, bore a very contrary sense, and I was charged to keep the indulgence secret from every one, yourself not excepted, and indeed yourself expressly named – as I can show in black and white, unless I have destroyed the letter. They must have changed their mind very swiftly, for the whole matter is still quite fresh; or rather, Henry's correspondent must have misconceived that part, as he seems to have misconceived the rest. To tell you the truth, sir,' he continued, getting visibly more easy, 'I had supposed this unexplained favour to a rebel was the effect of some application from yourself; and the injunction to secrecy among my family the result of a desire on your part to conceal your kindness. Hence I was the more careful to obey orders. It remains now to guess by what other channel indulgence can have flowed on so notorious an offender as myself; for I do not think your son need defend himself from what seems hinted at in Henry's letter. I have never yet heard of a Durrisdeer who was a turncoat or a spy,' says he proudly.

And so it seemed he had swum out of this danger unharmed; but this was to reckon without a blunder he had made, and without the pertinacity of Mr Henry, who was now to show he had something of his brother's spirit.

'You say the matter is still fresh?' says Mr Henry.

'It is recent,' says the Master, with a fair show of stoutness, and yet not without a quaver.

'Is it so recent as that?' asks Mr Henry, like a man a little puzzled, and spreading his letter forth again.

In all the letter there was no word as to the date; but how was the Master to know that?

'It seemed to come late enough for me,' says he, with a laugh. And at the sound of that laugh, which rang false, like a cracked bell, my lord looked at him again across the table, and I saw his old lips draw together close.

'No,' said Mr Henry, still glancing on his letter, 'but I remember your expression. You said it was very fresh.'

And here we had a proof of our victory, and the strongest instance yet of my lord's incredible indulgence; for what must he do but interfere to save his favourite from exposure!

'I think, Henry,' says he, with a kind of pitiful eagerness, 'I think we need dispute no more. We are all rejoiced at last to find your brother safe; we are all at one on that; and, as grateful subjects, we can do no less than drink to the King's health and bounty.'

Thus was the Master extricated; but at least he had been put to his defence, he had come lamely out, and the attraction of his personal danger was now publicly plucked away from him. My lord, in his heart of hearts, now knew his favourite to be a Government spy; and Mrs Henry (however she explained the tale) was notably cold in her behaviour to the discredited hero of romance. Thus in the best fabric of duplicity there is some weak point, if you can strike it, which will loosen all; and if, by this fortunate stroke, we had not shaken the idol, who can say how it might have gone with us at the catastrophe?

And yet at the time we seemed to have accomplished nothing. Before a day or two he had wiped off the ill results of his discomfiture, and, to all appearance, stood as high as ever. As for my Lord Durrisdeer, he was sunk in parental partiality; it was not so much love, which should be an active quality, as an apathy and torpor of his other powers; and forgiveness (so to misapply a noble word) flowed from him in sheer weakness, like the tears of senility. Mrs Henry's was a different case; and Heaven alone knows what he found to say to her, or how he persuaded her from her contempt. It is one of the worst things of sentiment, that the voice grows to be more important than the words, and the speaker than that which is spoken. But some excuse the Master must have found, or perhaps he had even struck upon some art to wrest this exposure to his own advantage; for after a time of coldness, it seemed as if things went worse than ever between him and Mrs Henry. They were then constantly together. I would not be thought to cast one shadow of blame, beyond what is due to a half-wilful blindness, on that unfortunate lady; but I do think, in these last days, she was playing very near the fire; and whether I be wrong or not in that, one thing is sure and quite sufficient: Mr Henry thought so. The poor gentleman sat for days in my room, so great a picture of distress that I could never venture to address him; yet it is to be thought he found some comfort even in my presence and the knowledge of my sympathy. There were times, too, when we talked, and a strange manner of talk it was; there was never a person named, nor an individual circumstance referred to; yet we had the same matter in our minds, and we were each aware of it. It is a strange art that can thus be practised; to talk for hours of a thing, and never name nor yet so much as hint at it. And I remember I wondered if it was by some such natural skill that the Master made love to Mrs Henry all day long (as he manifestly did), yet never startled her into reserve.

To show how far affairs had gone with Mr Henry, I will give some words of his, uttered (as I have cause not to forget) upon the 26th of February 1757. It was unseasonable weather, a cast back into winter: windless, bitter cold, the world all white with rime, the sky low and grey: the sea black and silent like a quarry-hole. Mr Henry sat close by the fire, and debated (as was now common with him) whether 'a man' should 'do things,' whether 'interference was wise,' and the like general propositions, which each of us particularly applied. I was by the window, looking out, when there passed below me the Master, Mrs Henry, and Miss Katharine, that now constant trio. The child was running to and fro, delighted with the frost; the Master spoke close in the lady's ear with what seemed (even from so far) a devilish grace of insinuation; and she on her part looked on the ground like a person lost in listening. I broke out of my reserve.

'If I were you, Mr Henry,' said I, 'I would deal openly with my lord.'

'Mackellar, Mackellar,' said he, 'you do not see the weakness of my ground. I can carry no such base thoughts to any one – to my father least of all; that would be to fall into the bottom of his scorn. The weakness of my ground,' he continued, 'lies in myself, that I am not one who engages love. I have their gratitude, they all tell me that;

I have a rich estate of it! But I am not present in their minds; they are moved neither to think with me nor to think for me. There is my loss!' He got to his feet, and trod down the fire. 'But some method must be found, Mackellar,' said he, looking at me suddenly over his shoulder; 'some way must be found. I am a man of a great deal of patience – far too much – far too much. I begin to despise myself. And yet, sure, never was a man involved in such a toil!' He fell back to his brooding.

'Cheer up,' said I. 'It will burst of itself.'

'I am far past anger now,' says he, which had so little coherency with my own observation that I let both fall.

ACCOUNT OF ALL THAT PASSED ON THE NIGHT OF FEBRUARY 27TH, 1757

On the evening of the interview referred to, the Master went abroad; he was abroad a great deal of the next day also, that fatal 27th; but where he went, or what he did, we never concerned ourselves to ask until next day. If we had done so, and by any chance found out, it might have changed all. But as all we did was done in ignorance, and should be so judged, I shall so narrate these passages as they appeared to us in the moment of their birth, and reserve all that I since discovered for the time of its discovery. For I have now come to one of the dark parts of my narrative, and must engage the reader's indulgence for my patron.

All the 27th that rigorous weather endured: a stifling cold; the folk passing about like smoking chimneys; the wide hearth in the hall piled high with fuel; some of the spring birds that had already blundered north into our neighbourhood besieging the windows of the house or trotting on the frozen turf like things distracted. About noon there came a blink of sunshine; showing a very pretty, wintry, frosty landscape of white hills and woods, with Crail's lugger waiting for a wind under the Craig Head, and the smoke mounting straight into the air from every farm and cottage. With the coming of night, the haze closed in overhead; it fell dark and still and starless, and exceeding cold: a night the most unseasonable, fit for strange events.

Mrs Henry withdrew, as was now her custom, very early. We had set ourselves of late to pass the evening with a game of cards; another mark that our visitor was wearying mightily of the life at Durrisdeer; and we had not been long at this when my old lord slipped from his place beside the fire, and was off without a word to seek the warmth of bed. The three thus left together had neither love nor courtesy to share; not one of us would have sat up one instant to oblige another; yet from the influence of custom, and as the cards had just been dealt, we continued the form of playing out the round. I should say we were late sitters; and though my lord had departed earlier than was his custom, twelve was already gone some time upon the clock, and the servants long ago in bed. Another thing I should say, that although I never saw the Master anyway affected with liquor, he had been drinking freely, and was perhaps (although he showed it not) a trifle heated.

Anyway, he now practised one of his transitions; and so soon as the door closed behind my lord, and without the smallest change of voice, shifted from ordinary civil talk into a stream of insult.

'My dear Henry, it is yours to play,' he had been saying, and now continued: 'It is a very strange thing how, even in so small a matter as a game of cards, you display your rusticity. You play, Jacob, like a bonnet-laird,[1] or a sailor in a tavern. The same dulness, the same petty greed, *cette lenteur d'hébêté qui me fait rager*;[2] it is strange I should have such a brother. Even Square-toes has a certain vivacity when his stake is imperilled; but the dreariness of a game with you I positively lack language to depict.'

Mr Henry continued to look at his cards, as though very maturely considering some play; but his mind was elsewhere.

'Dear God, will this never be done?' cries the Master. '*Quel lourdaud!*[3] But why do I trouble you with French expressions, which are lost on such an ignoramus? A *lourdaud*, my dear brother, is as we might say a bumpkin, a clown, a clodpole: a fellow without grace, lightness, quickness; any gift of pleasing, any natural brilliancy: such a one as you shall see, when you desire, by looking in the mirror. I tell you these things for your good, I assure you; and besides, Square-toes' (looking at me and stifling a yawn), 'it is one of my diversions in this very dreary spot to toast you and your master at the fire like chestnuts. I have great pleasure in your case, for I observe the nickname (rustic as it is) has always the power to make you writhe. But sometimes I have more trouble with this dear fellow here, who seems to have gone to sleep upon his cards. – Do you not see the applicability of the epithet I have just explained, dear Henry? Let me show you. For instance, with all those solid qualities which I delight to recognise in you, I never knew a woman who did not prefer me – nor, I think,' he continued, with the most silken deliberation, 'I think – who did not continue to prefer me.'

Mr Henry laid down his cards. He rose to his feet very softly, and seemed all the while like a person in deep thought. 'You coward!' he said gently, as if to himself. And then, with neither hurry nor any particular violence, he struck the Master in the mouth.

The Master sprang to his feet like one transfigured; I had never seen the man so beautiful. 'A blow!' he cried. 'I would not take a blow from God Almighty!'

'Lower your voice,' said Mr Henry. 'Do you wish my father to interfere for you again?'

'Gentlemen, gentlemen,' I cried, and sought to come between them.

The Master caught me by the shoulder, held me at arm's length, and still addressing his brother: 'Do you know what this means?' said he.

'It was the most deliberate act of my life,' says Mr Henry.

'I must have blood, I must have blood for this,' says the Master.

'Please God it shall be yours,' said Mr Henry; and he went to the wall and took down a pair of swords that hung there with others, naked. These he presented to the Master by the points. 'Mackellar shall see us play fair,' said Mr Henry. 'I think it very needful.'

'You need insult me no more,' said the Master, taking one of the swords at random. 'I have hated you all my life.'

'My father is but newly gone to bed,' said Mr Henry. 'We must go somewhere forth of the house.'

'There is an excellent place in the long shrubbery,' said the Master.

'Gentlemen,' said I, 'shame upon you both! Sons of the same mother, would you turn against the life she gave you?'

'Even so, Mackellar,' said Mr Henry, with the same perfect quietude of manner he had shown throughout.

'It is what I will prevent,' said I.

And now here is a blot upon my life. At these words of mine the Master turned his blade against my bosom; I saw the light run along the steel; and I threw up my arms and fell to my knees before him on the floor. 'No, no,' I cried, like a baby.

'We shall have no more trouble with him,' said the Master. 'It is a good thing to have a coward in the house.'

'We must have light,' said Mr Henry, as though there had been no interruption.

'This trembler can bring a pair of candles,' said the Master.

To my shame be it said, I was still so blinded with the flashing of that bare sword that I volunteered to bring a lantern.

'We do not need a l-l-lantern,' says the Master, mocking me. 'There is no breath of air. Come, get to your feet, take a pair of lights, and go before. I am close behind with this' – making the blade glitter as he spoke.

I took up the candlesticks and went before them, steps that I would give my hand to recall; but a coward is a slave at the best; and even as I went, my teeth smote each other in my mouth. It was as he had said: there was no breath stirring; a windless stricture of frost had bound the air; and as we went forth in the shine of the candles, the blackness was like a roof over our heads. Never a word was said; there was never a sound but the creaking of our steps along the frozen path. The cold of the night fell about me like a bucket of water; I shook as I went with more than terror; but my companions, bare-headed like myself, and fresh from the warm hall, appeared not even conscious of the change.

'Here is the place,' said the Master. 'Set down the candles.'

I did as he bid me, and presently the flames went up, as steady as in a chamber, in the midst of the frosted trees, and I beheld these two brothers take their places.

'The light is something in my eyes,' said the Master.

'I will give you every advantage,' replied Mr Henry, shifting his ground, 'for I think you are about to die.' He spoke rather sadly than otherwise, yet there was a ring in his voice.

'Henry Durie,' said the Master, 'two words before I begin. You are a fencer, you can hold a foil; you little know what a change it makes to hold a sword! And by that I know you are to fall. But see how strong is my situation! If you fall, I shift out of this country to where my money is before me. If I fall, where are you? My father, your wife – who is in love with me, as you very well know – your child even, who prefers me to yourself: – how will these avenge me! Had you thought of that, dear Henry?' He looked at his brother with a smile; then made a fencing-room salute.

Never a word said Mr Henry, but saluted too, and the swords rang together.

I am no judge of the play; my head, besides, was gone with cold and fear and horror; but it seems that Mr Henry took and kept the upper hand from the engagement, crowding in upon his foe with a contained and glowing fury. Nearer and nearer he crept upon the man, till of a sudden the Master leaped back with a little sobbing oath; and I believe the movement brought the light once more against his eyes. To it they went again, on the fresh ground; but now methought closer, Mr Henry pressing more outrageously, the Master beyond doubt with shaken confidence. For it is beyond doubt he now recognised himself for lost, and had some taste of the cold agony of fear; or he had never attempted the foul stroke. I cannot say I followed it, my untrained eye was never quick enough to seize details, but it appears he caught his brother's blade with his left hand, a practice not permitted. Certainly Mr Henry only saved himself by leaping on one side; as certainly the Master, lungeing in the air, stumbled on his knee, and before he could move, the sword was through his body.

I cried out with a stifled scream, and ran in; but the body was already fallen to the ground, where it writhed a moment like a trodden worm, and then lay motionless.

'Look at his left hand,' said Mr Henry.

'It is all bloody,' said I.

'On the inside?' said he.

'It is cut on the inside,' said I.

'I thought so,' said he, and turned his back.

I opened the man's clothes; the heart was quite still, it gave not a flutter.

'God forgive us, Mr Henry!' said I. 'He is dead.'

'Dead?' he repeated, a little stupidly; and then, with a rising tone,

'Dead? dead?' says he, and suddenly cast his bloody sword upon the ground.

'What must we do?' said I. 'Be yourself, sir. It is too late now: you must be yourself.'

He turned and stared at me. 'O, Mackellar!' says he, and put his face in his hands.

I plucked him by the coat. 'For God's sake, for all our sakes, be more courageous!' said I. 'What must we do?'

He showed me his face with the same stupid stare. 'Do?' says he. And with that his eye fell on the body, and 'O!' he cries out, with his hand to his brow, as if he had never remembered; and, turning from me, made off towards the house of Durrisdeer at a strange stumbling run.

I stood a moment mused; then it seemed to me my duty lay most plain on the side of the living; and I ran after him, leaving the candles on the frosty ground and the body lying in their light under the trees. But run as I pleased, he had the start of me, and was got into the house, and up to the hall, where I found him standing before the fire with his face once more in his hands, and as he so stood he visibly shuddered.

'Mr Henry, Mr Henry,' I said, 'this will be the ruin of us all.'

'What is this that I have done?' cries he, and then looking upon me with a countenance that I shall never forget, 'Who is to tell the old man?'[4] he said.

The word knocked at my heart; but it was no time for weakness. I went and poured him out a glass of brandy. 'Drink that,' said I, 'drink it down.' I forced him to swallow it like a child; and, being still perished with the cold of the night, I followed his example.

'It has to be told, Mackellar,' said he. 'It must be told.' And he fell suddenly in a seat – my old lord's seat by the chimney-side – and was shaken with dry sobs.

Dismay came upon my soul; it was plain there was no help in Mr Henry. 'Well,' said I, 'sit there, and leave all to me.' And taking a candle in my hand, I set forth out of the room in the dark house. There was no movement; I must suppose that all had gone unobserved; and I was now to consider how to smuggle through the rest with the like secrecy. It was no hour for scruples; and I opened my lady's door without so much as a knock, and passed boldly in.

'There is some calamity happened,' she cried, sitting up in bed.

'Madam,' said I, 'I will go forth again into the passage; and do you get as quickly as you can into your clothes. There is much to be done.'

She troubled me with no questions, nor did she keep me waiting. Ere I had time to prepare a word of that which I must say to her, she was on the threshold signing me to enter.

'Madam,' said I, 'if you cannot be very brave, I must go elsewhere; for if no one helps me to-night, there is an end of the house of Durrisdeer.'

'I am very courageous,' said she; and she looked at me with a sort of smile, very painful to see, but very brave too.

'It has come to a duel,' said I.

'A duel?' she repeated. 'A duel! Henry and—'

'And the Master,' said I. 'Things have been borne so long, things of which you know nothing, which you would not believe if I should tell. But to-night it went too far, and when he insulted you—'

'Stop,' said she. 'He? Who?'

'O! madam,' cried I, my bitterness breaking forth, 'do you ask me such a question? Indeed, then, I may go elsewhere for help; there is none here!'

'I do not know in what I have offended you,' said she. 'Forgive me; put me out of this suspense.'

But I dared not tell her yet; I felt not sure of her; and at the doubt, and under the sense of impotence it brought with it, I turned on the poor woman with something near to anger.

'Madam,' said I, 'we are speaking of two men: one of them insulted you, and you ask me which. I will help you to the answer. With one of these men you have spent all your hours: has the other reproached you? To one you have been always kind; to the other, as God sees me and judges between us two, I think not always: has his love ever failed you? To-night one of these two men told the other, in my hearing – the hearing of a hired stranger, – that you were in love with him. Before I say one word, you shall answer your own question:

Which was it? Nay, madam, you shall answer me another: If it has come to this dreadful end, whose fault is it?'

She stared at me like one dazzled. 'Good God!' she said once, in a kind of bursting exclamation; and then a second time in a whisper to herself: 'Great God! – In the name of mercy, Mackellar, what is wrong?' she cried. 'I am made up; I can hear all.'

'You are not fit to hear,' said I. 'Whatever it was, you shall say first it was your fault.'

'O!' she cried, with a gesture of wringing her hands, 'this man will drive me mad! Can you not put *me* out of your thoughts?'

'I think not once of you,' I cried. 'I think of none but my dear unhappy master.'

'Ah!' she cried, with her hand to her heart, 'is Henry dead?'

'Lower your voice,' said I. 'The other.'

I saw her sway like something stricken by the wind; and I know not whether in cowardice or misery, turned aside and looked upon the floor. 'These are dreadful tidings,' said I at length, when her silence began to put me in some fear; 'and you and I behove to be the more bold if the house is to be saved.' Still she answered nothing. 'There is Miss Katharine, besides,' I added: 'unless we bring this matter through, her inheritance is like to be of shame.'

I do not know if it was the thought of her child or the naked word shame that gave her deliverance; at least I had no sooner spoken than a sound passed her lips, the like of it I never heard; it was as though she had lain buried under a hill and sought to move that burthen. And the next moment she had found a sort of voice.

'It was a fight,' she whispered. 'It was not—?' and she paused upon the word.

'It was a fair fight on my dear master's part,' said I. 'As for the other, he was slain in the very act of a foul stroke.'

'Not now!' she cried.

'Madam,' said I, 'hatred of that man glows in my bosom like a burning fire; ay, even now he is dead. God knows, I would have stopped the fighting, had I dared. It is my shame I did not. But when I saw him fall, if I could have spared one thought from pitying of my master, it had been to exult in that deliverance.'

I do not know if she marked; but her next words were, 'My lord?'

'That shall be my part,' said I.

'You will not speak to him as you have to me?' she asked.

'Madam,' said I, 'have you not some one else to think of? Leave my lord to me.'

'Some one else?' she repeated.

'Your husband,' said I. She looked at me with a countenance illegible. 'Are you going to turn your back on him?' I asked.

Still she looked at me; then her hand went to her heart again. 'No,' said she.

'God bless you for that word!' I said. 'Go to him now, where he sits in the hall; speak to him – it matters not what you say; give him your hand; say, "I know all"; – if God gives you grace enough, say, "Forgive me."'

'God strengthen you, and make you merciful,' said she. 'I will go to my husband.'

'Let me light you there,' said I, taking up the candle.

'I will find my way in the dark,' she said, with a shudder, and I think the shudder was at me.

So we separated – she downstairs to where a little light glimmered in the hall-door, I along the passage to my lord's room. It seems hard to say why, but I could not burst in on the old man as I could on the young woman; with whatever reluctance, I must knock. But his old slumbers were light, or perhaps he slept not; and at the first summons I was bidden enter.

He, too, sat up in bed; very aged and bloodless he looked; and whereas he had a certain largeness of appearance when dressed for daylight, he now seemed frail and little, and his face (the wig being laid aside) not bigger than a child's. This daunted me; nor less, the haggard surmise of misfortune in his eye. Yet his voice was even peaceful as he inquired my errand. I set my candle down upon a chair, leaned on the bed-foot, and looked at him.

'Lord Durrisdeer,' said I, 'it is very well known to you that I am a partisan in your family.'

'I hope we are none of us partisans,' said he. 'That you love my son sincerely, I have always been glad to recognise.'

'O! my lord, we are past the hour of these civilities,' I replied. 'If we are to save anything out of the fire, we must look the fact in its bare countenance. A partisan I am; partisans we have all been; it is as a partisan that I am here in the middle of the night to plead before you. Hear me; before I go, I will tell you why.'

'I would always hear you, Mr Mackellar,' said he, 'and that at any hour, whether of the day or night, for I would be always sure you had a reason. You spoke once before to very proper purpose; I have not forgotten that.'

'I am here to plead the cause of my master,' I said. 'I need not tell you how he acts. You know how he is placed. You know with what generosity he has always met your other – met your wishes,' I corrected myself, stumbling at that name of son. 'You know – you must know – what he has suffered – what he has suffered about his wife.'

'Mr Mackellar!' cried my lord, rising in bed like a bearded lion.

'You said you would hear me,' I continued. 'What you do not know, what you should know, one of the things I am here to speak of, is the persecution he must bear in private. Your back is not turned before one whom I dare not name to you falls upon him with the most unfeeling taunts; twits him – pardon me, my lord – twits him with your partiality, calls him Jacob, calls him clown, pursues him with ungenerous raillery, not to be borne by man. And let but one of you appear, instantly he changes; and my master must smile and courtesy to the man who has been feeding him with insults; I know, for I have shared in some of it, and I tell you the life is insupportable. All these months it has endured; it began with the man's landing; it was by the name of Jacob that my master was greeted the first night.'

My lord made a movement as if to throw aside the clothes and rise. 'If there be any truth in this—' said he.

'Do I look like a man lying?' I interrupted, checking him with my hand.

'You should have told me at first,' he said.

'Ah, my lord! indeed I should, and you may well hate the face of this unfaithful servant!' I cried.

'I will take order,' said he, 'at once,' and again made the movement to rise.

Again I checked him. 'I have not done,' said I. 'Would God I had! All this my dear, unfortunate patron has endured without help or countenance. Your own best word, my lord, was only gratitude. O, but he was your son too! He had no other father. He was hated in the country, God knows how unjustly. He had a loveless marriage. He stood on all hands without affection or support – dear, generous, ill-fated, noble heart!'

'Your tears do you much honour and me much shame,' says my lord, with a palsied trembling. 'But you do me some injustice. Henry has been ever dear to me, very dear. James (I do not deny it, Mr Mackellar), James is perhaps dearer; you have not seen my James in quite a favourable light; he has suffered under his misfortunes; and we can only remember how great and how unmerited these were. And even now his is the more affectionate nature. But I will not speak of him. All that you say of Henry is most true; I do not wonder, I know him to be very magnanimous; you will say I trade upon the knowledge? It is possible; there are dangerous virtues: virtues that tempt the encroacher. Mr Mackellar, I will make it up to him; I will take order with all this. I have been weak; and, what is worse, I have been dull.'

'I must not hear you blame yourself, my lord, with that which I have yet to tell upon my conscience,' I replied. 'You have not been weak; you have been abused by a devilish dissembler. You saw yourself how he had deceived you in the matter of his danger; he has deceived you throughout in every step of his career. I wish to pluck him from your heart; I wish to force your eyes upon your other son; ah, you have a son there!'

'No, no,' said he, 'two sons – I have two sons.'

I made some gesture of despair that struck him; he looked at me with a changed face. 'There is much worse behind?' he asked, his voice dying as it rose upon the question.

'Much worse,' I answered. 'This night he said these words to Mr Henry: "I have never known a woman who did not prefer me to you, and I think who did not continue to prefer me."'

'I will hear nothing against my daughter,' he cried; and from his readiness to stop me in this direction, I conclude his eyes were not so dull as I had fancied, and he had looked not without anxiety upon the siege of Mrs Henry.

'I think not of blaming her,' cried I. 'It is not that. These words were said in my hearing to Mr Henry; and if you find them not yet plain enough, these others but a little after: "Your wife, who is in love with me." '

'They have quarrelled?' he said.

I nodded.

'I must fly to them,' he said, beginning once again to leave his bed.

'No, no!' I cried, holding forth my hands.

'You do not know,' said he. 'These are dangerous words.'

'Will nothing make you understand, my lord?' said I.

His eyes besought me for the truth.

I flung myself on my knees by the bedside. 'O, my lord,' cried I, 'think on him you have left; think of this poor sinner whom you begot, whom your wife bore to you, whom we have none of us strengthened as we could; think of him, not of yourself; he is the other sufferer – think of him! That is the door for sorrow – Christ's door, God's door: O! it stands open. Think of him, even as he thought of you. "*Who is to tell the old man?*" – these were his words. It was for that I came; that is why I am here pleading at your feet.'

'Let me get up,' he cried, thrusting me aside, and was on his feet before myself. His voice shook like a sail in the wind, yet he spoke with a good loudness; his face was like the snow, but his eyes were steady and dry. 'Here is too much speech,' said he. 'Where was it?'

'In the shrubbery,' said I.

'And Mr Henry?' he asked. And when I had told him he knotted his old face in thought.

'And Mr James?' says he.

'I have left him lying,' said I, 'beside the candles.'

'Candles?' he cried. And with that he ran to the window, opened it, and looked abroad. 'It might be spied from the road.'

'Where none goes by at such an hour,' I objected.

'It makes no matter,' he said. 'One might. – Hark!' cries he. 'What is that?'

It was the sound of men very guardedly rowing in the bay; and I told him so.

'The free-traders,' said my lord. 'Run at once, Mackellar; put these candles out. I will dress in the meanwhile; and when you return we can debate on what is wisest.'

I groped my way downstairs, and out at the door. From quite a far way off a sheen was visible, making points of brightness in the shrubbery; in so black a night it might have been remarked for miles; and I blamed myself bitterly for my incaution. How much more sharply when I reached the place! One of the candlesticks was overthrown, and that taper quenched. The other burned steadily by itself, and made a broad space of light upon the frosted ground. All within that circle seemed, by the force of contrast and the overhanging blackness, brighter than by day. And there was the blood-stain in the midst; and a little farther off Mr Henry's sword, the pommel of which was of silver; but of the body, not a trace. My heart thumped upon my ribs, the hair stirred upon my scalp, as I stood there staring – so strange was the sight, so dire the fears it wakened. I looked right and left; the ground was so hard, it told no story. I stood and listened till my ears ached, but the night was hollow about me like an empty church; not even a ripple stirred upon the shore; it seemed you might have heard a pin drop in the county.

I put the candle out, and the blackness fell about me groping dark; it was like a crown surrounding me; and I went back to the house of Durrisdeer, with my chin upon my shoulder, startling, as I went, with craven suppositions. In the door a figure moved to meet me, and I had near screamed with terror ere I recognised Mrs Henry.

'Have you told him?' says she.

'It was he who sent me,' said I. 'It is gone. – But why are you here?'

'It is gone!' she repeated. 'What is gone?'

'The body,' said I. 'Why are you not with your husband?'

'Gone?' said she. 'You cannot have looked. Come back.'

'There is no light now,' said I. 'I dare not.'

'I can see in the dark. I have been standing here so long – so long,' said she. 'Come, give me your hand.'

We returned to the shrubbery hand in hand, and to the fatal place.

'Take care of the blood,' said I.

'Blood?' she cried, and started violently back.

'I suppose it will be,' said I. 'I am like a blind man.'

'No,' said she, 'nothing! Have you not dreamed?'

'Ah, would to God we had!' cried I.

She spied the sword, picked it up, and seeing the blood, let it fall again with her hands thrown wide. 'Ah!' she cried, and then, with an instant courage, handled it the second time.[5] 'I will take it back and clean it properly,' says she, and again looked about her on all sides. 'It cannot be that he was dead?' she added.

'There was no flutter of his heart,' said I, and then remembering: 'Why are you not with your husband?'

'It is no use,' said she; 'he will not speak to me.'

'Not speak to you?' I repeated. 'Oh! you have not tried.'

'You have a right to doubt me,' she replied, with a gentle dignity.

At this, for the first time, I was seized with sorrow for her. 'God knows, madam,' I cried, 'God knows I am not so hard as I appear; on this dreadful night who can veneer his words? But I am a friend to all who are not Henry Durie's enemies.'

'It is hard, then, you should hesitate about his wife,' said she.

I saw all at once, like the rending of a veil, how nobly she had borne this unnatural calamity, and how generously my reproaches.

'We must go back and tell this to my lord,' said I.

'Him I cannot face,' she cried.

'You will find him the least moved of all of us,' said I.

'And yet I cannot face him,' said she.

'Well,' said I, 'you can return to Mr Henry; I will see my lord.'

As we walked back, I bearing the candlesticks, she the sword – a strange burthen for that woman – she had another thought. 'Should we tell Henry?' she asked.

'Let my lord decide,' said I.

My lord was nearly dressed when I came to his chamber. He heard me with a frown. 'The free-traders,' said he. 'But whether dead or alive?'

'I thought him—' said I, and paused, ashamed of the word.

'I know; but you may very well have been in error. Why should they remove him if not living?' he asked. 'O! here is a great door of hope. It must be given out that he departed – as he came – without any note of preparation. We must save all scandal.'

I saw he had fallen, like the rest of us, to think mainly of the house. Now that all the living members of the family were plunged in irremediable sorrow, it was strange how we turned to that conjoint abstraction of the family itself, and sought to bolster up the airy nothing of its reputation: not the Duries only, but the hired steward himself.

'Are we to tell Mr Henry?' I asked him.

'I will see,' said he. 'I am going first to visit him; then I go forth with you to view the shrubbery and consider.'

We went down-stairs into the hall. Mr Henry sat by the table with his head upon his hand, like a man of stone. His wife stood a little back from him, her hand at her mouth; it was plain she could not move him. My old lord walked very steadily to where his son was sitting; he had a steady countenance, too, but methought a little cold. When he was come quite up, he held out both his hands and said, 'My son!'

With a broken, strangled cry, Mr Henry leaped up and fell on his father's neck, crying and weeping, the most pitiful sight that ever a man witnessed. 'O! father,' he cried, 'you know I loved him; you know I loved him in the beginning; I could have died for him – you know that! I would have given my life for him and you. O! say you know that. O! say you can forgive me. O, father, father, what have I done – what have I done? And we used to be bairns together!' and wept and sobbed, and fondled the old man, and clutched him about the neck, with a passion of a child in terror.

And then he caught sight of his wife (you would have thought for the first time), where she stood weeping to hear him, and in a moment had fallen at her knees. 'And O my lass,' he cried, 'you must forgive me, too! Not your husband – I have only been the ruin of your life. But you knew me when I was a lad; there was no harm in Henry Durie then; he meant aye to be a friend to you. It's him – it's the old bairn that played with you – O, can ye never, never forgive him?'

Throughout all this my lord was like a cold, kind spectator with his wits about him. At the first cry, which was indeed enough to call the house about us, he had said to me over his shoulder, 'Close the door.' And now he nodded to himself.

'We may leave him to his wife now,' says he. 'Bring a light, Mr Mackellar.'

Upon my going forth again with my lord, I was aware of a strange phenomenon; for though it was quite dark, and the night not yet old, methought I smelt the morning. At the same time there went a tossing through the branches of the evergreens, so that they sounded like a quiet sea, and the air puffed at times against our faces, and the flame of the candle shook. We made the more speed, I believe, being surrounded by this bustle; visited the scene of the duel, where my lord looked upon the blood with stoicism; and passing farther on toward the landing-place, came at last upon some evidences of the truth. For, first of all, where was a pool across the path, the ice had been trodden in, plainly by more than one man's weight; next, and but a little farther, a young tree was broken, and down by the landing-place, where the traders' boats were usually beached, another stain of blood marked where the body must have been infallibly set down to rest the bearers.

The stain we set ourselves to wash away with the sea-water, carrying it in my lord's hat; and as we were thus engaged there came up a sudden moaning gust and left us instantly benighted.

'It will come to snow,' says my lord; 'and the best thing that we could hope. Let us go back now; we can do nothing in the dark.'

As we went houseward, the wind being again subsided, we were aware of a strong pattering noise about us in the night; and when we issued from the shelter of the trees, we found it raining smartly.

Throughout the whole of this, my lord's clearness of mind, no less than his activity of body, had not ceased to minister to my amazement. He set the crown upon it in the council we held on our return. The free-traders had certainly secured the Master, though whether dead or alive we were still left to our conjectures; the rain would, long before day, wipe out all marks of the transaction; by this we must profit. The Master had unexpectedly come after the fall of night; it must now be given out he had as suddenly departed before the break of day; and, to make all this plausible, it now only remained for me to mount into the man's chamber, and pack and conceal his baggage. True, we still lay at the discretion of the traders; but that was the incurable weakness of our guilt.

I heard him, as I said, with wonder, and hastened to obey. Mr and Mrs Henry were gone from the hall; my lord, for warmth's sake, hurried to his bed; there was still no sign of stir among the servants, and as I went up the tower stair, and entered the dead man's room, a horror of solitude weighed upon my mind. To my extreme surprise, it was all in the disorder of departure. Of his three portmanteaus, two were already locked; a third lay open and near full. At once there flashed upon me some suspicion of the truth. The man had been going, after all; he had but waited upon Crail, as Crail waited upon the wind; early in the night the seamen had perceived the weather changing; the boat had come to give notice of the change and call the passenger aboard, and the boat's crew had stumbled on him lying in his blood. Nay, and there was more behind. This pre-arranged departure shed some light upon his inconceivable insult of the night before; it was a parting shot, hatred being no longer checked by policy. And, for another thing, the nature of that insult, and the conduct of Mrs Henry, pointed to one conclusion, which I have never verified, and can now never verify until the great assize – the conclusion that he had at last forgotten himself, had gone too far in his advances, and had been rebuffed. It can never be verified, as I say; but as I thought of it that morning among his baggage, the thought was sweet to me like honey.

Into the open portmanteau I dipped a little ere I closed it. The most beautiful lace and linen, many suits of those fine plain clothes in which he loved to appear; a book or two, and those of the best, Cæsar's *Commentaries*, a volume of Mr Hobbes, the *Henriade* of M de Voltaire,[6] a book upon the Indies, one on the mathematics, far beyond where I have studied: these were what I observed with very mingled feelings. But in the open portmanteau, no papers of any description. This set me musing. It was possible the man was dead; but, since the traders had carried him away, not likely. It was possible he might still die of his wound; but it was also possible he might not. And in this latter case I was determined to have the means of some defence.

One after another I carried his portmanteaus to a loft in the top of the house which we kept locked; went to my own room for my keys, and, returning to the loft, had the gratification to find two that fitted pretty well. In one of the portmanteaus there was a shagreen[7] letter-case, which I cut open with my knife; and thenceforth (so far as any credit went) the man was at my mercy. Here was a vast deal of gallant correspondence, chiefly of his Paris days; and, what was more to the purpose, here were the copies of his own reports to the English Secretary, and the originals of the Secretary's answers: a most damning series: such as to publish would be to wreck the Master's honour and to set a price upon his life. I chuckled to myself as I ran through the documents; I rubbed my hands, I sang aloud in my glee. Day found me at the pleasing task; nor did I then remit my diligence, except in so far as I went to the window – looked out for a moment, to see the frost quite gone, the world turned black again, and the rain and the wind driving in the bay – and to assure myself that the lugger was gone from its anchorage, and the Master (whether dead or alive) now tumbling on the Irish Sea.

It is proper I should add in this place the very little I have subsequently angled out upon the doings of that night. It took me a long while to gather it; for we dared not openly ask, and the free-traders regarded me with enmity, if not with scorn. It was near six months before we even knew for certain that the man survived; and it was years before I learned from one of Crail's men, turned publican on his ill-gotten gain, some particulars which smack to me of truth. It seems the traders found the Master struggled on one elbow, and now staring round him, and now gazing at the candle, or at his hand, which was all bloodied, like a man stupid. Upon their coming, he would seem to have found his mind, bade them carry him aboard, and hold their tongues; and on the captain asking how he had come in such a pickle, replied with a burst of passionate swearing, and incontinently fainted. They held some debate, but they were momently looking for a wind, they were highly paid to smuggle him to France, and did not care to delay. Besides which, he was well enough liked by these abominable wretches: they supposed him under capital sentence, knew not in what mischief he might have got his wound, and judged it a piece of good-nature to remove him out of the way of danger. So he was taken aboard, recovered on the passage over, and was set ashore a convalescent at the Havre de Grace.[8] What is truly notable: he said not a word to any one of the duel, and not a trader knows to this day in what quarrel, or by the hand of what adversary, he fell. With any other man I should have set this down to natural decency; with him, to pride. He could not bear to avow, perhaps even to himself, that he had been vanquished by one whom he had so much insulted and whom he so cruelly despised.

SUMMARY OF EVENTS DURING THE MASTER'S SECOND ABSENCE

Of the heavy sickness which declared itself next morning I can think with equanimity, as of the last unmingled trouble that befell my master; and even that was perhaps a mercy in disguise; for what pains of the body could equal the miseries of his mind? Mrs Henry and I had the watching by the bed. My old lord called from time to time to take the news, but would not usually pass the door. Once, I remember, when hope was nigh gone, he stepped to the bedside, looked a while in his son's face, and turned away with a singular gesture of the head and hand thrown up, that remains upon my mind as something tragic; such grief and such a scorn of sublunary things were there expressed. But the most of the time Mrs Henry and I had the room to ourselves, taking turns by night, and bearing each other company by day, for it was dreary watching. Mr Henry, his shaven head bound in a napkin, tossed to and fro without remission, beating the bed with his hands. His tongue never lay; his voice ran continuously like a river, so that my heart was weary with the sound of it. It was notable, and to me inexpressibly mortifying, that he spoke all the while on matters of no import: comings and goings, horses – which he was ever calling to have saddled, thinking perhaps (the poor soul!) that he might ride away from his discomfort – matters of the garden, the salmon nets, and (what I particularly raged to hear) continually of his affairs, ciphering figures and holding disputation with the tenantry. Never a word of his father or his wife, nor of the Master, save only for a day or two, when his mind dwelled entirely in the past, and he supposed himself a boy again and upon some innocent child's play with his brother. What made this the more affecting: it appeared the Master had then run some peril of his life, for there was a cry – 'O! Jamie will be drowned – O, save Jamie!' which he came over and over with a great deal of passion.

This, I say, was affecting, both to Mrs Henry and myself; but the balance of my master's wanderings did him little justice. It seemed he had set out to justify his brother's calumnies; as though he was bent to prove himself a man of a dry nature, immersed in money-getting. Had I been there alone, I would not have troubled my thumb;[1] but all the while, as I listened, I was estimating the effect on the man's wife, and telling myself that he fell lower every day. I was the one person on the surface of the globe that comprehended him, and I was bound there should be yet another. Whether he was to die there and his virtues perish: or whether he should save his days and come back to that inheritance of sorrows, his right memory: I was bound he should be heartily lamented in the one case, and unaffectedly welcomed in the other, by the person he loved the most, his wife.

Finding no occasion of free speech, I bethought me at last of a kind of documentary disclosure; and for some nights, when I was off duty, and should have been asleep, I gave my time to the preparation of that which I may call my budget. But this I found to be the easiest portion of my task, and that which remained – namely, the presentation to my lady – almost more than I had fortitude to overtake. Several days I went about with my papers under my arm, spying for some juncture of talk to serve as introduction. I will not deny but that some offered; only when they did my tongue clove to the roof of my mouth; and I think I might have been carrying about my packet till this day, had not a fortunate accident delivered me from all my hesitations. This was at night, when I was once more leaving the room, the thing not yet done, and myself in despair at my own cowardice.

'What do you carry about with you, Mr Mackellar?' she asked. 'These last days, I see you always coming in and out with the same armful.'

I returned upon my steps without a word, laid the papers before her on the table, and left her to her reading. Of what that was, I am now to give you some idea; and the best will be to reproduce a letter of my own which came first in her budget, and of which (according to an excellent habitude) I have preserved the scroll. It will show, too, the moderation of my part in these affairs, a thing which some have called recklessly in question.

Durrisdeer,
1757.

HONOURED MADAM,

I trust I would not step out of my place without occasion; but I see how much evil has flowed in the past to all of your noble house from that unhappy and secretive fault of reticency, and the papers on which I venture to call your attention are family papers, and all highly worthy your acquaintance.

I append a schedule with some necessary observations,

And am,
Honoured Madam,
Your ladyship's obliged, obedient servant,
EPHRAIM MACKELLAR

Schedule of Papers.

A. Scroll of ten letters from Ephraim Mackellar to the Hon. James Durie, Esq., by courtesy Master of Ballantrae, during the latter's residence in Paris: under dates ... (*follow the dates*) ... *Nota*: to be read in connection with B and C.

B. Seven original letters from the said Mr of Ballantrae to the said E. Mackellar, under dates ... (*follow the dates*).

C. Three original letters from the said Mr of Ballantrae to the Hon. Henry Durie, Esq., under dates ... (*follow the dates*) ... *Nota*: given me by Mr Henry to answer: copies of my answers A 4, A 5, and A 9 of these productions. The purport of Mr Henry's communications, of which I can find no scroll, may be gathered from those of his unnatural brother.

D. A correspondence, original and scroll, extending over a period of three years till January of the current year, between the said Mr of Ballantrae and——, Under Secretary of State; twenty-seven in all. *Nota*: found among the Master's papers.

Weary as I was with watching and distress of mind, it was impossible for me to sleep. All night long I walked in my chamber, revolving what should be the issue, and sometimes repenting the temerity of my immixture in affairs so private; and with the first peep of the morning I was at the sick-room door. Mrs Henry had thrown open the shutters, and even the window, for the temperature was mild. She looked steadfastly before her; where was nothing to see, or only the blue of the morning creeping among woods. Upon the stir of my entrance she did not so much as turn about her face: a circumstance from which I augured very ill.

'Madam,' I began; and then again, 'Madam'; but could make no more of it. Nor yet did Mrs Henry come to my assistance with a word. In this pass I began gathering up the papers where they lay scattered on the table; and the first thing that struck me, their bulk appeared to have diminished. Once I ran them through, and twice; but the correspondence with the Secretary of State, on which I had reckoned so much against the future, was nowhere to be found. I looked in the chimney; amid the smouldering embers, black ashes of paper fluttered in the draught; and at that my timidity vanished.

'Good God, madam,' cried I, in a voice not fitting for a sick-room, 'Good God, madam, what have you done with my papers?'

'I have burned them,' said Mrs Henry, turning about. 'It is enough, it is too much, that you and I have seen them.'

'This is a fine night's work that you have done!' cried I. 'And all to save the reputation of a man that ate bread by the shedding of his comrades' blood, as I do by the shedding of ink.'

'To save the reputation of that family in which you are a servant, Mr Mackellar,' she returned, 'and for which you have already done so much.'

'It is a family I will not serve much longer,' I cried, 'for I am driven desperate. You have stricken the sword out of my hands; you have left us all defenceless. I had always these letters I could shake over his head; and now – what is to do? We are so falsely situate we dare not show the man the door; the country would fly on fire against us; and I had this one hold upon him – and now it is gone – now he may come back to-morrow, and we must all sit down with him to dinner, go for a stroll with him on the terrace, or take a hand at cards, of all things, to divert his leisure! No, madam! God forgive you, if He can find it in His heart; for I cannot find it in mine.'

'I wonder to find you so simple, Mr Mackellar,' said Mrs Henry. 'What does this man value reputation? But he knows how high we prize it; he knows we would rather die than make these letters public; and do you suppose he would not trade upon the knowledge? What you call your sword, Mr Mackellar, and which had been one indeed against a man of any remnant of propriety, would have been but a sword of paper against him. He would smile in your face at such a threat. He stands upon his degradation, he makes that his strength; it is in vain to struggle with such characters.' She cried out this last a little desperately, and then with more quiet: 'No, Mr Mackellar; I have thought upon this matter all night, and there is no way out of it. Papers or no papers, the door of this house stands open for him; he is the rightful heir, forsooth! If we sought to exclude him, all would redound against poor Henry, and I should see him stoned again upon the streets. Ah! if Henry dies, it is a different matter! They have broke the entail for their own good purposes; the estate goes to my daughter; and I shall see who sets a foot upon it. But if Henry lives, my poor Mr Mackellar, and that man returns, we must suffer: only this time it will be together.'

On the whole I was well pleased with Mrs Henry's attitude of mind; nor could I even deny there was some cogency in that which she advanced about the papers.

'Let us say no more about it,' said I. 'I can only be sorry I trusted a lady with the originals, which was an unbusinesslike proceeding at the best. As for what I said of leaving the service of the family, it was spoken with the tongue only; and you may set your mind at rest. I belong to Durrisdeer, Mrs Henry, as if I had been born there.'

I must do her the justice to say she seemed perfectly relieved; so that we began this morning, as we were to continue for so many years, on a proper ground of mutual indulgence and respect.

The same day, which was certainly predestinate to joy, we observed the first signal of recovery in Mr Henry; and about three of the following afternoon he found his mind again, recognising me by name with the strongest evidences of affection. Mrs Henry was also in the room, at the bed-foot; but it did not appear that he observed her. And indeed (the fever being gone) he was so weak that he made but the one effort and sank again into a lethargy. The course of his restoration was now slow, but equal; every day his appetite improved; every week we were able to remark an increase both of strength and flesh; and before the end of the month he was out of bed and had even begun to be carried in his chair upon the terrace.

It was perhaps at this time that Mrs Henry and I were the most uneasy in mind. Apprehension for his days was at an end; and a worse fear succeeded. Every day we drew consciously nearer to a day of reckoning; and the days passed on, and still there was nothing. Mr Henry bettered in strength, he held long talks with us on a great diversity of subjects, his father came and sat with him and went again; and still there was no reference to the late tragedy or to the former troubles which had brought it on. Did he remember, and conceal his dreadful knowledge? or was the whole blotted from his mind? This was the problem that kept us watching and trembling all day when we were in his company, and held us awake at night when we were in our lonely beds. We knew not even which alternative to hope for, both appearing so unnatural, and pointing so directly to an unsound brain. Once this fear offered, I observed his conduct with sedulous particularity. Something of the child he exhibited: a cheerfulness quite foreign to his previous character, an interest readily aroused, and then very tenacious, in small matters which he had heretofore despised. When he was stricken down, I was his only confidant, and I may say his only friend, and he was on terms of division with his wife; upon his recovery, all was changed, the past forgotten, the wife first and even single in his thoughts. He turned to her with all his emotions, like a child to its mother, and seemed secure of sympathy; called her in all his needs with something of that querulous familiarity that marks a certainty of indulgence; and I must say, in justice to the woman, he was never disappointed. To her, indeed, this changed behaviour was inexpressibly affecting; and I think she felt it secretly as a reproach;

so that I have seen her, in early days, escape out of the room that she might indulge herself in weeping. But to me the change appeared not natural; and viewing it along with all the rest, I began to wonder, with many head-shakings, whether his reason were perfectly erect.

As this doubt stretched over many years, endured indeed until my master's death, and clouded all our subsequent relations, I may well consider of it more at large. When he was able to resume some charge of his affairs, I had many opportunities to try him with precision. There was no lack of understanding, nor yet of authority; but the old continuous interest had quite departed; he grew readily fatigued, and fell to yawning; and he carried into money relations, where it is certainly out of place, a facility that bordered upon slackness. True, since we had no longer the exactions of the Master to contend against, there was the less occasion to raise strictness into principle or do battle for a farthing. True, again, there was nothing excessive in these relaxations, or I would have been no party to them. But the whole thing marked a change, very slight yet very perceptible; and though no man could say my master had gone at all out of his mind, no man could deny that he had drifted from his character. It was the same to the end, with his manner and appearance. Some of the heat of the fever lingered in his veins: his movements a little hurried, his speech notably more voluble, yet neither truly amiss. His whole mind stood open to happy impressions, welcoming these and making much of them; but the smallest suggestion of trouble or sorrow he received with visible impatience, and dismissed again with immediate relief. It was to this temper that he owed the felicity of his later days; and yet here it was, if anywhere, that you could call the man insane. A great part of this life consists in contemplating what we cannot cure; but Mr Henry, if he could not dismiss solicitude by an effort of the mind, must instantly and at whatever cost annihilate the cause of it; so that he played alternately the ostrich and the bull. It is to this strenuous cowardice of pain that I have to set down all the unfortunate and excessive steps of his subsequent career. Certainly this was the reason of his beating M'Manus, the groom, a thing so much out of all his former practice, and which awakened so much comment at the time.

It is to this, again, that I must lay the total loss of near upon two hundred pounds, more than the half of which I could have saved if his impatience would have suffered me. But he preferred loss or any desperate extreme to a continuance of mental suffering.

All this has led me far from our immediate trouble: whether he remembered or had forgotten his late dreadful act; and if he remembered, in what light he viewed it. The truth burst upon us suddenly, and was indeed one of the chief surprises of my life. He had been several times abroad, and was now beginning to walk a little with an arm, when it chanced I should be left alone with him upon the terrace. He turned to me with a singular furtive smile, such as schoolboys use when in fault; and says he, in a private whisper, and without the least preface: 'Where have you buried him?'

I could not make one sound in answer.

'Where have you buried him?' he repeated. 'I want to see his grave.'

I conceived I had best take the bull by the horns. 'Mr Henry,' said I, 'I have news to give that will rejoice you exceedingly. In all human likelihood, your hands are clear of blood. I reason from certain indices; and by these it should appear your brother was not dead, but was carried in a swound on board the lugger. But now he may be perfectly recovered.'

What there was in his countenance I could not read. 'James?' he asked.

'Your brother James,' I answered. 'I would not raise a hope that may be found deceptive, but in my heart I think it very probable he is alive.'

'Ah!' says Mr Henry; and suddenly rising from his seat with more alacrity than he had yet discovered, set one finger on my breast, and cried at me in a kind of screaming whisper, 'Mackellar' – these were his words – 'nothing can kill that man. He is not mortal. He is bound upon my back to all eternity – to all God's eternity!' says he, and, sitting down again, fell upon a stubborn silence.

A day or two after, with the same secret smile, and first looking about as if to be sure we were alone, 'Mackellar,' said he, 'when you have any intelligence, be sure and let me know. We must keep an eye upon him, or he will take us when we least expect.'

'He will not show face here again,' said I.

'O yes, he will,' said Mr Henry. 'Wherever I am, there will he be.' And again he looked all about him.

'You must not dwell upon this thought, Mr Henry,' said I.

'No,' said he, 'that is a very good advice. We will never think of it, except when you have news. And we do not know yet,' he added; 'he may be dead.'

The manner of his saying this convinced me thoroughly of what I had scarce ventured to suspect: that, so far from suffering any penitence for the attempt, he did but lament his failure. This was a discovery I kept to myself, fearing it might do him a prejudice with his wife. But I might have saved myself the trouble; she had divined it for herself, and found the sentiment quite natural. Indeed, I could not but say that there were three of us, all of the same mind; nor could any news have reached Durrisdeer more generally welcome than tidings of the Master's death.

This brings me to speak of the exception, my old lord. As soon as my anxiety for my own master began to be relaxed, I was aware of a change in the old gentleman, his father, that seemed to threaten mortal consequences. His face was pale and swollen; as he sat in the chimney-side with his Latin, he would drop off sleeping and the book roll in the ashes; some days he would drag his foot, others stumble in speaking. The amenity of his behaviour appeared more extreme; full of excuses for the least trouble, very thoughtful for all; to myself, of a most flattering civility. One day, that he had sent for his lawyer, and remained a long while private, he met me as he was crossing the hall with painful footsteps, and took me kindly by the hand. 'Mr Mackellar,' said he, 'I have had many occasions to set a proper value on your services; and to-day, when I re-cast my will, I have taken the freedom to name you for one of my executors. I believe you bear love enough to our house to render me this service.' At that very time he passed the greater portion of his days in slumber, from which it was often difficult to rouse him; seemed to have lost all count of years, and had several times (particularly on waking) called for his wife and for an old servant whose very gravestone was now green with moss. If I had been put to my oath, I must have declared he was incapable of testing;[2] and yet there was never a will drawn more sensible in every trait, or showing a more excellent judgment both of persons and affairs.

His dissolution, though it took not very long, proceeded by infinitesimal gradations. His faculties decayed together steadily; the power of his limbs was almost gone, he was extremely deaf, his speech had sunk into mere mumblings; and yet to the end he managed to discover something of his former courtesy and kindness, pressing the hand of any that helped him, presenting me with one of his Latin books, in which he had laboriously traced my name, and in a thousand ways reminding us of the greatness of that loss which it might almost be said we had already suffered. To the end, the power of articulation returned to him in flashes; it seemed he had only forgotten the art of speech as a child forgets his lesson, and at times he would call some part of it to mind. On the last night of his life he suddenly broke silence with these words from Virgil: 'Gnatique patrisque, alma, precor, miserere,'[3] perfectly uttered, and with a fitting accent. At the sudden clear sound of it we started from our several occupations; but it was in vain we turned to him; he sat there silent, and, to all appearance, fatuous. A little later he was had to bed with more difficulty than ever before; and some time in the night, without any mortal violence, his spirit fled.

At a far later period I chanced to speak of these particulars with a doctor of medicine, a man of so high a reputation that I scruple to adduce his name. By his view of it, father and son both suffered from the same affection: the father from the strain of his unnatural sorrows – the son, perhaps in the excitation of the fever; each had ruptured a vessel in the brain, and there was probably (my doctor added) some predisposition in the family to accidents of that description. The father sank, the son recovered all the externals of a healthy man; but it is like there was some destruction in those delicate tissues where the soul resides and does her earthly business; her heavenly, I would fain hope, cannot be thus obstructed by material accidents. And yet, upon a more mature opinion, it matters not one jot; for He who shall pass judgment on the records of our life is the same that formed us in frailty.

The death of my old lord was the occasion of a fresh surprise to us who watched the behaviour of his successor. To any considering mind, the two sons had between them slain their father, and he who took the sword might be even said to have slain him with his hand; but no such thought appeared to trouble my new lord. He was becomingly grave; I could scarce say sorrowful, or only with a pleasant sorrow; talking of the dead with a regretful cheerfulness, relating old examples of his character, smiling at them with a good conscience; and when the day of the funeral came round, doing the honours with exact propriety. I could perceive, besides, that he found a solid gratification in his accession to the title; the which he was punctilious in exacting.

And now there came upon the scene a new character, and one that played his part, too, in the story; I mean the present lord, Alexander, whose birth (17th July 1757) filled the cup of my poor master's happiness. There was nothing then left him to wish for; nor yet leisure for him to wish for it. Indeed, there never was a parent so fond and doting as he showed himself. He was continually uneasy in his son's absence. Was the child abroad? the father would be watching the clouds in case it rained. Was it night? he would rise out of his bed to observe its slumbers. His conversation grew even wearyful to strangers, since he talked of little but his son. In matters relating to the estate, all was designed with a particular eye to Alexander; and it would be: – 'Let us put it in hand at once, that the wood may be grown against Alexander's majority'; or, 'This will fall in again handsomely for Alexander's marriage.' Every day this absorption of the man's nature became more observable, with many touching and some very blameworthy particulars. Soon the child could walk abroad with him, at first on the terrace, hand in hand, and afterward at large about the policies; and this grew to be my lord's chief occupation. The sound of their two voices (audible a great way off, for they spoke loud) became familiar in the neighbourhood; and for my part I found it more agreeable than the sound of birds. It was pretty to see the pair returning full of briers, and the father as flushed and sometimes as bemuddled as the child, for they were equal sharers in all sorts of boyish entertainment, digging in the beach, damming of streams, and what not; and I have seen them gaze through a fence at cattle with the same childish contemplation.

The mention of these rambles brings me to a strange scene of which I was a witness. There was one walk I never followed myself without emotion, so often had I gone there upon miserable errands, so much had there befallen against the house of Durrisdeer. But the path lay handy from all points beyond the Muckle Ross; and I was driven, although much against my will, to take my use of it perhaps once in the two months. It befell when Mr Alexander was of the age of six or seven, I had some business on the far side in the morning, and entered the shrubbery, on my homeward way, about nine of a bright forenoon. It was that time of year when the woods are all in their spring colours, and thorns all in flower, and the birds in the high season of their singing. In contrast to this merriment, the shrubbery was only the more sad, and I the more oppressed by its associations. In this situation of spirit it struck me disagreeably to hear voices a little way in front, and to recognise the tones of my lord and Mr Alexander. I pushed ahead, and came presently into their view. They stood together in the open space where the duel was, my lord with his hand on his son's shoulder, and speaking with some gravity. At least, as he raised his head upon my coming, I thought I could perceive his countenance to lighten.

'Ah!' says he, 'here comes the good Mackellar. I have just been telling Sandie the story of this place, and how there was a man whom the devil tried to kill, and how near he came to kill the devil instead.'

I had thought it strange enough he should bring the child into that scene; that he should actually be discoursing of his act, passed measure. But the worst was yet to come: for he added, turning to his son – 'You can ask Mackellar; he was here and saw it.'

'Did you really see the devil?' asked the child.

'I have not heard the tale,' I replied; 'and I am in a press of business.' So far I said, sourly, fencing with the embarrassment of the position;

and suddenly the bitterness of the past, and the terror of that scene by candlelight, rushed in upon my mind. I bethought me that, for a difference of a second's quickness in parade, the child before me might have never seen the day; and the emotion that always fluttered round my heart in that dark shrubbery burst forth in words. 'But so much is true,' I cried, 'that I have met the devil in these woods, and seen him foiled here. Blessed be God that we escaped with life – blessed be God that one stone yet stands upon another in the walls of Durrisdeer! And, O! Mr Alexander, if ever you come by this spot, though it was a hundred years hence, and you came with the gayest and the highest in the land, I would step aside and remember a bit prayer.'

My lord bowed his head gravely. 'Ah!' says he, 'Mackellar is always in the right. Come, Alexander, take your bonnet off.' And with that he uncovered, and held out his hand. 'O Lord,' said he, 'I thank Thee, and my son thanks Thee, for Thy manifold great mercies. Let us have peace for a little; defend us from the evil man. Smite him, O Lord, upon the lying mouth!' The last broke out of him like a cry; and at that, whether remembered anger choked his utterance, or whether he perceived this was a singular sort of prayer, at least he suddenly came to a full stop; and, after a moment, set back his hat upon his head.

'I think you have forgot a word, my lord,' said I. '"Forgive us our trespasses, as we forgive them that trespass against us. For Thine is the kingdom, and the power, and the glory, for ever and ever. Amen."'

'Ah! that is easy saying,' said my lord. 'That is very easy saying, Mackellar. But for me to forgive! – I think I would cut a very silly figure if I had the affectation to pretend it.'

'The bairn, my lord!' said I, with some severity, for I thought his expressions little fitted for the ears of children.

'Why, very true,' said he. 'This is dull work for a bairn. Let's go nesting.'

I forget if it was the same day, but it was soon after, my lord, finding me alone, opened himself a little more on the same head.

'Mackellar,' he said, 'I am now a very happy man.'

'I think so indeed, my lord,' said I, 'and the sight of it gives me a light heart.'

'There is an obligation in happiness – do you not think so?' says he musingly.

'I think so indeed,' says I, 'and one in sorrow too. If we are not here to try to do the best, in my humble opinion the sooner we are away the better for all parties.'

'Ay, but if you were in my shoes, would you forgive him?' asks my lord.

The suddenness of the attack a little gravelled[4] me. 'It is a duty laid upon us strictly,' said I.

'Hut!' said he. 'These are expressions! Do you forgive the man yourself?'

'Well – no!' said I. 'God forgive me, I do not.'

'Shake hands upon that!' cries my lord, with a kind of joviality.

'It is an ill sentiment to shake hands upon,' said I, 'for Christian people. I think I will give you mine on some more evangelical occasion.'

This I said, smiling a little; but as for my lord, he went from the room laughing aloud.

For my lord's slavery to the child I can find no expression adequate. He lost himself in that continual thought: business, friends, and wife being all alike forgotten, or only remembered with a painful effort, like that of one struggling with a posset.[5] It was most notable in the matter of his wife. Since I had known Durrisdeer, she had been the burthen of his thought and the loadstone of his eyes; and now she was quite cast out. I have seen him come to the door of a room, look round, and pass my lady over as though she were a dog before the fire. It would be Alexander he was seeking, and my lady knew it well. I have heard him speak to her so ruggedly that I nearly found it in my heart to intervene: the cause would still be the same, that she had in some way thwarted Alexander. Without doubt this was in the nature of a judgment on my lady; without doubt she had the tables turned upon her, as only Providence can do it; she who had been cold so many years to every mark of tenderness, it was her part now to be neglected.

An odd situation resulted: that we had once more two parties in the house, and that now I was of my lady's. Not that ever I lost the love I bore my master. But, for one thing, he had the less use for my society. For another, I could not but compare the case of Mr Alexander with that of Miss Katharine; for whom my lord had never found the least attention. And for a third, I was wounded by the change he discovered to his wife, which struck me in the nature of an infidelity. I could not but admire, besides, the constancy and kindness she displayed. Perhaps her sentiment to my lord, as it had been founded from the first in pity, was that rather of a mother than a wife; perhaps it pleased her – if I may so say – to behold her two children so happy in each other; the more as one had suffered so unjustly in the past. But, for all that, and though I could never trace in her one spark of jealousy, she must fall back for society on poor neglected Miss Katharine; and I, on my part, came to pass my spare hours more and more with the mother and daughter. It would be easy to make too much of this division, for it was a pleasant family, as families go; still the thing existed; whether my lord knew it or not, I am in doubt. I do not think he did; he was bound up so entirely in his son; but the rest of us knew it, and in a manner suffered from the knowledge.

What troubled us most, however, was the great and growing danger to the child. My lord was his father over again; it was to be feared the son would prove a second Master. Time has proved these fears to have been quite exaggerate. Certainly there is no more worthy gentleman to-day in Scotland than the seventh Lord Durrisdeer. Of my own exodus from his employment it does not become me to speak, above all in a memorandum written only to justify his father . . .

[EDITOR'S NOTE. – *Five pages of Mr Mackellar's MS. are here omitted. I have gathered from their perusal an impression that Mr Mackellar, in his old age, was rather an exacting servant. Against the seventh Lord Durrisdeer (with whom, at any rate, we have no concern) nothing material is alleged.* – R. L. S.]

. . . But our fear at the time was lest he should turn out, in the person of his son, a second edition of his brother. My lady had tried to interject some wholesome discipline; she had been glad to give that up, and now looked on with secret dismay; sometimes she even spoke of it by hints; and sometimes, when there was brought to her knowledge some monstrous instance of my lord's indulgence, she would betray herself in a gesture or perhaps an exclamation. As for myself, I was haunted by the thought both day and night: not so much for the child's sake as for the father's. The man had gone to sleep, he was dreaming a dream, and any rough wakening must infallibly prove mortal. That he should survive the child's death was inconceivable; and the fear of its dishonour made me cover my face.

It was this continual pre-occupation that screwed me up at last to a remonstrance: a matter worthy to be narrated in detail. My lord and I sat one day at the same table upon some tedious business of detail; I have said that he had lost his former interest in such occupations; he was plainly itching to be gone, and he looked fretful, weary, and methought older than I had ever previously observed. I suppose it was the haggard face that put me suddenly upon my enterprise.

'My lord,' said I, with my head down, and feigning to continue my occupation – 'or, rather, let me call you again by the name of Mr Henry, for I fear your anger, and want you to think upon old times—'

'My good Mackellar!' said he; and that in tones so kindly that I had near forsook my purpose. But I called to mind that I was speaking for his good, and stuck to my colours.

'Has it never come in upon your mind what you are doing?' I asked.

'What I am doing?' he repeated; 'I was never good at guessing riddles.'

'What you are doing with your son?' said I.

'Well,' said he, with some defiance in his tone, 'and what am I doing with my son?'

'Your father was a very good man,' says I, straying from the direct path. 'But do you think he was a wise father?'

There was a pause before he spoke, and then: 'I say nothing against him,' he replied. 'I had the most cause perhaps; but I say nothing.'

'Why, there it is,' said I. 'You had the cause at least. And yet your father was a good man; I never knew a better, save on the one point, nor yet a wiser. Where he stumbled, it is highly possible another man should fall. He had the two sons—'

My lord rapped suddenly and violently on the table.

'What is this?' cried he. 'Speak out!'

'I will, then,' said I, my voice almost strangled with the thumping of my heart. 'If you continue to indulge Mr Alexander, you are following in your father's footsteps. Beware, my lord, lest (when he grows up) your son should follow in the Master's.'

I had never meant to put the thing so crudely; but in the extreme of fear there comes a brutal kind of courage, the most brutal indeed of all; and I burnt my ships with that plain word. I never had the answer. When I lifted my head my lord had risen to his feet, and the next moment he fell heavily on the floor. The fit or seizure endured not very long; he came to himself vacantly, put his hand to his head, which I was then supporting, and says he, in a broken voice: 'I have been ill,' and a little after: 'Help me.' I got him to his feet, and he stood pretty well, though he kept hold of the table. 'I have been ill, Mackellar,' he said again. 'Something broke, Mackellar – or was going to break, and then all swam away. I think I was very angry. Never you mind, Mackellar; never you mind, my man. I wouldnae hurt a hair upon your head. Too much has come and gone. It's a certain thing between us two. But I think, Mackellar, I will go to Mrs Henry – I think I will go to Mrs Henry,' said he, and got pretty steadily from the room, leaving me overcome with penitence.

Presently the door flew open, and my lady swept in with flashing eyes. 'What is all this?' she cried. 'What have you done to my husband? Will nothing teach you your position in this house? Will you never cease from making and meddling?'

'My lady,' said I, 'since I have been in this house I have had plenty of hard words. For a while they were my daily diet, and I swallowed them all. As for to-day, you may call me what you please; you will never find the name hard enough for such a blunder. And yet I meant it for the best.'

I told her all with ingenuity, even as it is written here; and when she had heard me out, she pondered, and I could see her animosity fall. 'Yes,' she said, 'you meant well indeed. I have had the same thought myself, or the same temptation rather, which makes me pardon you. But, dear God, can you not understand that he can bear no more? He can bear no more!' she cried. 'The cord is stretched to snapping. What matters the future if he have one or two good days?'

'Amen,' said I. 'I will meddle no more. I am pleased enough that you should recognise the kindness of my meaning.'

'Yes,' said my lady; 'but when it came to the point, I have to suppose your courage failed you; for what you said was said cruelly.' She paused, looking at me; then suddenly smiled a little, and said a singular thing: 'Do you know what you are, Mr Mackellar? You are an old maid.'

No more incident of any note occurred in the family until the return of that ill-starred man, the Master. But I have to place here a second extract from the memoirs of Chevalier Burke, interesting in itself, and highly necessary for my purpose. It is our only sight of the Master on his Indian travels; and the first word in these pages of Secundra Dass. One fact, it is to observe, appears here very clearly, which if we had known some twenty years ago, how many calamities and sorrows had been spared! – that Secundra Dass spoke English.

ADVENTURE OF CHEVALIER BURKE IN INDIA

Extracted from his Memoirs

. . . Here was I, therefore, on the streets of that city, the name of which I cannot call to mind, while even then I was so ill acquainted with its situation that I knew not whether to go south or north. The alert being sudden, I had run forth without shoes or stockings; my hat had been struck from my head in the mellay;[1] my kit was in the hands of the English; I had no companion but the cipaye,[2] no weapon but my sword, and the devil a coin in my pocket. In short, I was for all the world like one of those calendars[3] with whom Mr Galland[4] has made us acquainted in his elegant tales. These gentlemen, you will remember, were for ever falling in with extraordinary incidents; and I was myself upon the brink of one so astonishing that I protest I cannot explain it to this day.

The cipaye was a very honest man; he had served many years with the French colours, and would have let himself be cut to pieces for any of the brave countrymen of Mr Lally.[5] It is the same fellow (his name has quite escaped me) of whom I have narrated already a surprising instance of generosity of mind – when he found Mr de Fessac and myself upon the ramparts, entirely overcome with liquor, and covered us with straw while the commandant was passing by. I consulted him, therefore, with perfect freedom. It was a fine question what to do; but we decided at last to escalade a garden wall, where we could certainly sleep in the shadow of the trees, and might perhaps find an occasion to get hold of a pair of slippers and a turban. In that part of the city we had only the difficulty of the choice, for it was a quarter consisting entirely of walled gardens, and the lanes which divided them were at that hour of the night deserted. I gave the cipaye a back, and we had soon dropped into a large enclosure full of trees. The place was soaking with the dew, which, in that country, is exceedingly unwholesome, above all to whites; yet my fatigue was so extreme that I was already half asleep, when the cipaye recalled me to my senses. In the far end of the enclosure a bright light had suddenly shone out, and continued to burn steadily among the leaves. It was a circumstance highly unusual in such a place and hour; and, in our situation, it behoved us to proceed with some timidity. The cipaye was sent to reconnoitre, and pretty soon returned with the intelligence that we had fallen extremely amiss, for the house belonged to a white man, who was in all likelihood English.

'Faith,' says I, 'if there is a white man to be seen, I will have a look at him; for, the Lord be praised! there are more sorts than the one!'

The cipaye led me forward accordingly to a place from which I had a clear view upon the house. It was surrounded with a wide verandah; a lamp, very well trimmed, stood upon the floor of it, and on either side of the lamp there sat a man, cross-legged, after the Oriental manner. Both, besides, were bundled up in muslin like two natives; and yet one of them was not only a white man, but a man very well known to me and the reader, being indeed that very Master of Ballantrae of whose gallantry and genius I have had to speak so often. Word had reached me that he was come to the Indies, though we had never met, and I heard little of his occupations. But, sure, I had no sooner recognised him, and found myself in the arms of so old a comrade, than I supposed my tribulations were quite done. I stepped plainly forth into the light of the moon, which shone exceeding strong, and hailing Ballantrae by name, made him in a few words master of my grievous situation. He turned, started the least thing in the world, looked me fair in the face while I was speaking, and when I had done addressed himself to his companion in the barbarous native dialect. The second person, who was of an extraordinary delicate appearance, with legs like walking canes and fingers like the stalk of a tobacco-pipe,* now rose to his feet.

'The Sahib,' says he, 'understands no English language. I under-

* *Note by Mr Mackellar.* – Plainly Secundra Dass. – E. McK.

stand it myself, and I see you make some small mistake – O! which may happen very often. But the Sahib would be glad to know how you come in a garden?'

'Ballantrae!' I cried, 'have you the damned impudence to deny me to my face?'

Ballantrae never moved a muscle, staring at me like an image in a pagoda.

'The Sahib understands no English language,' says the native, as glib as before. 'He be glad to know how you come in a garden?'

'O! the divil fetch him,' says I. 'He would be glad to know how I come in a garden, would he? Well, now, my dear man, just have the civility to tell the Sahib, with my kind love, that we are two soldiers here whom he never met and never heard of, but the cipaye is a broth of a boy, and I am a broth of a boy myself; and if we don't get a full meal of meat, and a turban, and slippers, and the value of a gold mohur[6] in small change as a matter of convenience, bedad, my friend, I could lay my finger on a garden where there is going to be trouble.'

They carried their comedy so far as to converse a while in Hindustanee; and then says the Hindu, with the same smile, but sighing as if he were tired of the repetition, 'The Sahib would be glad to know how you come in a garden?'

'Is that the way of it?' says I, and laying my hand on my sword-hilt I bade the cipaye draw.

Ballantrae's Hindu, still smiling, pulled out a pistol from his bosom, and though Ballantrae himself never moved a muscle I knew him well enough to be sure he was prepared.

'The Sahib thinks you better go away,' says the Hindu.

Well, to be plain, it was what I was thinking myself; for the report of a pistol would have been, under Providence, the means of hanging the pair of us.

'Tell the Sahib I consider him no gentleman,' says I, and turned away with a gesture of contempt.

I was not gone three steps when the voice of the Hindu called me back. 'The Sahib would be glad to know if you are a dam low Irishman,' says he; and at the words Ballantrae smiled and bowed very low.

'What is that?' says I.

'The Sahib say you ask your friend Mackellar,' says the Hindu. 'The Sahib he cry quits.'

'Tell the Sahib I will give him a cure for the Scots fiddle when next we meet,' cried I.

The pair were still smiling as I left.

There is little doubt some flaws may be picked in my own behaviour; and when a man, however gallant, appeals to posterity with an account of his exploits, he must almost certainly expect to share the fate of Cæsar and Alexander, and to meet with some detractors. But there is one thing that can never be laid at the door of Francis Burke: he never turned his back on a friend . . .

(Here follows a passage which the Chevalier Burke has been at the pains to delete before sending me his manuscript. Doubtless it was some very natural complaint of what he supposed to be an indiscretion on my part; though, indeed, I can call none to mind. Perhaps Mr Henry was less guarded; or it is just possible the Master found the means to examine my correspondence, and himself read the letter from Troyes: in revenge for which this cruel jest was perpetrated on Mr Burke in his extreme necessity. The Master, for all his wickedness, was not without some natural affection; I believe he was sincerely attached to Mr Burke in the beginning; but the thought of treachery dried up the springs of his very shallow friendship, and his detestable nature appeared naked. – E.McK.)

THE ENEMY IN THE HOUSE

It is a strange thing that I should be at a stick for a date – the date, besides, of an incident that changed the very nature of my life, and sent us all into foreign lands. But the truth is, I was stricken out of all my habitudes, and find my journals very ill redd-up,* the day not indicated sometimes for a week or two together, and the whole fashion of the thing like that of a man near desperate. It was late in March at least, or early in April, 1764. I had slept heavily, and wakened with a premonition of some evil to befall. So strong was this upon my spirit that I hurried down-stairs in my shirt and breeches, and my hand (I remember) shook upon the rail. It was a cold, sunny morning, with a thick white frost; the blackbirds sang exceeding sweet and loud about the house of Durrisdeer, and there was a noise of the sea in all the chambers. As I came by the doors of the hall, another sound arrested me – of voices talking. I drew nearer, and stood like a man dreaming. Here was certainly a human voice, and that in my own master's house, and yet I knew it not; certainly human speech, and that in my native land; and yet, listen as I pleased, I could not catch one syllable. An old tale started up in my mind of a fairy wife (or perhaps only a wandering stranger), that came to the place of my fathers some generations back, and stayed the matter of a week, talking often in a tongue that signified nothing to the hearers; and went again, as she had come, under cloud of night, leaving not so much as a name behind her. A little fear I had, but more curiosity; and I opened the hall-door, and entered.

* Ordered.

The supper-things still lay upon the table; the shutters were still closed, although day peeped in the divisions; and the great room was lighted only with a single taper and the shining of the fire. Close in the chimney sat two men. The one that was wrapped in a cloak and wore boots, I knew at once: it was the bird of ill omen back again. Of the other, who was set close to the red embers, and made up into a bundle like a mummy, I could but see that he was an alien, of a darker hue than any man of Europe, very frailly built, with a singular tall forehead, and a secret eye. Several packets and a small valise were on the floor; and to judge by the smallness of this luggage, and by the condition of the Master's boots, grossly patched by some unscrupulous country cobbler, evil had not prospered.

He rose upon my entrance; our eyes crossed; and I know not why it should have been, but my courage rose like a lark on a May morning.

'Ha!' said I, 'is this you?' – and I was pleased with the unconcern of my own voice.

'It is even myself, worthy Mackellar,' says the Master.

'This time you have brought the black dog[1] visibly upon your back,' I continued.

'Referring to Secundra Dass?' asked the Master. 'Let me present you. He is a native gentleman of India.'

'Hum!' said I. 'I am no great lover either of you or your friends, Mr Bally. But I will let a little daylight in, and have a look at you.' And so saying, I undid the shutters of the eastern window.

By the light of the morning I could perceive the man was changed. Later, when we were all together, I was more struck to see how lightly time had dealt with him; but the first glance was otherwise.

'You are getting an old man,' said I.

A shade came upon his face. 'If you could see yourself,' said he, 'you would perhaps not dwell upon the topic.'

'Hut!' I returned, 'old age is nothing to me. I think I have been always old; and I am now, I thank God, better known and more respected. It is not every one that can say that, Mr Bally! The lines in *your* brow are calamities; your life begins to close in upon you like a prison; death will soon be rapping at the door; and I see not from what source you are to draw your consolations.'

Here the Master addressed himself to Secundra Dass in Hindustanee, from which I gathered (I freely confess, with a high degree of pleasure) that my remarks annoyed him. All this while, you may be sure, my mind had been busy upon other matters, even while I rallied my enemy; and chiefly as to how I should communicate secretly and quickly with my lord. To this, in the breathing-space now given me, I turned all the forces of my mind; when, suddenly shifting my eyes, I was aware of the man himself standing in the doorway, and, to all appearance, quite composed. He had no sooner met my looks than he stepped across the threshold. The Master heard him coming, and advanced upon the other side; about four feet apart, these brothers came to a full pause, and stood exchanging steady looks, and then my lord smiled, bowed a little forward, and turned briskly away.

'Mackellar,' says he, 'we must see to breakfast for these travellers.'

It was plain the Master was a trifle disconcerted; but he assumed the more impudence of speech and manner. 'I am as hungry as a hawk,' says he. 'Let it be something good, Henry.'

My lord turned to him with the same hard smile. 'Lord Durrisdeer,' says he.

'O! never in the family,' returned the Master.

'Every one in this house renders me my proper title,' says my lord. 'If it please you to make an exception, I will leave you to consider what appearance it will bear to strangers, and whether it may not be translated as an effect of impotent jealousy.'

I could have clapped my hands together with delight: the more so as my lord left no time for any answer, but, bidding me with a sign to follow him, went straight out of the hall.

'Come quick,' says he; 'we have to sweep vermin from the house.' And he sped through the passages, with so swift a step that I could scarce keep up with him, straight to the door of John Paul, the which he opened without summons and walked in. John was, to all appearance, sound asleep, but my lord made no pretence of waking him.

'John Paul,' said he, speaking as quietly as ever I heard him, 'you served my father long, or I would pack you from the house like a dog. If in half an hour's time I find you gone, you shall continue to receive your wages in Edinburgh. If you linger here or in St Bride's – old man, old servant, and altogether – I shall find some very astonishing way to make you smart for your disloyalty. Up and begone. The door you let them in by will serve for your departure. I do not choose my son shall see your face again.'

'I am rejoiced to find you bear the thing so quietly,' said I, when we were forth again by ourselves.

'Quietly!' cries he, and put my hand suddenly against his heart, which struck upon his bosom like a sledge.[2]

At this revelation I was filled with wonder and fear. There was no constitution could bear so violent a strain – his least of all, that was unhinged already; and I decided in my mind that we must bring this monstrous situation to an end.

'It would be well, I think, if I took word to my lady,' said I. Indeed, he should have gone himself, but I counted – not in vain – on his indifference.

'Ay,' says he, 'do. I will hurry breakfast: we must all appear at the table, even Alexander; it must appear we are untroubled.'

I ran to my lady's room, and with no preparatory cruelty disclosed my news.

'My mind was long ago made up,' said she. 'We must make our packets secretly to-day, and leave secretly to-night. Thank Heaven, we have another house! The first ship that sails shall bear us to New York.'

'And what of him?' I asked.

'We leave him Durrisdeer,' she cried. 'Let him work his pleasure upon that.'

'Not so, by your leave,' said I. 'There shall be a dog at his heels that can hold fast. Bed he shall have, and board, and a horse to ride upon, if he behave himself; but the keys – if you think well of it, my lady – shall be left in the hands of one Mackellar. There will be good care taken; trust him for that.'

'Mr Mackellar,' she cried, 'I thank you for that thought. All shall be left in your hands. If we must go into a savage country, I bequeath it to you to take our vengeance. Send Macconochie to St Bride's, to arrange privately for horses and to call the lawyer. My lord must leave procuration.'

At that moment my lord came to the door, and we opened our plan to him.

'I will never hear of it,' he cried; 'he would think I feared him. I will stay in my own house, please God, until I die. There lives not the man can beard me out of it. Once and for all, here I am, and here I stay, in spite of all the devils in hell.' I can give no idea of the vehemency of his words and utterance; but we both stood aghast, and I in particular, who had been a witness of his former self-restraint.

My lady looked at me with an appeal that went to my heart and recalled me to my wits. I made her a private sign to go, and when my lord and I were alone, went up to him where he was racing to and fro in one end of the room like a half-lunatic, and set my hand firmly on his shoulder.

'My lord,' says I, 'I am going to be the plain-dealer once more; if for the last time, so much the better, for I am grown weary of the part.'

'Nothing will change me,' he answered. 'God forbid I should refuse to hear you; but nothing will change me.' This he said firmly, with no signal of the former violence, which already raised my hopes.

'Very well,' said I. 'I can afford to waste my breath.' I pointed to a chair, and he sat down and looked at me. 'I can remember a time when my lady very much neglected you,' said I.

'I never spoke of it while it lasted,' returned my lord, with a high flush of colour; 'and it is all changed now.'

'Do you know how much?' I said. 'Do you know how much it is all changed? The tables are turned, my lord! It is my lady that now courts you for a word, a look – ay, and courts you in vain. Do you know with whom she passes her days while you are out gallivanting in the policies? My lord, she is glad to pass them with a certain dry old grieve* of the name of Ephraim Mackellar; and I think you may be able to remember what that means, for I am the more in a mistake or you were once driven to the same company yourself.'

'Mackellar!' cries my lord, getting to his feet. 'O my God, Mackellar!'

* Land steward.

'It is neither the name of Mackellar nor the name of God that can change the truth,' said I; 'and I am telling you the fact. Now for you, that suffered so much, to deal out the same suffering to another, is that the part of any Christian? But you are so swallowed up in your new friend that the old are all forgotten. They are all clean vanished from your memory. And yet they stood by you at the darkest; my lady not the least. And does my lady ever cross your mind? Does it ever cross your mind what she went through that night? – or what manner of a wife she has been to you thenceforward? – or in what kind of a position she finds herself to-day? Never. It is your pride to stay and face him out, and she must stay along with you. O! my lord's pride – that's the great affair! And yet she is the woman, and you are a great hulking man! She is the woman that you swore to protect; and, more betoken, the own mother of that son of yours!'

'You are speaking very bitterly, Mackellar,' said he; 'but, the Lord knows, I fear you are speaking very true. I have not proved worthy of my happiness. Bring my lady back.'

My lady was waiting near at hand to learn the issue. When I brought her in, my lord took a hand of each of us, and laid them both upon his bosom. 'I have had two friends in my life,' said he. 'All the comfort ever I had, it came from one or other. When you two are in a mind, I think I would be an ungrateful dog—' He shut his mouth very hard, and looked on us with swimming eyes. 'Do what ye like with me,' says he, 'only don't think—' He stopped again. 'Do what ye please with me: God knows I love and honour you.' And dropping our two hands, he turned his back and went and gazed out of the window. But my lady ran after, calling his name, and threw herself upon his neck in a passion of weeping.

I went out and shut the door behind me, and stood and thanked God from the bottom of my heart.

At the breakfast board, according to my lord's design, we were all met. The Master had by that time plucked off his patched boots and made a toilet suitable to the hour; Secundra Dass was no longer bundled up in wrappers, but wore a decent plain black suit, which misbecame him strangely; and the pair were at the great window, looking forth, when the family entered. They turned; and the black man (as they had already named him in the house) bowed almost to his knees, but the Master was for running forward like one of the family. My lady stopped him, curtseying low from the far end of the hall, and keeping her children at her back. My lord was a little in front: so there were the three cousins of Durrisdeer face to face. The hand of time was very legible on all; I seemed to read in their changed faces a *memento mori*; and what affected me still more, it was the wicked man that bore his years the handsomest. My lady was quite transfigured into the matron, a becoming woman for the head of a great tableful of children and dependants. My lord was grown slack in his limbs; he stooped; he walked with a running motion, as though he had learned again from Mr Alexander; his face was drawn; it seemed a trifle longer than of old; and it wore at times a smile very singularly mingled, and which (in my eyes) appeared both bitter and pathetic. But the Master still bore himself erect, although perhaps with effort; his brow barred about the centre with imperious lines, his mouth set as for command. He had all the gravity and something of the splendour of Satan in the *Paradise Lost*. I could not help but see the man with admiration, and was only surprised that I saw him with so little fear.

But indeed (as long as we were at the table) it seemed as if his authority were quite vanished and his teeth all drawn. We had known him a magician that controlled the elements; and here he was, transformed into an ordinary gentleman, chatting like his neighbours at the breakfast board. For now the father was dead, and my lord and lady reconciled, in what ear was he to pour his calumnies? It came upon me in a kind of vision how hugely I had overrated the man's subtlety. He had his malice still; he was false as ever; and, the occasion being gone that made his strength, he sat there impotent; he was still the viper, but now spent his venom on a file.[3] Two more thoughts occurred to me while yet we sat at breakfast: the first, that he was abashed – I had almost said, distressed – to find his wickedness quite unavailing; the second, that perhaps my lord was in the right, and we did amiss to fly from our dismasted enemy. But my poor master's leaping heart came in my mind, and I remembered it was for his life we played the coward.

When the meal was over, the Master followed me to my room, and, taking a chair (which I had never offered him), asked me what was to be done with him.

'Why, Mr Bally,' said I, 'the house will still be open to you for a time.'

'For a time?' says he. 'I do not know if I quite take your meaning.'

'It is plain enough,' said I. 'We keep you for our reputation; as soon as you shall have publicly disgraced yourself by some of your misconduct, we shall pack you forth again.'

'You are become an impudent rogue,' said the Master, bending his brows at me dangerously.

'I learned in a good school,' I returned. 'And you must have perceived yourself that with my old lord's death your power is quite departed. I do not fear you now, Mr Bally; I think even – God forgive me – that I take a certain pleasure in your company.'

He broke out in a burst of laughter, which I clearly saw to be assumed.

'I have come with empty pockets,' says he, after a pause.

'I do not think there will be any money going,' I replied. 'I would advise you not to build on that.'

'I shall have something to say on the point,' he returned.

'Indeed?' said I. 'I have not a guess what it will be, then.'

'O! you affect confidence,' said the Master. 'I have still one strong position – that you people fear a scandal, and I enjoy it.'

'Pardon me, Mr Bally,' says I. 'We do not in the least fear a scandal against you.'

He laughed again. 'You have been studying repartee,' he said. 'But speech is very easy, and sometimes very deceptive. I warn you fairly: you will find me vitriol in the house. You would do wiser to pay money down and see my back.' And with that he waved his hand to me and left the room.

A little after, my lord came with the lawyer, Mr Carlyle; a bottle of old wine was brought, and we all had a glass before we fell to business. The necessary deeds were then prepared and executed, and the Scots estates made over in trust to Mr Carlyle and myself.

'There is one point, Mr Carlyle,' said my lord, when these affairs had been adjusted, 'on which I wish that you would do us justice. This sudden departure coinciding with my brother's return will be certainly commented on. I wish you would discourage any conjunction of the two.'

'I will make a point of it, my lord,' said Mr Carlyle. 'The Mas— Mr Bally does not, then, accompany you?'

'It is a point I must approach,' said my lord. 'Mr Bally remains at Durrisdeer, under the care of Mr Mackellar; and I do not mean that he shall even know our destination.'

'Common report, however—' began the lawyer.

'Ah! but, Mr Carlyle, this is to be a secret quite among ourselves,' interrupted my lord. 'None but you and Mackellar are to be made acquainted with my movements.'

'And Mr Bally stays here? Quite so,' said Mr Carlyle. 'The powers you leave—' Then he broke off again. 'Mr Mackellar, we have a rather heavy weight upon us.'

'No doubt, sir,' said I.

'No doubt,' said he. 'Mr Bally will have no voice?'

'He will have no voice,' said my lord; 'and, I hope, no influence. Mr Bally is not a good adviser.'

'I see,' said the lawyer. – 'By the way, has Mr Bally means?'

'I understand him to have nothing,' replied my lord. 'I give him table, fire, and candle in this house.'

'And in the matter of an allowance? If I am to share the responsibility, you will see how highly desirable it is that I should understand your views,' said the lawyer. 'On the question of an allowance?'

'There will be no allowance,' said my lord. 'I wish Mr Bally to live very private. We have not always been gratified with his behaviour.'

'And in the matter of money,' I added, 'he has shown himself an infamous bad husband. Glance your eye upon that docket, Mr Carlyle, where I have brought together the different sums the man has drawn from the estate in the last fifteen or twenty years. The total is pretty.'

Mr Carlyle made the motion of whistling. 'I had no guess of this,' said he. 'Excuse me once more, my lord, if I appear to push you; but it is really desirable I should penetrate your intentions. Mr Mackellar might die, when I should find myself alone upon this trust. Would it not be rather your lordship's preference that Mr Bally should – ahem – should leave the country?'

My lord looked at Mr Carlyle. 'Why do you ask that?' said he.

'I gather, my lord, that Mr Bally is not a comfort to his family,' says the lawyer, with a smile.

My lord's face became suddenly knotted. 'I wish he was in hell!' cried he, and filled himself a glass of wine, but with a hand so tottering that he spilled the half into his bosom. This was the second time that, in the midst of the most regular and wise behaviour, his animosity had spurted out. It startled Mr Carlyle, who observed my lord thenceforth with covert curiosity; and to me it restored the certainty that we were acting for the best in view of my lord's health and reason.

Except for this explosion the interview was very successfully conducted. No doubt Mr Carlyle would talk, as lawyers do, little by little. We could thus feel we had laid the foundations of a better feeling in the country, and the man's own misconduct would certainly complete what we had begun. Indeed, before his departure, the lawyer showed us there had already gone abroad some glimmerings of the truth.

'I should perhaps explain to you, my lord,' said he, pausing, with his hat in his hand, 'that I have not been altogether surprised with your lordship's dispositions in the case of Mr Bally. Something of this nature oozed out when he was last in Durrisdeer. There was some talk of a woman at St Bride's, to whom you had behaved extremely handsome, and Mr Bally with no small degree of cruelty. There was the entail, again, which was much controverted. In short, there was no want of talk, back and forward; and some of our wiseacres took up a strong opinion. I remained in suspense, as became one of my cloth; but Mr Mackellar's docket here has finally opened my eyes. – I do not think, Mr Mackellar, that you and I will give him that much rope.'

The rest of that important day passed prosperously through. It was our policy to keep the enemy in view, and I took my turn to be his watchman with the rest. I think his spirits rose as he perceived us to be so attentive, and I know that mine insensibly declined. What chiefly daunted me was the man's singular dexterity to worm himself into our troubles. You may have felt (after a horse accident) the hand of a bone-setter artfully divide and interrogate the muscles, and settle strongly on the injured place? It was so with the Master's tongue, that was so cunning to question; and his eyes, that were so quick to observe. I seemed to have said nothing, and yet to have let all out. Before I knew where I was the man was condoling with me on my lord's neglect of my lady and myself, and his hurtful indulgence to his son. On this last point I perceived him (with panic fear) to return repeatedly. The boy had displayed a certain shrinking from his uncle; it was strong in my mind his father had been fool enough to indoctrinate the same, which was no wise beginning: and when I looked upon the man before me, still so handsome, so apt a speaker, with so great a variety of fortunes to relate, I saw he was the very personage to captivate a boyish fancy. John Paul had left only that morning; it was not to be supposed he had been altogether dumb upon his favourite subject: so that here would be Mr Alexander in the part of Dido, with a curiosity inflamed to hear; and there would be the Master, like a diabolical Æneas,[4] full of matter the most pleasing in the world to any youthful ear, such as battles, sea-disasters, flights, the forests of the West, and (since his later voyage) the ancient cities of the Indies. How cunningly these baits might be employed, and what an empire might be so founded, little by little, in the mind of any boy, stood obviously clear to me. There was no inhibition, so long as the man was in the house, that would be strong enough to hold these two apart; for if it be hard to charm serpents, it is no very difficult thing to cast a glamour[5] on a little chip of manhood not very long in breeches. I recalled an ancient sailor-man who dwelt in a lone house beyond the Figgate Whins (I believe, he called it after Portobello), and how the boys would troop out of Leith on a Saturday, and sit and listen to his swearing tales, as thick as crows about a carrion: a thing I often remarked as I went by, a young student, on my own more meditative holiday diversion. Many of these boys went, no doubt, in the face of an express command; many feared, and even hated, the old brute of whom they made their hero; and I have seen them flee from him when he was tipsy, and stone him when he was drunk. And yet there they came each Saturday! How much more easily would a boy like Mr Alexander fall under the influence of a high-looking, high-spoken gentleman-adventurer, who should conceive the fancy to entrap him; and the influence gained, how easy to employ it for the child's perversion!

I doubt if our enemy had named Mr Alexander three times before I perceived which way his mind was aiming – all this train of thought and memory passed in one pulsation through my own – and you may say I started back as though an open hole had gaped across a pathway. Mr Alexander: there was the weak point, there was the Eve in our perishable paradise; and the serpent was already hissing on the trail.

I promise you, I went the more heartily about the preparations; my last scruple gone, the danger of delay written before me in huge characters. From that moment forth I seem not to have sat down or breathed. Now I would be at my post with the Master and his Indian; now in the garret buckling a valise; now sending forth Macconochie by the side postern and the wood-path to bear it to the trysting-place; and, again, snatching some words of counsel with my lady. This was the *verso* of our life in Durrisdeer that day; but on the *recto* all appeared quite settled, as of a family at home in its paternal seat; and what perturbation may have been observable, the Master would set down to the blow of his unlooked-for coming, and the fear he was accustomed to inspire.

Supper went creditably off, cold salutations passed, and the company trooped to their respective chambers. I attended the Master to the last. We had put him next door to his Indian, in the north wing; because that was the most distant and could be severed from the body of the house with doors. I saw he was a kind friend or a good master (whichever it was) to his Secundra Dass – seeing to his comfort; mending the fire with his own hand, for the Indian complained of cold; inquiring as to the rice on which the stranger made his diet; talking with him pleasantly in the Hindustanee, while I stood by, my candle in my hand, and affected to be overcome with slumber. At length the Master observed my signals of distress. 'I perceive,' says he, 'that you have all your ancient habits: early to bed and early to rise. Yawn yourself away!'

Once in my own room, I made the customary motions of undressing, so that I might time myself; and when the cycle was complete, set my tinder-box ready, and blew out my taper. The matter of an hour afterward I made a light again, put on my shoes of list[6] that I had worn by my lord's sick-bed, and set forth into the house to call the voyagers. All were dressed and waiting – my lord, my lady, Miss Katharine, Mr Alexander, my lady's woman Christie; and I observed the effect of secrecy even upon quite innocent persons, that one after another showed in the chink of the door a face as white as paper. We slipped out of the side postern into a night of darkness, scarce broken by a star or two; so that at first we groped and stumbled and fell among the bushes. A few hundred yards up the wood-path Macconochie was waiting us with a great lantern; so the rest of the way we went easy enough, but still in a kind of guilty silence. A little beyond the abbey the path debouched on the main road; and some quarter of a mile farther, at the place called Eagles, where the moors begin, we saw the lights of the two carriages stand shining by the wayside. Scarce a word or two was uttered at our parting, and these regarded business: a silent grasping of hands, a turning of faces aside, and the thing was over; the horses broke into a trot, the lamplight sped like Will-o'-the-Wisp upon the broken moorland, it dipped beyond Stony Brae; and there were Macconochie and I alone with our lantern on the road. There was one thing more to wait for, and that was the reappearance of the coach upon Cartmore. It seems they must have pulled up upon the summit, looked back for a last time, and seen our lantern not yet moved away from the place of separation. For a lamp was taken from a carriage, and waved three times up and down by way of a farewell. And then they were gone indeed, having looked their last on the kind roof of Durrisdeer, their faces toward a barbarous country. I never knew before the greatness of that vault of night in which we two poor serving-men – the one old, and the one elderly – stood for the first time deserted; I had never felt before my own dependency upon the countenance of others. The sense of isolation burned in my bowels like a fire. It seemed that we who remained at home were the true exiles, and that Durrisdeer and Solwayside, and all that made my country native, its air good to me, and its language welcome, had gone forth and was far over the sea with my old masters.

The remainder of that night I paced to and fro on the smooth highway, reflecting on the future and the past. My thoughts, which at first dwelled tenderly on those who were just gone, took a more manly temper as I considered what remained for me to do. Day came upon the inland mountain-tops, and the fowls began to cry, and the smoke of homesteads to arise in the brown bosom of the moors, before I turned my face homeward, and went down the path to where the roof of Durrisdeer shone in the morning by the sea.

At the customary hour I had the Master called, and awaited his coming in the hall with a quiet mind. He looked about him at the empty room and the three covers set.

'We are a small party,' said he. 'How comes that?'

'This is the party to which we must grow accustomed,' I replied.

He looked at me with a sudden sharpness. 'What is all this?' said he.

'You and I and your friend Mr Dass are now all the company,' I replied. 'My lord, my lady, and the children, are gone upon a voyage.'

'Upon my word!' said he. 'Can this be possible? I have indeed fluttered your Volscians in Corioli![7] But this is no reason why our breakfast should go cold. Sit down, Mr Mackellar, if you please' – taking, as he spoke, the head of the table, which I had designed to occupy myself – 'and as we eat, you can give me the details of this evasion.'

I could see he was more affected than his language carried, and I determined to equal him in coolness. 'I was about to ask you to take the head of the table,' said I; 'for though I am now thrust into the position of your host, I could never forget that you were, after all, a member of the family.'

For a while he played the part of entertainer, giving directions to

Macconochie, who received them with an evil grace, and attending specially upon Secundra. 'And where has my good family withdrawn to?' he asked carelessly.

'Ah! Mr Bally, that is another point,' said I. 'I have no orders to communicate their destination.'

'To me,' he corrected.

'To any one,' said I.

'It is the less pointed,' said the Master; '*c'est de bon ton*: my brother improves as he continues. And I, dear Mr Mackellar?'

'You will have bed and board, Mr Bally,' said I. 'I am permitted to give you the run of the cellar, which is pretty reasonably stocked. You have only to keep well with me, which is no very difficult matter, and you shall want neither for wine nor a saddle-horse.'

He made an excuse to send Macconochie from the room.

'And for money?' he inquired. 'Have I to keep well with my good friend Mackellar for my pocket-money also? This is a pleasing return to the principles of boyhood.'

'There was no allowance made,' said I; 'but I will take it on myself to see you are supplied in moderation.'

'In moderation?' he repeated. 'And you will take it on yourself?' He drew himself up, and looked about the hall at the dark rows of portraits. 'In the name of my ancestors, I thank you,' says he; and then, with a return to irony, 'But there must certainly be an allowance for Secundra Dass?' he said. 'It is not possible they have omitted that?'

'I will make a note of it, and ask instructions when I write,' said I.

And he, with a sudden change of manner, and leaning forward with an elbow on the table – 'Do you think this entirely wise?'

'I execute my orders, Mr Bally,' said I.

'Profoundly modest,' said the Master; 'perhaps not equally ingenuous. You told me yesterday my power was fallen with my father's death. How comes it, then, that a peer of the realm flees under cloud of night out of a house in which his fathers have stood several sieges? that he conceals his address, which must be a matter of concern to his Gracious Majesty and to the whole republic? and that he should leave me in possession, and under the paternal charge of his invaluable Mackellar? This smacks to me of a very considerable and genuine apprehension.'

I sought to interrupt him with some not very truthful denegation; but he waved me down, and pursued his speech.

'I say, it smacks of it,' he said; 'but I will go beyond that, for I think the apprehension grounded. I came to this house with some reluctancy. In view of the manner of my last departure, nothing but necessity could have induced me to return. Money, however, is that which I must have. You will not give with a good grace; well, I have the power to force it from you. Inside of a week, without leaving Durrisdeer, I will find out where these fools are fled to. I will follow; and when I have run my quarry down, I will drive a wedge into that family that shall once more burst it into shivers. I shall see then whether my Lord Durrisdeer' (said with indescribable scorn and rage) 'will choose to buy my absence; and you will all see whether, by that time, I decide for profit or revenge.'

I was amazed to hear the man so open. The truth is, he was consumed with anger at my lord's successful flight, felt himself to figure as a dupe, and was in no humour to weigh language.

'Do you consider *this* entirely wise?' said I, copying his words.

'These twenty years I have lived by my poor wisdom,' he answered with a smile that seemed almost foolish in its vanity.

'And come out a beggar in the end,' said I, 'if beggar be a strong enough word for it.'

'I would have you to observe, Mr Mackellar,' cried he, with a sudden imperious heat, in which I could not but admire him, 'that I am scrupulously civil: copy me in that, and we shall be the better friends.'

Throughout this dialogue I had been incommoded by the observation of Secundra Dass. Not one of us, since the first word, had made a feint of eating: our eyes were in each other's faces – you might say, in each other's bosoms; and those of the Indian troubled me with a certain changing brightness, as of comprehension. But I brushed the fancy aside, telling myself once more he understood no English; only, from the gravity of both voices, and the occasional scorn and anger in the Master's, smelled out there was something of import in the wind.

For the matter of three weeks we continued to live together in the house of Durrisdeer: the beginning of that most singular chapter of my life – what I must call my intimacy with the Master. At first he was somewhat changeable in his behaviour: now civil, now returning to his old manner of flouting me to my face; and in both I met him half-way. Thanks be to Providence, I had now no measure to keep with the man; and I was never afraid of black brows, only of naked swords. So that I found a certain entertainment in these bouts of incivility, and was not always ill inspired in my rejoinders. At last (it was at supper) I had a droll expression that entirely vanquished him. He laughed again and again; and 'Who would have guessed,' he cried, 'that this old wife had any wit under his petticoats?'

'It is no wit, Mr Bally,' said I: 'a dry Scots humour, and something of the driest.' And, indeed, I never had the least pretension to be thought a wit.

From that hour he was never rude with me, but all passed between us in a manner of pleasantry. One of our chief times of daffing* was when he required a horse, another bottle, or some money. He would approach me then after the manner of a schoolboy, and I would carry it on by way of being his father: on both sides, with an infinity of mirth. I could not but perceive that he thought more of me, which tickled that poor part of mankind, the vanity. He dropped, besides (I must suppose unconsciously), into a manner that was not only familiar, but even friendly; and this, on the part of one who had so long detested me, I found the more insidious. He went little abroad; sometimes even refusing invitations. 'No,' he would say, 'what do I care for these thick-headed bonnet-lairds? I will stay at home, Mackellar; and we shall share a bottle quietly, and have one of our good talks.' And, indeed, meal-time at Durrisdeer must have been a delight to any one, by reason of the brilliancy of the discourse. He would often express

* Fooling.

wonder at his former indifference to my society. 'But, you see,' he would add, 'we were upon opposite sides. And so we are to-day; but let us never speak of that. I would think much less of you if you were not staunch to your employer.' You are to consider he seemed to me quite impotent for any evil; and how it is a most engaging form of flattery when (after many years) tardy justice is done to a man's character and parts. But I have no thought to excuse myself. I was to blame; I let him cajole me, and, in short, I think the watch-dog was gone sound asleep, when he was suddenly aroused.

I should say the Indian was continually travelling to and fro in the house. He never spoke, save in his own dialect and with the Master; walked without sound; and was always turning up where you would least expect him, fallen into a deep abstraction, from which he would start (upon your coming) to mock you with one of his grovelling obeisances. He seemed so quiet, so frail, and so wrapped in his own fancies, that I came to pass him over without much regard, or even to pity him for a harmless exile from his country. And yet without doubt the creature was still eavesdropping; and without doubt it was through his stealth and my security that our secret reached the Master.

It was one very wild night, after supper, and when we had been making more than usually merry, that the blow fell on me.

'This is all very fine,' says the Master, 'but we should do better to be buckling our valise.'

'Why so?' I cried. 'Are you leaving?'

'We are all leaving to-morrow in the morning,' said he. 'For the port of Glascow first, thence for the province of New York.'

I suppose I must have groaned aloud.

'Yes,' he continued, 'I boasted; I said a week, and it has taken me near twenty days. But never mind; I shall make it up; I will go the faster.'

'Have you the money for this voyage?' I asked.

'Dear and ingenuous personage, I have,' said he. 'Blame me, if you choose, for my duplicity; but while I have been wringing shillings from my daddy, I had a stock of my own put by against a rainy day. You will pay for your own passage, if you choose to accompany us on our flank march; I have enough for Secundra and myself, but not more – enough to be dangerous, not enough to be generous. There is, however, an outside seat upon the chaise which I will let you have upon a moderate commutation; so that the whole menagerie can go together – the house-dog, the monkey, and the tiger.'

'I go with you,' said I.

'I count upon it,' said the Master. 'You have seen me foiled; I mean you shall see me victorious. To gain that I will risk wetting you like a sop in this wild weather.'

'And at least,' I added, 'you know very well you could not throw me off.'

'Not easily,' said he. 'You put your finger on the point with your usual excellent good sense. I never fight with the inevitable.'

'I suppose it is useless to appeal to you?' said I.

'Believe me, perfectly,' said he.

'And yet, if you would give me time, I could write—' I began.

'And what would be my Lord Durrisdeer's answer?' asks he.

'Ay,' said I, 'that is the rub.'

'And, at any rate, how much more expeditious that I should go myself!' says he. 'But all this is quite a waste of breath. At seven to-morrow the chaise will be at the door. For I start from the door, Mackellar; I do not skulk through woods and take my chaise upon the wayside – shall we say, at Eagles?'

My mind was now thoroughly made up. 'Can you spare me quarter of an hour at St Bride's?' said I. 'I have a little necessary business with Carlyle.'

'An hour, if you prefer,' said he. 'I do not seek to deny that the money for your seat is an object to me; and you could always get the first to Glascow with saddle-horses.'

'Well,' said I, 'I never thought to leave old Scotland.'

'It will brisken you up,' says he.

'This will be an ill journey for some one,' I said. 'I think, sir, for you. Something speaks in my bosom; and so much it says plain – that this is an ill-omened journey.'

'If you take to prophecy,' says he, 'listen to that.'

There came up a violent squall off the open Solway, and the rain was dashed on the great windows.

'Do ye ken what that bodes, warlock?' said he, in a broad accent: 'that there'll be a man Mackellar unco sick at sea.'

When I got to my chamber, I sat there under a painful excitation, hearkening to the turmoil of the gale, which struck full upon that gable of the house. What with the pressure on my spirits, the eldritch[8] cries of the wind among the turret-tops, and the perpetual trepidation of the masoned house, sleep fled my eyelids utterly. I sat by my taper, looking on the black panes of the window, where the storm appeared continually on the point of bursting in its entrance; and upon that empty field I beheld a perspective of consequences that made the hair to rise upon my scalp. The child corrupted, the home broken up, my master dead, or worse than dead, my mistress plunged in desolation – all these I saw before me painted brightly on the darkness; and the outcry of the wind appeared to mock at my inaction.

MR MACKELLAR'S JOURNEY WITH THE MASTER

The chaise came to the door in a strong drenching mist. We took our leave in silence: the house of Durrisdeer standing with drooping gutters and windows closed, like a place dedicate to melancholy. I observed the Master kept his head out, looking back on these splashed walls and glimmering roofs, till they were suddenly swallowed in the mist; and I must suppose some natural sadness[1] fell upon the man at this departure; or was it some prevision of the end? At least, upon our mounting the long brae from Durrisdeer, as we walked side by side in the wet, he began first to whistle and then to sing the saddest of our country tunes, which sets folk weeping in a tavern, *Wandering Willie.*[2] The set of words he used with it I have not heard elsewhere, and could never come by any copy; but some of them which were the most appropriate to our departure linger in my memory. One verse began—

> Home was home then, my dear, full of kindly faces;
> Home was home then, my dear, happy for the child.

And ended somewhat thus—

> Now, when day dawns on the brow of the moorland,
> Lone stands the house, and the chimney-stone is cold,
> Lone let it stand, now the folks are all departed,
> The kind hearts, the true hearts, that loved the place of old.

I could never be a judge of the merit of these verses; they were so hallowed by the melancholy of the air, and were sung (or rather 'soothed') to me by a master-singer at a time so fitting. He looked in my face when he had done, and saw that my eyes watered.

'Ah! Mackellar,' said he, 'do you think I have never a regret?'

'I do not think you could be so bad a man,' said I, 'if you had not all the machinery to be a good one.'

'No, not all,' says he: 'not all. You are there in error. The malady of not wanting, my evangelist.' But methought he sighed as he mounted again into the chaise.

All day long we journeyed in the same miserable weather: the mist besetting us closely, the heavens incessantly weeping on my head. The road lay over moorish hills, where was no sound but the crying of moor-fowl in the wet heather and the pouring of the swollen burns. Sometimes I would doze off in slumber, when I would find myself plunged at once in some foul and ominous nightmare, from the which I would awake strangling. Sometimes, if the way was steep and the wheels turning slowly, I would overhear the voices from within, talking in that tropical tongue which was to me as inarticulate as the piping of the fowls. Sometimes, at a longer ascent, the Master would set foot to ground and walk by my side, mostly without speech. And all the time, sleeping or waking, I beheld the same black perspective of approaching ruin; and the same pictures rose in my view, only they were now painted upon hill-side mist. One, I remember, stood before me with the colours of a true illusion. It showed me my lord seated at a table in a small room; his head, which was at first buried in his hands, he slowly raised, and turned upon me a countenance from which hope had fled. I saw it first on the black window-panes, my last night in Durrisdeer; it haunted and returned upon me half the voyage through; and yet it was no effect of lunacy, for I have come to a ripe old age with no decay of my intelligence; nor yet (as I was then tempted to suppose) a heaven-sent warning of the future, for all manner of calamities befell, not that calamity – and I saw many pitiful sights, but never that one.

It was decided we should travel on all night; and it was singular, once the dusk had fallen, my spirits somewhat rose. The bright lamps, shining forth into the mist and on the smoking horses and the hodding[3] post-boy, gave me perhaps an outlook intrinsically more cheerful than what day had shown; or perhaps my mind had become wearied of its melancholy. At least, I spent some waking hours, not without satisfaction in my thoughts, although wet and weary in my body; and fell at last into a natural slumber without dreams. Yet I must have been at work even in the deepest of my sleep; and at work with at least a measure of intelligence. For I started broad awake, in the very act of crying out to myself

'Home was home then, my dear, happy for the child,'

stricken to find in it an appropriateness, which I had not yesterday observed, to the Master's detestable purpose in the present journey.

We were then close upon the city of Glascow, where we were soon breakfasting together at an inn, and where (as the devil would have it) we found a ship in the very article of sailing. We took our places in the cabin; and, two days after, carried our effects on board. Her name was the *Nonesuch*, a very ancient ship, and very happily named. By all accounts this should be her last voyage; people shook their heads upon the quays, and I had several warnings offered me by strangers in the street to the effect that she was rotten as a cheese, too deeply loaden, and must infallibly founder if we met a gale. From this it fell out we were the only passengers; the Captain, M'Murtrie, was a silent, absorbed man, with the Glascow or Gaelic accent; the mates ignorant rough seafarers, come in through the hawsehole;[4] and the Master and I were cast upon each other's company.

The *Nonesuch* carried a fair wind out of the Clyde, and for near upon a week we enjoyed bright weather and a sense of progress. I found myself (to my wonder) a born seaman, in so far at least as I was never sick; yet I was far from tasting the usual serenity of my health. Whether it was the motion of the ship on the billows, the confinement, the salted food, or all of these together, I suffered from a blackness of spirit and a painful strain upon my temper. The nature of my errand on that ship perhaps contributed; I think it did no more; the malady (whatever it was) sprang from my environment; and if the ship were not to blame, then it was the Master. Hatred and fear are ill bedfellows; but (to my shame be it spoken) I have tasted those in other places, lain down and got up with them, and eaten and drunk with them, and yet never before, nor after, have I been so poisoned through and through, in soul and body, as I was on board the *Nonesuch*. I freely confess my enemy set me a fair example of forbearance; in our worst days displayed the most patient geniality, holding me in conversation as long as I would suffer, and when I had rebuffed his civility, stretching himself on deck to read. The book he had on board with him was Mr Richardson's famous *Clarissa*,[5] and among other small attentions he would read me passages aloud; nor could any elocutionist have given with greater potency the pathetic portions of that work. I would retort upon him with passages out of the Bible, which was all my library – and very fresh to me, my religious duties (I grieve to say it) being always and even to this day extremely neglected. He tasted the merits of the work like the connoisseur he was; and would sometimes take it from my hand, turn the leaves over like a man that knew his way, and give me, with his fine declamation, a Roland for my Oliver.[6] But it was singular how little he applied his reading to himself; it passed high above his head like summer thunder; Lovelace and Clarissa, the tales of David's generosity, the psalms of his penitence, the solemn questions of the Book of Job, the touching poetry of Isaiah – they were to him a source of entertainment only, like the scraping of a fiddle in a change-house. This outer sensibility and inner toughness set me against him; it seemed of a piece with that impudent grossness which I knew to underlie the veneer of his fine manners; and sometimes my gorge rose against him as though he were deformed – and sometimes I would draw away as though from something partly spectral. I had moments when I thought of him as of a man of pasteboard – as though, if one should strike smartly through the buckram[7] of his countenance, there would be found a mere vacuity within. This horror (not merely fanciful, I think) vastly increased my detestation of his neighbourhood; I began to feel something shiver within me on his drawing near; I had at times a longing to cry out; there were days when I thought I could have struck him. This frame of mind was doubtless helped by shame, because I had dropped during our last days at Durrisdeer into a certain toleration of the man; and if any one had then told me I should drop into it again, I must have laughed in his face. It is possible he remained unconscious of this extreme fever of my resentment; yet I think he was too quick; and rather that he had fallen, in a long life of idleness, into a positive need of company, which obliged him to confront and tolerate my unconcealed aversion. Certain, at least, that he loved the note of his own tongue, as, indeed, he entirely loved all the parts and properties of himself; a sort of imbecility which almost necessarily attends on wickedness. I have seen him driven, when I proved recalcitrant, to long discourses with the skipper; and this, although the man plainly testified his weariness, fiddling miserably with both hand and foot, and replying only with a grunt.

After the first week out we fell in with foul winds and heavy weather. The sea was high. The *Nonesuch* being an old-fashioned ship, and badly loaden, rolled beyond belief; so that the skipper trembled for his masts, and I for my life. We made no progress on our course. An unbearable ill-humour settled on the ship: men, mates, and master, girding at one another all day long. A saucy word on the one hand, and a blow on the other, made a daily incident. There were times when the whole crew refused their duty; and we of the afterguard were twice got under arms – being the first time that ever I bore weapons – in the fear of mutiny.

In the midst of our evil season sprang up a hurricane of wind; so that all supposed she must go down. I was shut in the cabin from noon of one day till sundown of the next; the Master was somewhere lashed on deck; Secundra had eaten of some drug and lay insensible; so you may say I passed these hours in an unbroken solitude. At first I was terrified beyond motion, and almost beyond thought, my mind appearing to be frozen. Presently there stole in on me a ray of comfort. If the *Nonesuch* foundered, she would carry down with her into the deeps of that unsounded sea the creature whom we all so feared and hated; there would be no more Master of Ballantrae, the fish would sport among his ribs; his schemes all brought to nothing, his harmless enemies at peace. At first, I have said, it was but a ray of comfort; but it had soon grown to be broad sunshine. The thought of the man's death, of his deletion from this world, which he embittered for so many, took possession of my mind. I hugged it; I found it sweet in my belly. I conceived the ship's last plunge, the sea bursting upon all sides into the cabin, the brief mortal conflict there, all by myself, in that closed place; I numbered the horrors, I had almost said with satisfaction; I felt I could bear all and more, if the *Nonesuch* carried down with her, overtook by the same ruin, the enemy of my poor master's house. Towards noon of the second day the screaming of the wind abated; the ship lay not so perilously over, and it began to be clear to me that we were past the height of the tempest. As I hope for mercy, I was singly disappointed. In the selfishness of that vile, absorbing passion of hatred, I forgot the case of our innocent ship-mates, and thought but of myself and my enemy. For myself, I was already old; I had never been young, I was not formed for the world's pleasures, I had few affections; it mattered not the toss of a silver tester[8] whether I was drowned there and then in the Atlantic, or dribbled out a few more years, to die, perhaps no less terribly, in a deserted sick-bed. Down I went upon my knees – holding on by the locker, or else I had been instantly dashed across the tossing cabin – and, lifting up my voice in the midst of that clamour of the abating hurricane, impiously prayed for my own death. 'O God!' I cried, 'I would be liker a man if I rose and struck this creature down; but Thou madest me a coward from my mother's womb. O Lord, Thou madest me so, Thou knowest my weakness, Thou knowest that any face of death will set me shaking in my shoes. But, lo! here is Thy servant ready, his mortal weakness laid aside. Let me give my life for this creature's; take the two of them, Lord! take the two, and have mercy on the innocent!' In some such words as these, only yet more irreverent and with more sacred adjurations, I continued to pour forth my spirit. God heard me not, I must suppose in mercy; and I was still absorbed in my agony of supplication when some one, removing the tarpaulin cover, let the light of the sunset pour into the cabin. I stumbled to my feet ashamed, and was seized with surprise to find myself totter and ache like one that had been stretched upon the rack. Secundra Dass, who had slept off the effects of his drug, stood in a corner not far off, gazing at me with wild eyes; and from the open skylight the captain thanked me for my supplications.

'It's you that saved the ship, Mr Mackellar,' says he. 'There is no craft of seamanship that could have kept her floating: well may we say, "Except the Lord the city keep, the watchmen watch in vain"![9]

I was abashed by the captain's error; abashed, also, by the surprise and fear with which the Indian regarded me at first, and the obsequious civilities with which he soon began to cumber me. I know now that he must have overheard and comprehended the peculiar nature of my prayers. It is certain, of course, that he at once disclosed the matter to his patron; and looking back with greater knowledge, I can now understand what so much puzzled me at the moment, those singular and (so to speak) approving smiles with which the Master honoured me. Similarly, I can understand a word that I remember to have fallen from him in conversation that same night; when, holding up his hand and smiling, 'Ah! Mackellar,' said he, 'not every man is so great a coward as he thinks he is – nor yet so good a Christian.' He did not guess how true he spoke! For the fact is, the thoughts which had come to me in the violence of the storm retained their hold upon my spirit; and the words that rose to my lips unbidden in the instancy of prayer continued to sound in my ears: with what shameful consequences it is fitting I should honestly relate; for I could not support a part of such disloyalty as to describe the sins of others and conceal my own.

The wind fell, but the sea hove ever the higher. All night the *Nonesuch* rolled outrageously; the next day dawned, and the next, and brought no change. To cross the cabin was scarce possible; old experienced seamen were cast down upon the deck, and one cruelly mauled in the concussion; every board and block in the old ship cried out aloud; and the great bell by the anchor-bitts[10] continually and dolefully rang. One of these days the Master and I sate alone together at the break of the poop. I should say the *Nonesuch* carried a high, raised poop. About the top of it ran considerable bulwarks, which made the ship unweatherly: and these, as they approached the front on each side, ran down in a fine, old-fashioned, carven scroll to join the bulwarks of the waist. From this disposition, which seems designed rather for ornament than use, it followed there was a discontinuance of protection: and that, besides, at the very margin of the elevated part where (in certain movements of the ship) it might be the most needful. It was here we were sitting: our feet hanging down, the

Master betwixt me and the side, and I holding on with both hands to the grating of the cabin skylight; for it struck me it was a dangerous position, the more so as I had continually before my eyes a measure of our evolutions in the person of the Master, which stood out in the break of the bulwarks against the sun. Now his head would be in the zenith and his shadow fall quite beyond the *Nonesuch* on the farther side; and now he would swing down till he was underneath my feet, and the line of the sea leaped high above him like the ceiling of a room. I looked on upon this with a growing fascination, as birds are said to look on snakes. My mind, besides, was troubled with an astonishing diversity of noises; for now that we had all sails spread in the vain hope to bring her to the sea, the ship sounded like a factory with their reverberations. We spoke first of the mutiny with which we had been threatened; this led us on to the topic of assassination; and that offered a temptation to the Master more strong than he was able to resist. He must tell me a tale, and show me at the same time how clever he was, and how wicked. It was a thing he did always with affectation and display; generally with a good effect. But this tale, told in a high key in the midst of so great a tumult, and by a narrator who was one moment looking down at me from the skies and the next peering up from under the soles of my feet – this particular tale, I say, took hold upon me in a degree quite singular.

'My friend the count,' it was thus that he began his story, 'had for an enemy a certain German baron, a stranger in Rome. It matters not what was the ground of the count's enmity; but as he had a firm design to be revenged, and that with safety to himself, he kept it secret even from the baron. Indeed, that is the first principle of vengeance; and hatred betrayed is hatred impotent. The count was a man of a curious, searching mind; he had something of the artist; if anything fell for him to do, it must always be done with an exact perfection, not only as to the result, but in the very means and instruments, or he thought the thing miscarried. It chanced he was one day riding in the outer suburbs, when he came to a disused by-road branching off into the moor which lies about Rome. On the one hand was an ancient Roman tomb; on the other a deserted house in a garden of evergreen trees. This road brought him presently into a field of ruins, in the midst of which, in the side of a hill, he saw an open door, and, not far off, a single stunted pine no greater than a currant-bush. The place was desert and very secret; a voice spoke in the count's bosom that there was something here to his advantage. He tied his horse to the pine-tree, took his flint and steel in his hand to make a light, and entered into the hill. The doorway opened on a passage of old Roman masonry, which shortly after branched in two. The count took the turning to the right, and followed it, groping forward in the dark, till he was brought up by a kind of fence, about elbow-high, which extended quite across the passage. Sounding forward with his foot, he found an edge of polished stone, and then vacancy. All his curiosity was now awakened, and, getting some rotten sticks that lay about the floor, he made a fire. In front of him was a profound well; doubtless some neighbouring peasant had once used it for his water, and it was he that had set up the fence. A long while the count stood leaning on the rail and looking down into the pit. It was of Roman foundation, and, like all that nation set their hands to, built as for eternity; the sides were still straight, and the joints smooth; to a man who should fall in, no escape was possible. "Now," the count was thinking, "a strong impulsion brought me to this place. What for? what have I gained? why should I be sent to gaze into this well?" when the rail of the fence gave suddenly under his weight, and he came within an ace of falling headlong in. Leaping back to save himself, he trod out the last flicker of his fire, which gave him thenceforward no more light, only an incommoding smoke. "Was I sent here to my death?" says he, and shook from head to foot. And then a thought flashed in his mind. He crept forth on hands and knees to the brink of the pit, and felt above him in the air. The rail had been fast to a pair of uprights; it had only broken from the one, and still depended from the other. The count set it back again as he had found it, so that the place meant death to the first comer, and groped out of the catacomb like a sick man. The next day, riding in the Corso with the baron, he purposely betrayed a strong pre-occupation. The other (as he had designed) inquired into the cause; and he, after some fencing, admitted that his spirits had been dashed by an unusual dream. This was calculated to draw on the baron – a superstitious man, who affected the scorn of superstition. Some rallying followed, and then the count, as if suddenly carried away, called on his friend to beware, for it was of him that he had dreamed. You know enough of human nature, my excellent Mackellar, to be certain of one thing: I mean that the baron did not rest till he had heard the dream. The count, sure that he would never desist, kept him in play till his curiosity was highly inflamed, and then suffered himself, with seeming reluctance, to be overborne. "I warn you," says he, "evil will come of it; something tells me so. But since there is to be no peace either for you or me except on this condition, the blame be on your own head! This was the dream: – I beheld you riding, I know not where, yet I think it must have been near Rome, for on your one hand was an ancient tomb, and on the other a garden of evergreen trees. Methought I cried and cried upon you to come back in a very agony of terror; whether you heard me I know not, but you went doggedly on. The road brought you to a desert place among ruins, where was a door in a hill-side, and hard by the door a misbegotten pine. Here you dismounted (I still crying on you to beware), tied your horse to the pine-tree, and entered resolutely in by the door. Within, it was dark; but in my dream I could still see you, and still besought you to hold back. You felt your way along the right-hand wall, took a branching passage to the right, and came to a little chamber, where was a well with a railing. At this – I know not why – my alarm for you increased a thousandfold, so that I seemed to scream myself hoarse with warnings, crying it was still time, and bidding you begone at once from that vestibule. Such was the word I used in my dream, and it seemed then to have a clear significancy; but to-day, and awake, I profess I know not what it means. To all my outcry you rendered not the least attention, leaning the while upon the rail and looking down intently in the water. And then there was made to you a communication; I do not think I even gathered what it was, but the fear of it plucked me clean out of my slumber, and I awoke shaking and sobbing. And now," continues the count, "I thank you from my heart for your insistency. This dream lay on me like a load; and now I have told it in plain words and in the broad daylight, it seems no great matter." – "I do not know," says the baron. "It is in some points strange. A communication, did you say! O! it is an odd dream. It will make a story to amuse our friends." – "I am not so sure," says the count. "I am sensible of some reluctancy. Let us rather forget it." – "By all means," says the baron. And (in fact) the dream was not again referred to. Some days after, the count proposed a ride in the fields, which the baron (since they were daily growing faster friends) very readily accepted. On the way back to Rome, the count led them insensibly by a particular route. Presently he reined in his horse, clapped his hand before his eyes, and cried out aloud. Then he showed his face again (which was now quite white, for he was a consummate actor), and stared upon the baron. "What ails you?" cries the baron. "What is wrong with you?" – "Nothing," cries the count. "It is nothing. A seizure, I know not what. Let us hurry back to Rome." But in the meanwhile the baron had looked about him; and there, on the left-hand side of the way as they went back to Rome, he saw a dusty by-road with a tomb upon the one hand and a garden of evergreen trees upon the other. – "Yes," says he, with a changed voice. "Let us by all means hurry back to Rome. I fear you are not well in health." – "O, for God's sake!" cried the count, shuddering, "back to Rome and let me get to bed." They made their return with scarce a word; and the count, who should by rights have gone into society, took to his bed and gave out he had a touch of country fever. The next day the baron's horse was found tied to the pine, but himself was never heard of from that hour. – And now, was that a murder?' says the Master, breaking sharply off.

'Are you sure he was a count?' I asked.

'I am not certain of the title,' said he, 'but he was a gentleman of family: and the Lord deliver you, Mackellar, from an enemy so subtile!'

These last words he spoke down at me, smiling from high above; the next, he was under my feet. I continued to follow his evolutions with a childish fixity; they made me giddy and vacant, and I spoke as in a dream.

'He hated the baron with a great hatred?' I asked.

'His belly moved when the man came near him,' said the Master.

'I have felt that same,' said I.

'Verily!' cries the Master. 'Here is news indeed! I wonder – do I flatter myself? or am I the cause of these ventral perturbations?'

He was quite capable of choosing out a graceful posture, even with no one to behold him but myself, and all the more if there were any element of peril. He sat now with one knee flung across the other, his arms on his bosom, fitting the swing of the ship with an exquisite balance, such as a feather-weight might overthrow. All at once I had the vision of my lord at the table, with his head upon his hands; only now, when he showed me his countenance, it was heavy with reproach. The words of my own prayer – *I were liker a man if I struck this creature down* – shot at the same time into my memory. I called my energies together, and (the ship then heeling downward toward my enemy) thrust at him swiftly with my foot. It was written I should have the guilt of this attempt without the profit. Whether from my own uncertainty or his incredible quickness, he escaped the thrust, leaping to his feet and catching hold at the same moment of a stay.

I do not know how long a time passed by: I lying where I was upon the deck, overcome with terror and remorse and shame: he standing with the stay in his hand, backed against the bulwarks, and regarding me with an expression singularly mingled. At last he spoke.

'Mackellar,' said he, 'I make no reproaches, but I offer you a bargain. On your side, I do not suppose you desire to have this exploit made public; on mine, I own to you freely I do not care to draw my breath in a perpetual terror of assassination by the man I sit at meat with. Promise me – but no,' says he, breaking off, 'you are not yet in the quiet possession of your mind; you might think I had extorted the promise from your weakness; and I would leave no door open for casuistry to come in – that dishonesty of the conscientious. Take time to meditate.'

With that he made off up the sliding deck like a squirrel, and plunged into the cabin. About half an hour later he returned – I still lying as he had left me.

'Now,' says he, 'will you give me your troth as a Christian, and a faithful servant of my brother's, that I shall have no more to fear from your attempts?'

'I give it you,' said I.

'I shall require your hand upon it,' says he.

'You have the right to make conditions,' I replied, and we shook hands.

He sat down at once in the same place and the old perilous attitude.

'Hold on!' cried I, covering my eyes. 'I cannot bear to see you in that posture. The least irregularity of the sea might plunge you overboard.'

'You are highly inconsistent,' he replied, smiling, but doing as I asked. 'For all that, Mackellar, I would have you to know you have risen forty feet in my esteem. You think I cannot set a price upon fidelity? But why do you suppose I carry that Secundra Dass about the world with me? Because he would die or do murder for me to-morrow; and I love him for it. Well, you may think it odd, but I like you the better for this afternoon. I thought you were magnetised with the Ten Commandments; but no – God damn my soul!' – he cries, 'the old wife has blood in his body after all! Which does not change the fact,' he continued, smiling again, 'that you have done well to give your promise; for I doubt if you would ever shine in your new trade.'

'I suppose,' said I, 'I should ask your pardon and God's for my attempt. At any rate, I have passed my word, which I will keep faithfully. But when I think of those you persecute—' I paused.

'Life is a singular thing,' said he, 'and mankind a very singular people. You suppose yourself to love my brother. I assure you, it is merely custom. Interrogate your memory; and when first you came to Durrisdeer, you will find you considered him a dull, ordinary youth. He is as dull and ordinary now, though not so young. Had you instead fallen in with me, you would to-day be as strong upon my side.'

'I would never say you were ordinary, Mr Bally,' I returned; 'but here you prove yourself dull. You have just shown your reliance on my word – in other terms, that is, my conscience – the same which starts instinctively back from you, like the eye from a strong light.'

'Ah!' says he, 'but I mean otherwise. I mean had I met you in my youth. You are to consider I was not always as I am to-day; nor (had

I met in with a friend of your description) should I have ever been so.'

'Hut, Mr Bally,' says I, 'you would have made a mock of me; you would never have spent ten civil words on such a Square-toes.'

But he was now fairly started on his new course of justification, with which he wearied me throughout the remainder of the passage. No doubt in the past he had taken pleasure to paint himself unnecessarily black, and made a vaunt of his wickedness, bearing it for a coat-of-arms. Nor was he so illogical as to abate one item of his old confessions. 'But now that I know you are a human being,' he would say, 'I can take the trouble to explain myself. For I assure you I am human too, and have my virtues like my neighbours.' I say, he wearied me, for I had only the one word to say in answer: twenty times I must have said it: 'Give up your present purpose and return with me to Durrisdeer: then I will believe you.'

Thereupon he would shake his head at me. 'Ah! Mackellar, you might live a thousand years and never understand my nature,' he would say. 'This battle is now committed, the hour of reflection quite past, the hour for mercy not yet come. It began between us when we span a coin in the hall of Durrisdeer, now twenty years ago; we have had our ups and downs, but never either of us dreamed of giving in; and as for me, when my glove is cast, life and honour go with it.'

'A fig for your honour!' I would say. 'And by your leave, these warlike similitudes are something too high-sounding for the matter in hand. You want some dirty money; there is the bottom of your contention; and as for your means, what are they? to stir up sorrow in a family that never harmed you, to debauch (if you can) your own nephew, and to wring the heart of your born brother! A footpad that kills an old granny in a woollen mutch[11] with a dirty bludgeon, and that for a shilling piece and a paper of snuff – there is all the warrior that you are.'

When I would attack him thus (or somewhat thus) he would smile, and sigh like a man misunderstood. Once, I remember, he defended himself more at large, and had some curious sophistries, worth repeating, for a light upon his character.

'You are very like a civilian to think war consists in drums and banners,' said he. 'War (as the ancients said very wisely) is *ultima ratio.* When we take our advantage unrelentingly, then we make war. Ah! Mackellar, you are a devil of a soldier in the steward's room at Durrisdeer, or the tenants do you sad injustice!'

'I think little of what war is or is not,' I replied. 'But you weary me with claiming my respect. Your brother is a good man, and you are a bad one – neither more nor less.'

'Had I been Alexander—' he began.

'It is so we all dupe ourselves,' I cried. 'Had I been St Paul, it would have been all one; I would have made the same hash of that career that you now see me making of my own.'

'I tell you,' he cried, bearing down my interruption, 'had I been the least petty chieftain in the Highlands, had I been the least king of naked negroes in the African desert, my people would have adored me. A bad man, am I? Ah! but I was born for a good tyrant! Ask Secundra Dass; he will tell you I treat him like a son. Cast in your lot with me to-morrow, become my slave, my chattel, a thing I can command as I command the powers of my own limbs and spirit – you will see no more that dark side that I turn upon the world in anger. I must have all or none. But where all is given I give it back with usury. I have a kingly nature: there is my loss!'

'It has been hitherto rather the loss of others,' I remarked, 'which seems a little on the hither side of royalty.'

'Tilly-vally!'[12] cried he. 'Even now, I tell you, I would spare that family in which you take so great an interest: yes, even now – to-morrow I would leave them to their petty welfare, and disappear in that forest of cut-throats and thimble-riggers that we call the world. I would do it to-morrow!' says he. 'Only – only—'

'Only what?' I asked.

'Only they must beg it on their bended knees. I think in public, too,' he added, smiling. 'Indeed, Mackellar, I doubt if there be a hall big enough to serve my purpose for that act of reparation.'

'Vanity, vanity!' I moralised. 'To think that this great force for evil should be swayed by the same sentiment that sets a lassie mincing to her glass!'

'O! there are double words for everything: the word that swells, the word that belittles; you cannot fight me with a word!' said he. 'You said the other day that I relied on your conscience: were I in your humour of detraction, I might say I built upon your vanity. It is your pretension to be *un homme de parole*;[13] 'tis mine not to accept defeat. Call it vanity, call it virtue, call it greatness of soul – what signifies the expression? But recognise in each of us a common strain: that we both live for an idea.'

It will be gathered from so much familiar talk, and so much patience on both sides, that we now lived together upon excellent terms. Such was again the fact, and this time more seriously than before. Apart from disputations such as that which I have tried to reproduce, not only consideration reigned, but, I am tempted to say, even kindness. When I fell sick (as I did shortly after our great storm), he sat by my berth to entertain me with his conversation, and treated me with excellent remedies, which I accepted with security. Himself commented on the circumstance. 'You see,' says he, 'you begin to know me better. A very little while ago, upon this lonely ship, where no one but myself has any smattering of science, you would have made sure I had designs upon your life. And, observe, it is since I found you had designs upon my own that I have shown you most respect. You will tell me if this speaks of a small mind.' I found little to reply. In so far as regarded myself, I believed him to mean well; I am, perhaps, the more a dupe of his dissimulation, but I believed (and I still believe) that he regarded me with genuine kindness. Singular and sad fact! so soon as this change began, my animosity abated, and these haunting visions of my master passed utterly away. So that, perhaps, there was truth in the man's last vaunting word to me, uttered on the twenty-second day of July, when our long voyage was at last brought almost to an end, and we lay becalmed at the sea end of the vast harbour of New York, in a gasping heat, which was presently exchanged for a surprising waterfall of rain. I stood on the poop, regarding the green shores near at hand, and now and then the light smoke of the little town, our destination. And as I was even then devising how to steal a march on my familiar enemy, I was conscious of a shade of embarrassment when he approached me with his hand extended.

'I am now to bid you farewell,' said he, 'and that for ever. For now you go among my enemies, where all your former prejudices will revive. I never yet failed to charm a person when I wanted; even you, my good friend – to call you so for once – even you have now a very different portrait of me in your memory, and one that you will never quite forget. The voyage has not lasted long enough, or I should have wrote the impression deeper. But now all is at an end, and we are again at war. Judge by this little interlude how dangerous I am; and tell those fools' – pointing with his finger to the town – 'to think twice and thrice before they set me at defiance.'

PASSAGES AT NEW YORK

I have mentioned I was resolved to steal a march upon the Master; and this, with the complicity of Captain M'Murtrie, was mighty easily effected: a boat being partly loaded on the one side of our ship, and the Master placed on board of it, the while a skiff put off from the other, carrying me alone. I had no more trouble in finding a direction to my lord's house, whither I went at top speed, and which I found to be on the outskirts of the place, a very suitable mansion, in a fine garden, with an extraordinary large barn, byre, and stable, all in one. It was here my lord was walking when I arrived; indeed, it had become his chief place of frequentation, and his mind was now filled with farming. I burst in upon him breathless, and gave him my news: which was indeed no news at all, several ships having outsailed the *Nonesuch* in the interval.

'We have been expecting you long,' said my lord; 'and indeed, of late days, ceased to expect you any more. I am glad to take your hand again, Mackellar. I thought you had been at the bottom of the sea.'

'Ah! my lord, would God I had!' cried I. 'Things would have been better for yourself.'

'Not in the least,' says he grimly. 'I could not ask better. There is a long score to pay, and now – at last – I can begin to pay it.'

I cried out against his security.

'O!' says he, 'this is not Durrisdeer, and I have taken my precautions. His reputation awaits him; I have prepared a welcome for my brother. Indeed, fortune has served me; for I found here a merchant of Albany who knew him after the '45, and had mighty convenient suspicions of a murder: some one of the name of Chew it was, another

Albanian. No one here will be surprised if I deny him my door; he will not be suffered to address my children, nor even to salute my wife: as for myself, I make so much exception for a brother that he may speak to me. I should lose my pleasure else,' says my lord, rubbing his palms.

Presently he bethought himself, and set men off running, with billets, to summon the magnates of the province. I cannot recall what pretext he employed; at least, it was successful; and when our ancient enemy appeared upon the scene, he found my lord pacing in front of his house under some trees of shade, with the Governor upon one hand and various notables upon the other. My lady, who was seated in the verandah, rose with a very pinched expression and carried her children into the house.

The Master, well dressed, and with an elegant walking-sword, bowed to the company in a handsome manner and nodded to my lord with familiarity. My lord did not accept the salutation, but looked upon his brother with bended brows.

'Well, sir,' says he at last, 'what ill wind brings you hither of all places, where (to our common disgrace) your reputation has preceded you?'

'Your lordship is pleased to be civil,' cries the Master, with a fine start.

'I am pleased to be very plain,' returned my lord; 'because it is needful you should clearly understand your situation. At home, where you were so little known, it was still possible to keep appearances; that would be quite vain in this province; and I have to tell you that I am quite resolved to wash my hands of you. You have already ruined me almost to the door, as you ruined my father before me; – whose heart you also broke. Your crimes escape the law; but my friend the Governor has promised protection to my family. Have a care, sir!' cries my lord, shaking his cane at him: 'if you are observed to utter two words to any of my innocent household, the law shall be stretched to make you smart for it.'

'Ah!' says the Master, very slowly. 'And so this is the advantage of a foreign land! These gentlemen are unacquainted with our story, I perceive. They do not know that I am the true Lord Durrisdeer; they do not know you are my younger brother, sitting in my place under a sworn family compact, they do not know (or they would not be seen with you in familiar correspondence) that every acre is mine before God Almighty – and every doit of the money you withhold from me, you do it as a thief, a perjurer, and a disloyal brother!'

'General Clinton,'[1] I cried, 'do not listen to his lies. I am the steward of the estate, and there is not one word of truth in it. The man is a forfeited rebel turned into a hired spy: there is his story in two words.'

It was thus that (in the heat of the moment) I let slip his infamy.

'Fellow,' said the Governor, turning his face sternly on the Master, 'I know more of you than you think for. We have some broken ends of your adventures in the provinces, which you will do very well not to drive me to investigate. There is the disappearance of Mr Jacob Chew with all his merchandise; there is the matter of where you came ashore from with so much money and jewels, when you were picked up by a Bermudan out of Albany. Believe me, if I let these matters lie, it is in commiseration for your family, and out of respect for my valued friend, Lord Durrisdeer.'

There was a murmur of applause from the provincials.

'I should have remembered how a title would shine out in such a hole as this,' says the Master, white as a sheet: 'no matter how unjustly come by. It remains for me, then, to die at my lord's door, where my dead body will form a very cheerful ornament.'

'Away with your affectations!' cries my lord. 'You know very well I have no such meaning; only to protect myself from calumny, and my home from your intrusion. I offer you a choice. Either I shall pay your passage home on the first ship, when you may perhaps be able to resume your occupations under Government, although God knows I would rather see you on the highway! Or, if that likes you not, stay here and welcome! I have inquired the least sum on which body and soul can be decently kept together in New York; so much you shall have, paid weekly; and if you cannot labour with your hands to better it, high time you should betake yourself to learn. The condition is – that you speak with no member of my family except myself,' he added.

I do not think I have ever seen any man so pale as was the Master; but he was erect and his mouth firm.

'I have been met here with some very unmerited insults,' said he, 'from which I have certainly no idea to take refuge by flight. Give me your pittance; I take it without shame, for it is mine already – like the shirt upon your back; and I choose to stay until these gentlemen shall understand me better. Already they must spy the cloven hoof, since with all your pretended eagerness for the family honour, you take a pleasure to degrade it in my person.'

'This is all very fine,' says my lord; 'but to us who know you of old, you must be sure it signifies nothing. You take that alternative out of which you think that you can make the most. Take it, if you can, in silence; it will serve you better in the long-run, you may believe me, than this ostentation of ingratitude.'

'O, gratitude, my lord!' cries the Master, with a mounting intonation, and his forefinger very conspicuously lifted up. 'Be at rest: it will not fail you. It now remains that I should salute these gentlemen whom we have wearied with our family affairs.'

And he bowed to each in succession, settled his walking-sword, and took himself off, leaving every one amazed at his behaviour, and me not less so at my lord's.

We were now to enter on a changed phase of this family division. The Master was by no manner of means so helpless as my lord supposed, having at his hand, and entirely devoted to his service, an excellent artist in all sorts of goldsmith work. With my lord's allowance, which was not so scanty as he had described it, the pair could support life; and all the earnings of Secundra Dass might be laid upon one side for any future purpose. That this was done, I have no doubt. It was in all likelihood the Master's design to gather a sufficiency, and then proceed in quest of that treasure which he had buried long before among the mountains; to which, if he had confined himself, he would have been more happily inspired. But unfortunately for himself and all of us, he took counsel of his anger. The public disgrace of his arrival – which I sometimes wonder he could manage to survive – rankled in his bones; he was in that humour when a man – in the words of the old adage – will cut off his nose to spite his face; and he must make himself a public spectacle in the hopes that some of the disgrace might spatter on my lord.

He chose, in a poor quarter of the town, a lonely, small house of boards, overhung with some acacias. It was furnished in front with a sort of hutch opening, like that of a dog's kennel, but about as high as a table from the ground, in which the poor man that built it had formerly displayed some wares; and it was this which took the Master's fancy and possibly suggested his proceedings. It appears, on board the pirate ship he had acquired some quickness with the needle – enough, at least, to play the part of tailor in the public eye; which was all that was required by the nature of his vengeance. A placard was hung above the hutch, bearing these words in something of the following disposition:

JAMES DURIE,
FORMERLY MASTER OF BALLANTRAE.
CLOTHES NEATLY CLOUTED.

SECUNDRA DASS,
DECAYED GENTLEMAN OF INDIA.
FINE GOLDSMITH WORK.

Underneath this, when he had a job, my gentleman sat withinside tailor-wise and busily stitching. I say, when he had a job; but such customers as came were rather for Secundra, and the Master's sewing would be more in the manner of Penelope's.[2] He could never have designed to gain even butter to his bread by such a means of livelihood: enough for him that there was the name of Durie dragged in the dirt on the placard, and the sometime heir of that proud family set up cross-legged in public for a reproach upon his brother's meanness. And in so far his device succeeded that there was murmuring in the town and a party formed highly inimical to my lord. My lord's favour with the Governor laid him more open on the other side; my lady (who was never so well received in the colony) met with painful innuendoes; in a party of women, where it would be the topic most natural to introduce, she was almost debarred from the naming of needle-work; and I have seen her return with a flushed countenance, and vow that she would go abroad no more.

In the meanwhile my lord dwelled in his decent mansion, immersed in farming; a popular man with his intimates, and careless or unconscious of the rest. He laid on flesh; had a bright, busy face; even the heat seemed to prosper with him; and my lady – in despite of her own annoyances – daily blessed Heaven her father should have left her such a paradise. She had looked on from a window upon the Master's humiliation; and from that hour appeared to feel at ease. I was not so sure myself; as time went on, there seemed to me a something not quite wholesome in my lord's condition. Happy he was, beyond a doubt, but the grounds of this felicity were secret; even in the bosom of his family he brooded with manifest delight upon some private thought; and I conceived at last the suspicion (quite unworthy of us both) that he kept a mistress somewhere in the town. Yet he went little abroad, and his day was very fully occupied; indeed, there was but a single period, and that pretty early in the morning, while Mr Alexander was at his lesson-book, of which I was not certain of the disposition. It should be borne in mind, in the defence of that which I now did, that I was always in some fear my lord was not quite justly in his reason; and with our enemy sitting so still in the same town with us, I did well to be upon my guard. Accordingly I made a pretext, had the hour changed at which I taught Mr Alexander the foundation of ciphering and the mathematic, and set myself instead to dog my master's footsteps.

Every morning, fair or foul, he took his gold-headed cane, set his hat on the back of his head – a recent habitude, which I thought to indicate a burning brow – and betook himself to make a certain circuit. At the first his way was among pleasant trees and beside a graveyard, where he would sit a while, if the day were fine, in meditation. Presently the path turned down to the water-side, and came back along the harbour-front and past the Master's booth. As he approached this second part of his circuit, my Lord Durrisdeer began to pace more leisurely, like a man delighted with the air and scene; and before the booth, half-way between that and the water's edge, would pause a little, leaning on his staff. It was the hour when the Master sate within upon his board and plied his needle. So these two brothers would gaze upon each other with hard faces; and then my lord move on again, smiling to himself.

It was but twice that I must stoop to that ungrateful necessity of playing spy. I was then certain of my lord's purpose in his rambles and of the secret source of his delight. Here was his mistress: it was hatred and not love that gave him healthful colours. Some moralists might have been relieved by the discovery; I confess that I was dismayed. I found this situation of two brethren not only odious in itself, but big with possibilities of further evil; and I made it my practice, in so far as many occupations would allow, to go by a shorter path and be secretly present at their meeting. Coming down one day a little late, after I had been near a week prevented, I was struck with surprise to find a new development. I should say there was a bench against the Master's house, where customers might sit to parley with the shopman; and here I found my lord seated, nursing his cane and looking pleasantly forth upon the bay. Not three feet from him sate the Master, stitching. Neither spoke; nor (in this new situation) did my lord so much as cast a glance upon his enemy. He tasted his neighbourhood, I must suppose, less indirectly in the bare proximity of person; and, without doubt, drank deep of hateful pleasures.

He had no sooner come away than I openly joined him.

'My lord, my lord,' said I, 'this is no manner of behaviour.'

'I grow fat upon it,' he replied: and not merely the words, which were strange enough, but the whole character of his expression, shocked me.

'I warn you, my lord, against this indulgency of evil feeling,' said I. 'I know not to which it is more perilous, the soul or the reason; but you go the way to murder both.'

'You cannot understand,' said he. 'You had never such mountains of bitterness upon your heart.'

'And if it were no more,' I added, 'you will surely goad the man to some extremity.'

'To the contrary; I am breaking his spirit,' says my lord.

Every morning for hard upon a week my lord took his same place upon the bench. It was a pleasant place, under the green acacias, with a sight upon the bay and shipping, and a sound (from some way off) of mariners singing at their employ. Here the two sate without speech or any external movement, beyond that of the needle, or the Master biting off a thread, for he still clung to his pretence of industry; and here I made a point to join them, wondering at myself and my companions. If any of my lord's friends went by, he would hail them cheerfully, and cry out he was there to give some good advice to his brother, who was now (to his delight) grown quite industrious. And even this the Master accepted with a steady countenance; what was in his mind, God knows, or perhaps Satan only.

All of a sudden, on a still day of what they call the Indian Summer, when the woods were changed into gold and pink and scarlet, the Master laid down his needle and burst into a fit of merriment. I think he must have been preparing it a long while in silence, for the note in itself was pretty naturally pitched; but breaking suddenly from so extreme a silence, and in circumstances so averse from mirth, it sounded ominously on my ear.

'Henry,' said he, 'I have for once made a false step, and for once you have had the wit to profit by it. The farce of the cobbler ends to-day; and I confess to you (with my compliments) that you have had the best of it. Blood will out; and you have certainly a choice idea of how to make yourself unpleasant.'

Never a word said my lord; it was just as though the Master had not broken silence.

'Come,' resumed the Master, 'do not be sulky; it will spoil your attitude. You can now afford (believe me) to be a little gracious; for I have not merely a defeat to accept. I had meant to continue this performance till I had gathered enough money for a certain purpose; I confess ingenuously I have not the courage. You naturally desire my absence from this town; I have come round by another way to the same idea. And I have a proposition to make; or, if your lordship prefers, a favour to ask.'

'Ask it,' says my lord.

'You may have heard that I had once in this country a considerable treasure,' returned the Master; 'it matters not whether or no – such is the fact; and I was obliged to bury it in a spot of which I have sufficient indications. To the recovery of this has my ambition now come down; and, as it is my own, you will not grudge it me.'

'Go and get it,' says my lord. 'I make no opposition.'

'Yes,' said the Master; 'but to do so I must find men and carriage. The way is long and rough, and the country infested with wild Indians. Advance me only so much as shall be needful: either as a lump sum, in lieu of my allowance; or, if you prefer it, as a loan, which I shall repay on my return. And then, if you so decide, you may have seen the last of me.'

My lord stared him steadily in the eyes; there was a hard smile upon his face, but he uttered nothing.

'Henry,' said the Master, with a formidable quietness, and drawing at the same time somewhat back – 'Henry, I had the honour to address you.'

'Let us be stepping homeward,' says my lord to me, who was plucking at his sleeve; and with that he rose, stretched himself, settled his hat, and, still without a syllable of response, began to walk steadily along the shore.

I hesitated a while between the two brothers, so serious a climax did we seem to have reached. But the Master had resumed his occupation, his eyes lowered, his hand seemingly as deft as ever; and I decided to pursue my lord.

'Are you mad?' I cried, so soon as I had overtook him. 'Would you cast away so fair an opportunity?'

'Is it possible you should still believe in him?' inquired my lord, almost with a sneer.

'I wish him forth of this town!' I cried. 'I wish him anywhere and anyhow but as he is.'

'I have said my say,' returned my lord, 'and you have said yours. There let it rest.'

But I was bent on dislodging the Master. That sight of him patiently returning to his needlework was more than my imagination could digest. There was never a man made, and the Master the least of any, that could accept so long a series of insults. The air smelt blood to me. And I vowed there should be no neglect of mine if, through any chink of possibility, crime could be yet turned aside. That same day, therefore, I came to my lord in his business room, where he sat upon some trivial occupation.

'My lord,' said I, 'I have found a suitable investment for my small economies. But these are unhappily in Scotland; it will take some time to lift them, and the affair presses. Could your lordship see his way to advance me the amount against my note?'

He read me a while with keen eyes. 'I have never inquired into the state of your affairs, Mackellar,' says he. 'Beyond the amount of your caution, you may not be worth a farthing, for what I know.'

'I have been a long while in your service, and never told a lie, nor yet asked a favour for myself,' said I, 'until to-day.'

'A favour for the Master,' he returned quietly. 'Do you take me for a fool, Mackellar? Understand it once and for all, I treat this beast in my own way; fear nor favour shall not move me; and before I am hoodwinked, it will require a trickster less transparent than yourself. I ask service, loyal service; not that you should make and mar behind my back, and steal my own money to defeat me.'

'My lord,' said I, 'these are very unpardonable expressions.'

'Think once more, Mackellar,' he replied; 'and you will see they fit the fact. It is your own subterfuge that is unpardonable. Deny (if you can) that you designed this money to evade my orders with, and I will ask your pardon freely. If you cannot, you must have the resolution to hear your conduct go by its own name.'

'If you think I had any design but to save you—' I began.

'O! my old friend,' said he, 'you know very well what I think! Here is my hand to you with all my heart; but of money, not one rap.'

Defeated upon this side, I went straight to my room, wrote a letter, ran with it to the harbour, for I knew a ship was on the point of sailing; and came to the Master's door a little before dusk. Entering without the form of any knock, I found him sitting with his Indian at a simple meal of maize porridge with some milk. The house within was clean and poor; only a few books upon a shelf distinguished it, and (in one corner) Secundra's little bench.

'Mr Bally,' said I, 'I have near five hundred pounds laid by in Scotland, the economies of a hard life. A letter goes by yon ship to have it lifted. Have so much patience till the return ship comes in, and it is all yours, upon the same condition you offered to my lord this morning.'

He rose from the table, came forward, took me by the shoulders, and looked me in the face, smiling.

'And yet you are very fond of money!' said he. 'And yet you love money beyond all things else, except my brother.'

'I fear old age and poverty,' said I, 'which is another matter.'

'I will never quarrel for a name. Call it so,' he replied. – 'Ah! Mackellar, Mackellar, if this were done from any love to me, how gladly would I close upon your offer!'

'And yet,' I eagerly answered – 'I say it to my shame, but I cannot see you in this poor place without compunction. It is not my single thought, nor my first; and yet it's there! I would gladly see you delivered. I do not offer it in love, and far from that; but, as God judges me – and I wonder at it too! – quite without enmity.'

'Ah!' says he, still holding my shoulders, and now gently shaking me, 'you think of me more than you suppose. "And I wonder at it too,"' he added, repeating my expression and, I suppose, something of my voice. 'You are an honest man, and for that cause I spare you.'

'Spare me?' I cried.

'Spare you,' he repeated, letting me go and turning away. And then, fronting me once more: 'You little know what I would do with it, Mackellar! Did you think I had swallowed my defeat indeed? Listen: my life has been a series of unmerited cast-backs. That fool, Prince Charlie, mismanaged a most promising affair: there fell my first fortune. In Paris I had my foot once more high up on the ladder: that time it was an accident; a letter came to the wrong hand, and I was bare again. A third time I found my opportunity; I built up a place for myself in India with an infinite patience; and then Clive[3] came, my rajah was swallowed up, and I escaped out of the convulsion, like another Æneas,[4] with Secundra Dass upon my back. Three times I have had my hand upon the highest station: and I am not yet three-and-forty. I know the world as few men know it when they come to die – Court and camp, the East and the West; I know where to go, I see a thousand openings. I am now at the height of my resources, sound of health, of inordinate ambition. Well, all this I resign; I care not if I die, and the world never hear of me; I care only for one thing, and that I will have. Mind yourself; lest, when the roof falls, you too should be crushed under the ruins.'

As I came out of his house, all hope of intervention quite destroyed, I was aware of a stir on the harbour-side, and, raising my eyes, there was a great ship newly come to anchor. It seems strange I could have looked upon her with so much indifference, for she brought death to the brothers of Durrisdeer. After all the desperate episodes of this contention, the insults, the opposing interests, the fraternal duel in the shrubbery, it was reserved for some poor devil in Grub Street, scribbling for his dinner, and not caring what he scribbled, to cast a spell across four thousand miles of the salt sea, and send forth both these brothers into savage and wintry deserts, there to die. But such a thought was distant from my mind; and while all the provincials were fluttered about me by the unusual animation of their port, I passed throughout their midst on my return homeward, quite absorbed in the recollection of my visit and the Master's speech.

The same night there was brought to us from the ship a little packet of pamphlets. The next day my lord was under engagement to go with the Governor upon some party of pleasure; the time was nearly due, and I left him for a moment alone in his room and skimming through the pamphlets. When I returned, his head had fallen upon the table, his arms lying abroad amongst the crumpled papers.

'My lord, my lord!' I cried as I ran forward, for I supposed he was in some fit.

He sprang up like a figure upon wires, his countenance deformed with fury, so that in a strange place I should scarce have known him. His hand at the same time flew above his head, as though to strike me down. 'Leave me alone!' he screeched, and I fled, as fast as my shaking legs would bear me, for my lady. She, too, lost no time; but when we returned, he had the door locked within, and only cried to us from the other side to leave him be. We looked in each other's faces, very white – each supposing the blow had come at last.

'I will write to the Governor to excuse him,' says she. 'We must keep our strong friends.' But when she took up the pen it flew out of her fingers. 'I cannot write,' said she. 'Can you?'

'I will make a shift, my lady,' said I.

She looked over me as I wrote. 'That will do,' she said, when I had done. 'Thank God, Mackellar, I have you to lean upon! But what can it be now? What, what can it be?'

In my own mind I believed there was no explanation possible, and none required; it was my fear that the man's madness had now simply burst forth its way, like the long-smothered flames of a volcano; but to this (in mere mercy to my lady) I durst not give expression.

'It is more to the purpose to consider our own behaviour,' said I. 'Must we leave him there alone?'

'I do not dare disturb him,' she replied. 'Nature may know best; it may be Nature that cries to be alone; and we grope in the dark. O yes, I would leave him as he is.'

'I will, then, despatch this letter, my lady, and return here, if you please, to sit with you,' said I.

'Pray do,' cries my lady.

All afternoon we sat together, mostly in silence, watching my lord's door. My own mind was busy with the scene that had just passed, and its singular resemblance to my vision. I must say a word upon this, for the story has gone abroad with great exaggeration, and I have even seen it printed, and my own name referred to for particulars. So much was the same: here was my lord in a room, with his head upon the table, and when he raised his face, it wore such an expression as distressed me to the soul. But the room was different, my lord's attitude at the table not at all the same, and his face, when he disclosed it, expressed a painful degree of fury instead of that haunting despair which had always (except once, already referred to) characterised it in the vision. There is the whole truth at last before the public; and if the differences be great, the coincidence was yet enough to fill me with uneasiness. All afternoon, as I say, I sat and pondered upon this quite to myself; for my lady had trouble of her own, and it was my last thought to vex her with fancies. About the midst of our time of waiting, she conceived an ingenious scheme, had Mr Alexander fetched, and bid him knock at his father's door. My lord sent the boy about his business, but without the least violence, whether of manner or expression; so that I began to entertain a hope the fit was over.

At last, as the night fell and I was lighting a lamp that stood there trimmed, the door opened and my lord stood within upon the threshold. The light was not so strong that we could read his countenance; when he spoke, methought his voice a little altered, but yet perfectly steady.

'Mackellar,' said he, 'carry this note to its destination with your own hand. It is highly private. Find the person alone when you deliver it.'

'Henry,' says my lady, 'you are not ill?'

'No, no,' says he querulously, 'I am occupied. Not at all; I am only occupied. It is a singular thing a man must be supposed to be ill when he has any business! Send me supper to this room, and a basket of wine: I expect the visit of a friend. Otherwise I am not to be disturbed.'

And with that he once more shut himself in.

The note was addressed to one Captain Harris, at a tavern on the port-side. I knew Harris (by reputation) for a dangerous adventurer, highly suspected of piracy in the past, and now following the rude business of an Indian trader. What my lord should have to say to him, or he to my lord, it passed my imagination to conceive: or yet how my lord had heard of him, unless by a disgraceful trial from which the man was recently escaped. Altogether I went upon the errand with reluctance, and from the little I saw of the Captain, returned from it with sorrow. I found him in a foul-smelling chamber, sitting by a guttering candle and an empty bottle; he had the remains of a military carriage, or rather perhaps it was an affectation, for his manners were low.

'Tell my lord, with my service, that I will wait upon his lordship in the inside of half an hour,' says he, when he had read the note; and then had the servility, pointing to his empty bottle, to propose that I should buy him liquor.

Although I returned with my best speed, the Captain followed close upon my heels; and he stayed late into the night. The cock was crowing a second time when I saw (from my chamber window) my lord lighting him to the gate, both men very much affected with their potations, and sometimes leaning one upon the other to confabulate. Yet the next morning my lord was abroad again early with a hundred pounds of money in his pocket. I never supposed that he returned with it; and yet I was quite sure it did not find its way to the Master, for I lingered all morning within view of the booth. That was the last time my Lord Durrisdeer passed his own enclosure till we left New York; he walked in his barn, or sat and talked with his family, all much as usual; but the town saw nothing of him, and his daily visits to the Master seemed forgotten. Nor yet did Harris reappear; or not until the end.

I was now much oppressed with a sense of the mysteries in which we had begun to move. It was plain, if only from his change of habitude, my lord had something on his mind of a grave nature; but what it was, whence it sprang, or why he should now keep the house and garden, I could make no guess at. It was clear, even to probation, the pamphlets had some share in this revolution; I read all I could find, and they were all extremely insignificant, and of the usual kind of party scurrility; even to a high politician, I could spy out no particular matter of offence, and my lord was a man rather indifferent on public questions. The truth is, the pamphlet which was the spring of this affair lay all the time on my lord's bosom. There it was that I found it at last, after he was dead, in the midst of the north wilderness: in such a place, in such dismal circumstances, I was to read for the first time these idle, lying words of a Whig pamphleteer declaiming against indulgency to Jacobites: – 'Another notorious Rebel, the *M—r* of *B—e*, is to have his Title restored,' the passage ran. 'This Business has been long in hand, since he rendered some very disgraceful Services in Scotland and France. His Brother, *L—d D—r*, is known to be no better than himself in Inclination; and the supposed Heir, who is now to be set aside, was bred up in the most detestable Principles. In the old Phrase, it is *six of the one and half a dozen of the other*; but the Favour of such a Reposition is too extreme to be passed over.' A man in his right wits could not have cared two straws for a tale so manifestly false; that Government should ever entertain the notion was inconceivable to any reasoning creature, unless possibly the fool that penned it; and my lord, though never brilliant, was ever remarkable for sense. That he should credit such a rodomontade, and carry the pamphlet on his bosom and the words in his heart, is the clear proof of the man's lunacy. Doubtless the mere mention of Mr Alexander, and the threat directly held out against the child's succession, precipitated that which had so long impended. Or else my master had been truly mad for a long time, and we were too dull or too much used to him, and did not perceive the extent of his infirmity.

About a week after the day of the pamphlets I was late upon the harbour-side, and took a turn towards the Master's, as I often did. The door opened, a flood of light came forth upon the road, and I beheld a man taking his departure with friendly salutations. I cannot say how singularly I was shaken to recognise the adventurer Harris. I could not but conclude it was the hand of my lord that had brought him there; and prolonged my walk in very serious and apprehensive thought. It was late when I came home, and there was my lord making up his portmanteau for a voyage.

'Why do you come so late?' he cried. 'We leave to-morrow for Albany, you and I together; and it is high time you were about your preparations.'

'For Albany, my lord?' I cried. 'And for what earthly purpose?'

'Change of scene,' said he.

And my lady, who appeared to have been weeping, gave me the signal to obey without more parley. She told me a little later (when we found occasion to exchange some words) that he had suddenly announced his intention after a visit from Captain Harris, and her best endeavours, whether to dissuade him from the journey, or to elicit some explanation of its purpose, had alike proved unavailing.

THE JOURNEY IN THE WILDERNESS

We made a prosperous voyage up that fine river of the Hudson, the weather grateful, the hills singularly beautified with the colours of the autumn. At Albany we had our residence at an inn, where I was not so blind and my lord not so cunning but what I could see he had some design to hold me prisoner. The work he found for me to do was not so pressing that we should transact it apart from necessary papers in the chamber of an inn; nor was it of such importance that I should be set upon as many as four or five scrolls of the same document. I submitted in appearance; but I took private measures on my own side, and had the news of the town communicated to me daily by the politeness of our host. In this way I received at last a piece of intelligence for which, I may say, I had been waiting. Captain Harris (I was told) with 'Mr Mountain, the trader,'[1] had gone by up the river in a boat. I would have feared the landlord's eye, so strong the sense of some complicity upon my master's part oppressed me. But I made out to say I had some knowledge of the Captain, although none of Mr Mountain, and to inquire who else was of the party. My informant knew not; Mr Mountain had come ashore upon some needful purchases; had gone round the town buying, drinking, and prating; and it seemed the party went upon some likely venture, for he had spoken much of great things he would do when he returned. No more was known, for none of the rest had come ashore, and it seemed they were pressed for time to reach a certain spot before the snow should fall.

And sure enough, the next day there fell a sprinkle even in Albany; but it passed as it came, and was but a reminder of what lay before us. I thought of it lightly then, knowing so little as I did of that inclement province: the retrospect is different; and I wonder at times if some of the horror of these events which I must now rehearse flowed not from the foul skies and savage winds to which we were exposed, and the agony of cold that we must suffer.

The boat having passed by, I thought at first we should have left the town. But no such matter. My lord continued his stay in Albany, where he had no ostensible affairs, and kept me by him, far from my due employment, and making a pretence of occupation. It is upon this passage I expect, and perhaps deserve, censure. I was not so dull but what I had my own thoughts. I could not see the Master intrust himself into the hands of Harris, and not suspect some underhand contrivance. Harris bore a villainous reputation, and he had been tampered with in private by my lord; Mountain, the trader, proved, upon inquiry, to be another of the same kidney; the errand they were all gone upon being the recovery of ill-gotten treasures, offered in itself a very strong incentive to foul play; and the character of the country where they journeyed promised impunity to deeds of blood. Well: it is true I had all these thoughts and fears, and guesses of the Master's fate. But you are to consider I was the same man that sought to dash him from the bulwarks of a ship in the mid-sea; the same that, a little before, very impiously but sincerely offered God a bargain, seeking to hire God to be my bravo.[2] It is true again that I had a good deal melted towards our enemy. But this I always thought of as a weakness of the flesh, and even culpable; my mind remaining steady and quite bent against him. True, yet again, that it was one thing to assume on my own shoulders the guilt and danger of a criminal attempt, and another to stand by and see my lord imperil and besmirch himself. But this was the very ground of my inaction. For (should I anyway stir in the business) I might fail indeed to save the Master, but I could not miss to make a byword of my lord.

Thus it was that I did nothing; and upon the same reasons, I am still strong to justify my course. My lord had carried with him several introductions to chief people of the town and neighbourhood; others he had before encountered in New York: with this consequence, that he went much abroad, and I am sorry to say was altogether too convivial in his habits. I was often in bed, but never asleep, when he returned; and there was scarce a night when he did not betray the influence of liquor. By day he would still lay upon me endless tasks, which he showed considerable ingenuity to fish up and renew, in the manner of Penelope's web.[3] I never refused, as I say, for I was hired to do his bidding; but I took no pains to keep my penetration under a bushel, and would sometimes smile in his face.

'I think I must be the devil and you Michael Scott,'[4] I said to him one day. 'I have bridged Tweed and split the Eildons; and now you set me to the rope of sand.'

He looked at me with shining eyes, and looked away again, his jaw chewing, but without words.

'Well, well, my lord,' said I, 'your will is my pleasure. I will do this thing for the fourth time; but I would beg of you to invent another task against to-morrow, for by my troth, I am weary of this one.'

'You do not know what you are saying,' returned my lord, putting on his hat and turning his back to me. 'It is a strange thing you should take a pleasure to annoy me. A friend – but that is a different affair. It is a strange thing. I am a man that has had ill-fortune all my life through. I am still surrounded by contrivances. I am always treading in plots,' he burst out. 'The whole world is banded against me.'

'I would not talk wicked nonsense if I were you,' said I; 'but I will tell you what I *would* do – I would put my head in cold water, for you had more last night than you could carry.'

'Do ye think that?' said he, with a manner of interest highly awakened. 'Would that be good for me? It's a thing I never tried.'

'I mind the days when you had no call to try, and I wish, my lord, that they were back again,' said I. 'But the plain truth is, if you continue to exceed, you will do yourself a mischief.'

'I don't appear to carry drink the way I used to,' said my lord. 'I get overtaken, Mackellar. But I will be more upon my guard.'

'That is what I would ask of you,' I replied. 'You are to bear in mind that you are Mr Alexander's father: give the bairn a chance to carry his name with some responsibility.'

'Ay, ay,' said he. 'Ye're a very sensible man, Mackellar, and have been long in my employ. But I think, if you have nothing more to say to me I will be stepping. If you have nothing more to say?' he added, with that burning, childish eagerness that was now so common with the man.

'No, my lord, I have nothing more,' said I, dryly enough.

'Then I think I will be stepping,' says my lord, and stood and looked at me, fidgeting with his hat, which he had taken off again. 'I suppose you will have no errands? No? I am to meet Sir William Johnson,[5] but I will be more upon my guard.' He was silent for a time, and then, smiling: 'Do you call to mind a place, Mackellar – it's a little below Eagles – where the burn runs very deep under a wood of rowans? I mind being there when I was a lad – dear, it comes over me like an old song! – I was after the fishing, and I made a bonny cast. Eh, but I was happy. I wonder, Mackellar, why I am never happy now?'

'My lord,' said I, 'if you would drink with more moderation you would have the better chance. It is an old byword that the bottle is a false consoler.'

'No doubt,' said he, 'no doubt. Well, I think I will be going.'

'Good-morning, my lord,' said I.

'Good-morning, good-morning,' said he, and so got himself at last from the apartment.

I give that for a fair specimen of my lord in the morning; and I must have described my patron very ill if the reader does not perceive a notable falling off. To behold the man thus fallen: to know him accepted among his companions for a poor, muddled toper, welcome (if he were welcome at all) for the bare consideration of his title; and to recall the virtues he had once displayed against such odds of fortune; was not this a thing at once to rage and to be humbled at?

In his cups, he was more excessive. I will give but the one scene, close upon the end, which is strongly marked upon my memory to this day, and at the time affected me almost with horror.

I was in bed, lying there awake, when I heard him stumbling on the stair and singing. My lord had no gift of music, his brother had all the graces of the family, so that when I say singing, you are to understand a manner of high, carolling utterance, which was truly neither speech nor song. Something not unlike is to be heard upon the lips of children, ere they learn shame; from those of a man grown elderly it had a strange effect. He opened the door with noisy precaution; peered in, shading his candle; conceived me to slumber; entered, set his light upon the table, and took off his hat. I saw him very plain; a high, feverish exultation appeared to boil in his veins, and he stood and smiled and smirked upon the candle. Presently he lifted up his arm, snapped his fingers, and fell to undress. As he did so, having once more forgot my presence, he took back to his singing; and now I could hear the words, which were these from the old song of the *Twa Corbies*[6] endlessly repeated:

> 'And over his banes when they are bare
> The wind sall blaw for evermair!'

I have said there was no music in the man. His strains had no logical succession except in so far as they inclined a little to the minor mode; but they exercised a rude potency upon the feelings, and followed the words, and signified the feelings of the singer with barbaric fitness. He took it first in the time and manner of a rant; presently this ill-favoured gleefulness abated, he began to dwell upon the notes more feelingly, and sank at last into a degree of maudlin pathos that was to me scarce bearable. By equal steps, the original briskness of his acts declined; and when he was stripped to his breeches, he sat on the bedside and fell to whimpering. I know nothing less respectable than the tears of drunkenness, and turned my back impatiently on this poor sight.

But he had started himself (I am to suppose) on that slippery descent of self-pity; on the which, to a man unstrung by old sorrows and recent potations, there is no arrest except exhaustion. His tears continued to flow, and the man to sit there, three parts naked, in the cold air of the chamber. I twitted myself alternately with inhumanity and sentimental weakness, now half rising in my bed to interfere, now reading myself lessons of indifference and courting slumber, until, upon a sudden, the *quantum mutatus ab illo*[7] shot into my mind; and calling to remembrance his old wisdom, constancy, and patience, I was overborne with a pity almost approaching the passionate, not for my master alone, but for the sons of man.

At this I leaped from my place, went over to his side and laid a hand on his bare shoulder, which was cold as stone. He uncovered his face and showed it me all swollen and begrutten* like a child's; and at the sight my impatience partially revived.

'Think shame to yourself,' said I. 'This is bairnly conduct. I might have been snivelling myself, if I had cared to swill my belly with wine. But I went to my bed sober like a man. Come: get into yours, and have done with this pitiable exhibition.'

'O, Mackellar,' said he, 'my heart is wae!'

'Wae?' cried I. 'For a good cause, I think. What words were these you sang as you came in? Show pity to others, we then can talk of pity to yourself. You can be the one thing or the other, but I will be no party to half-way houses. If you're a striker, strike, and if you're a bleater, bleat!'

'Ay!' cries he, with a burst, 'that's it – strike! that's talking! Man, I've stood it all too long. But when they laid a hand upon the child, when the child's threatened' – his momentary vigour whimpering off – 'my child, my Alexander!' – and he was at his tears again.

I took him by the shoulders and shook him. 'Alexander!' said I. 'Do you even think of him? Not you! Look yourself in the face like a brave man, and you'll find you're but a self-deceiver. The wife, the friend, the child, they're all equally forgot, and you sunk in a mere bog of selfishness.'

'Mackellar,' said he, with a wonderful return to his old manner and appearance, 'you may say what you will to me, but one thing I never was – I was never selfish.'

'I will open your eyes in your despite,' said I. 'How long have we been here? and how often have you written to your family? I think this is the first time you were ever separate: have you written at all? Do they know if you are dead or living?'

I had caught him here too openly; it braced his better nature; there was no more weeping, he thanked me very penitently, got to bed, and was soon fast asleep; and the first thing he did the next morning was to sit down and begin a letter to my lady: a very tender letter it

* Tear-marked.

was too, though it was never finished. Indeed, all communication with New York was transacted by myself; and it will be judged I had a thankless task of it. What to tell my lady, and in what words, and how far to be false and how far cruel, was a thing that kept me often from my slumber.

All this while, no doubt, my lord waited with growing impatiency for news of his accomplices. Harris, it is to be thought, had promised a high degree of expedition; the time was already overpast when word was to be looked for; and suspense was a very evil counsellor to a man of an impaired intelligence. My lord's mind throughout this interval dwelled almost wholly in the wilderness, following that party with whose deeds he had so much concern. He continually conjured up their camps and progresses, the fashion of the country, the perpetration in a thousand different manners of the same horrid fact, and that consequent spectacle of the Master's bones lying scattered in the wind. These private, guilty considerations I would continually observe to peep forth in the man's talk, like rabbits from a hill.[8] And it is the less wonder if the scene of his meditations began to draw him bodily.

It is well known what pretext he took. Sir William Johnson had a diplomatic errand in these parts; and my lord and I (from curiosity, as was given out) went in his company. Sir William was well attended and liberally supplied. Hunters brought us venison, fish was taken for us daily in the streams, and brandy ran like water. We proceeded by day and encamped by night in the military style; sentinels were set and changed; every man had his named duty; and Sir William was the spring of all. There was much in this that might at times have entertained me; but, for our misfortune, the weather was extremely harsh, the days were in the beginning open, but the nights frosty from the first. A painful keen wind blew most of the time, so that we sat in the boat with blue fingers, and at night, as we scorched our faces at the fire, the clothes upon our back appeared to be of paper. A dreadful solitude surrounded our steps; the land was quite dispeopled, there was no smoke of fires; and save for a single boat of merchants on the second day, we met no travellers. The season was indeed late, but this desertion of the waterways impressed Sir William himself; and I have heard him more than once express a sense of intimidation. 'I have come too late, I fear;

they must have dug up the hatchet,' he said; and the future proved how justly he had reasoned.

I could never depict the blackness of my soul upon this journey. I have none of those minds that are in love with the unusual: to see the winter coming and to lie in the field so far from any house, oppressed me like a nightmare; it seemed, indeed, a kind of awful braving of God's power; and this thought, which I daresay only writes me down a coward, was greatly exaggerated by my private knowledge of the errand we were come upon. I was besides encumbered by my duties to Sir William, whom it fell upon me to entertain; for my lord was quite sunk into a state bordering on *pervigilium*,[9] watching the woods with a rapt eye, sleeping scarce at all, and speaking sometimes not twenty words in a whole day. That which he said was still coherent; but it turned almost invariably upon the party for whom he kept his crazy look-out. He would tell Sir William often, and always as if it were a new communication, that he had 'a brother somewhere in the woods,' and beg that the sentinels should be directed 'to inquire for him.' 'I am anxious for news of my brother,' he would say. And sometimes, when we were under way, he would fancy he spied a canoe far off upon the water or a camp on the shore, and exhibit painful agitation. It was impossible but Sir William should be struck with these singularities; and at last he led me aside, and hinted his uneasiness. I touched my head and shook it; quite rejoiced to prepare a little testimony against possible disclosures.

'But in that case,' cries Sir William, 'is it wise to let him go at large?'

'Those that know him best,' said I, 'are persuaded that he should be humoured.'

'Well, well,' replied Sir William, 'it is none of my affairs. But if I had understood, you would never have been here.'

Our advance into this savage country had thus uneventfully proceeded for about a week, when we encamped for a night at a place where the river ran among considerable mountains clothed in wood. The fires were lighted on a level space at the water's edge; and we supped and lay down to sleep in the customary fashion. It chanced the night fell murderously cold; the stringency of the frost seized and bit me through my coverings, so that pain kept me wakeful; and I was afoot again before the peep of day, crouching by the fires or trotting to and fro at the stream's edge, to combat the aching of my limbs. At last dawn began to break upon hoar woods and mountains, the sleepers rolled in their robes, and the boisterous river dashing among spears of ice. I stood looking about me, swaddled in my stiff coat of a bull's fur, and the breath smoking from my scorched nostrils, when, upon a sudden, a singular, eager cry rang from the borders of the wood. The sentries answered it, the sleepers sprang to their feet; one pointed, the rest followed his direction with their eyes, and there, upon the edge of the forest, and betwixt two trees, we beheld the figure of a man reaching forth his hands like one in ecstasy. The next moment he ran forward, fell on his knees at the side of the camp, and burst in tears.

This was John Mountain, the trader, escaped from the most horrid perils; and his first word, when he got speech, was to ask if we had seen Secundra Dass.

'Seen what?' cries Sir William.

'No,' said I, 'we have seen nothing of him. Why?'

'Nothing?' says Mountain. 'Then I was right after all.' With that he struck his palm upon his brow. 'But what takes him back?' he cried. 'What takes the man back among dead bodies? There is some damned mystery here.'

This was a word which highly aroused our curiosity, but I shall be more perspicacious if I narrate these incidents in their true order. Here follows a narrative which I have compiled out of three sources, not very consistent in all points:

First, a written statement by Mountain, in which everything criminal is cleverly smuggled out of view;

Second, two conversations with Secundra Dass; and

Third, many conversations with Mountain himself, in which he was pleased to be entirely plain; for the truth is he regarded me as an accomplice.

NARRATIVE OF THE TRADER, MOUNTAIN

The crew that went up the river under the joint command of Captain Harris and the Master numbered in all nine persons, of whom (if I except Secundra Dass) there was not one that had not merited the gallows. From Harris downward the voyagers were notorious in that colony for desperate, bloody-minded miscreants; some were reputed pirates, the most hawkers of rum; all ranters and drinkers; all fit associates, embarking together without remorse, upon this treacherous and murderous design. I could not hear there was much discipline or any set captain in the gang; but Harris and four others, Mountain himself, two Scotsmen – Pinkerton and Hastie – and a man of the name of Hicks, a drunken shoemaker, put their heads together and agreed upon the course. In a material sense, they were well enough provided; and the Master in particular brought with him a tent where he might enjoy some privacy and shelter.

Even this small indulgence told against him in the minds of his companions. But indeed he was in a position so entirely false (and even ridiculous) that all his habit of command and arts of pleasing were here thrown away. In the eyes of all, except Secundra Dass, he figured as a common gull and designated victim; going unconsciously to death; yet he could not but suppose himself the contriver and the leader of the expedition; he could scarce help but so conduct himself; and at the least hint of authority or condescension, his deceivers would be laughing in their sleeves. I was so used to see and to conceive him in a high, authoritative attitude, that when I had conceived his position on this journey, I was pained and could have blushed. How soon he may have entertained a first surmise, we cannot know; but it was long, and the party had advanced into the wilderness beyond the reach of any help, ere he was fully awakened to the truth.

It fell thus. Harris and some others had drawn apart into the woods for consultation, when they were startled by a rustling in the brush. They were all accustomed to the arts of Indian warfare, and Mountain had not only lived and hunted, but fought and earned some reputation, with the savages. He could move in the woods without noise, and follow a trail like a hound; and upon the emergence of this alert, he was deputed by the rest to plunge into the thicket for intelligence. He was soon convinced there was a man in his close neighbourhood, moving with precaution but without art among the leaves and branches; and coming shortly to a place of advantage, he was able to observe Secundra Dass crawling briskly off with many backward glances. At this he knew not whether to laugh or cry; and his accomplices, when he had returned and reported, were in much the same dubiety. There was now no danger of an Indian onslaught; but on the other hand, since Secundra Dass was at the pains to spy upon them, it was highly probable he knew English, and if he knew English it was certain the whole of their design was in the Master's knowledge. There was one singularity in the position. If Secundra Dass knew and concealed his knowledge of English, Harris was a proficient in several of the tongues of India, and as his career in that part of the world had been a great deal worse than profligate, he had not thought proper to remark upon the circumstance. Each side had thus a spy-hole on the counsels of the other. The plotters, so soon as this advantage was explained, returned to camp; Harris, hearing the Hindustani was once more closeted with his master, crept to the side of the tent; and the rest, sitting about the fire with their tobacco, awaited his report with impatience. When he came at last, his face was very black. He had overheard enough to confirm the worst of his suspicions. Secundra Dass was a good English scholar; he had been some days creeping and listening, the Master was now fully informed of the conspiracy, and the pair proposed on the morrow to fall out of line at a carrying place and plunge at a venture in the woods: preferring the full risk of famine, savage beasts, and savage men to their position in the midst of traitors.

What, then, was to be done? Some were for killing the Master on the spot; but Harris assured them that would be a crime without profit, since the secret of the treasure must die along with him that buried it. Others were for desisting at once from the whole enterprise and making for New York; but the appetising name of treasure, and the thought of the long way they had already travelled, dissuaded the majority. I imagine they were dull fellows for the most part. Harris, indeed, had some acquirements, Mountain was no fool, Hastie was an educated man; but even these had manifestly failed in life, and the rest were the dregs of colonial rascality. The conclusion they reached, at least, was more the offspring of greed and hope than reason. It was to temporise, to be wary and watch the Master, to be silent and supply no further aliment to his suspicions, and to depend entirely (as well as I make out) on the chance that their victim was as greedy, hopeful, and irrational as themselves, and might, after all, betray his life and treasure.

Twice in the course of the next day Secundra and the Master must have appeared to themselves to have escaped; and twice they were circumvented. The Master, save that the second time he grew a little pale, displayed no sign of disappointment, apologised for the stupidity with which he had fallen aside, thanked his recapturers as for a service, and rejoined the caravan with all his usual gallantry and cheerfulness of mien and bearing. But it is certain he had smelled a rat; for from thenceforth he and Secundra spoke only in each other's ear, and Harris listened and shivered by the tent in vain. The same night it was announced they were to leave the boats and proceed by foot, a circumstance which (as it put an end to the confusion of the portages) greatly lessened the chances of escape.

And now there began between the two sides a silent contest, for life on the one hand, for riches on the other. They were now near that quarter of the desert in which the Master himself must begin to play the part of guide; and using this for a pretext of persecution, Harris and his men sat with him every night about the fire, and laboured to entrap him into some admission. If he let slip his secret, he knew well it was the warrant for his death; on the other hand, he durst not refuse their questions, and must appear to help them to the best of his capacity, or he practically published his mistrust. And yet Mountain assures me the man's brow was never ruffled. He sat in the midst of these jackals, his life depending by a thread, like some easy, witty householder at home by his own fire; an answer he had for everything – as often as not, a jesting answer; avoided threats, evaded insults; talked, laughed, and listened with an open countenance; and, in short, conducted himself in such a manner as must have disarmed suspicion, and went near to stagger knowledge. Indeed, Mountain confessed to me they would soon have disbelieved the Captain's story, and supposed their designated victim still quite innocent of their designs; but for the fact that he continued (however ingeniously) to give the slip to questions, and the yet stronger confirmation of his repeated efforts to escape. The last of these, which brought things to a head, I am now to relate. And first I should say that by this time the temper of Harris's companions was utterly worn out; civility was scarce pretended; and, for one very significant circumstance, the Master and Secundra had been (on some pretext) deprived of weapons. On their side, however, the threatened pair kept up the parade of friendship handsomely; Secundra was all bows, the Master all smiles; and on the last night of the truce he had even gone so far as to sing for the diversion of the company. It was observed that he had also eaten with unusual heartiness, and drank deep, doubtless from design.

At least, about three in the morning, he came out of the tent into the open air, audibly mourning and complaining, with all the manner of a sufferer from surfeit. For some while, Secundra publicly attended on his patron, who at last became more easy, and fell asleep on the frosty ground behind the tent, the Indian returning within. Some time after, the sentry was changed; had the Master pointed out to him, where he lay in what is called a robe of buffalo: and thenceforth kept an eye upon him (he declared) without remission. With the first of the dawn, a draught of wind came suddenly and blew open one side the corner of the robe; and with the same puff, the Master's hat whirled in the air and fell some yards away. The sentry thinking it remarkable the sleeper should not awaken, thereupon drew near; and the next moment, with a great shout, informed the camp their prisoner was escaped. He had left behind his Indian, who (in the first vivacity of the surprise) came near to pay the forfeit of his life, and was, in fact, inhumanly mishandled; but Secundra, in the midst of threats and cruelties, stuck to it with extraordinary loyalty, that he was quite ignorant of his master's plans, which might indeed be true, and of the manner of his escape, which was demonstrably false. Nothing was therefore left to the conspirators but to rely entirely on the skill of

Mountain. The night had been frosty, the ground quite hard; and the sun was no sooner up than a strong thaw set in. It was Mountain's boast that few men could have followed that trail, and still fewer (even of the native Indians) found it. The Master had thus a long start before his pursuers had the scent, and he must have travelled with surprising energy for a pedestrian so unused, since it was near noon before Mountain had a view of him. At this conjuncture the trader was alone, all his companions following, at his own request, several hundred yards in the rear; he knew the Master was unarmed; his heart was besides heated with the exercise and lust of hunting; and seeing the quarry so close, so defenceless, and seeming so fatigued, he vaingloriously determined to effect the capture with his single hand. A step or two farther brought him to one margin of a little clearing; on the other, with his arms folded and his back to a huge stone, the Master sat. It is possible Mountain may have made a rustle, it is certain, at least, the Master raised his head and gazed directly at that quarter of the thicket where his hunter lay; 'I could not be sure he saw me,' Mountain said; 'he just looked my way like a man with his mind made up, and all the courage ran out of me like rum out of a bottle.' And presently, when the Master looked away again, and appeared to resume those meditations in which he had sat immersed before the trader's coming, Mountain slunk stealthily back and returned to seek the help of his companions.

And now began the chapter of surprises, for the scout had scarce informed the others of his discovery, and they were yet preparing their weapons for a rush upon the fugitive, when the man himself appeared in their midst, walking openly and quietly, with his hands behind his back.

'Ah, men!' says he, on his beholding them. 'Here is a fortunate encounter. Let us get back to camp.'

Mountain had not mentioned his own weakness or the Master's disconcerting gaze upon the thicket, so that (with all the rest) his return appeared spontaneous. For all that, a hubbub arose; oaths flew, fists were shaken, and guns pointed.

'Let us get back to camp,' said the Master. 'I have an explanation to make, but it must be laid before you all. And in the meanwhile I would put up these weapons, one of which might very easily go off and blow away your hopes of treasure. I would not kill,' says he, smiling, 'the goose with the golden eggs.'

The charm of his superiority once more triumphed; and the party, in no particular order, set off on their return. By the way, he found occasion to get a word or two apart with Mountain.

'You are a clever fellow and a bold,' says he, 'but I am not so sure that you are doing yourself justice. I would have you to consider whether you would not do better, ay, and safer, to serve me instead of serving so commonplace a rascal as Mr Harris. Consider of it,' he concluded, dealing the man a gentle tap upon the shoulder, 'and don't be in haste. Dead or alive, you will find me an ill man to quarrel with.'

When they were come back to the camp, where Harris and Pinkerton stood guard over Secundra, these two ran upon the Master like viragoes, and were amazed out of measure when they were bidden by their comrades to 'stand back and hear what the gentleman had to say.' The Master had not flinched before their onslaught; nor, at this proof of the ground he had gained, did he betray the least sufficiency.

'Do not let us be in haste,' says he. 'Meat first and public speaking after.'

With that they made a hasty meal: and as soon as it was done, the Master, leaning on one elbow, began his speech. He spoke long, addressing himself to each except Harris, finding for each (with the same exception) some particular flattery. He called them 'bold, honest blades,' declared he had never seen a more jovial company, work better done, or pains more merrily supported. 'Well, then,' says he, 'some one asks me, Why the devil I ran away? But that is scarce worth answer, for I think you all know pretty well. But you know only pretty well: that is a point I shall arrive at presently, and be you ready to remark it when it comes. There is a traitor here: a double traitor: I will give you his name before I am done; and let that suffice for now. But here comes some other gentleman and asks me, "Why, in the devil, I came back?" Well, before I answer that question, I have one to put to you. It was this cur here, this Harris, that speaks Hindustani?' cries he, rising on one knee and pointing fair at the man's face, with a gesture indescribably menacing; and when he had been answered in the affirmative, 'Ah!' says he, 'then are all my suspicions verified, and I did rightly to come back. Now, men, hear the truth for the first time.' Thereupon he launched forth in a long story, told with extraordinary skill, how he had all along suspected Harris, how he had found the confirmation of his fears, and how Harris must have misrepresented what passed between Secundra and himself. At this point he made a bold stroke with excellent effect. 'I suppose,' says he, 'you think you are going shares with Harris, I suppose you think you will see to that yourselves; you would naturally not think so flat a rogue could cozen you. But have a care! These half-idiots have a sort of cunning, as the skunk has its stench; and it may be news to you that Harris has taken care of himself already. Yes, for him the treasure is all money in the bargain. You must find it or go starve. But he has been paid beforehand; my brother paid him to destroy me; look at him, if you doubt – look at him, grinning and gulping, a detected thief!' Thence, having made this happy impression, he explained how he had escaped, and thought better of it, and at last concluded to come back, lay the truth before the company, and take his chance with them once more: persuaded as he was, they would instantly depose Harris and elect some other leader. 'There is the whole truth,' said he: 'and, with one exception, I put myself entirely in your hands. What is the exception? There he sits,' he cried, pointing once more to Harris; 'a man that has to die! Weapons and conditions are all one to me; put me face to face with him, and if you give me nothing but a stick, in five minutes I will show you a sop of broken carrion, fit for dogs to roll in.'

It was dark night when he made an end; they had listened in almost perfect silence; but the firelight scarce permitted any one to judge, from the look of his neighbours, with what result of persuasion or conviction. Indeed, the Master had set himself in the brightest place, and kept his face there, to be the centre of men's eyes: doubtless on a profound calculation. Silence followed for a while, and presently the whole party became involved in disputation: the Master lying on his back, with his hands knit under his head and one knee flung across the other, like a person unconcerned in the result. And here, I daresay, his bravado carried him too far and prejudiced his case. At least, after a cast or two back and forward, opinion settled finally against him. It's possible he hoped to repeat the business of the pirate ship, and be himself, perhaps, on hard enough conditions, elected leader; and things went so far that way that Mountain actually threw out the proposition. But the rock he split upon was Hastie. This fellow was not well liked, being sour and slow, with an ugly, glowering disposition, but he had studied some time for the Church at Edinburgh College, before ill-conduct had destroyed his prospects, and he now remembered and applied what he had learned. Indeed, he had not proceeded very far, when the Master rolled carelessly upon one side, which was done (in Mountain's opinion) to conceal the beginnings of despair upon his countenance. Hastie dismissed the most of what they had heard as nothing to the matter: what they wanted was the treasure. All that was said of Harris might be true, and they would have to see to that in time. But what had that to do with the treasure? They had heard a vast of words; but the truth was just this, that Mr Durie was damnably frightened and had several times run off. Here he was – whether caught or come back was all one to Hastie: the point was to make an end of the business. As for the talk of deposing and electing captains, he hoped they were all free men and could attend their own affairs. That was dust flung in their eyes, and so was the proposal to fight Harris. 'He shall fight no one in this camp, I can tell him that,' said Hastie. 'We had trouble enough to get his arms away from him, and we should look pretty fools to give them back again. But if it's excitement the gentleman is after, I can supply him with more than perhaps he cares about. For I have no intention to spend the remainder of my life in these mountains; already I have been too long; and I propose that he should immediately tell us where that treasure is, or else immediately be shot. And there,' says he, producing his weapon, 'there is the pistol that I mean to use.'

'Come, I call you a man,' cries the Master, sitting up and looking at the speaker with an air of admiration.

'I didn't ask you to call me anything,' returned Hastie; 'which is it to be?'

'That's an idle question,' said the Master. 'Needs must when the devil drives. The truth is we are within easy walk of the place, and I will show it you to-morrow.'

With that, as if all were quite settled, and settled exactly to his mind, he walked off to his tent, whither Secundra had preceded him.

I cannot think of these last turns and wriggles of my old enemy, except with admiration; scarce even pity is mingled with the sentiment, so strongly the man supported, so boldly resisted his misfortunes. Even at that hour, when he perceived himself quite lost, when he saw he had but effected an exchange of enemies, and overthrown Harris to set Hastie up, no sign of weakness appeared in his behaviour, and he withdrew to his tent, already determined (I must suppose) upon affronting the incredible hazard of his last expedient, with the same easy, assured, genteel expression and demeanour as he might have left a theatre withal to join a supper of the wits. But doubtless within, if we could see there, his soul trembled.

Early in the night word went about the camp that he was sick; and the first thing the next morning he called Hastie to his side, and inquired most anxiously if he had any skill in medicine. As a matter of fact, this was a vanity of that fallen divinity student's, to which he had cunningly addressed himself. Hastie examined him; and being flattered, ignorant, and highly suspicious, knew not in the least whether the man was sick or malingering. In this state he went forth again to his companions; and (as the thing which would give himself most consequence either way) announced that the patient was in a fair way to die.

'For all that,' he added, with an oath, 'and if he bursts by the wayside, he must bring us this morning to the treasure.'

But there were several in the camp (Mountain among the number) whom this brutality revolted. They would have seen the Master pistolled, or pistolled him themselves, without the smallest sentiment of pity; but they seemed to have been touched by his gallant fight and unequivocal defeat the night before; perhaps, too, they were even already beginning to oppose themselves to their new leader: at least, they now declared that (if the man was sick) he should have a day's rest in spite of Hastie's teeth.

The next morning he was manifestly worse, and Hastie himself began to display something of humane concern, so easily does even the pretence of doctoring awaken sympathy. The third the Master called Mountain and Hastie to the tent, announced himself to be dying, gave them full particulars as to the position of the cache, and begged them to set out incontinently on the quest, so that they might see if he deceived them, and (if they were at first unsuccessful) he should be able to correct their error.

But here arose a difficulty on which he doubtless counted. None of these men would trust another, none would consent to stay behind. On the other hand, although the Master seemed extremely low, spoke scarce above a whisper, and lay much of the time insensible, it was still possible it was a fraudulent sickness; and if all went treasure-hunting, it might prove they had gone upon a wild-goose chase, and return to find their prisoner flown. They concluded, therefore, to hang idling round the camp, alleging sympathy to their reason; and certainly, so mingled are our dispositions, several were sincerely (if not very deeply) affected by the natural peril of the man whom they callously designed to murder. In the afternoon, Hastie was called to the bedside to pray: the which (incredible as it must appear) he did with unction; about eight at night the wailing of Secundra announced that all was over; and before ten, the Indian, with a link stuck in the ground, was toiling at the grave. Sunrise of next day beheld the Master's burial, all hands attending with great decency of demeanour; and the body was laid in the earth, wrapped in a fur robe, with only the face uncovered; which last was of a waxy whiteness, and had the nostrils plugged according to some Oriental habit of Secundra's. No sooner was the grave filled than the lamentations of the Indian once more struck concern to every heart; and it appears this gang of murderers, so far from resenting his outcries, although both distressful and (in such a country) perilous to their own safety, roughly but kindly endeavoured to console him.

But if human nature is even in the worst of men occasionally kind, it is still, and before all things, greedy; and they soon turned from the mourner to their own concerns. The cache of the treasure being hard by, although yet unidentified, it was concluded not to break camp; and the day passed, on the part of the voyagers, in unavailing exploration of the woods, Secundra the while lying on his master's grave. That night they placed no sentinel, but lay all together about the fire, in the customary woodman fashion, the heads outward, like the spokes of a wheel. Morning found them in the same disposition; only Pinkerton, who lay on Mountain's right, between him and Hastie, had (in the hours of darkness) been secretly butchered, and there lay, still wrapped as to his body in his mantle, but offering above that ungodly and horrific spectacle of the scalped head. The gang were that morning as pale as a company of phantoms, for the pertinacity of Indian war (or, to speak more correctly, Indian murder) was well known to all. But they laid the chief blame on their unsentinelled posture; and, fired with the neighbourhood of the treasure, determined to continue where they were. Pinkerton was buried hard by the Master; the survivors again passed the day in exploration, and returned in a mingled humour of anxiety and hope, being partly certain they were now close on the discovery of what they sought, and on the other hand (with the return of darkness) infected with the fear of Indians. Mountain was the first sentry; he declares he neither slept nor yet sat down, but kept his watch with a perpetual and straining vigilance, and it was even with unconcern that (when he saw by the stars his time was up) he drew near the fire to awaken his successor. This man (it was Hicks the shoemaker) slept on the lee side of the circle, something farther off in consequence than those to windward, and in a place darkened by the blowing smoke. Mountain stooped and took him by the shoulder; his hand was at once smeared by some adhesive wetness; and (the wind at the moment veering) the firelight shone upon the sleeper, and showed him, like Pinkerton, dead and scalped.

It was clear they had fallen in the hands of one of those matchless Indian bravos, that will sometimes follow a party for days, and in spite of indefatigable travel, and unsleeping watch, continue to keep up with their advance, and steal a scalp at every resting-place. Upon this discovery, the treasure-seekers, already reduced to a poor half-dozen, fell into mere dismay, seized a few necessaries, and, deserting the remainder of their goods, fled outright into the forest. Their fire they left still burning, and their dead comrade unburied. All day they ceased not to flee, eating by the way, from hand to mouth; and since they feared to sleep, continued to advance at random even in the hours of darkness. But the limit of man's endurance is soon reached; when they rested at last it was to sleep profoundly; and when they woke, it was to find that the enemy was still upon their heels, and death and mutilation had once more lessened and deformed their company.

By this they had become light-headed, they had quite missed their path in the wilderness, their stores were already running low. With the further horrors it is superfluous that I should swell this narrative, already too prolonged. Suffice it to say that when at length a night passed by innocuous, and they might breathe again in the hope that the murderer had at last desisted from pursuit, Mountain and Secundra were alone. The trader is firmly persuaded their unseen enemy was some warrior of his own acquaintance, and that he himself was spared by favour. The mercy extended to Secundra he explains on the ground that the East Indian was thought to be insane; partly from the fact that, through all the horrors of the flight, and while others were casting away their very food and weapons, Secundra continued to stagger forward with a mattock on his shoulder, and partly because, in the last days, and with a great degree of heat and fluency, he perpetually spoke with himself in his own language. But he was sane enough when it came to English.

'You think he will be gone quite away?' he asked, upon their blest awakening in safety.

'I pray God so, I believe so, I dare to believe so,' Mountain had replied almost with incoherence, as he described the scene to me.

And indeed he was so much distempered that until he met us, the next morning, he could scarce be certain whether he had dreamed, or whether it was a fact, that Secundra had thereupon turned directly about and returned without a word upon their footprints, setting his face for these wintry and hungry solitudes, along a path whose every stage was mile-stoned with a mutilated corpse.

Mountain's story, as it was laid before Sir William Johnson and my lord, was shorn, of course, of all the earlier particulars, and the expedition described to have proceeded uneventfully, until the Master sickened. But the latter part was very forcibly related, the speaker visibly thrilling to his recollections; and our then situation, on the fringe of the same desert, and the private interests of each, gave him an audience prepared to share in his emotions. For Mountain's intelligence not only changed the world for my Lord Durrisdeer, but materially affected the designs of Sir William Johnson.

These I find I must lay more at length before the reader. Word had reached Albany of dubious import; it had been rumoured some hostility was to be put in act; and the Indian diplomatist had, thereupon, sped into the wilderness, even at the approach of winter, to nip that mischief in the bud. Here, on the borders, he learned that he was come too late; and a difficult choice was thus presented to a man (upon the whole) not any more bold than prudent. His standing with the painted braves may be compared to that of my Lord President Culloden[10] among the chiefs of our own Highlanders at the 'forty-five; that is as much as to say, he was, to these men, reason's only speaking-trumpet, and counsels of peace and moderation, if they were to prevail at all, must prevail singly through his influence. If, then, he should return, the province must lie open to all the abominable tragedies of Indian war – the houses blaze, the wayfarer be cut off, and the men of the woods collect their usual disgusting spoil of human scalps. On the other side, to go farther forth, to risk so small a party deeper in the desert, to carry words of peace among warlike savages already rejoicing to return to war: here was an extremity from which it was easy to perceive his mind revolted.

'I have come too late,' he said more than once, and would fall into a deep consideration, his head bowed in his hands, his foot patting the ground.

At length he raised his face and looked upon us, that is to say, upon my lord, Mountain, and myself, sitting close round a small fire, which had been made for privacy in one corner of the camp.

'My lord, to be quite frank with you, I find myself in two minds,' said he. 'I think it very needful I should go on, but not at all proper I should any longer enjoy the pleasure of your company. We are here still upon the water-side; and I think the risk to southward no great matter. Will not yourself and Mr Mackellar take a single boat's crew and return to Albany?'

My lord, I should say, had listened to Mountain's narrative, regarding him throughout with a painful intensity of gaze; and, since the tale concluded, had sat as in a dream. There was something very daunting in his look; something to my eyes not rightly human; the face, lean, and dark, and aged, the mouth painful, the teeth disclosed in a perpetual rictus; the eyeball swimming clear of the lids upon a field of blood-shot white. I could not behold him myself without a jarring irritation, such as, I believe, is too frequently the uppermost feeling on the sickness of those dear to us. Others, I could not but remark, were scarce able to support his neighbourhood – Sir William eviting to be near him, Mountain dodging his eye, and, when he met it, blenching and halting in his story. At this appeal, however, my lord appeared to recover his command upon himself.

'To Albany?' said he, with a good voice.

'Not short of it, at least,' replied Sir William. 'There is no safety nearer hand.'

'I would be very sweir* to return,' says my lord. 'I am not afraid – of Indians,' he added, with a jerk.

'I wish that I could say so much,' returned Sir William, smiling; 'although, if any man durst say it, it should be myself. But you are to keep in view my responsibility, and that as the voyage has now become highly dangerous, and your business – if you ever had any,' says he, – 'brought quite to a conclusion by the distressing family intelligence you have received, I should be hardly justified if I even suffered you to proceed, and run the risk of some obloquy if anything regrettable should follow.'

My lord turned to Mountain. 'What did he pretend he died of?' he asked.

'I don't think I understand your honour,' said the trader, pausing, like a man very much affected, in the dressing of some cruel frost-bites.

For a moment my lord seemed at a full stop; and then, with some

* Unwilling.

irritation, 'I ask you what he died of. Surely that's a plain question,' said he.

'O! I don't know,' said Mountain. 'Hastie even never knew. He seemed to sicken natural, and just pass away.'

'There it is, you see!' concluded my lord, turning to Sir William.

'Your lordship is too deep for me,' replied Sir William.

'Why,' says my lord, 'this is a matter of succession; my son's title may be called in doubt; and the man being supposed to be dead of nobody can tell what, a great deal of suspicion would be naturally roused.'

'But, God damn me, the man's buried!' cried Sir William.

'I will never believe that,' returned my lord, painfully trembling. 'I'll never believe it!' he cried again, and jumped to his feet. 'Did he *look* dead?' he asked of Mountain.

'Look dead?' repeated the trader. 'He looked white. Why, what would he be at? I tell you, I put the sods upon him.'

My lord caught Sir William by the coat with a hooked hand. 'This man has the name of my brother,' says he, 'but it's well understood that he was never canny.'

'Canny?' says Sir William. 'What is that?'

'He's not of this world,' whispered my lord, 'neither him nor the black deil that serves him. I have struck my sword throughout his vitals,' he cried; 'I have felt the hilt dirl* on his breastbone,[11] and the hot blood spirt in my very face, time and again, time and again!' he repeated, with a gesture indescribable. 'But he was never dead for that,' said he, and sighed aloud. 'Why should I think he was dead now? No, not till I see him rotting,' says he.

Sir William looked across at me with a long face. Mountain forgot his wounds, staring and gaping.

'My lord,' said I, 'I wish you would collect your spirits.' But my throat was so dry, and my own wits so scattered, I could add no more.

'No,' says my lord, 'it's not to be supposed that he would understand me. Mackellar does, for he kens all, and has seen him buried before now. This is a very good servant to me, Sir William, this man Mackellar;

* Ring.

he buried him with his own hands – he and my father – by the light of two siller candlesticks. The other man is a familiar spirit; he brought him from Coromandel.[13] I would have told ye this long syne, Sir William, only it was in the family.' These last remarks he made with a kind of a melancholy composure, and his time of aberration seemed to pass away. 'You can ask yourself what it all means,' he proceeded. 'My brother falls sick, and dies, and is buried, or so they say; and all seems very plain. But why did the familiar go back? I think ye must see for yourself it's a point that wants some clearing.'

'I will be at your service, my lord, in half a minute,' said Sir William, rising. – 'Mr Mackellar, two words with you'; and he led me without the camp, the frost crunching in our steps, the trees standing at our elbow, hoar with frost, even as on that night in the Long Shrubbery. 'Of course, this is midsummer madness,' said Sir William, as soon as we were gotten out of hearing.

'Why, certainly,' said I. 'The man is mad. I think that manifest.'

'Shall I seize and bind him?' asked Sir William. 'I will upon your authority. If these are all ravings, that should certainly be done.'

I looked down upon the ground, back at the camp, with its bright fires and the folk watching us, and about me on the woods and mountains; there was just the one way that I could not look, and that was in Sir William's face.

'Sir William,' said I at last, 'I think my lord not sane, and have long thought him so. But there are degrees in madness; and whether he should be brought under restraint – Sir William, I am no fit judge,' I concluded.

'I will be the judge,' said he. 'I ask for facts. Was there, in all that jargon, any word of truth or sanity? Do you hesitate?' he asked. 'Am I to understand you have buried this gentleman before?'

'Not buried,' said I; and then, taking up courage at last, 'Sir William,' said I, 'unless I were to tell you a long story, which much concerns a noble family (and myself not in the least), it would be impossible to make this matter clear to you. Say the word, and I will do it, right or wrong. And, at any rate, I will say so much, that my lord is not so crazy as he seems. This is a strange matter, into the tail of which you are unhappily drifted.'

'I desire none of your secrets,' replied Sir William; 'but I will be plain, at the risk of incivility, and confess that I take little pleasure in my present company.'

'I would be the last to blame you,' said I, 'for that.'

'I have not asked either for your censure or your praise, sir,' returned Sir William. 'I desire simply to be quit of you; and to that effect, I put a boat and complement of men at your disposal.'

'This is fairly offered,' said I, after reflection. 'But you must suffer me to say a word upon the other side. We have a natural curiosity to learn the truth of this affair; I have some of it myself; my lord (it is very plain) has but too much. The matter of the Indian's return is enigmatical.'

'I think so myself,' Sir William interrupted, 'and I propose (since I go in that direction) to probe it to the bottom. Whether or not the man has gone like a dog to die upon his master's grave, his life, at least, is in great danger, and I propose, if I can, to save it. – There is nothing against his character?'

'Nothing, Sir William,' I replied.

'And the other?' he said. 'I have heard my lord, of course; but, from the circumstances of his servant's loyalty, I must suppose he had some noble qualities.'

'You must not ask me that!' I cried. 'Hell may have noble flames. I have known him a score of years, and always hated, and always admired, and always slavishly feared him.'

'I appear to intrude again upon your secrets,' said Sir William, 'believe me, inadvertently. Enough that I will see the grave, and (if possible) rescue the Indian. Upon these terms, can you persuade your master to return to Albany?'

'Sir William,' said I, 'I will tell you how it is. You do not see my lord to advantage; it will seem even strange to you that I should love him; but I do, and I am not alone. If he goes back to Albany, it must be by force, and it will be the death-warrant of his reason, and perhaps his life. That is my sincere belief; but I am in your hands, and ready to obey, if you will assume so much responsibility as to command.'

'I will have no shred of responsibility; it is my single endeavour to avoid the same,' cried Sir William. 'You insist upon following this journey up; and be it so! I wash my hands of the whole matter.'

With which word he turned upon his heel and gave the order to break camp; and my lord, who had been hovering near by, came instantly to my side.

'Which is it to be?' said he.

'You are to have your way,' I answered. 'You shall see the grave.'

The situation of the Master's grave was, between guides, easily described; it lay, indeed, beside a chief landmark of the wilderness, a certain range of peaks, conspicuous by their design and altitude, and the source of many brawling tributaries to that inland sea, Lake Champlain. It was therefore possible to strike for it direct, instead of following back the blood-stained trail of the fugitives, and to cover, in some sixteen hours of march, a distance which their perturbed wanderings had extended over more than sixty. Our boats we left under a guard upon the river; it was, indeed, probable we should return to find them frozen fast; and the small equipment with which we set forth upon the expedition included not only an infinity of furs to protect us from the cold, but an arsenal of snow-shoes to render travel possible, when the inevitable snow should fall. Considerable alarm was manifested at our departure; the march was conducted with soldierly precaution, the camp at night sedulously chosen and patrolled; and it was a consideration of this sort that arrested us, the second day, within not many hundred yards of our destination – the night being already imminent, the spot in which we stood well qualified to be a strong camp for a party of our numbers; and Sir William, therefore, on a sudden thought, arresting our advance.

Before us was the high range of mountains toward which we had been all day deviously drawing near. From the first light of the dawn, their silver peaks had been the goal of our advance across a tumbled lowland forest, thrid with rough streams, and strewn with monstrous boulders; the peaks (as I say) silver, for already at the higher altitudes the snow fell nightly; but the woods and the low ground only breathed upon with frost. All day heaven had been charged with ugly vapours, in the which the sun swam and glimmered like a shilling-piece; all day the wind blew on our left cheek barbarous cold, but very pure to breathe. With the end of the afternoon, however, the wind fell; the clouds, being no longer reinforced, were scattered or drunk up; the sun set behind us with some wintry splendour, and the white brow of the mountains shared its dying glow.

It was dark ere we had supper; we ate in silence, and the meal was scarce despatched before my lord slunk from the fireside to the margin of the camp; whither I made haste to follow him. The camp was on high ground, overlooking a frozen lake, perhaps a mile in its longest measurement; all about us the forest lay in heights and hollows; above rose the white mountains; and higher yet, the moon rode in a fair sky. There was no breath of air; nowhere a twig creaked; and the sounds of our own camp were hushed and swallowed up in the surrounding stillness. Now that the sun and the wind were both gone down, it appeared almost warm, like a night of July: a singular illusion of the sense, when earth, air, and water were strained to bursting with the extremity of frost.

My lord (or what I still continued to call by his loved name) stood with his elbow in one hand, and his chin sunk in the other, gazing before him on the surface of the wood. My eyes followed his, and rested almost pleasantly upon the frosted contexture of the pines, rising in moonlit hillocks, or sinking in the shadow of small glens. Hard by, I told myself, was the grave of our enemy, now gone where the wicked cease from troubling, the earth heaped for ever on his once so active limbs. I could not but think of him as somehow fortunate to be thus done with man's anxiety and weariness, the daily expense of spirit, and that daily river of circumstance to be swum through, at any hazard, under the penalty of shame or death. I could not but think how good was the end of that long travel; and with that, my mind swung at a tangent to my lord. For was not my lord dead also? a maimed soldier, looking vainly for discharge, lingering derided in the line of battle? A kind man, I remembered him; wise, with a decent pride, a son perhaps too dutiful, a husband only too loving, one that could suffer and be silent, one whose hand I loved to press. Of a sudden, pity caught in my windpipe with a sob; I could have wept aloud to remember and behold him; and standing thus by his elbow, under the broad moon, I prayed fervently either that he should be released, or I strengthened to persist in my affection.

'O God,' said I, 'this was the best man to me and to himself, and now I shrink from him. He did no wrong, or not till he was broke with sorrows; these are but his honourable wounds that we begin to shrink from. O cover them up, O take him away, before we hate him!'

I was still so engaged in my own bosom when a sound broke suddenly upon the night. It was neither very loud nor very near; yet, bursting as it did from so profound and so prolonged a silence, it startled the camp like an alarm of trumpets. Ere I had taken breath, Sir William was beside me, the main part of the voyagers clustered at his back, intently giving ear. Methought, as I glanced at them across my shoulder, there was a whiteness, other than moonlight, on their cheeks; and the rays of the moon reflected with a sparkle on the eyes of some, and the shadows lying black under the brows of others (according as they raised or bowed the head to listen) gave to the group a strange air of animation and anxiety. My lord was to the front, crouching a little forth, his hand raised as for silence: a man turned to stone. And still the sounds continued, breathlessly renewed with a precipitate rhythm.

Suddenly Mountain spoke in a loud, broken whisper, as of a man relieved. 'I have it now,' he said; and, as we all turned to hear him, 'the Indian must have known the cache,' he added. 'That is he – he is digging out the treasure.'

'Why, to be sure!' exclaimed Sir William. 'We were geese not to have supposed so much.'

'The only thing is,' Mountain resumed, 'the sound is very close to our old camp. And, again, I do not see how he is there before us, unless the man had wings!'

'Greed and fear are wings,' remarked Sir William. 'But this rogue has given us an alert, and I have a notion to return the compliment. – What say you, gentlemen, shall we have a moonlight hunt?'

It was so agreed; dispositions were made to surround Secundra at his task; some of Sir William's Indians hastened in advance; and a strong guard being left at our headquarters, we set forth along the uneven bottom of the forest; frost crackling, ice sometimes loudly splitting under foot; and overhead the blackness of pine-woods and the broken brightness of the moon. Our way led down into a hollow of the land; and as we descended, the sounds diminished and had almost died away. Upon the other slope it was more open, only dotted with a few pines, and several vast and scattered rocks that made inky shadows in the moonlight. Here the sounds began to reach us more distinctly; we could now perceive the ring of iron, and more exactly estimate the furious degree of haste with which the digger plied his instrument. As we neared the top of the ascent, a bird or two winged aloft and hovered darkly in the moonlight; and the next moment we were gazing through a fringe of trees upon a singular picture.

A narrow plateau, overlooked by the white mountains, and encompassed nearer hand by woods, lay bare to the strong radiance of the moon. Rough goods, such as make the wealth of foresters, were sprinkled here and there upon the ground in meaningless disarray. About the midst, a tent stood, silvered with frost: the door open, gaping on the black interior. At the one end of this small stage lay what seemed the tattered remnants of a man. Without doubt we had arrived upon the scene of Harris's encampment; there were the goods scattered in the panic of flight; it was in yon tent the Master breathed his last; and the frozen carrion that lay before us was the body of the drunken shoemaker. It was always moving to come upon the theatre of any tragic incident; to come upon it after so many days, and to find it (in the seclusion of a desert) still unchanged, must have impressed the mind of the most careless. And yet it was not that which struck us into pillars of stone; but the sight (which yet we had been half expecting) of Secundra ankle-deep in the grave of his late master. He had cast the main part of his raiment by, yet his frail arms and shoulders glistered in the moonlight with a copious sweat; his face was contracted with anxiety and expectation; his blows resounded on the grave, as thick as sobs; and behind him, strangely deformed and ink-black upon the frosty ground, the creature's shadow repeated and parodied his swift gesticulations. Some night-birds arose from the boughs upon our coming, and then settled back; but Secundra, absorbed in his toil, heard or heeded not at all.

I heard Mountain whisper to Sir William, 'Good God! it's the grave! He's digging him up!' It was what we had all guessed, and yet to hear it put in language thrilled me. Sir William violently started.

'You damned sacrilegious hound!' he cried. 'What's this?'

Secundra leaped in the air, a little breathless cry escaped him, the tool flew from his grasp, and he stood one instant staring at the speaker. The next, swift as an arrow, he sped for the woods upon the farther side; and the next again, throwing up his hands with a violent gesture of resolution, he had begun already to retrace his steps.

'Well, then, you come, you help—' he was saying. But by now my lord had stepped beside Sir William; the moon shone fair upon his face, and the words were still upon Secundra's lips, when he beheld and recognised his master's enemy. 'Him!' he screamed, clasping his hands, and shrinking on himself.

'Come, come!' said Sir William. 'There is none here to do you harm, if you be innocent; and if you be guilty, your escape is quite cut off. Speak, what do you here among the graves of the dead and the remains of the unburied?'

'You no murderer?' inquired Secundra. 'You true man? You see me safe?'

'I will see you safe, if you be innocent,' returned Sir William. 'I have said the thing, and I see not wherefore you should doubt it.'

'These all murderers,' cried Secundra, 'that is why! He kill – murderer,' pointing to Mountain; 'these two hire-murderers,' pointing to my lord and myself – 'all gallows-murderers! Ah! I see you all swing in a rope. Now I go save the Sahib; he see you swing in a rope. The Sahib,' he continued, pointing to the grave, 'he not dead. He bury, he not dead.'

My lord uttered a little noise, moved nearer to the grave, and stood and stared in it.

'Buried and not dead?' exclaimed Sir William. 'What kind of rant is this?'

'See, Sahib,' said Secundra. 'The Sahib and I alone with murderers; try all way to escape, no way good. Then try this way: good way in warm climate, good way in India; here, in this dam cold place, who can tell? I tell you pretty good hurry: you help, you light a fire, help rub.'

'What is the creature talking of?' cried Sir William. 'My head goes round.'

'I tell you I bury him alive,' said Secundra. 'I teach him swallow his tongue. Now dig him up pretty good hurry, and he not much worse. You light a fire.'

Sir William turned to the nearest of his men. 'Light a fire,' said he. 'My lot seems to be cast with the insane.'

'You good man,' returned Secundra. 'Now I go dig the Sahib up.'

He returned as he spoke to the grave, and resumed his former toil. My lord stood rooted, and I at my lord's side, fearing I knew not what.

The frost was not yet very deep, and presently the Indian threw aside his tool, and began to scoop the dirt by handfuls. Then he disengaged a corner of a buffalo robe; and then I saw hair catch among his fingers: yet a moment more, and the moon shone on something white. A while Secundra crouched upon his knees, scraping with delicate fingers, breathing with puffed lips; and when he moved aside, I beheld the face of the Master wholly disengaged. It was deadly white, the eyes closed, the ears and nostrils plugged, the cheeks fallen, the nose sharp as if in death; but for all he had lain so many days under the sod, corruption had not approached him, and (what strangely affected all of us) his lips and chin were mantled with a swarthy beard.

'My God!' cried Mountain, 'he was as smooth as a baby when we laid him there!'

'They say hair grows upon the dead,' observed Sir William; but his voice was thick and weak.

Secundra paid no heed to our remarks, digging swift as a terrier in the loose earth. Every moment the form of the Master, swathed in his buffalo robe, grew more distinct in the bottom of that shallow trough; the moon shining strong, and the shadows of the standers-by, as they drew forward and back, falling and flitting over his emergent countenance. The sight held us with a horror not before experienced.

I dared not look my lord in the face; but for as long as it lasted, I never observed him to draw breath; and a little in the background one of the men (I know not whom) burst into a kind of sobbing.

'Now,' said Secundra, 'you help me lift him out.'

Of the flight of time I have no idea; it may have been three hours, and it may have been five, that the Indian laboured to reanimate his master's body. One thing only I know, that it was still night, and the moon was not yet set, although it had sunk low, and now barred the plateau with long shadows, when Secundra uttered a small cry of satisfaction: and, leaning swiftly forth, I thought I could myself perceive a change upon that icy countenance of the unburied. The next moment I beheld his eyelids flutter; the next they rose entirely, and the week-old corpse looked me for a moment in the face.

So much display of life I can myself swear to. I have heard from others that he visibly strove to speak, that his teeth showed in his beard, and that his brow was contorted as with an agony of pain and effort. And this may have been; I know not, I was otherwise engaged. For at that first disclosure of the dead man's eyes my Lord Durrisdeer fell to the ground, and when I raised him up he was a corpse.

Day came, and still Secundra could not be persuaded to desist from his unavailing efforts. Sir William, leaving a small party under my command, proceeded on his embassy with the first light; and still the Indian rubbed the limbs and breathed in the mouth of the dead body. You would think such labours might have vitalised a stone; but, except for that one moment (which was my lord's death), the black spirit of the Master held aloof from its discarded clay; and by about the hour of noon, even the faithful servant was at length convinced. He took it with unshaken quietude.

'Too cold,' said he, 'good way in India, no good here.' And, asking for some food, which he ravenously devoured as soon as it was set before him, he drew near to the fire and took his place at my elbow. In the same spot, as soon as he had eaten, he stretched himself out, and fell into a childlike slumber, from which I must arouse him, some hours afterwards, to take his part as one of the mourners at the double funeral. It was the same throughout; he seemed to have outlived at once, and with the same effort, his grief for his master and his terror of myself and Mountain.

One of the men left with me was skilled in stone-cutting; and before Sir William returned to pick us up, I had chiselled on a boulder this inscription, with a copy of which I may fitly bring my narrative to a close:

J. D.
HEIR TO A SCOTTISH TITLE,
A MASTER OF THE ARTS AND GRACES,
ADMIRED IN EUROPE, ASIA, AMERICA,
IN WAR AND PEACE,
IN THE TENTS OF SAVAGE HUNTERS AND THE
CITADELS OF KINGS, AFTER SO MUCH
ACQUIRED, ACCOMPLISHED, AND
ENDURED, LIES HERE FOR-
GOTTEN.

H. D.
HIS BROTHER,
AFTER A LIFE OF UNMERITED DISTRESS,
BRAVELY SUPPORTED,
DIED ALMOST IN THE SAME HOUR,
AND SLEEPS IN THE SAME GRAVE
WITH HIS FRATERNAL ENEMY.

THE PIETY OF HIS WIFE AND ONE OLD
SERVANT RAISED THIS STONE
TO BOTH.

APPENDIX

Stevenson's 'Note to *The Master of Ballantrae*' (1893–4)

In late 1893 and early 1894 Stevenson thought of writing prefaces for the proposed Edinburgh Edition, and he started drafting an essay on *The Master of Ballantrae.* Earlier in 1893 he had written a piece on *Treasure Island* ('My First Book'), and he began one on *Kidnapped* before dropping the whole plan on the advice of Colvin and Baxter. Two drafts of the essay on *The Master* exist and have seen the light of day in three separate publications, reprinted below. For the textual history of these fragments, see Roger Swearingen's *The Prose Writings of Robert Louis Stevenson: A Guide* (1980), pp. 192–3.

The first (I) is the initial draft, from a transcription by Graham Balfour, included in the Edinburgh Edition, 21 (1896), as 'The Genesis of "The Master of Ballantrae"'. The second (II) comprises those portions of the revised draft which do not overlap with anything in the first draft, up to but excluding the last two pages: these fragments were first published in 1921 and reprinted in the Vailima Edition, 26 (1923), as 'Note to "The Master of Ballantrae"'. The third (III) represents the final two pages of the revised draft which appeared for the first time in Elsie Noble Caldwell, *Last Witness for Robert Louis Stevenson* (Norman, Oklahoma, 1960), pp. 117–19. They are reproduced by permission of The Huntington Library, San Marino, California, where they are held as HM 20535.

I

I was walking one night in the verandah of a small house in which I lived, outside the hamlet of Saranac. It was winter; the night was very dark; the air extraordinary clear and cold, and sweet with the purity of forests. From a good way below, the river was to be heard contending with ice and boulders: a few lights appeared, scattered unevenly among the darkness, but so far away as not to lessen the sense of isolation. For the making of a story here were fine conditions. I was besides moved with the spirit of emulation, for I had just finished my third or fourth perusal of *The Phantom Ship*. 'Come,' said I to my engine, 'let us make a tale, a story of many years and countries, of the sea and the land, savagery and civilisation; a story that shall have the same large features and may be treated in the same summary elliptic method as the book you have been reading and admiring.' I was here brought up with a reflection exceedingly just in itself, but which, as the sequel shows, I failed to profit by. I saw that Marryat, not less than Homer, Milton, and Virgil, profited by the choice of a familiar and legendary subject; so that he prepared his readers on the very title-page; and this set me cudgelling my brains, if by any chance I could hit upon some similar belief to be the centre-piece of my own meditated fiction. In the course of this vain search there cropped up in my memory a singular case of a buried and resuscitated fakir, which I had been often told by an uncle of mine, then lately dead, Inspector-General John Balfour.[1]

On such a fine frosty night, with no wind and the thermometer below zero, the brain works with much vivacity; and the next moment I had seen the circumstance transplanted from India and the tropics to the Adirondack wilderness and the stringent cold of the Canadian border. Here then, almost before I had begun my story, I had two countries, two of the ends of the earth involved: and thus though the notion of the resuscitated man failed entirely on the score of general acceptation, or even (as I have since found) acceptability, it fitted at once with my design of a tale of many lands; and this decided me to consider further of its possibilities. The man who should thus be buried was the first question: a good man, whose return to life would be hailed by the reader and the other characters with gladness? This trenched upon the Christian picture and was dismissed. If the idea, then, was to be of any use at all for me, I had to create a kind of evil genius to his friends and family, take him through many disappearances, and make this final restoration from the pit of death, in the icy

American wilderness, the last and grimmest of the series. I need not tell my brothers of the craft that I was now in the most interesting moments of an author's life; the hours that followed that night upon the balcony, and the following nights and days, whether walking abroad or lying wakeful in my bed, were hours of unadulterated joy. My mother, who was then living with me alone, perhaps had less enjoyment; for, in the absence of my wife, who is my usual helper in these times of parturition, I must spur her up at all seasons to hear me relate and try to clarify my unformed fancies.

And while I was groping for the fable and the characters required, behold, I found them lying ready and nine years old in my memory. Pease porridge hot, pease porridge cold, pease porridge in the pot, nine years old. Was there ever a more complete justification of the rule of Horace? Here, thinking of quite other things, I had stumbled on the solution, or perhaps I should rather say (in stagewright phrase) the Curtain or final Tableau of a story conceived long before on the moors between Pitlochry and Strathardle, conceived in the Highland rain, in the blend of the smell of heather and bog-plants, and with a mind full of the *Atholl Correspondence* and the *Memoirs of the Chevalier de Johnstone*. So long ago,[2] so far away it was, that I had first evoked the faces and the mutual tragic situation of the men of Durrisdeer.

My story was now world-wide enough: Scotland, India, and America being all obligatory scenes. But of these India was strange to me except in books; I had never known any living Indian save a Parsee, a member of my club in London, equally civilised and (to all seeing) equally occidental with myself. It was plain, thus far, that I should have to get into India and out of it again upon a foot of fairy lightness; and I believe this first suggested to me the idea of the Chevalier Burke for a narrator. It was at first intended that he should be Scottish, and I was then filled with fears that he might prove only the degraded shadow of my own Alan Breck. Presently, however, it began to occur to me it would be like my Master to curry favour with the Prince's Irishmen; and that an Irish refugee would have a particular reason to find himself in India with his countryman, the unfortunate Lally. Irish, therefore, I decided he should be, and then, all of a sudden, I was aware of a tall shadow across my path, the shadow of Barry Lyndon.[3] No man (in Lord Foppington's[4] phrase) of a nice morality could go very deep with my Master: in the original idea of this story conceived in Scotland, this companion had been besides intended to be worse than the bad elder son with whom (as it was then meant) he was to visit Scotland; if I took an Irishman, and a very bad Irishman, in the midst of the eighteenth century, how was I to evade Barry Lyndon? The wretch besieged me, offering his services; he gave me excellent references; he proved that he was highly fitted for the work I had to do; he, or my own evil heart, suggested it was easy to disguise his ancient livery with a little lace and a few frogs and buttons, so that Thackeray himself should hardly recognise him. And then of a sudden there came to me memories of a young Irishman, with whom I was once intimate, and had spent long nights walking and talking with, upon a very desolate coast in a bleak autumn: I recalled him as a youth of an extraordinary moral simplicity – almost vacancy; plastic to any influence, the creature of his admirations: and putting such a youth in fancy into the career of a soldier of fortune, it occurred to me that he would serve my turn as well as Mr Lyndon, and in place of entering into competition with the Master, would afford a slight though a distinct relief. I know not if I have done him well, though his moral dissertations always highly entertained me: but I own I have been surprised to find that he reminded some critics of Barry Lyndon after all . . .

II

An account of how a story arose in the writer's mind, from and towards what points the course of invention travelled, what facts were utilised, what were easy and what were hard, and how the finished work looks in the eyes of its begetter, has always seemed to me excellent reading for the curious. Placed in front, I should be inclined to judge it an impertinence; placed as a rear guard to the volume, it may serve a useful purpose on occasion. The story may be read, and it may lack yet half an hour of your accustomed bedtime; or you may have bought the volume to beguile the tedium of a journey, and have come to the last page some way short of your expected destination; at such time no one would care to embark on matter entirely new, and yet he might be ready enough to dwell a little longer from a new standpoint on the same train of thought which he has been following so long. The magician after he has prepared his sleight of hand will sometimes afford a second, and a fresh, pleasure by explaining the method of his dexterity. As some such after-piece, for an empty moment, it is hoped this note may be regarded.

It was the case of Marquis of Tullibardine[5] that first struck me; the situation of a younger brother succeeding in this underhand, irregular fashion, and under an implied contract of seniority, to his elder's place and future, struck me as so full of bitterness, and the mental relations of a family thus circumstanced so fruitful of misjudgment and domestic animosity, it took my fancy then as a drama in a nutshell, to be solved between four persons and within four walls; with my new incident and with my new aim, I saw myself, and rejoiced to be, committed to great spaces and voyages, and a long evolution of time. But in the matter of the characters involved, I determined to adhere to the original four actors. With four characters – two brothers, a father, and a heroine (all nameless but in a determined relation) I was to carry the reader to and fro in space over a good half of the world, and sustain his interest in time through the extent of a generation.

Surely, beyond the worsted lace of his gentility, and a trick of Celtic boastfulness, my poor chevalier, eminently proud of his degradation, unaffectedly unconscious of his genuine merit, is a creature utterly distinct, in the essential part of him, from the brute whom Thackeray disinterred out of the *Newgate Calendar* and set re-existing, for the time of the duration of the English language.

The need of a confidant for Mr Henry led to the introduction of Mackellar, for it was only to a servant that a man such as I conceived Mr Henry, could unbosom; and no sooner had he begun to take on lineament, than I perceived the uses of the character, and was at once tempted to intrust to him the part of a spokesman. Nothing more pleases me than for one of my puppets to display himself in his own language; in no other way than this of the dramatic monologue, are humorous and incongruous traits so persuasively presented. The narration, put in the mouth of the land steward, would supply, as if by the way and accidentally, a certain subdued element of comedy, much to be desired, and scarce otherwise, except by violence, to be introduced. Besides which, the device enabled me to view my heroine from the outside, which was doubly desirable. First, and generally, because I am always afraid of my women, who are not admired in my home circle; second, and particularly, because I should be thus enabled to pass over without realisation an ugly and delicate business – the Master's courtship of his brother's wife. Accordingly, and perfectly satisfied with myself, I hastily wrote and re-wrote the first half of my story down to the end of the duel, through the eyes and in the words of the good Ephraim. Cowardice is always punished; I had no sooner got this length, I had no sooner learned to appreciate the advantages of my method, than I was brought face to face with its defects and fell into a panic fear of the conclusion. How, with a narrator like Mackellar, should I transact the melodrama in the wilderness? How, with his style, so full of disabilities, attack a passage which must be either altogether seizing or altogether silly and absurd? The first half was already in type, when I made up my mind to have it thus done, and recommence the tale in the third person. Friends advised, one this way, one that; my publishers were afraid of the delay; indolence had doubtless a voice; I had besides a natural love for the documentary method in narration; and I ended by committing myself to the impersonation of Mackellar, and suffering the publication to proceed.

I was doubtless right and wrong; the book has suffered and has gained in consequence; gained in relief and verisimilitude, suffered in fire, force and (as one of my critics has well said) in 'large dramatic rhythm.' The same astute and kindly judge complains of 'the dredging machine of Mr Mackellar's memory, shooting out the facts bucketful by bucketful'; and I understand the ground of his complaint, although my sense is otherwise. The realism I love is that of method; not only that all in a story may possibly have come to pass, but that all might naturally be recorded – a realism that justifies the book itself as well as the fable it commemorates.

III

. . . known that? is a captious question that has often marred my pleasure in fine scenes of fiction. I must confess, however, that my choice of the first person made this Master of Ballantrae, before I was done with it, a burthen and a nightmare. I never thought of the business in the Wilderness but I fell back aghast; and when the remainder of the book, down to the departure from New York, had been finished in the adorable island of Tahiti, and I found myself after another voyage face to face in the suburbs of Honolulu with the first page of my conclusion, I came near to confessing a defeat. Months passed before I could see how to attack the problem, how the pen of Mackellar was to relate a series of incidents so highly coloured, so excessive, and so tragic; the magazine was already on my heels, when desperation helped me; and in a few days of furious industry the novel was, for good or evil rushed to its last word. Some violence was done; Mackellar would scarcely have so written, yet I think that on the whole and in view of the extreme difficulty of the passage, I shall be thought to have preserved the note beyond expectation.

With James Durie himself I never had a moment's stick; I had no model in my eye, whatever, he rose before me, and took shape, and justification, as when a whistler unconsciously and note by note recalls a melody. I have been at school and college with Mackellar and with Henry; the chronicle, as I have said, was drawn from the possibilities of a callow youth who went long since to the bad; my old Durrisdeer was founded on the face of an old gentleman whom I once loved, although I scarcely knew him, but for the Master I had no original, which is perhaps another way of confessing that the original was no other than myself. We have all a certain attitude toward our own character and part in life; we desire more or less identity between the essence and the seeming; we put the two in different relations of cause and effect, some living up to the appearance, others trimming the appearance to the life; and the secret of the Master is principally this, that he is indifferent to that problem. A live man, a full man, in every other point a human man, he has this one element of inhumanity.

Abjectly fond of admiration, he is careless, how or for what he is admired in error; whether for a fact or for a lie, or (whether by different people) for incongruous pretensions. An unveracious [error for *avaricious*? MS clearly *unveracious*] vanity, monstrous in its exactions, and unusual, although far from unparalleled, in its unveracity. Of such are the persons (one of whom was known to me) who pass themselves off as authors of other people's books. It is in short a very ordinary and despicable character magnified. But if the question were put to me, I should have to own that this magnitude improves even on myself. It is my only ground with Mr Hole, whose illustrations convey other points I can't find language to [commend?], that his Master is not my Master; mine had a more slender body, a larger, a finer and darker countenance, attitudes more precise and more theatrical; and more of the fairy prince, and more of Satan; and the black mole on his cheek (I could not tell you why) was an essential part of him.

The story told to Mackellar on board the *Nonesuch* was, it may amuse the reader to learn, a dream I had in Papeete, when I supposed myself to be reading a tale of Edgar Allan Poe's; it was only in the [? – word undecipherable] of the next day that I perceived its suitability to its present purpose.

I have said very little about Clementina,[6] because I have said so little of her in the text. She was one of my ungrateful children, for I am rarely on a fond [sound?] footing with my daughters. I had a model for her; dull people think they can do wonders with a model, it is a fine illusion; this is my model, and she has not been drawn – and this is my heroine, and she has never been entirely animate. A certain correspondent wrote to protest against a copying blunder in the original text; I had made Clementina thrust a sword 'up to the hilt' in the frosty ground;[7] the folly of the statement, equal to the worst in Victor Hugo, shows that I was regarding her modestly from the outside. When a character lives, when the writer feels and reveals him from within, such flights are quite impossible; the author is conscious of, he receives [?] every effort, he feels, he estimates the resistance; the thing done, is done by him; and he is brought to a pause by a physical impossibility even as if it were he himself, and not his puppet, that had emerged to violate the laws of nature.

NOTES

I am particularly indebted to *The Letters of Robert Louis Stevenson*, 8 vols., ed. Bradford A. Booth and Ernest Mehew (New Haven and London, 1994–5); all references to Stevenson's letters are to this edition. I must also acknowledge debts to the *Oxford English Dictionary (OED)*, the *Dictionary of National Biography (DNB)*, the *Encyclopedia Britannica*, and Trevor Royle, *The Macmillan Companion to Scottish Literature* (London and Basingstoke, 1983).

DEDICATION

1. *Sir Percy Florence and Lady Shelley*: The Stevensons became friendly with the Shelleys soon after moving to Bournemouth in 1885. The son of the poet and his wife were some thirty years older than Stevenson, close to his own parents in age. Sir Percy was a keen amateur photographer and yachtsman.

PREFACE

1. *PREFACE:* In the first days of 1888 Stevenson asked his old friend Charles Baxter to play along with a fiction. Baxter's legal firm would find itself in charge of Mackellar's memoirs on the date at which their seal was to be broken, one hundred years after the death of Mackellar's master, Henry Durie (*Letters* 6, 99). Baxter obliged, but Stevenson then dropped the whole idea for the tale's first publication ('a little too like Scott'). In May 1894 however he recalled it to favour and expressed the intention of including it in the Edinburgh Edition. 'It will give you,' he told Baxter, 'what I should so much like you to have, another corner of your own in that lofty monument'

(*Letters* 8, 290). It was first published in the Appendix to the Edinburgh Edition, 28 (1898).

2. *Mr Johnstone Thomson, W. S.*: Stevenson and Baxter had long before created the characters of Thomson and Johnstone, 'a pair of dissolute and disreputable Church elders who wrote to each other in broad Scots' (see Ernest Mehew's Introduction to *Letters* 1, 40–44). One of the Scots poems in *Underwoods* (1887) purports to be an extract from a letter of Mr Thomson to Mr Johnstone, 'The Scotsman's Return from Abroad'.

3. *the Piranesis*: Etchings by the Italian artist Giovanni Battista Piranesi (1720–78) may well have adorned Baxter's dining-room. In 1884 Stevenson himself had been given some by their mutual friend W. E. Henley, of which his favourite was 'The Tomb of Caecilia Metella' (*Letters* 4, 265).

4. *Law's 'Memorials'*: Robert Law (*c.* 1628–*c.* 1690), covenanting preacher and author of *Memorialls, or The Memorable Things that fell out within this Island of Brittain from 1638 to 1684*. Scott similarly claims them as a source in his Introduction (1830) to *The Bride of Lammermoor* (1819), the novel that contains the Master of Ravenswood.

5. *In 1783*: This is incorrect, the closing scenes of the novel being set towards the end of 1764.

6. *Ephraim Mackellar*: Stevenson first thought of naming Mackellar 'Naphtali' after the biblical son of Jacob and Bilhah, Rachel's maid (*Letters* 6, 81). His second thought of 'Ephraim' associates him with the pattern of succession in which a younger son inherits before his elder brother. The best-known instance of this is the tale of Jacob and Esau, to which the novel explicitly alludes. In blessing Joseph's two sons, the dying Jacob chooses to lay his right hand on the head of Ephraim and not the first-born Manasseh (Genesis xlviii).

7. *nothing so noble as baldness*: There was a long-standing joke between Stevenson and his cousin Bob, shared with their friends Baxter and Henley, in which 'bald' was a term of approval (*Letters* 3, 323, note 2).

SUMMARY OF EVENTS DURING THE MASTER'S WANDERINGS

1. *The Duries of Durrisdeer and Ballantrae*: Durisdeer [sic] and Ballantrae are both real places in south-west Scotland, and Stevenson passed a night at the latter on a walking-tour in January 1876 ('A Winter's Walk in Carrick and Galloway' was first published in 1896 after his death). Durisdeer is in Nithsdale, north of Dumfries; Ballantrae is on the west coast, south of Girvan. The district round Dumfries had some painful associations for Stevenson. In

September 1873 he went there with his father when their relations were deeply troubled by disagreements over religious belief. They paid their respects to the tombstones in the churchyard at Irongray, seven miles from Dumfries ('Lord Irongray' was a name that Stevenson toyed with for this novel), and also to Covenanter tombstones in the woods. He imagined the house of Durrisdeer as being close to Kircudbright Bay on the Solway Firth, the nearby town of St Bride's being modelled on Kircudbright. The district provides the major setting for one of Stevenson's favourite Scott novels, *Redgauntlet* (1824); 'Durisdeer' is mentioned in a verse that Darsie Latimer sings in 'Chapter Ninth'. Carol Mills points out some of the echoes of Scott (see Select Bibliography).

2. *David First*: Born 1084, he divided the kingdom of Scotland with his elder brother in 1107 and became sole ruler in 1124. After an unsuccessful invasion of England, he devoted himself to politics and piety, dying at Carlisle in 1153.

3. *Kittle*: Touchy, difficult, awkward.

4. *Thomas of Ercildoune*: Thirteenth-century poet and seer, known as 'The Rhymer', who lived at Erceldoune (Earlston) in Berwickshire. He is supposed to have predicted the death of Alexander III, the Battle of Bannockburn, and the accession of James VI to the throne of Great Britain.

5. *to tie*: To marry.

6. *waur*: Worse.

7. *unco*: Strange, remarkable, terrible (see also pp. 22, 152).

8. *Prince Charlie's landing*: On 23 July 1745 the grandson of the deposed King James II and VII, Prince Charles Edward (1720–88), landed with seven companions, mainly Irish exiles, at Eriskay in the Outer Hebrides. Despite a mixed reception in the Highlands, the support of the clans enabled him to take Perth and Edinburgh and proclaim his father James VIII of Scotland. The government forces were defeated at Prestonpans and Carlisle was captured, but without sufficient English (and French) support Charles's officers persuaded him to call off the invasion of England at Derby on Black Friday, 6 December. The retreating army won a further victory at Falkirk the following January, but amid bitter dissension between Charles and his general, Lord George Murray (see note 17 below), the exhausted Scots forces were finally crushed by the Duke of Cumberland at Culloden on 16 April 1746. After months of hiding, Charles eventually escaped to the Continent. This was the end of the Stuart cause, and much else (see note 18). William Ferguson observes that 'far from being a "Scotch rebellion", as it seemed to most Englishmen, the '45 was more like a Scottish civil war' (*Scotland 1689 to the Present* (Edinburgh and London, 1968), p. 153).

9. *King James . . . King George*: In his Note on the novel Stevenson said that he had in mind 'the case of Marquis of Tullibardine' (see Appendix, p. 225). Created 1st Duke of Atholl in 1703, John Murray opposed the Union of 1707. Of the four sons who survived to declare their allegiances in 1715, the eldest and the two youngest supported the Jacobite rising and suffered the consequences. William, Marquis of Tullibardine and heir to his father's title and estates, was disinherited, and in 1724 the unattainted second son, James, who had remained loyal to King George, succeeded his father as the 2nd Duke of Atholl. In 1745 he was again to be found on the government side, accompanying the Duke of Cumberland to Scotland, while his two remaining brothers fought for Prince Charles Edward. The elder brother William was arrested after Culloden and died in the Tower in 1746. The youngest surviving brother, Lord George Murray, was the leading general of the Jacobite army (see note 17). (*The Scots Peerage*, ed. Sir James Balfour Paul (Edinburgh, 1904), I, 478–88.)

10. *cadet*: Younger son.

11. *the hall*: Stevenson advised *Scribner's* that their illustrator, William Hole, would get 'a broad hint for the Hall at Durrisdeer' from Robert William Billings's *Baronial and Ecclesiastical Antiquities of Scotland* (1845–52), a book which he knew as a child; he pointed in particular to Craigievar Castle, Aberdeenshire, and Pinkie House in Musselburgh, Midlothian (*Letters* 6, 101).

12. '*I could not love you, dear, so well, loved I not honour more*': The last two lines of 'Song: To Lucasta, Going to the Wars', by the Cavalier poet Richard Lovelace (1618–57/8). Note the later reference to the infamous fictional Lovelace of Samuel Richardson's *Clarissa* (p. 156).

13. *my Lord President*: Duncan Forbes of Culloden (1685–1747), lawyer and advocate, succeeded to the family estates on the death of his brother in 1734. Loyal to the Hanoverian cause, he was appointed successively MP for Inverness, lord advocate and in 1737 lord president of the court of session. In 1745 he tried, not without some success, to persuade the Highland chiefs against supporting the Jacobite cause. He steered clear of the conflict himself and retreated to Skye with forces loyal to King George. After Culloden he protested against the cruelties of the Duke of Cumberland, who described him as 'that old woman who talked to me about humanity' (*DNB*). Memoirs of Forbes were among the books Stevenson asked his father to send to Davos in the winter of 1880–81, when he was enthusiastically plotting a book on Scottish history, and the section he planned on 'The Heroic Age' devoted a chapter to Forbes (*Letters* 3, 126–7, 136). See also p. 207, where Forbes is compared to Sir William Johnson in his efforts to reason with the 'natives'.

14. *Carlisle*: Besieged and swiftly captured by Charles's forces on their march south in November 1745.

15. *passageing*: Moving sideways (equestrian).

16. *Sir Thomas Sullivan*: An Irishman, one of the 'seven men of Moidart' who landed with the Prince on the west coast of Scotland (see note 38 below).

17. *my Lord George*: For the family background of Lord George Murray (1694–1760), see note 9 above. During the uprising of 1715 he served with the Jacobites under his brother, the Marquis of Tullibardine. He escaped to the Continent, but was later pardoned and returned to Scotland. He was persuaded again to support the Jacobite cause in 1745, and established himself as Charles's leading general. He was mainly responsible for the victories at Prestonpans and Falkirk, but his relations with the Prince were always vexed. Charles took his advice to retreat from Derby with great reluctance, and ignored his opposition to making a stand against Cumberland at Culloden. The Chevalier de Johnstone served as Murray's aide-de-camp during the early stages of the campaign and remained a stout admirer, claiming that 'Had Prince Charles slept during the whole of the expedition, and allowed Lord George to act for him, according to his own judgment, there is every reason for supposing he would have found the crown of Great Britain on his head, when he awoke' (*A Memoir of the 'Forty-Five*, ed. B. Rawson, 2nd edn. (1958), p. 122). A modern historian has called him 'a commander of genius' (Ferguson, *Scotland 1689 to the Present*, p. 151). He died in exile on the Continent in 1760.

18. *Culloden*: See note 8 above. William Ferguson writes: 'Much more than Jacobitism died at Culloden. Thereafter the disintegration of the old Highland society, already advanced in some quarters, was accelerated. The patriarchal authority of the chiefs and great territorial magnates was gradually transformed into landlordism' (*Scotland 1689 to the Present*, p. 154).

19. *up the gait*: Up the road.

20. *lichtit*: Alighted.

21. *wirra, wirra*: An (Irish) exclamation of sorrow or lament.

22. *Non vi sed sæpe cadendo*: From Bishop Latimer's aphorism (itself the adaptation of a line from Ovid's poem of exile, *Epistulae ex ponto*): '*Gutta cavat lapidem, non vi sed sæpe cadendo*. The drop of rain maketh a hole in the stone, not by violence, but by oft falling' (*Seventh Sermon before Edward VI*, 1549).

23. *scaur*: Steep hill.

24. *sneckdraw*: Crafty, sly person (cf. *Kidnapped* (Ch. 16): 'There's many a lying sneckdraw sits close in kirk').

25. *Claverhouse*: John Graham of Claverhouse, 1st Viscount Dundee ('Bonnie Dundee'), led the campaign against the militant Covenanters in south-west Scotland from 1677 to the decisive Battle of Bothwell Brig on 22 June 1679. He then took a leading role in the suppression of the Covenanting conventicles, earning the name 'Bloody Clavers'. He was killed fighting for the deposed King James at the Battle of Killiecrankie in 1689.

Stevenson was fascinated by the Covenanters from an early age, his imagination steeped in stories of 'The Killing-Time'. His interest declares itself most explicitly in 'Thrawn Janet', 'The Tale of Tod Lapraik' (in *Catriona*) and the fragment of *Heathercat*, and in his essays 'The Pentland Rising' and 'The Coast of Fife'. See Kenneth Gelder, 'Stevenson and the Covenanters', *Scottish Literary Journal*, 11.1 (December 1984), 56–70, and his edition of *Robert Louis Stevenson: The Scottish Stories and Essays* (Edinburgh, 1989).

26. *pargeted*: Plastered.

27. *Edinburgh College*: The University, sometimes referred to as the College of King James, founded in 1583 by royal charter granted by James VI.

28. *thrapples*: Throats.

29. *fleering and flyting*: Scornful laughter and quarrelling.

30. *wabster*: Weaver.

31. *dreigh*: Doleful, miserable.

32. *chapping*: Knocking.

33. *lum*: Chimney.

34. *poother*: Gunpowder.

35. *gaed gyte*: Went mad.

36. *straucht*: Straight.

37. *wynd*: Narrow, often winding lane leading off a main street.

38. *one of the Prince's Irishmen*: Mackellar follows the Chevalier de Johnstone's hostility to the Irishmen 'whose baseness of soul corresponded to the obscurity of their birth . . . But the Prince blindly adopted their opinions' (*A Memoir of the 'Forty-Five*, p. 127).

39. *Ettenheim*: German town on the Ettenbach, under the western slope of the Black Forest.

THE MASTER'S WANDERINGS

1. *From the Memoirs of the Chevalier de Burke*: In February 1888 Stevenson told his editor at *Scribner's*: 'I think the Chevalier's narration very important and in its place; it not only prepares the end, it thoroughly prepares the reader for the Master himself when he is to come upon the stage. And it is highly desirable there should be no ambiguity. Also I confess the Chevalier himself amuses me. I rather think I am fond of that gentleman.' (*Letters* 6, 115)

2. *Ruthven*: The site of a fort between Stirling and Inverness, captured by the Prince's troops before Culloden, and after it the rallying-point for the defeated forces before their final dispersal. 'Our separation at Ruthven was truly affecting,' the Chevalier de Johnstone remembers. 'We bade one another an eternal adieu. No one could tell whether the scaffold would not be his fate' (*A Memoir of the 'Forty-Five*, p. 131).

3. *Alan Black Stewart*: Alan Breck, as Mackellar points out, the glamorous Highlander with whom David Balfour strikes up an intimate friendship in *Kidnapped* (1886).

4. *colewort*: Cabbage.

5. *the Great Minch*: The stretch of sea separating mainland Scotland from the Isle of Lewis, the northernmost of the Western Isles.

6. *Teach his name*: Mackellar rightly points out in his Note on p. 47 that this could not have been 'the celebrated *Blackbeard*'. Nevertheless, Stevenson has modelled him on the Edward Teach or Thatch, commonly known as Blackbeard, who cruised along the Spanish Main, then north along the coast of Carolina and Virginia, terrorizing the planters, until he was shot and decapitated in a violent show-down in 1718. Stevenson knew of him from *A General History of the Robberies and Murders of the most notorious Pyrates* (1724). He would have been pleased to discover that its supposed author, 'Captain Charles Johnson', was in fact Daniel Defoe, whom he much admired.

7. *crowder*: Fiddler (who draws crowds).

8. *boltsprit*: Obsolete form of bowsprit: 'a large spar or boom running out from the stem of a vessel, to which . . . the foremast stays are fastened' (*OED*).

9. *taffrail*: 'the aftermost portion of the poop-rail' (*OED*).

10. *'Hell, hell!'* Stevenson borrowed this from Defoe's Blackbeard, who 'aim'd at making his Men believe he was a Devil incarnate; for being one Day at Sea, and a little flushed with drink: – *Come*, says he, *let us make a Hell of our own, and try how long we can bear it*; . . .' He then fills several pots of brimstone in the hold and sets them on fire (*A General History of . . . Pyrates*, p. 100).

11. *dirk*: Dagger.

12. *companion*: Ladder from deck to cabin.

13. *a pirate by the name of Roberts*: Defoe describes the Set of Articles agreed by Captain Roberts and his crew, 'for the better Conversation of their Society, and doing Justice to one another' in his *General History of . . . Pyrates*, pp. 169–72.

14. *foul*: Of a ship, 'having the bottom overgrown with seaweed, shell-fish, etc.' (*OED*).

15. '*port de carénage*': Place for careening a ship (turning it over on one side for cleaning, caulking and repairing).

16. *moon-calf*: Congenital idiot, born fool; also used of Ransome, the doomed cabin-boy of the *Covenant* (*Kidnapped*, Ch. 5).

17. *any French settlement*: At this date the French were hoping to establish a chain of settlements from Quebec to New Orleans that would shut the British into a narrow strip of the eastern seaboard. Their ambitions for control of North America were to be destroyed in the Seven Years' War (1756–63).

18. *the horse*: 'a wooden frame on which soldiers were made to ride as a punishment' (*OED*).

19. *The town of Albany . . . at that time*: Albany occupied a position of strategic importance throughout the colonial period, on the edge of Iroquois country to the north and at the head of navigation on the Hudson River.

20. *Governor Clinton*: George Clinton (1686–1761), Governor of New York 1743–53. See 'Passages at New York', note 1.

21. *Crown Point . . . Lake Champlain*: The French built a fort at Crown Point on Lake Champlain in 1731, and another at Ticonderoga in 1755 (the place-name that inspired one of Stevenson's best-known poems, published in the December 1887 issue of *Scribner's*, as he was beginning this novel). Both were captured by General Amherst in 1759. Named after the first governor of French Canada, the lake lies mainly between the States of New York and Vermont, extending slightly over the Canadian border, just to the east of the Adirondack Mountains. It was the main gateway between French Canada and the English settlements (see also p. 212).

22. *portages*: Tracks over which boats are carried from one river or lake to another.

23. *bilged*: Stove in (of the bottom or 'bilge' of a boat or ship).

24. *The labours of Hercules, so finely described by Homer*: But they are not. The Chevalier's knowledge of the Classics is as shaky as Mackellar's is sound.

25. *touchwood*: 'the soft white substance into which wood is converted by the action of certain fungi' (*OED*).

26. *chairman*: Man whose occupation it is to wheel or carry persons in chairs.

PERSECUTIONS ENDURED BY MR HENRY

1. *brown study*: 'a state of mental abstraction or musing' (*OED*).
2. *Criffel*: A summit overlooking Carse Bay on the Solway Firth.
3. *the Scots Fund*: This was supposed to support the Jacobite exiles.
4. *the pathetic air of Shule Aroon*: An Irish or Anglo-Irish ballad, also known as 'Shule Agra(h),' both meaning 'Go/come/move, my love.' The verses are normally composed of three rhyming lines of English and an unvarying fourth line of Gaelic which is repeated in the wholly Gaelic four-line refrain. P. W. Joyce prints a fairly standard version of words and music in his collection of *Old Irish Folk Music and Songs* (London and Dublin, 1909), where he says that it 'belongs to the time of the "Wild Geese" or Irish Brigade (between 1691 and 1745), when thousands of young Irishmen went to the Continent to enlist in the armies there, chiefly French' (pp. 236–7). For further references to this popular ballad, see Alisoun Gardner-Medwin, 'Miss Reburn's Ballads: a nineteenth-century repertoire from Ireland', in *Ballad Studies*, ed. E. B. Lyle (Cambridge and Ipswich, 1976), pp. 99–100, and note 16, p. 206. Sir Walter Scott heard a younger sister of Maria Edgeworth sing a version on their visit to Abbotsford in 1823 (J. G. Lockhart, *Memoirs of the Life of Sir Walter Scott*, Vol. 5 (Edinburgh and London, 1837), pp. 306–7), and Stephen Dedalus is supposed to sing another in the 'Ithaca' section of James Joyce's *Ulysses*. (This note owes a particular debt to Hugh Shields for his generous advice; also to Emer Nolan, Clíona Ó Gallchoir, Shane Murphy, Erich Poppe and William Gillies for various kinds of assistance.) See also note 18 below.
5. *bairnly kickshaw*: Childish trifle.
6. *Mr Lally*: Comte Thomas Arthur de Lally, Baron de Tollendal (1702–66), son of an Irish Jacobite who married a French lady of noble family. He was involved in several Jacobite plots and in 1745 accompanied Charles Edward to Scotland, serving as his aide-de-camp at the battle of Falkirk. When war broke out with England in 1756 he was given command of the French expedition to India. He was not a success. He surrendered at the siege of Pondicherry in 1761 and was sent to England as a prisoner of war. Accused of treason and cowardice in France, he insisted on going to stand trial, only to be convicted and executed after many delays. See also note 20 below.
7. *the Muckleross*: Western headland at the entrance to Kircudbright Bay.
8. *lugger*: 'a small vessel with . . . four-cornered cut sails, set fore and aft, and may have two or three masts' (*OED*).

9. *brailed up*: Furled up by means of the 'brails', small ropes fastened to edges of sails.
10. *swithering*: Hesitating.
11. *toised*: Eyed up and down. This is a rare word adapted by Stevenson from the French *toiser* (*toise* is a French measurement, equivalent to just over six feet); he uses it again in *St Ives* (Ch. 19) (1894).
12. *precisian*: 'one who is rigidly precise or punctilious in the observance of rules or forms' (*OED*).
13. *'Sneck up'*: Though 'sneck' is a good Scots word for 'latch' or 'lock', and the local folk think of Henry Durie as a 'sneckdraw' (p. 17), the Master is using a widespread colloquialism meaning 'go hang yourself, away with you' (*OED*, 'snick', *v.* 1). Scott uses it in *Kenilworth* ('Bidding the steward go snick up', Ch. 29), and it is the expletive that Sir Toby Belch levels at the killjoy steward with ideas above his station in *Twelfth Night* (II.3.94). The Master's style of bleeding the family dry is not quite Sir Toby's, but it is a nice literary hit to identify Mackellar with Malvolio. Poor Mackellar attracts another of Sir Toby's exclamations on p. 167, again from the Master. Stevenson throws off the phrase himself in a mock-abusive letter to William Archer from Saranac Lake in November 1887 (*Letters* 6, 54).
14. *the elder brother of the parable*: Henry has assumed the position of the elder brother in the parable of the prodigal son (Luke xv. 11–32). On hearing of the lavish reception accorded his younger brother, he angrily reminds their father that he has served him faithfully for years without any special reward.
15. *policies*: The enclosed grounds of a large house.
16. *trepanned*: Kidnapped (David Balfour uses the words interchangeably in *Kidnapped*, Chs. 5, 27).
17. *parallel*: Siege-trench running parallel to face of works being attacked.
18. *the same air as I had heard the Colonel whistle*: See note 4 above. In the version of 'Shule Aroon' printed by P. W. Joyce the third of the five verses corresponds to the one sung by the Master:

> I'll dye my petticoats, I'll dye them red,
> And round the world I'll beg my bread,
> Until my parents would wish me dead,
> *Is go dee tu mavourneen slaun.*

(In modern spelling the last line would be: *Is go dté tú mo mhúirnín slán.*) The distinctly English flavour of Stevenson's fourth line corresponds to versions recorded in Hampshire, Lancashire and elsewhere (see *Journal of the Folk Song Society*, Vol. 3 (1908–9), p. 29, and Vol. 5 (1914–16), pp. 180–81.

19. *Belvedere*: Summer-house positioned on an eminence.
20. *the French Indies*: Over the period in which the novel is set, the imperial ambitions of France and Britain collided violently, both in India and in North America, spurred on by the Seven Years' War in Europe (1756–63). Before this, French interests in India had been vigorously promoted by Joseph François Dupleix, governor-general of all French establishments from 1742, with power-bases in Pondicherry and, after 1746, Madras. Dupleix had ambitions to subjugate the whole of Southern India by the manipulation of native rulers, but in 1754 he was recalled by a French government anxious to make peace. With the outbreak of war in Europe in 1756, hostilities in India were renewed, and the timing of the Master's plans for making a fortune there coincides with the French expedition led by Lally (see note 6 above), the other name most memorably associated with France's Indian aspirations.
21. *break the entail and alienate a piece of land*: The principle of entail ensures the succession of a landed estate, so that it cannot be bequeathed at pleasure by any one possessor; 'alienation' is a legal term for the transference of ownership to another.
22. *Cockermouth*: Town in Cumbria, a short distance across the Solway Firth.
23. *point-de-vice*: Neatly turned-out.
24. *shog*: Jolt.

ACCOUNT OF ALL THAT PASSED ON THE NIGHT OF FEBRUARY 27TH, 1757

1. *bonnet-laird*: 'a petty proprietor in Scotland, wearing a bonnet like the humbler classes' (*OED*).
2. *cette lenteur d'hébété qui me fait rager*: 'this sluggish torpor that drives me mad.'
3. *lourdaud*: Oaf.
4. '*Who is to tell the old man?*' In the background of ballad and folk-tale on which this scene draws, one may hear the question that marks the turning-point of 'The Twa Brothers'. The man or boy who has dealt his brother a mortal wound (in most versions, by accident) asks what he will say to the father – and mother, and sister, and true-love (*The English and Scottish Popular Ballads*, 5 Vols., ed. F. J. Child (Boston and New York, 1882–98), I, ii, 435).
5. *and then . . . handled it the second time*: In the serial and first editions this sentence concluded: 'and thrust it to the hilt into the frozen ground' (see Textual Variants). Stevenson confessed to the French translator Marcel Schwob that this was 'one of my inconceivable blunders, an exaggeration to

stagger Hugo' (*Letters* 7, 69). See also Stevenson's remarks in the third fragment from his Note on the novel (Appendix, p. 228).

6. *Cæsar's Commentaries, a volume of Mr Hobbes, the Henriade of M de Voltaire*: These suggest the Master's interests in military strategy, power politics, and rationalist philosophy. Julius Caesar wrote *Commentaries* on the Gallic War (58–52 BC) and on the Civil War against Pompey which concluded in 48 BC. Voltaire's *La Henriade* is an epic poem published in 1728 (the revision of an earlier version with a different title); it is devoted to the exploits of Henry of Navarre, later Henry IV of France, one of the many heroic figures whom the Master fails to emulate.

7. *shagreen*: 'a species of untanned leather with a rough granular surface, prepared from the skin of the horse, ass, etc., or of the shark, seal, etc., and frequently dyed green' (*OED*).

8. *Havre de Grace*: Normandy seaport on the Seine estuary, much assaulted by the English. Named 'the harbour of grace' by Francis I in 1516 after an old chapel dedicated to Notre-Dame-de-Grâce, it is now more simply known as 'Le Havre'.

SUMMARY OF EVENTS DURING THE MASTER'S SECOND ABSENCE

1. *troubled my thumb*: Concerned myself.

2. *testing*: 'the making of a will; the disposing of property by will' (*OED*).

3. *Gnatique patrisque, alma, precor, miserere*: 'Take pity on a son and father, I beg you, gracious lady' (Virgil, *Aeneid* 6, 116–17). Aeneas pleads with the Sibyl to be allowed to descend to the underworld and greet his father Anchises (see Introduction, p. xiv).

3. *gravelled*: Confounded.

4. *posset*: Poisoned drink.

ADVENTURE OF CHEVALIER BURKE IN INDIA

1. *mellay*: Fight, skirmish (French, *mêlée*).

2. *cipaye* (French): Sepoy, a native Indian soldier serving under European command.

3. *calendars*: Presumably the Chevalier is referring to the 'calenders', 'a mendicant order of dervishes in Turkey and Persia' (*OED*), familiar to English readers from the *Arabian Nights*.

4. *Mr Galland*: Antoine Galland (1646–1715) was responsible for introducing the *Arabian Nights* to Europe through his French translation of 1704–17.
5. *Mr Lally*: See 'Persecutions Endured by Mr Henry', notes 6 and 20.
6. *mohur*: Chief gold coin of British India.

THE ENEMY IN THE HOUSE

1. *the black dog*: Melancholy, gloom.
2. *sledge*: Sledge-hammer.
3. *spent his venom on a file*: Proverbial expression derived from one of Aesop's Fables in which a serpent 'fond a file which she beganne to gnawe with her teethe' (trans. William Caxton, 1484); hence 'to make an attempt that can result only in vexatious failure' (*OED*).
4. *Dido . . . Æneas*: Aeneas masters Dido with his story of the fall of Troy in Book 2 of Virgil's *Aeneid*. For further references to this epic piece of narration, see 'Passages at New York', note 4, and 'The Journey in the Wilderness', note 7.
5. *a glamour*: Spell, enchantment: according to the *OED*, 'originally Scottish, introduced into the literary language by Scott'.
6. *list*: Made of cheap cloth.
7. *fluttered your Volscians in Corioli!* An allusion to the final bravura boast of Shakespeare's Caius Martius, 'That, like an eagle in a dove-cote, I/Flutter'd your Volscians in Corioles./Alone I did it.' (*Coriolanus*, V.6. 114–16)
8. *eldritch*: Weird, unearthly.

MR MACKELLAR'S JOURNEY WITH THE MASTER

1. *some natural sadness*: A faint echo of the farewell to Eden at the close of Milton's *Paradise Lost*: 'Some natural tears they dropped . . .' (12, 645).
2. *Wandering Willie*: The lines cited here are taken from two verses that Stevenson himself included in a letter to Charles Baxter from Tautira, while working on this section of the novel, 8 or 9 November 1888. He boasts of their superiority to Burns's version, 'Here awa', there awa' wandering, Willie' (first printed in *Poems*, 1792).

> Home no more home to me, whither shall I wander?
> Hunger my driver, I go where I must.

Cold blows the winter wind over hill and heather;
  Thick drives the rain, and my roof is in the dust.
Loved of wise men was the shade of my roof-tree,
  The true word of welcome was spoken in the door.
Dear days of old, with the faces in the firelight,
  Kind folks of old, you come again no more.

Home was home then, my dear, full of kindly faces:
  Home was home then, my dear, happy for the child.
Fire and the windows bright glittered on the moorland,
  Song, tuneful song, built a palace in the wild.
Now when day dawns on the brow of the moorland,
  Lone stands the house and the chimney stone is cold.
Lone let it stand, now the folks are all departed,
  The kind hearts, the true hearts, that loved the house of old.

Stevenson's poem was first published, with an additional stanza, in *Songs of Travel*, Vol. 14 of the Edinburgh Edition (1895). See *Robert Louis Stevenson: Collected Poems*, ed. Janet Adam Smith, 2nd edn. (London, 1971), p. 256.

3. *hodding*: Jogging up and down in the saddle.

4. *hawsehole*: Hole cut in the bows of a ship for cable to pass through.

5. *Mr Richardson's famous 'Clarissa'*: Samuel Richardson's novel (1748–9) boasts an evidently appropriate model for the Master in the villainous and seductive Lovelace (cf. the allusion to the Cavalier Lovelace on p. 13).

6. *a Roland for my Oliver*: Charlemagne's two leading Paladins or Peers fought a long and indecisive duel before swearing eternal friendship. Oliver's prudence failed to save Roland from the disaster at Roncesvalles or Roncevaux, subject of the twelfth-century *Chanson de Roland*. The story of their duel was retold in *La Légende des Siècles* (first series, 1859) by Victor Hugo, whom Stevenson much admired.

7. *buckram*: A kind of coarse linen or cloth, with the added association of 'men in buckram', meaning non-existent persons, after Falstaff's 'four rogues in buckram' (*1 Henry IV*, II.4).

8. *tester*: Colloquial term for a sixpence.

9. '*Except the Lord the city keep, the watchmen watch in vain!*' Psalm 127, v.1.

10. *anchor-bitts*: Pair of posts on ship's deck for fastening the cable while the ship rides at anchor.

11. *mutch*: Night-cap.

12. '*Tilly-vally!*' 'Nonsense!' An exclamation of uncertain origin but distinctly literary provenance (cf. Shakespeare, *2 Henry IV*, II.5.90; *Twelfth Night*, II.3.79;

Scott, *The Antiquary*, Ch. 6). For another echo of *Twelfth Night*, see 'Persecutions Endured by Mr Henry', note 13.
13. *un homme de parole*: A man of your word.

PASSAGES AT NEW YORK

1. *General Clinton*: Stevenson asked his editor at *Scribner's* to verify the name of the Governor of New York in 1764, and the serial version carried the correct name of Cadwallader Colden, Governor from 1761 to 1776. In volume form, however, the name reverted to the incorrect 'Clinton'; this may have been inadvertent, but it is possible that on second thought Stevenson opted for historical error so as to preserve fictional continuity with the Clinton who was Governor at the time of the Master's first visit to New York (see 'The Master's Wanderings', note 20).
2. *sewing . . . in the manner of Penelope's*: The faithful wife of Odysseus unpicked at night the web that she wove by day, to avoid reaching the conclusion that would leave her at the mercy of her suitors (see also p. 188).
3. *Clive*: Robert Lord Clive (1725–74) laid the foundations of the British Empire in India, and so claims consideration as a modern hero on a par with the classical Aeneas whom the Master mentions at the end of this same sentence. Clive had three spells in India. He began as a humble clerk in the East India Company in 1744 and returned to Britain nine years later as a military hero; going out again in 1756, he defeated the French the next year at the battle of Plassey, and for the next four years served as Governor of Bengal; he resumed this post in 1765, but ill-health drove him home after only two years. His administrative and military success did not protect him from prejudice, conspiracy and official enquiry, and he committed suicide in 1774.
4. *like another Æneas*: In their flight from Troy by night Aeneas carried his father Anchises on his back (see 'The Enemy in the House', note 4, and 'The Journey in the Wilderness', note 7).

THE JOURNEY IN THE WILDERNESS

1. *Mountain, the trader*: In October 1888 Stevenson sent an urgent request from Tahiti to his *Scribner's* editor for a couple of books that he needed for background to the final chapters of the novel. In February 1889 he acknowledged receipt of Alexander Henry's *Travels and Adventures in Canada and the Indian Territories 1760–76* (1809) – 'just what I wanted by a blessed providence', 'that admirable book' (*Letters* 6, 247, 259).

2. *bravo*: Assassin.

3. *Penelope's web*: See 'Passages at New York', note 2.

4. '*I must be the devil and you Michael Scott*': Twelfth-century Scottish astrologer and mathematician reputed to be a black magician. He figures in Dante's *Inferno*, Scott's *The Lay of the Last Minstrel* and James Hogg's *The Three Perils of Man* (1822), where he is called 'the Master'. The allusions here are explained by a note of Scott's to *The Lay of the Last Minstrel* (1805), Canto II, xiii:

> Michael Scott was, once upon a time, much embarrassed by a spirit, for whom he was under the necessity of finding constant employment. He commanded him to build a *cauld*, or dam-head, across the Tweed at Kelso; it was accomplished in one night, and still does honour to the infernal architect. Michael next ordered that Eildon hill, which was then a uniform cone, should be divided into three. Another night was sufficient to part its summit into the three picturesque peaks which it now bears. At length the enchanter conquered this indefatigable demon, by employing him in the hopeless and endless task of making ropes out of sea-sand.

5. *Sir William Johnson*: Born in Ireland in 1715, Johnson emigrated to America in his twenties, colonized some land west of Schenectady and won the enduring respect of the Indian tribes with whom he traded. His influence served to sustain the often precarious relations between Indians and colonists, and in 1756 he was appointed colonel and sole superintendent of Indian affairs. After the defeat of the French his negotiations with the volatile tribes culminated in the treaty of Fort Stanwix in 1768. He was well rewarded by a grateful monarch. He left a valuable memoir on the 'Languages, Customs, and Manners of the Indian Six Nations' and his correspondence with British and colonial governments has been described as 'absolutely essential to a proper understanding of the history of the state [of New York] and of America generally' (*DNB*). He died in 1774. Like Clive of India, Sir William is another 'modern hero' whose name and fame cast a shade over the Master.

6. *the old song of the Twa Corbies*: Scott printed this grim little ballad, of which Henry sings the closing lines, in *Minstrelsy of the Scottish Border* (1803). Scott and others have compared it to the more tender English ballad of 'The Three Ravens', in which hawk and hound and female figure remain loyal to the dead man, denying the ravens their prey.

As I was walking all alane,
I heard twa corbies making a mane;
The tane unto t'other say,
'Where sall we gang and dine to-day?'

'In behint yon auld fail* dyke,
'I wot there lies a new-slain knight;
'And naebody kens that he lies there,
'But his hawk, his hound, and lady fair.

'His hound is to the hunting gane,
'His hawk to fetch the wild-fowl hame,
'His lady's ta'en another mate,
'So we may make our dinner sweet.

'Ye'll sit on his white hause-bane,†
'And I'll pike out his bonny blue een;
'Wi' ae lock o' his gowden hair,
'We'll theek‡ our nest when it grows bare.

'Mony a one for him makes mane,
'But nane sall ken where he is gane;
'O'er his white banes, when they are bare,
'The wind sall blaw for evermair.'

(Text from *The English and Scottish Popular Ballads*, 5 Vols., ed. F. J. Child (Boston and New York, 1882–98), 1, i, 253).

7. *quantum mutatus ab illo*: 'how changed from the man he once was'. The phrase comes from Aeneas's description of the ghost of Hector which appears to him on the night of the fall of Troy (Virgil, *Aeneid* 2, 274). See 'The Enemy in the House', note 4 and 'Passages at New York', note 4.

8. *like rabbits from a hill*: Compare David Balfour's last view of his uncle Ebenezer, alone in the house of Shaws – 'the peak of a nightcap, bobbing up and down and back and forward, like the head of a rabbit from a burrow' (*Kidnapped*, Ch. 30).

9. *pervigilium*: Watching through the night.

10. *my Lord President Culloden*: Duncan Forbes of Culloden; see 'Summary of Events During the Master's Wanderings', note 13.

* turf
† collar-bone
‡ thatch

11. '*I have felt the hilt dirl on his breastbone*': Henry tries to summon Alan Breck's bravura, this being virtually a repetition of the threat Alan issues to Ebenezer Balfour near the end of *Kidnapped*: 'Before your jottering finger could find the trigger, the hilt would dirl on your breast bane' (Ch. 29).
12. *Coromandel*: The Coromandel Coast, Eastern seaboard of India from Cape Calimere to the mouth of the Kistna river, site of conflict between the French and the English, and of some of Clive's greatest exploits (see 'Passages at New York', note 3).

APPENDIX

1. *Inspector-General John Balfour*: In his essay 'The Coast of Fife', written in the spring of 1888 for publication in *Scribner's Magazine* the following October, Stevenson recalled 'the tall figure and the white locks of the last Englishman in Delhi, my uncle Dr Balfour, who was still walking his hospital rounds, while the troops from Meerut clattered and cried "Deen, Deen" along the streets of the imperial city' (i.e. in the Mutiny of 1857).
2. *So long ago*: Fanny Stevenson dates this as the summer of 1881 when she and Louis spent two months at Pitlochry and he wrote two of his finest Scots tales, 'Thrawn Janet' and 'The Merry Men' (Prefatory Note to the Tusitala Edition, 10 (1924)). The previous winter in Davos he had been avidly consuming material for the book(s) he planned to write on Scottish history from 1700 onwards (see *Letters* 3, 124–40). This helps to explain his references to 'the *Atholl Correspondence*' (see 'Summary of Events During the Master's Wanderings', note 9) and the *Memoirs of the Chevalier de Johnstone*, aide-de-camp to the Young Pretender, first published in 1820 (see 'Summary of Events During the Master's Wanderings', notes 17 and 38, and 'The Master's Wanderings', note 1).
3. *Barry Lyndon*: Scoundrel-hero of Thackeray's novel *The Memoirs of Barry Lyndon, Esquire, by Himself* (1852).
4. *Lord Foppington*: A character in Vanbrugh's play *The Relapse* (1696).
5. *the case of Marquis of Tullibardine*: See 'Summary of Events During the Master's Wanderings', note 9.
6. *Clementina*: Stevenson's discarded name for Alison Graeme.
7. *'up to the hilt' in the frosty ground*: See 'Account of All That Passed on the Night of February 27th, 1757', note 5.

TEXTUAL VARIANTS

The text of the Edinburgh Edition printed here has the benefit of authorial revisions to the first serial publication in *Scribner's Magazine* and the first editions in book form, American and English (see Note on the Text). Stevenson retouched the tale twice, between serial issue and first edition, then again, more lightly, for the Edinburgh Edition. The revisions mainly take the form of deletions. He chose, for example, to relieve the Master of a certain meanness of spirit by obscuring the reason for a quarrel with the Chevalier that had been quite clear in the serial, at least according to the Chevalier (see below on pp. 50). But his most concentrated amendments are to the serial version of the quarrel and duel, the section entitled 'Account of All That Passed on the Night of February 27th, 1757' (the sixth instalment). They are presumably among the 'final corrections on the earlier parts, against book form' which Stevenson mentions in a letter to Burlingame from Honolulu in April 1889 (*Letters* 6, 283). The most significant changes involve the stiffening of Mackellar's authority in this crisis. In the serial Lord Durrisdeer rebukes him ('You must have more command'), and Mrs Henry reassures him ('you need not be afraid with me'): both of these are excised in revision, as if Mackellar himself were censoring these affronts to his self-assurance. There is a notable tempering of his exchanges with Mrs Henry: some asperity is lost but also a warm handshake. Later on Mackellar is deprived of a flourishing description of fire-light (p. 134) and a sentence of fine writing about the sea (p. 157). In other words Stevenson was concerned to preserve a certain level of desiccation in his main narrator which the serial version had at moments slightly jeopardized.

The following passages from *Scribner's* serial and Cassell's first English edition represent the most significant differences from the text of the Edinburgh Edition. Those from *Scribner's* were revised for the first edition; those from the first edition were revised for the Edinburgh Edition. Page and line numbers refer to the beginning of the equivalent passages in the present text.

Page and line

50, 27 I awaked the next morning very early, to find Ballantrae already up and tampering with the packets; not that at the moment I suspected his good faith; though I observed the man to be confused, on my awaking, and to begin with a sullen spirit a conversation that came very near to end in blows. (*Scribner's*)

50, 35 . . . and as for myself he fubbed me off unhandsomely, and any gentleman would have resented his behavior. Had I found him openly claim a greater share, I might have let that pass; for an Irishman is always generous. But he gulled me, made a parade of generosity, gave me the more part of the gold; and it was at last only by an accident and some boggling in his sleight of hand, that I discovered he had kept for himself some valuable jewels, worth upwards of a thousand pounds. (*Scribner's*)

86, 10 . . . and the money paid over to our leech and sent by some private carriage into France. Or so he said; though I have suspected since it did not go so far. (First edition)

96, 33 I opened the man's clothes; my hand was as steady as ever, and all my fear fallen from me; nothing left but a great commiseration. The heart was quite still, it gave not a flutter. (*Scribner's*)

98, 13 'I am very courageous,' said she.

'I think so,' said I, holding up the candle to scrutinize her face; 'I pray God so!' I set down the light upon the chimney. 'And another thing, Mrs Henry,' I added, pointing at her with my finger: 'when so much is lost already, we can do no more but save what remains. The best now is very little; you and I must try for it.'

'I will, Mackellar, good Mackellar,' said she. 'But no more suspense!' and she laid her hand on my shoulder and looked at me with a sort of smile, very painful for me to see, but very brave too.

'It has come to a duel,' said I. (*Scribner's*)

100, 11 'God bless you for that word!' I said. 'Go to him now, where he sits in the hall; speak to him – it matters not what you say; give him your hand; say, "I know all"; – if God gives you grace enough, say "Forgive me."'

'Nay,' said she, 'may God forgive us all, and you not least, Mr Mackellar, for a harsh judger and a cruel tongue.'

'Pray rather I may be helped in what remains to do,' said I. 'For it seems to me that I am innocent of the least offence in this matter, and yet have the most dreadful part of it.'

'You say very true, Mr Mackellar,' said she. 'God strengthen you, and make you merciful. I will go to my husband; I shall not be more backward in my duty than yourself, and I will try to be more kind.'

'Let me light you there,' said I, taking up the candle. (*Scribner's*)

103, 13 His eyes and his face and his clasped hands besought me for the truth. (*Scribner's*)

103, 23 His voice shook like a sail in the wind, yet he spoke with a good loudness; his face was like the snow, but his eyes were steady and dry. I beheld him with a wonder I could not hide. I had looked for him to die under the blow, and he bore it with more constancy than he had received the news of his son's safety.

'I ask you where it was,' he repeated. 'You must have more command.'

'In the shrubbery,' said I.

'And Mr Henry?' he asked. And when I had told him he knotted his old face in thought.

'And Mr James?' says he.

'I have left him lying,' said I, 'beside the candles.'

'Candles?' he cried, with a more spirited briskness than I had ever remarked upon his lips. 'This is highly imprudent.' And with that he ran to the window, opened it, and looked abroad. (*Scribner's*)

104, 34 'I can see in the dark. I have been standing here so long – so long,' said she. 'Come; give me your arm; you need not be afraid with me.' (*Scribner's*)

105, 5 'Ah, would to God we had!' cried I.

She laid her hand upon my arm. 'Continue to be brave,' she said, 'for you and I must help each other.' (*Scribner's*)

105, 7 'Ah!' she cried. And then, with an instant courage, handled it the second time, and thrust it to the hilt into the frozen ground. (First edition)

105, 14 'Not speak to you?' I repeated. 'O, you have not tried!'

'I know you think you have a right to doubt me,' she replied, with a gentle dignity; 'but I will prove to you before I have done that I am more worthy of your pity.' (*Scribner's*)

105, 20 'It is hard, then, you should hesitate about his wife,' said she. 'But here is my hand, Mr Mackellar, if you will take it; for I think you have a loyal nature.'

I gave her mine with a sudden warmth of friendship; for I saw all at once, like the rending of a veil, how nobly she had borne this unnatural calamity, and how generously my reproaches. (*Scribner's*)

106, 14 His wife stood a little back from him, her hand at her mouth; and she made us a quick signal of defeat; it was plain she could not move him. (*Scribner's*)

106, 26 'And we used to be bairns together. O, he was a bonny lad!' (*Scribner's*)

124, 33 . . . it was her part now to be neglected: the more praise to her that she played it well. (First edition)

130, 22 Word had reached me that he was come to the Indies; but it appeared he kept with the English party, for we had never met and I heard little of his occupations. (*Scribner's*)

134, 21 . . . and the great room was lighted only with a single taper and some lurching reverberation of the fire. (First edition)

148, 6 'This smacks to me of a very considerable and genuine apprehension. But I will go beyond that . . .' (*Scribner's*)

157, 20 . . . in the fear of mutiny. All this to the piping of the ropes and the perpetual perilous rolling of the ship. (*Scribner's*)

187, 32 . . . and upon the same reasons, I am still strong to justify my course. We lived meanwhile in Albany, but though alone together in a strange place, had little traffic beyond formal salutations. (First edition)

READ MORE IN PENGUIN

In every corner of the world, on every subject under the sun, Penguin represents quality and variety – the very best in publishing today.

For complete information about books available from Penguin – including Puffins, Penguin Classics and Arkana – and how to order them, write to us at the appropriate address below. Please note that for copyright reasons the selection of books varies from country to country.

In the United Kingdom: Please write to *Dept. EP, Penguin Books Ltd, Bath Road, Harmondsworth, West Drayton, Middlesex UB7 0DA*

In the United States: Please write to *Consumer Services, Penguin Putnam Inc., 405 Murray Hill Parkway, East Rutherford, New Jersey 07073-2136.* VISA and MasterCard holders call 1-800-631-8571 to order Penguin titles

In Canada: Please write to *Penguin Books Canada Ltd, 10 Alcorn Avenue, Suite 300, Toronto, Ontario M4V 3B2*

In Australia: Please write to *Penguin Books Australia Ltd, 487 Maroondah Highway, Ringwood, Victoria 3134*

In New Zealand: Please write to *Penguin Books (NZ) Ltd, Private Bag 102902, North Shore Mail Centre, Auckland 10*

In India: Please write to *Penguin Books India Pvt Ltd, 11 Community Centre, Panchsheel Park, New Delhi 110017*

In the Netherlands: Please write to *Penguin Books Netherlands bv, Postbus 3507, NL-1001 AH Amsterdam*

In Germany: Please write to *Penguin Books Deutschland GmbH, Metzlerstrasse 26, 60594 Frankfurt am Main*

In Spain: Please write to *Penguin Books S. A., Bravo Murillo 19, 1°B, 28015 Madrid*

In Italy: Please write to *Penguin Italia s.r.l., Via Vittorio Emanuele 45/a, 20094 Corsico, Milano*

In France: Please write to *Penguin France, 12, Rue Prosper Ferradou, 31700 Blagnac*

In Japan: Please write to *Penguin Books Japan Ltd, Iidabashi KM-Bldg, 2-23-9 Koraku, Bunkyo-Ku, Tokyo 112-0004*

In South Africa: Please write to *Penguin Books South Africa (Pty) Ltd, P.O. Box 751093, Gardenview, 2047 Johannesburg*